It's A Thin Line

W9-BVM-914

Other books by Kimberla Lawson Roby

BEHIND CLOSED DOORS

HERE AND NOW

CASTING THE FIRST STONE

It's A Thin Line

KIMBERLA LAWSON ROBY

DAFINA BOOKS
Kensington Publishing Corp.
http://www.kensingtonbooks.com

DAFINA BOOKS are published by

Kensington Publishing Corp.
850 Third Avenue
New York, NY 10022

Copyright © 2001 by Kimberla Lawson Roby

All rights reserved. No part of this book may be reproduced in any form or by any means without the prior written consent of the Publisher, excepting brief quotes used in reviews.

If you purchased this book without a cover, you should be aware that this book is stolen property. It was reported as "unsold and destroyed" to the Publisher and neither the Author nor the Publisher has received any payment for this "stripped book."

All Kensington Titles, Imprints, and Distributed Lines are available at special quantity discounts for bulk purchases for sales promotions, premiums, fund-raising, and educational or institutional use. Special book excerpts or customized printings can also be created to fit specific needs. For details, write or phone the office of the Kensington special sales manager: Kensington Publishing Corp., 850 Third Avenue, New York, NY 10022, attn: Special Sales Department, Phone: 1-800-221-2647.

Dafina and the Dafina logo Reg. U.S. Pat. & TM Off.

First hardcover printing: May 2001
First trade paperback printing: October 2002
First Dafina mass market printing: October 2003

10 9 8 7 6 5 4 3 2 1

Printed in the United States of America

To every woman who has ever experienced domestic violence.

To every family member who has ever given care to an ill or elderly loved one.

To every human being who has ever concealed a deep, dark childhood secret.

Acknowledgments

As always I thank God for blessing me with the opportunity to write and for giving me everything I need and so much more.

To my wonderful husband, Will. You continue to be the most understanding and caring person as I deal with Mom's illness. There have been so many nights when I have left the nursing facility in tears only to arrive home and find you waiting with open arms. I am so thankful that I married a man who loves me as much as I love him. You are the best.

To my mom, Arletha Stapleton, who is the joy of my life and who still fills my heart with happiness on a daily basis. You are a remarkable, loving woman, and your faith is so fascinating. Thank you for showing me that God will never place anything on me that I cannot bear and that if I truly keep my faith in Him, I'll never have a thing to worry about.

My brother, Willie Stapleton, Jr., for staying in my corner during not just the good times but through all the sad and trying times as well. I have watched you grow in so many ways since Mom's illness, and I am so proud of you. I have always loved you, but the bond that we share now has risen to a whole new level. And to my youngest brother, Michael Stapleton—I love you so very much.

To my little nephews and niece, Michael Jamaal Young,

Malik James Stapleton, and Alana Denise Lawson. I am here for you always.

My aunt, Fannie Haley, for helping me in every way you can with Mom—from washing her clothing, to praying with her, to lifting my spirits during our many conversations. You never criticize or complain, and I couldn't have made it through the year 2000 without you. You are like my second mother, and I love you so much.

My uncle, Ben Tennin, my mom's twin for truly loving her as much as you love yourself and for being there every morning without fail. I love you from the bottom of my heart.

My uncle and aunt, Clifton and Vernell Tennin for making sure Mom receives a home-cooked meal on a weekly basis. It means so much to her and me. You are both so incredibly caring, and I love you dearly.

Lori Whitaker Thurman—my friend, my sister in spirit. You have always been so dependable and caring, but the way you stepped in during my tour and every other time I needed to travel to promote my work was far beyond the call of duty. You have your own mom to look after as well as your own work to complete, so making sure my mom was okay and that she had everything she needed shows that you genuinely went out of your way to be there for me. It is no wonder the nurses and CNAs at the nursing facility assumed you were Mom's blood daughter, because you have certainly earned that role. Not ever will I forget what you have done. And to Ulysses, for standing by you, the way every husband should.

Kelli Tunson Bullard—my friend, my sister in spirit for finalizing the title of this book. I still wish you hadn't moved to Atlanta—partly because my phone bill is sky-high every month (smile), but mostly because I really miss being able to see you, Brian and the girls, Kiara (Will's and my little goddaughter), Kaprisha, and KaSondra. But you know you really have a true friend in someone when the relationship is able to remain the same even when it's long distance.

To Evelyn Barmore and Susan Saylor who continue to work around my erratic schedule without any complaints. I appreciate both of you more than you could ever know.

To the rest of my family members and friends, my mom's friends, coworkers, and church members who continue to visit and call her. It is so easy for everyone to forget about a person who has been ill for such a long period of time, and I appreciate all of your thoughtfulness.

To the entire staff at P.A. Peterson Center for all the care that you have given my mom. Most of you have become great friends, and it is a joy to spend time with each of you every weeknight and on the weekends. I appreciate everything that you do.

On the publishing side:

To Peggy Hicks, my publicist, my sister, my soul mate. What are the chances that two women could meet while working for the same company, become best friends, leave corporate America to start businesses of their own and then, ultimately work together in the publishing arena? We've done everything together for the last sixteen years, and isn't it so amazing how the tradition is still continuing. You are absolutely the best publicist any author could have, and you have made all the difference when it comes to promoting my work. I love you, and I appreciate your knowledge and commitment in the highest possible capacity. And to Steven Hicks who may as well be my brother, and Lauren Chapple who is nothing less than a niece. Thank you for always rooting on my behalf.

My agent, Elaine Koster. What a wonderful three years we have had. You possess what every successful agent must have—professionalism, charisma, personality, and a very caring attitude. You are the whole package, and while I've said it many times before, you have made my publishing life so much easier. And for that, I am totally indebted.

To Julie Snively, Edith Lee Webster, and everyone else at the *Rockford Register Star* who publicize my career on a year-round basis! Thank you for everything.

To Karen Thomas, Laurie Parkin, and everyone else at Kensington Publishing who worked hard to make this book the best that it could be.

E. Lynn Harris for your unwavering, unconditional support of me as an author. You are such a wonderful friend, and I am so proud of your much deserved success. Love and blessings.

To all of my author friends: Eric Jerome Dickey, Shandra Hill, Patricia Haley, Lolita Files, Victoria Christopher Murray, Yolanda Joe, Veronda Johnson, Veraunda Jackson, Timm McCann, Kieja Shapodee, Colin Channer, Deborah Gregory, Trevy McDonald, Franklin White, Victor McGlothin, Vincent Alexander, Carl Weber, Camika Spencer, Tajuana "TJ" Butler, Francis Ray, Rochelle Alers, C. Kelly Robinson, and all of the rest of my colleagues in this industry.

And words simply cannot express my gratitude toward all of the book clubs situated throughout the country. You go out of your way to support my work, and you have played such a crucial part in building my reading audience. I appreciate being given the opportunity to attend some of your discussions, and I hope to see all of you very soon.

To all of the African-American, independent bookstore owners and staff members who still hand sell my novels to their customers. I sincerely appreciate your support, because without you, my career would not have been possible.

And, of course, to all of my readers everywhere. You are the most important of all, and please know that I will never, ever forget that.

Much love,
Kimberla Lawson Roby

E-mail: *kim@kimroby.com*
Web site: *http://www.kimroby.com*

Chapter 1

Sydney Taylor wondered if she and her husband, Wesley, would ever see eye to eye in terms of their sexual relations. They'd been having these problems in the bedroom for over a year now, and it was starting to cause an uncomfortable strain on their marriage. A marriage that had always been ideal and very happy until Wesley realized how infrequent their lovemaking had become. Sydney genuinely didn't want it to be this way, but it was just that she was under so much stress, trying to meet multiple freelance writing deadlines. Not to mention transporting their daughter, Victoria, to every after-school activity that Covington Park Jr. High School seemed to offer. On most days, Sydney didn't know whether she was coming or going, and her schedule had become so hectic that it felt like she was trying to squeeze thirty hours into a normal twenty-four-hour day.

But Wesley didn't seem to care about any of that,

and for the most part had decided that she simply didn't desire him anymore, and that making love to him just wasn't important to her. She tried to explain to him that she loved him from the bottom of her heart and that things would eventually get better, but she had to admit that they hadn't. As a matter of fact, the infrequency was worse than ever before, and the reason why Wesley had turned his back to her so abruptly just a few minutes ago.

She didn't know what was wrong with her, because the evening had started out with such great intentions. Victoria was spending the night with her two cousins at their grandmother's, and Sydney and Wesley had planned a quiet, candlelight dinner at home. But maybe it was the fact that she was desperately fighting to meet a very critical deadline and wasn't able to relax by the time Wesley arrived home from work. He'd phoned her early in the afternoon and asked if it would be better for him to pick up a meal for them from Big Italy's, and she'd quickly agreed when she realized she wasn't going to have time to cook anything the way she'd planned. And Wesley was okay with that, since his number one priority wasn't whether they ate a home-cooked meal or take-out in the first place. What he wanted was to make love and hadn't hesitated to let her know that as soon as they'd finished eating dinner.

Sydney had lit the candles on the dining room table, as they'd discussed the day before, and she'd even lit a few in their bedroom on top of the armoire, the dresser, and one on each nightstand. The setting was absolutely perfect, but for some reason when her husband tried to kiss her, she just didn't seem to have any energy, and while she would never ever admit it to him, she didn't have one ounce of desire for him. It wasn't that she desired any other man, but she simply couldn't stop thinking about all the work she still needed to complete before the weekend was over with.

They'd gotten completely undressed, and Wesley had tried to turn her on to the best of his ability, but for some reason it hadn't worked. She'd decided that she would feign her excitement and enthusiasm, so that he wouldn't feel bad, but it wasn't long before he moved away from her and asked her what her problem was. She didn't know how to respond to him, and it wasn't long before he turned away from her in complete silence.

She wanted to say something to him, but she didn't know how to approach him without causing a huge argument. They'd had major blow-ups over this very situation before, and she just didn't feel like going through any of that again. But she knew she couldn't just leave things the way they were, especially since they'd vowed never to go to sleep angry with each other and hadn't since the day they were married fourteen years ago.

She glanced over at him again and found the nerve to speak.

"Sweetie, I am so sorry," she said, holding her breath.

But Wesley ignored her apology. He didn't even grunt.

"Wesley, talk to me," she pleaded.

Wesley sat up on the side of the bed and looked back at his wife.

"What is there to talk about, Sydney? Huh? I mean, what exactly do you think we need to say to each other?"

"We need to talk about this problem that we have."

"No," he said in a hostile tone. "*We* don't have a problem. It's you who has the problem. 'I've got such a bad headache; oh, I'm so stressed out; oh, I'm so exhausted; oh, I don't know where the time went; oh, Victoria isn't asleep yet,'" he said, mocking Sydney's usual excuses in a female tone of voice.

She just looked at him, sort of feeling sorry for the way things were between them, but slightly irritated because he just didn't understand everything she was going through.

"Wesley, do you think I'm lying when I say those things? Because when I say I'm tired and stressed out, I really do mean it. I know that doesn't help things, but I can't help the way I feel."

"That's fine and great, but exactly where do I fit into this stressful schedule you seem to have every day of the week? Because it's almost as if the only thing I'm good for is bringing home my paycheck."

"What are you talking about?" she asked, becoming angry.

"You know exactly what I'm talking about. It's not like I stuttered," he said sarcastically.

"You know, if you would stop messing up every room in the house, and I wouldn't have to pick up behind you and Victoria every day, maybe I would have way more energy than I do. And it's not like you're the only person bringing a paycheck into this household. Do you think I'm working this hard just for the sake of burning myself out?"

"Whatever, Sydney. You can go around and about all you want to, but that still doesn't change the fact that our sex life is nonexistent and you're not trying to do a damn thing to make it better. I'm sick of begging you for sex, and I'm sick of having this same tired conversation about it. Hell, I may as well buy some blow-up doll, because right now, I'd have a better chance of getting excitement from it than I am from you," he said, standing up.

Sydney sighed with frustration. "I can't believe you feel that way. After all the years we've been together. And it's not like we've *just* married, but we've always been happily married."

"Well, being happily married isn't enough when there's not enough lovemaking going on. I mean, what exactly do you expect me to do?"

"I expect you to work with me on this. Geez. You're

acting like you want to go out and get it from someone else."

"You said it. I didn't."

"What the hell does that mean?" she asked, sitting up on the side of the bed.

"I don't want to discuss this anymore, and I think the best thing for you to do is get your rest, and the best thing for me to do is go sleep in the family room."

Wesley left the bedroom, and Sydney felt tears flowing down her face.

She hated when things turned this bad between them, and she didn't know what was happening to their relationship. It seemed as though they were drifting further and further apart, and it was all because of this sex issue. She wanted to make love to him, but she just didn't have the energy to do so. Maybe she needed to see her gynecologist. Maybe she needed her testosterone level checked. Maybe she had some female problem that had caused her sexual desire to drop to an all-time low. She'd read articles about women who fit into this category, and wondered if maybe her problem really was a medical one.

She lay there for almost a half-hour tossing a thousand thoughts through her mind. She couldn't come up with a solution, but she did know one thing, and that was that she wouldn't be able to stand waking up in a different room than Wesley. It was one thing when one of them traveled for business and their separation couldn't be helped, but it just didn't seem right, sleeping separately when they were both sleeping under the same roof. She had a lot of pride, and it was hard making up with Wesley after they had an argument. Normally, he was the one who usually called a truce whenever they had a disagreement, but rarely did he make the first move when it came to this subject.

She heard him flipping through the channels on the

television, and decided that she had to muster up the courage to go talk with him. She needed to make things right with him, and she wasn't going to rest until she did.

She wrapped a blanket around herself, strolled down the hallway, and walked into the family room. Wesley glanced over at her and then turned his focus back to *Trading Places,* one of his favorite Eddie Murphy reruns. He wasn't going to make this easy for her. She knew that without question.

She dropped down on the sofa so close to him that there was no room for him to move away. But he still didn't say anything and continued watching the big-screen television.

"Wesley, how long are you going to be mad at me?" she asked, laying her head on his shoulder.

"I'm sick of this, Sydney, and you know this isn't right."

"Baby, I'm sorry," she said. "I don't know what's wrong with me, but what I do know is that I love you, and I couldn't stand it if we weren't together. When I tell you I'm tired, I'm really telling you the truth. But I do admit that it seems like I'm tired and stressed all the time. I'm thinking that maybe I need to see my doctor."

"Maybe you should, because this once a week or once every two weeks stuff isn't working for me."

"Wesley, we just made love three days ago on Tuesday, so why are you trying to make it seem like it's been longer than that?"

At first Wesley didn't say anything, but then he smiled and looked at her. "Woman, my penis doesn't know what day of the week it is, and it definitely doesn't know how many days have gone by since it got taken care of."

They both laughed, and then hugged each other tightly for longer than usual.

"Baby," Wesley said, sighing in a serious tone. "I'm

sorry for getting so upset, but can I help it if I desire my beautiful wife every day of the week?"

Maybe he couldn't, but she'd been sure that marrying a man ten years her senior would basically guarantee that he wouldn't want to have sex every time he looked at her. It was almost insane, and now that he was forty-six, his desire was becoming stronger as the years continued on. Most women would have thought this was the greatest thing in the world, but she just couldn't keep up with his pace. It wasn't that she didn't enjoy sex with him because when they did make love, it was the best feeling she'd ever experienced. It was just that she had too much on her plate, and needed to rearrange some things so that she could spend more time with her wonderful husband. And it wouldn't hurt to spend just a little more time with Victoria as well. She'd been trying so hard to build her career as a writer, because her ultimate goal was to write a novel and hopefully sell it to a major publishing house in New York. That was probably a long way down the road, but these magazine articles she was writing would help prove her writing ability when it came time to submit her book-length manuscript, and the reason she had to work as hard as she could getting her name out there.

Wesley pulled his wife into his arms and kissed her passionately. To his surprise, she kissed him back with such force and desire that he didn't know what had come over her, and he couldn't believe that this was the same woman he'd argued with less than ten minutes ago. Sydney pulled away from him, stood up, dropped the blanket she was wrapped in onto the floor, and gazed at him with total fire in her eyes. Wesley picked up the TV selector and turned it off, then picked up the remote pad for the stereo system and started the first track of one of his jazz CDs.

He stood, and they held each other close, dancing to

the beautiful music, neither of them covered with one stitch of clothing. They kissed until Wesley began lowering himself onto his knees, kissing every part of Sydney's long, toned body on the way down. She moaned with much pleasure and wished that this feeling she was experiencing would never come to an end. It was so amazing, that she couldn't help but wonder how any woman could pass up a chance at making love with a man who loved her as much as Wesley loved her, and one who knew specifically how to satisfy her sexually. He was absolutely the best, and the thought of him giving this satisfaction to any other woman was completely out of the question, and the reason why she was going to have to get her priorities in line when it came to him. They had a loving, committed marriage, and there was no way she was going to throw away the best thing that had ever happened to her. The best thing that could happen to any woman who wanted the man of her dreams.

Sydney gazed down at her husband, who was still on his knees, grabbed the sides of his head, and moaned at a high volume. She begged him to stop, not wanting this to end so quickly, but in a matter of seconds, she exploded uncontrollably.

Wesley stood up, turned the front of her body toward the sofa, and eased inside her from behind.

"Oh, my goodness," Sydney wailed.

"Oh, baby," Wesley complimented her.

He moved his muscular body in a circular motion with ease, then faster. And faster. Then, she clutched the back of the sofa with both hands and moved her body like she knew he wanted her to. They both moaned with pleasure and Wesley loved her in a more forceful manner than before, reaching for his much-awaited climax. His eyes rolled upward, toward the back of his head, with his body shivering and hovering comfortably over Sydney's.

They settled onto the seat of the sofa, their bodies wrapped together as one. This was the way their love-making was supposed to be, and the way it always had been whenever they were fortunate enough to find an opportunity to engage in it. There was this problem with frequency, but never a problem with quality or satisfaction. There was no doubt about it, they were good together and it was clear that they were in fact meant to be together. They were soul mates and neither of them ever questioned that whole philosophy. They'd met the same day Sydney graduated from the university with a journalism degree. She'd gone out with a few of her friends to a nightclub in the city, and it just so happened that Wesley was a friend of a friend of a friend. They'd been attracted to each other from the very beginning, and it wasn't long before they danced to a few songs and ended up spending the entire evening at their own separate table. They dated for weeks and months, but they'd both known from the start that they were destined to become man and wife. The love and spiritual connection between them had been obvious to everyone around them, and the idea of them living their lives together forever was inevitable.

Then there was their beautiful, twelve-year-old daughter, Victoria, who was the model child on most occasions or at least when her lovely adolescence wasn't causing major turmoil for her and Sydney's close-knit, mother-daughter relationship. Her father spoiled her, but there were times when Victoria saw her mother as the enemy—especially when she couldn't have everything the way she wanted it, exactly when she wanted. There were days when she was sure that Sydney was trying to "control" her life, but Sydney always assured her that she wasn't simply *trying* to control her life, but that instead, she was in fact actually doing it. And that as long as she was living under their roof, was still a minor and unable to take care of herself, not a whole lot was going to change. Maybe within reason, but when it came to serious issues, situations that could ruin her life or tamper with her well-being, she and her father were always going to have a certain level of control. Whether Victoria liked it or not, that's just the way things were going to be.

Sydney wanted to be the best wife, the best mother, and the best writer. She wanted to be the same super-woman that every other New Millennium woman needed to be. But she was going to have to rearrange her priorities, she was going to have to work on spending more time intimately with Wesley, more quality time with Victoria, and unfortunately maybe less time writing. She'd still work hard to meet her deadlines, but maybe she wouldn't take on so many projects, all at the same time.

"Now that's what I'm talking about," Wesley finally commented.

"Oh, really?" Sydney added.

"Yes, really. And you wonder why I want it so much. No man could get used to going without something that feels this good."

"It can't be that good," she said, teasing him. "Is it?"

"You know how good it is, and that's why you try to ration it to me. A form of control is what it is."

They both laughed.

"No it's not," Sydney insisted. "I would never use sex to control you."

"Yeah, right. All women use sex as a weapon. Especially when they find out the man is hooked on it."

"So, since you're so hooked, does that mean I don't have to worry about you going somewhere else to get it?" she said playfully, yet somewhat serious.

"Look, baby, I know I get upset—"

"That's an understatement," she interrupted.

"Okay, I practically go ballistic," he said, chuckling. "But understand this. I don't want anyone else. I don't want to make love with anyone else, and I could never love anyone the way that I love you."

"I know I haven't been giving you enough of my time, but I promise things are going to be changing around here. You and Victoria mean everything to me, and I don't want you to ever think otherwise," she said.

They chatted and held each other for a long while, until finally drifting off to sleep.

Chapter 2

"I think it's so wonderful that CPMA honors ten minority high school seniors every year with two-thousand-dollar college scholarships," Lori Sanders said to Gina Harris.

"It really is," Gina agreed with her coworker, and then turned to her husband, Phillip, who didn't seem to be having a very good time. "Isn't it, honey?" she asked him.

"Yeah, I guess," Phillip answered without even looking at her.

Gina didn't know what Phillip's problem was, and with all the paranoia he seemed to be consumed with, she knew it could be just about anything. It wasn't worth trying to find out right now, because it would only make him angrier in the end.

"So, Gina," Michael Wilson said. "Word is, you're the most qualified candidate for that MIS director position everybody in the department has been drooling over for the last few weeks."

"Oh, I don't know about that," Gina commented modestly and wished he would leave this whole subject alone. She hadn't mentioned any of this to Phillip, because she knew it was going to send him into one of his unexplainable rages. She'd gotten a promotion a few years back, and Phillip had done everything in the book to make her feel like she didn't deserve it. He insisted that the only reason she kept working for these promotions was so that she could rub his face in them. He didn't like the fact that she earned more money than him, and had made it clear on several occasions that he pretty much despised her for it.

"Well, everyone else knows you are even if you don't. I've been at the company longer than you, and even I have to admit that you're still the best person for the job."

Everyone at the table nodded their heads in agreement. All except Phillip.

Michael continued with his words of praise, and then turned his attention to Phillip. "So, Phillip, how does it feel to be living with a woman who's beautiful and intelligent?"

"What, are you saying, that I'm not intelligent, and that I should feel privileged to be married to Gina?" he asked nastily.

Everyone at the table looked around at each other, obviously not knowing what to say. Gina felt like crawling inside her own skin. She was so embarrassed and sorry for Phillip's behavior. She didn't know why he was being so mean to all of her coworkers, but she wished he would stop it. She wished he would never have agreed to come, if all he was going to do was ruin the evening for everyone else. But then there was no way he was letting her out of the house to go to an event like this without him, and it was only luck that he'd allowed them to attend at all.

"I'm not saying anything like that," Michael answered. "I was only trying to give you a compliment. You're a lucky man, and you should be proud of your wife and her accomplishments."

Phillip stared at Michael but didn't respond. Then he looked away from the table like he didn't want to be bothered with anyone who was sitting there. He freaked out like this every time he was in the company of degreed professionals, and Gina didn't know what she could do to make him feel more comfortable. She'd told him a thousand times that having a degree was a wonderful thing, but it didn't mean that a person was any better than someone who didn't have one. But Phillip had barely graduated from high school, and Gina knew he felt as though he wasn't equal to her colleagues, who in most cases, were armed with no less than a master's degree.

The servers brought out baskets of bread and salad with house dressing. Then they served prime rib for those who preferred red meat, and grilled chicken for those who didn't. The food was wonderful, as always, whenever Gina attended conferences and dinners at the Hyatt Regency in The McCormick Place, a huge convention center situated near Lake Shore Drive.

Phillip ate his meal in silence, but everyone else chatted about work and anything else they could think of. Gina answered questions mostly, because she didn't want Phillip to think she was having too good of a time. He was obviously having a horrible time, and she knew she was going to have hell to pay on the way home if it looked like she was ignoring him. She was going to have to deal with him one way or the other anyhow, but maybe if she didn't do a lot of laughing and didn't appear to be enjoying herself, it wouldn't be as bad.

The scholarships were presented to five African-American students, two Asian, two Latino, and one East Indian. When the program was over, everyone convened outside the banquet facility to pick up their coats. Gina tried to make small talk with Phillip, but he really didn't have much to say to her. No more than what he had to, anyway.

They strolled through the lobby and then out to the valet area. Phillip pulled the claim check from his pocket and gave it to the valet person on duty.

"Since the twins are at Mom's, we should have reserved a hotel room and spent the night," Gina offered, trying to smooth things over.

Phillip turned toward her, and frowned. "For what, Gina? So you can make me feel worse than those idiot coworkers of yours did? And it seems to me that you should be asking that son-of-a-bitch Michael up to a room, because that's who you he-he'd and ha-ha'd with all night anyway."

"Phillip, what are you talking about?"

"Play dumb if you want to. I may not have a college degree, but I'm not stupid, Gina."

Gina loathed these jealous tendencies of Phillip's. It was almost as if he expected her to sit like some child who could only speak when spoken to, and he never expected her to have conversations with any man she could think of. He didn't even like her communicating with her brother, Rick, for that matter. And to be honest, sometimes he seemed to have a problem with her visiting her mother, and her sister, Sydney, as well.

She had to calm him down. She didn't know how she was going to do it, but she didn't want to argue with him all the way back to Covington Park and then again once they arrived at their home. She'd wanted this to be an elegant evening out and a nice, quiet, romantic rest of the evening in their bedroom. She'd been looking forward to getting out of the house and going to this event, because she really thought they needed a change of pace and atmosphere. But now, she wasn't so sure if bringing Phillip to this scholarship dinner had been the wisest decision to make. And she certainly hadn't planned on Michael bringing up her promotion possibility like he had.

The valet attendant pulled their pure white, BMW 535 in front of the hotel and stepped out of it. Phillip didn't bother opening the door for Gina, walked around to the driver's side, tipped the attendant, and before Gina could barely close her door, he pulled off. They drove onto 94 and headed to the south suburbs in silence. But it wasn't long before Phillip went off.

"So, are you screwing that asshole Michael?" he demanded an answer.

"What? No! What kind of question is that?"

"Don't play dumb with me, Gina. Bitches like you mess around on men like me all the time."

"Why are you calling me a bitch, Phillip, and why are you always accusing me of messing around on you, when you know I'm not?"

Phillip changed lanes abruptly, and Gina had to hold on to the dashboard to keep herself balanced. He was driving like a psychopath, and he was scaring her to no end. She couldn't believe that all of this was happening simply because she'd had a conversation with Michael, one of her most dedicated coworkers. The ironic part was, their relationship was strictly platonic, and not once had Michael ever approached her in an improper manner.

"Phillip, what's the matter with you?"

"There's nothing wrong with me, but I'll be damned if I'm going to let you laugh and talk with your other man right up in my face, and then let you get away with it."

Get away with it? What did he mean by that? Gina was more terrified now than she'd been in a very long time. They'd had some physical problems during the first couple years of their marriage, but after the twins were born, things had become one hundred percent better between them. Phillip had been a proud father, and he'd basically treated her like a queen from that day forward. Sure, they'd had their ups and downs over the last couple of years, and he'd gotten physical with her a few times here and there, but she'd learned what to say, what not to say, what to do, and what she shouldn't in order to avoid pissing him off. She understood him well, she thought, and she wasn't sure at all why he was acting as if he was losing his natural mind right now.

"Honey. Look," she pleaded with him. "I don't know what I did wrong, but I promise you, there's nothing going on between Michael and me. I love you and only you."

Phillip laughed like she'd just told a very funny joke, and slammed on the accelerator.

"Phillip, please stop it," she begged loudly. "You're going to kill us if you keep driving like this. Why are you doing this?"

"You weren't acting like you were afraid of anything when you were talking to your man at the table. Now were you?"

"Michael is not my man, Phillip," she tried to convince him.

"Don't deny that again, Gina. You know I hate a liar more than I hate anything else," he said matter-of-factly.

Gina wanted to plead with him again, but she decided that it was best to stay calm and quiet for the rest of the ride. She didn't know what was going to happen when they arrived home, but she was already praying that God would remove this paranoia from his twisted mind. He was so jealous and possessive, but she hadn't seen him act this way in a very long while. Although, now that she thought about it, he had had a couple of drinks, and alcohol did seem to increase his suspicion of her and other men. Once when he'd been drinking at a wedding reception they'd gone to, he accused her of staring at the groom, his cousin's new husband. He saw what he wanted to, and there was no telling him any different.

Phillip drove into the subdivision, into the driveway of their tri-level home, waited for the garage to open, and drove inside. They both stepped out of the car, and Gina continued praying like she never had before.

She walked through the door, shut off the security system, and Phillip walked in behind her.

"So, how long have you been screwing Michael?" Phillip started. "Huh?"

"I told you, I'm not doing anything with Michael. We work in the same department, and that's it."

"I thought I told you that I don't want to hear any more of your lies," he said, pulling a beer from the refrigerator.

Gina walked through the hallway and up to their bedroom without responding. She was so worried about what Phillip was going to do, that she slipped on the top stair. When she caught her balance, she entered the bedroom and heard Phillip walking up the stairway behind her.

"You know what? I ought to throw your ass down those stairs for treating me like you did tonight. You talked to that son-of-a-bitch like I wasn't even there. And then he made that funky comment about you being so intelligent, like I was some illiterate fool. That's why he had that funky grin on his face. He wanted me to know he was knockin' the boots and that he has been for a long time."

Gina didn't know whether to beg for forgiveness or keep her mouth shut. She couldn't win for losing, and she didn't know what to do to make him understand that all of this was nothing more than something he'd fabricated in his mind.

She sighed deeply. "Honey—"

But Phillip didn't wait for her to finish her sentence. He tossed his half-empty beer can across the room and hit her in her stomach.

She wailed with pain and dropped down on the bed. Phillip rushed over to her and forced her back to her feet by her hair.

"Bitch, you thought you were so smart. You might have a degree, but you're about as stupid as they come. Frontin' that white boy in my face like that."

"Phillip, stop it," she pleaded, the same as she had for the last hour or so.

"I'll bet you didn't tell Mikey to stop when he was rammin' his dick inside you. Now did you?" he asked, slamming her down on the bed.

Gina screamed and scooted her body, trying to move away from him, but he yanked her by her feet, pulling her off the bed, down on her tail bone. She wailed again in pain, but Phillip couldn't have cared less.

"Get up off of that floor, Gina. I mean, get up, right now," he yelled.

"Phillip, I'm hurt," she said, crying uncontrollably. "Please don't do this."

"Don't do what?" he said, kicking her in her hip.

She screamed loudly.

"I said get up," he yelled again, and this time, he pulled her up by her throat.

"I'm sorry, Phillip," she said, gasping for breath. "I'm so sorry."

"Yeah, you better be, because I'm not playing with you. You've got one more time to let me catch you messing around with another man, and I promise you, Gina, I *will* kill you. And believe me when I say that no one will ever find out what happened to you."

He slung her on the bed and walked out of the bedroom.

She curled her body in the fetal position and cried like she'd just been diagnosed with some form of cancer and there wasn't anything the doctors could do about it. She thanked God that her babies, Carl and Caitlin, had spent the night with their grandmother and hadn't had to witness yet another violent episode between their parents. They were safe, and that gave her at least some peace of mind. They'd witnessed a few slaps and shoves here and there, but they'd never seen their father beat their mother down the way he just had. She didn't know what was happening to Phillip. She loved him, God help her, because he was her children's father, but she hated him for physically abusing her. She was frightened for her life, but she was tired of living in this invisible prison he was trying to keep her in. He didn't like her family or friends visiting, and he had a huge fit every time he heard her having a decent conversation on the phone with any of them. Her sister, Sydney, couldn't stand the ground that Phillip walked on, and only tolerated him because she knew Gina loved him. Delores, Gina's mother, wasn't aware of all the beatings. She'd known about the incidents that had taken place early in their marriage, but she was totally in the dark about recent events. And Gina wanted to keep it that way. Their mother had been diagnosed with what they believed was a benign brain tumor called a meningioma, and while it hadn't grown since they accidentally discovered it eighteen months ago, Gina didn't want to worry her mother unnecessarily. The sort of worry that would cause her mother to lose sleep at night. Who she wanted to call, though, was her brother, but she always decided against that ever since the time she had and Rick had threatened to bury Phillip six feet under if he ever found out that he was beating his sister again.

She felt so stupid for being in this situation and for staying in this marriage for as long as she had. She seemed to have everything together from a career standpoint, but she just couldn't find the courage to stand up to Phillip so she could leave him. She couldn't even use the same excuse that abused housewives use, since she earned more than enough money to make it on her own. She didn't even need child support from him, and it definitely wasn't good to have her children living in this abusive environment. Phillip hadn't beat the children, but who was to say what might happen if he continued to come home in one of his drunken, jealous rages. She didn't want to be in this situation, and she wasn't sure if she stayed because she did in fact love this man who treated her like an animal, or if it was the fact that he'd promised her over and over that he really would kill her if she even thought about trying to leave him. She thought about leaving all the time, but she couldn't take the chance that Phillip might do exactly what he said he would. Her children needed their mother too much for her to take any unnecessary risks.

Gina wondered when this night would be over with, but most of all, she wondered how many more times Phillip was going to have to hurt her before she finally woke up and did something about it. Maybe it was as simple as getting him professional help. She didn't know what the future held for them or their children, but she had a very eerie feeling about all of this in general. She had a feeling that things were going to get worse instead of better.

Chapter 3

Rick Mathis turned the lock inside the front door of the condo, opened it, and waited for his fiancée, Samantha, to enter before him. They'd just returned from seeing some romantic flick that he hadn't cared that much about seeing, but it hadn't been as boring as he'd expected. Come to think of it, he'd actually thought it had a pretty good plot, but more importantly, it had certainly placed Samantha in a very passionate mood. He could tell by the way she'd held and caressed his hand on the way home, and how she'd looked at him when they were leaving the cinema.

Samantha dropped her purse in the chair and lit multiple candles in the living room. Rick took out a bottle of Chardonnay, filled two wineglasses, and brought them to the sculptured glass coffee table. Then they both sat down on the sofa and relaxed for a few minutes.

"So, what do you want to do for the rest of the

evening?" Samantha asked, smiling, and smoothing her fingers under his chin.

"What do you think?" he responded, knowing she already knew the answer to his question. It was what he always wanted to do every Friday evening. He enjoyed making love to her on other days of the week and did, but it always seemed different when he didn't have to think about rising for work the next morning. He was a customer service supervisor for one of the leading Chicago clothing distribution centers, but he never had to work weekends. Of course, they'd wanted him to the first couple of years he'd been employed with the company, but it wasn't long before he earned enough time to pass weekend hours off to the supervisors at a lower level.

Rick picked up his wineglass and took a couple of sips. Samantha did the same, but Rick removed her glass from her hand and sat both of them down on the table. "Come here," he instructed while pulling her closer to him by her arm.

They didn't speak a word to each other, but shared a long-awaited intimate kiss. Samantha was the best thing ever, and he'd never met a woman who could satisfy his every need the way she did. She looked good, she could cook just about anything one could think of, she kept the condo immaculate, and she didn't have a burning desire to have a house full of children. Even better, she had a top accounting position that earned her a great salary. She had the whole package, and there wasn't anything he could see that needed changing. Sure, she'd thrown the idea of marriage up to him a few times, but things were perfect the way they were, and the reason he'd kept insisting that they had plenty of time to say "I do." It was just a piece of paper anyway, and it wasn't going to change the way they felt about each other one bit. They loved each other, they were engaged, and they lived a very happy life.

He'd been hesitant about having her move into his condo, but since he didn't want to lose her, he figured he really didn't have much choice. She'd basically told him that—either they were going to move closer toward making a permanent commitment, or they were going to have to go their separate ways—which was the same thing she'd told him when she'd wanted to get engaged. He'd held out for as long as he could, but when he'd seen for sure that she was serious about ending their relationship, he'd hurried to tell her that she could give up her apartment and make her home with him. That was one year ago, and to his surprise, things were still going well.

Rick pulled Samantha's sweater over her head, and she returned the favor by helping him remove his. He unhooked her bra and immediately caressed her breasts with his hand on one and his tongue on the other. She arched her back in a sensual manner, allowing him to have his way with her. Then Rick slipped off her pants and underwear and stroked his hand back and forth between her legs all the while sucking each of her breasts.

"Please, sweetheart," she requested.

"Please what?" Rick asked, teasing her.

"Baby, please," she continued.

"Please what?"

"Give it to me."

"You don't really want it?" he said, still tormenting her.

"I do, baby. Please," she said, breathing loudly.

"I think I'll let you give it to me instead," he said, standing up. Then he removed the rest of his clothing and stretched out on his back. Samantha climbed on top backward, eased down on him, and moved her body up, down, and around. She continued that same sequence in a rough, lustful fashion, and Rick didn't know how long he was going to be able to stand all of this. He wanted to wait until she received total satisfaction, but she always drove him insane whenever she rode him in this manner. It was as if she was a different person when they made love and not at all like the very well-educated, decent woman he'd always known her to be. Her coworkers and family members would have been amazed at the things she did in the bedroom let alone the things she said. But then, they'd probably have a few heart attacks over what every other person in the country did and said when they were having sex as well.

Samantha groaned louder and more often, while still rolling her body round and round, up and down, and Rick knew it was just a matter of time before she got what she'd been working so hard for. He worked right along with her, pulling and pushing her buttocks up and down, and pushing himself in and out of her.

"Oh, yes," Samantha shouted. "Oh, my," she continued until they both climaxed. Then she turned to face him, and extended her body across his.

"You're the best, you know that," he said, completely out of breath.

"I know," she boasted. "And don't you forget it."

"Oh, so it's like that, huh?"

"It's exactly like that," she said, slightly laughing.

"I hear you."

They were silent for a few minutes.

"Sweetheart," Samantha began. "As much as I hate to bring this up, we really do need to discuss it."

Now why did she always have to ruin everything with all this talk about getting married? She hadn't said one word, but he already knew where this conversation was heading. Couldn't she have waited a few more minutes before bringing all this up, allowing him some time to savor the moment? It wouldn't have made any difference, because it wasn't like they were going right to sleep. It was almost as if she enjoyed turning him on and then dropping a bomb all at the same time. He didn't understand why she couldn't just leave well enough alone and why she couldn't be happy with the existing conditions. He was happy, and he didn't see any reason why she shouldn't be either. He was committed to her. Maybe not the way she wanted him to be, but he was faithful to her, and he brought all of his money home. What more could a woman ask for? He'd been the ideal man ever since he met her, and it just seemed to him that she should be jumping up and down about it. Especially since the ratio of men to women was at least ten to one. She was living the good life, and didn't even know it. But then maybe she did know it after all, and her unhappiness was probably due to the fact that a man could give his woman the world but she would still wake up the next morning asking for something more.

"Rick, are you listening to me?"

"Yeah, I'm listening. What is it?" He played ignorant.

"We've been engaged for two years, we've been living together for a year, and I don't think it's right for us to keep living in sin the way we are. You say that you love me, I have no doubt that I love you, so why can't we just make all of this legal?"

There was that infamous "L" word again. She'd said these same words over and over for so long now, he wondered if she could actually speak them in her sleep. He didn't know how many times he was going to have to tell her, but his feelings about tying the knot hadn't changed since the day she brought this subject up last weekend. Did she think something miraculous had happened since then? Maybe it was the sex she'd just given him. His brother-in-law, Wesley, swore that Sydney always used sex to control him, and maybe Samantha had been having conversations with her.

"Samantha, I'm not feeling any of this at all. I've told you how I feel about getting married, so why do you insist on bringing this up all the time?"

"Because, Rick, I don't want to keep living like this. I need to know that our relationship is permanent."

"We've only been living together for a year, and I don't think we should just go jumping into marriage so quickly. It's just not the right time."

"When is the right time? And what do you mean 'jumping into it'? You make it sound like you'd be signing your life away or something."

"That's pretty much what you do when you sign on the dotted line, don't you?" he said and burst out laughing.

Samantha pushed against his chest as hard as she could and lifted her body away from him. Then she started gathering up her clothes. "You think this is all a joke, but I'm tired of living like this. As a matter of fact, I'm telling you, that I *won't* continue living like this forever."

"Why are you getting so upset over nothing? It's not like I'm out with some other woman. I'm here with you all the time. You know I don't want anyone else, so what's the big deal?" he said, realizing that he was losing ground.

"What's the big deal?" she repeated his question, squinting her eyes in anger.

Rick didn't like the way she was looking at him.

"I'll tell you what the big deal is. Either you're going to commit or I'm moving out, because I'm not about to spend the rest of my life shacking up with you."

"Oh, so what you're saying is that you practically begged to move in here, but now you're ready to pack your shit and leave. I don't believe I'm hearing this."

"What do you expect me to do, Rick? Keep living here without any form of security whatsoever, leaving the relationship wide open, so you can leave me whenever you get ready? No, I'm sorry, but I'm not having it. I've seen too many of my girlfriends go through that very thing, and in every situation, some man had promised them that he was going to marry them, and then of course didn't."

"Why are you comparing our situation to everyone else's?" he asked, wanting to know why women always had to play the comparison game when they were trying to get their way with something.

"Because, when it comes to men making promises about marriage, the story is always the same. There might be a few who follow through on their word, but not very many."

"Well, I'm telling you, baby, when the time is right, we will get married. Story-book wedding and all if you want it."

"That's not good enough, Rick. You are going to have to make a commitment or things aren't going to work between us."

"Look," Rick said in an angry tone. "You do whatever it is you feel you have to do. I've told you for the last time how I feel about this."

Samantha gathered up her shoes, picked up her purse, and headed toward the stairway. She didn't say another word to him. Didn't even look in his direction. Now he wished he'd never allowed her to move in with him. He'd known it was going to be a disaster, but since things had gone so well for almost twelve months, he'd started thinking that maybe things really would work out for the best. But, now, she was pressing him about something that he wasn't ready to do, and wasn't going to until he was good and ready.

She really pissed him off when she went on one of these tangents of hers, and it was at times like these when he wondered if he was in fact in love with her or not. Maybe it was just the sex. Or maybe it was the idea of being in love with her that fascinated him. He didn't know, but right now he wasn't sure about anything. He wasn't even sure if they should remain engaged, let alone think about getting married. He didn't like it when she tried to force him to do something he wasn't ready to do, and he couldn't understand why this ball and chain attachment was so important to her. Why it was so important to practically every woman living on earth? It wasn't that he wanted his freedom to mess around with other women, because he didn't. But at the same time, he didn't like the idea of being so attached to someone else that you lost your own independence. He'd seen a number of men go out like that, and he didn't want to end up in the same predicament. She said she didn't want any children, but the next thing you knew, she'd be planning to have a whole army of little ones. Even worse, he could see both of them walking around with huge bellies because of how lazy they'd become, and how their six children would tire them out so terribly, that the idea of making love would be totally out of the question.

"Oh, *hellll* no," Rick blurted out before he realized it. "I don't think so," he said.

Then he flipped on the television.

Chapter 4

Rick parked his silver Expedition in front of his mother's house and saw Sydney and Wesley pulling their black Jeep Cherokee Limited into the driveway. It was Saturday morning and they were all there for the delicious breakfast Delores always cooked for them one Saturday out of every month. It had been sort of a tradition after they'd each grown up and moved out of the house, and it was good for the entire family to spend quality time together.

"Hey, sis, what's up?" Rick said, walking toward his eldest sister and hugging her.

"Hey, Rick," she said, smiling at him.

"Hey, Wes, man, how's it going with you?" Rick said, shaking Wesley's hand.

"It's all good, brother-in-law, what's up with you?" Wesley asked.

"Everything's good on this end, but it'll be even better once I get in here and get some of what Mom is cooking."

They all laughed and walked through the garage, which was already open. They could hear the twins playing and Victoria talking to her grandmother. Then they walked through the door leading into the kitchen.

"Hey, Mom, how are you?" Sydney said, hugging her mother and kissing her on the cheek. Rick and Wesley did the same. Then, they exchanged hugs and greetings with the children.

"So, is everybody doing okay?" Delores asked, placing inside the stove a tray of sausages she'd just finished frying.

"We're all fine," Sydney answered. "Just waiting to eat the best breakfast in town."

"It'll all be ready in a little while," Delores confirmed.

"Can I help you with anything?" Sydney asked, even though she knew her mother always took pride in cooking the entire breakfast on her own. She always asked, though, just for the sake of being considerate.

"No, I'm fine. You just make yourself comfortable."

"So, Carl and Caitlin, did you guys have fun spending the night over here?" Sydney asked.

"Yep," they answered in unison. "Victoria played a lot of games with us, and we watched television real late."

"Well, that's good. Victoria, when we finish breakfast, you need to get dressed right away, so we can get to our hair appointment. And as a matter of fact, you could be taking your shower now while Granny is still cooking."

"Okay, but can I go to the movies with Sabrina and Marlene this afternoon?"

"I guess so, as long as it's not rated R."

"It's not. We haven't decided which one we're going to see yet, but they're all PG-13."

"You won't be thirteen until next month, so I guess that means you can't see those either," Wesley interrupted playfully.

"Daddy," she whined. "That's only a few weeks away."

"I'm just kidding with you," he said, grabbing her around her neck.

"We want to go, too," Carl commented.

"Yeah," Caitlin agreed.

"The movies we're going to see aren't for little kids," Victoria quickly responded.

"Yes, they are. If you can go to the movies, then we can, too." Caitlin complained.

"I think you guys are going to a birthday party, aren't you?" Sydney asked.

"Oh yeah," Carl remembered. "And it's going to be a lot more fun than your movie, Victoria," he boasted.

"Whatever, Carl," Victoria said and went upstairs to get cleaned up.

"I wonder where Gina is, anyway," Sydney said.

"Probably can't get out," Rick said sarcastically.

"Rick!" Delores scolded and shook her head in disagreement, not wanting the children to pick up on the fact that their uncle was referring to their possessive father.

"Okay, Mom," Rick said, laughing.

"And anyway, where is Samantha?" Delores asked him.

"Yeah, where is Samantha?" Sydney wanted to know as well.

"She didn't feel like coming," he answered but didn't discuss any details. The last thing he wanted was for them to learn that his relationship was resting on very shaky ground, and that he and his fiancée were having some very serious problems over this marriage thing.

"Why not?" Delores wanted to know.

"She just didn't. I guess she didn't feel like getting dressed," he lied.

"Well, call her and ask her if she wants me to send her a plate." Delores continued.

"I will, right before I leave."

Everyone's attention turned toward the door when they saw it opening. It was Gina.

"Mom," Caitlin said, running over to her mother. Carl did the same, and Gina hugged them both together.

"How are my babies doing this morning? Did you have a good time last night?"

"Yep, but Victoria won't take us to the movies with her," Caitlin reiterated.

"You have a birthday party to go to," Gina reminded her.

"I know, but we could go with her after that," Caitlin said.

"The party will probably start around the same time Victoria is going to the movies," Gina tried to reason with her.

Caitlin wasn't satisfied, but she didn't push the issue any further. She and Carl left the room to go upstairs into the spare bedroom.

"Hi, Mom," Gina said, hugging her mother. Then, she spoke to and embraced Sydney and Wesley.

"How's it going, baby brother," she said to Rick and hugged him.

"I'm fine, sis. What's going on with you?"

"Everything is fine," she said, knowing that she'd experienced the worst night of her life.

"You look tired," Delores said to her middle child.

"You're not sick, are you?" Sydney asked suspiciously.

"No, I'm not sick," Gina responded defensively. "It's not a crime to be tired or to just get up and throw something on, is it?"

"No. And I didn't mean anything by it either. I was just asking."

Gina turned her attention to her mother.

"So, Mom, do you need me to finish up anything for you?"

"No, I'm almost finished. And where's Phillip at this morning?"

"Oh, he didn't feel like coming."

"What is this thing with everybody not feeling up to coming to breakfast? I only do this once per month. Is it my cooking? Maybe Samantha and Phillip don't like it."

"That's not it, Mom," Gina assured her. "He just didn't feel like coming."

Delores looked over at Sydney and then turned back toward the stove, not wanting to say anything else.

Gina felt uncomfortable with all of these questions, because she knew that they were all thinking the worst about Phillip. Not one of them cared for him all that much, and she hated having to make excuses for his absence. She wished that Phillip could attend these family get-togethers a little more often than he had been. But he just didn't want to, and after last night, there was no way he was going to come and socialize with the likes of her family members. He was still overly upset about her possible promotion and the fact that he still insisted that she was having an affair with her coworker. She didn't know what she was going to do or how she was going to convince him that none of what he was believing was true. He'd made his mind up about what was going on, and whenever he did that, there was usually no way to change what he was thinking. He hadn't even said anything to her when she'd told him she was coming to get the children this morning, and if it hadn't been for the fact that she had to pick them up, he probably wouldn't have allowed her to come to her mother's for breakfast at all. He'd stopped her on a few other occasions, and to eliminate any confusion in the household, she'd stayed at home like he instructed her to.

Wesley and Rick conversed about the NFL draft picks and decided that they'd go back over to Wesley and Sydney's to watch them this afternoon. Sydney and Gina talked about the children, work, and made a bunch of small talk until Delores announced that breakfast was ready to be served.

Sydney called the children downstairs, and everyone lined up along the counter to fix their plates. As usual, Delores had outdone herself and prepared a most mouth-watering spread. Eggs scrambled in butter, grits, country sausage patties and links, homemade biscuits and white gravy, and her tasty cheddar cheese, hash brown casserole.

They all sat down at the dining room table and passed around two pitchers, one filled with fresh-squeezed orange juice, and the other with milk.

Rick forked up a helping of eggs, but Delores stopped him before he could take a bite of it.

"You know the rules," she said and Rick lowered his utensil back on his plate. They hadn't said grace yet.

"Sorry," he said, smiling.

"Lord, we sit before You this morning, just wanting to thank You for another beautiful day," Delores began. "We thank You for waking us up in our right minds, for putting food on our table, and for bringing us all together once again as a family. And Lord, please bless those in our family who couldn't be here with us as well. These and many other blessings I ask in Your son, Jesus's name. Amen."

"Amen," they all said in unison.

Everyone complimented Delores on how good everything was, and it wasn't long before they'd all eaten so much that everyone rested back in their chairs like they couldn't move. It was always this way whenever Delores cooked anything, and the reason her meals weren't ideal for anyone who was claiming to be on any diets. It just wasn't possible to pass up Delores's cooking once a person had been given the opportunity to sample it. She was just that good, and Sydney had been trying to encourage her mother for the longest time to think about starting a catering business—especially since she was retiring from the post office in a couple of months. Delores wasn't sure if it was something she wanted to do or not, but Sydney had decided that she would keep talking about it, hoping it would help her to agree to it.

They all sat conversing with each other for a while, and then Sydney began removing the dishes from the table, scraped them, and loaded everything into the dishwasher. Rick and Wesley walked into the family room, and the children all went upstairs to gather together their belongings.

"So, Mom, what are you going to do today?" Sydney asked Delores.

"The church is having that fund-raiser for the homeless, and since I'm on the committee, I'll probably spend the rest of the day working with that."

"I'm thinking I'll probably go to the mall after I drop Victoria off at the movies. Wesley and Rick are planning to watch the football drafts at our house anyway. What about you, Gina? What are you doing this afternoon?"

"Taking the kids to that birthday party and that's about it."

"Why don't you let Phillip drop them off, so you can come shopping with me."

Gina hesitated, and Sydney already knew she was getting ready to make some excuse in terms of why Phillip couldn't take them and, of course, why she couldn't go with her.

"I think Phillip has somewhere he has to be this afternoon, and I don't think he'll be back in time to drop the twins off."

"Well, maybe you can drop them off, and he can

pick them up," Sydney said, wanting to know how she was going to respond to this suggestion.

"No, I don't think so. I don't need to be buying anything anyway."

"Oh, well, let me know if you get home and change your mind," Sydney said, knowing full well that Gina wasn't going to change her mind about going. Maybe if it had been left up to just her, but the truth of the matter was, Phillip wasn't about to let her hang out with her own sister on a nice Saturday afternoon.

"Well, I guess we'd better go," Sydney said when she saw Victoria walk into the kitchen with her duffel bag. "Honey, are you ready?" she asked Wesley.

"Whenever you are," he answered.

"Well, Mom, thanks for the breakfast, and I'll give you a call later on tonight," Sydney said, hugging her mother good-bye.

They all said their good-byes, and before long, everyone drove to their various destinations.

As soon as the twins had taken their baths and dressed themselves, Gina drove them over to their schoolmate's birthday celebration. Phillip hadn't been home when they'd arrived from Delores's, but he'd pulled into the driveway just as Gina and the children were backing out. He'd asked where they were going, and she'd told him that she was dropping the children off at the birthday party they'd been invited to. He'd told her that he'd be waiting for her when she got back, and she'd been relieved to know that he didn't seem to be as angry as he had been earlier this morning. She hoped things were going to be better between them, and that this whole having-an-affair-with-Michael business had somehow become only a figment of his imagination.

She told the children to call when the party was over

with, and then drove back home. Phillip was waiting for her in the bedroom, and called down to her as soon as he heard her step inside the house.

She didn't know what to expect, and she wished this nervous feeling in her stomach would disappear. She took a deep breath and headed upstairs. When she walked into the room, Phillip was sitting on the bed with his face buried inside his hands.

Gina stared at him in silence.

"I really messed up, didn't I?"

Gina still didn't say anything. It wasn't that she didn't want to, but she didn't want to chance saying the wrong thing, which could ultimately send him into another unnecessary rage.

"But it's just that those people you work with always try to make me feel like I'm not as good as the rest of them or like you could be doing so much better if you'd married someone else."

"Phillip, you're no less than any of those people or me," she said, trying to pacify him.

"Well, they make me feel that way, and then that damn Michael made it seem like you and him had something going on."

Gina didn't agree with that at all, but didn't dare contradict what he was saying. She should have, but she knew better.

Phillip stood up and walked over to Gina. He pulled her into his arms. "Gina, you make me so crazy when you give other men more attention than you give me. It was almost like you and him didn't care whether I was at the table or not."

"Phillip I don't want any other man. I'm married to you, and I've always loved only you," she said, resting the side of her face on his shoulder with tears rolling down her face. She didn't know if her tears were from relief because he'd had a change in attitude or from exhaustion because she was so tired of riding this emotional roller coaster with him.

"I don't know what's wrong with me. It's just that I love you so much, and I couldn't stand it if you left me for someone else. I wouldn't be able to deal with that."

"I'm not going to leave you, Phillip, and you've got to stop thinking that I'm messing around on you, because I'm not. I never have, and I never will."

"What can I say?" he asked. "I'm sorry, and I'll try to think before I react the next time. And the other thing that bothered me is that you hadn't told me about this promotion you might be getting. And it makes me think you're hiding things from me."

Was he serious? She hadn't told him, because she'd known all along that he was going to throw an insane fit. The idea of her success and the amount of money she brought into their household made him sick to his stomach, and she wasn't about to tell him that if she received the promotion, she'd be earning even more money than she already was. He was so jealous of her master's degree and her career, and she tried hard not to bring up either subject. He was so insecure about his own educational background, and the fact that he worked as a manual laborer always made him feel as though he wasn't as good as the next person. He earned over forty thousand dollars a year, but it wasn't enough to make him feel worthy, she guessed. They lived a very comfortable life, and as far as she was concerned, that's all that should have mattered to him. But it wasn't enough. He had a problem, and it had become progressively worse as the years had gone on. The more she earned, the more controlling and abusive he became. The beatings didn't take place on a daily basis. Sometimes months passed by and their relationship seemed almost normal, but whenever the paranoia set in, Phillip became a terrifying maniac. If her family only knew some of the abuse she had gone through. If her coworkers only knew that she wasn't the strong, intelligent, woman they thought she was when it came to her lifestyle on the home front.

"Honey, I didn't say anything, because I didn't think it was that important, and it's not that big of a promotion anyway," she said, knowing it was what she'd been working so hard for ever since joining the company.

"But you know I don't like you keeping things from me," he said.

"I'm sorry. I should have told you about it."

"Well, you don't know if you're going to get it anyway, and it's not like you have to take it."

She closed her eyes. How was she going to turn down the chance at becoming director of an entire department? Who would be silly enough to do something like that? She didn't want to make any more problems between them, so she went along with what he was saying.

"I probably won't get it anyway, because there are people who have been there longer than I have."

"You make enough anyway, and I don't think it's a good idea for you to take another job that will take away the time you need to spend here with me and the kids."

"Let's not talk about this anymore, okay," she suggested.

Phillip tilted her chin up and kissed her. "Baby, I need you so badly. I need to make love to you right now."

Gina didn't know how she felt about that, but she wasn't in a position to tell him no. Maybe it would make things better between them, and he'd forget all about his ludicrous insinuation concerning her coworker, Michael. She didn't know how she was going to feel during or after, but since she didn't have any choice in the matter, she decided that she would force herself to enjoy him. That she would moan with great desire and satisfaction the way he expected her to. That she would choose a different man, some gorgeous actor, to fantasize about while this whole sex act between them was in progress. Something she always had to do whenever they made what Phillip truly believed was love.

Chapter 5

"I don't know what's going on with Gina and Phillip, but she's been acting awfully distant ever since we saw her at breakfast a couple of weeks ago," Sydney said, driving onto the freeway. She and Delores were on their way to a Bottomless Closet fund-raiser and fashion show. They always supported the event because the proceeds went toward helping single mothers who were trying to enter the workforce. Marshall Fields donated brand-new clothing, so that the women could dress for success when they went on job interviews, but sometimes they donated evening attire as well. Which was the reason why Sydney and Delores were going. They'd gone the year before and had found evening dresses priced near two hundred dollars, but ended up paying only twenty-five dollars for each of them.

"I sure hope Phillip isn't putting his hands on Gina again," Delores said worriedly.

"Well, all I know is that something isn't right. I called her this morning at work to see if she was coming to the fund-raiser this evening, but she claimed she had to work late. I don't know whether she really did or if she was just telling me that, but I'd almost be willing to bet that Phillip wouldn't have allowed her to come anyway. He controls everything that has to do with Gina, and I don't know why she puts up with that. It's always been that way from the very beginning, but it seems like things have gotten worse than they used to be. She seems so squirrelly and defensive all the time. It's almost like she's afraid of him."

"She's always been afraid of him," Delores added. "You can tell that whenever you see them together. And my poor grandbabies are watching all of that."

"Gina doesn't have to stay in that situation, Mom. She makes more than enough money, so it's not like she needs Phillip to take care of her or those children."

"Maybe it's just not that easy, because I think there's more to the story. Gina's not telling us everything that's going on in that house. For all we know, Phillip could be jumping on her all the time. She used to call Rick a lot when she and Phillip first got together, but after Rick threatened him, she never called him again concerning their problems."

"Well, if he is fighting her, then she needs to get rid of him."

Delores sighed. "I hate to even think about him putting his hands on my baby. It brings tears to my eyes. Gina is so intelligent, and it's hard for me to believe that she would allow some man to keep her down the way Phillip is doing."

"He doesn't even want Gina spending time with you, me, or anybody else in the family. That girl doesn't even have any friends to turn to, because Phillip pretty much isolated Gina from all of them as soon as they were married."

"He only does that so he doesn't have to worry about anybody talking some sense into her. If you notice, all insecure men like him never want other people around."

Sydney stopped at a four-way stop sign, then drove another half mile and turned into the Ramada Suites Hotel, where the event was taking place. "Well, Mom, all we can do is be here for Gina, but we can't make her talk until she's ready."

"I'm afraid that when she does, something terrible will have happened. You need to talk to your sister. Maybe she'll open up if it's just the two of you. Take her to lunch or something, because it definitely has to be some time during the day when Phillip won't know about it."

"I don't know. You saw how defensive she got at breakfast when I said she looked tired. She's always defensive whenever you ask her anything about herself."

"Well, all you can do is try, and if she still doesn't open up, then there's nothing else you can do."

"I'll see if we can go to lunch sometime this week," Sydney told Delores and they both stepped out of the car and headed toward the hotel entrance.

"Honey, it's going to take a little longer than I thought," Gina explained. "We had a major system crash this afternoon, and I can't leave until we get things back on track."

"Who is we, Gina?" Phillip asked suspiciously.

"Half of our entire department. I promise I'll be there as soon as we get finished. If you need anything, then all you have to do is call me at my desk, and if you don't get an answer, then it means I'm in the computer room, and you can call me on my cell phone."

"It's already six-thirty, so what am I supposed to do

about feeding the twins?" he asked as if he didn't know one thing about cooking or fast-food restaurants.

"All you have to do is get them a couple of Happy Meals, and they'll be fine."

"What about me? What am I supposed to do while you're messing around at work?"

"Honey, all I can say is that I'm sorry, and that I'll make it up to you."

"Hmmph. And you've got the nerve to be wanting that promotion? If you're having to stay this late at work now, what's it going to be like when you're running the whole department? It's not going to work. I can tell you that right now. I won't stand for you putting some career before me and my kids."

Gina didn't know what to say, but she knew she needed to get back to work. The other team members were obviously becoming impatient as they waited for her, and they were starting to gaze toward where she was talking on the phone.

"Phillip, I'll be there as soon as I can, so please don't be upset with me. Okay?"

"Why would I be upset?" he asked sarcastically. "You make it sound like you're doing something you shouldn't be. Is that asshole Michael there, too? You say you're staying over to fix some computer problem, but I don't know *what* you're doing. It's not like I'm there to see for myself."

She didn't know what she was going to do if Phillip somehow decided that she'd stayed at work late just so she could mess around on him. She hated being in this situation, but she needed her job and couldn't slack when it came to taking care of her responsibilities. Phillip enjoyed the lifestyle they lived, so he never went as far as telling her she couldn't work, but at the same time, he didn't like the fact that, when she worked, he couldn't keep close tabs on her. He couldn't monitor or control her in the least little bit, and that was the only time when she felt like she was free to do what she wanted. She could say what she wanted without stepping on egg shells.

"Phillip, I have to go, okay. I'll call you in a little while if we still don't have this crash taken care of."

"Yeah, whatever," he said and hung up the phone.

Gina closed her eyes, took a deep breath, and hoped this situation at work would be taken care of very quickly. Because if it wasn't, she didn't even want to imagine what the consequences were going to be.

Everyone worked as quickly and as diligently as they could, until finally everything was back on track. They were all noticeably exhausted, and within minutes, they each grabbed purses, keys, blazers, all other personal belongings, and headed out the door.

Gina sat inside her car, turned the key in the ignition, noticed the digital clock on the dash, and panicked. She couldn't believe it was 10:30 P.M. Phillip had called her at eight, and she'd tried to explain that they were almost finished. He hadn't sounded like he was overly upset, but she'd told him that she would be home no later than nine-thirty. It would now take her at least a half-hour to drive from Naperville, which meant she wouldn't make it inside the house until eleven or after.

She punched in her home phone number on her cell phone. It rang a few times, but the voice mail system answered instead of Phillip. She wondered where he was, and she hoped nothing had happened with one of the children. She didn't know what to think. Maybe he was just sleeping, but she knew that wasn't possible, because Phillip was like a parent who never slept when their children were out late somewhere. She tried the number again, but all she heard was her own outgoing message again.

She drove as fast as she could, praying all the way

that everything was all right. She hoped Phillip wasn't purposely not answering the phone just so she'd be worried. He'd done that a couple of other times, but with Phillip she just couldn't be sure.

As she turned into the subdivision, she saw lights shining in the kitchen and upstairs in their bedroom. Phillip's BMW was parked in its normal spot, so it wasn't like he'd left or anything. She hurried into the house, and called out to him. No one answered. She walked closer to the stairway, preparing to head upstairs, until she heard something move over in the living room.

"You think I'm stupid, don't you?" Phillip said, walking out of the dark room and right next to where Gina was standing.

He startled her, and she didn't know how to respond.

"Oh, you don't have anything to say to that, do you?" he continued.

"Phillip, you know I've been at work, and I came straight home as soon as I left there," she began.

"I called your lying ass three hours ago, and you said you were going to be here at nine-thirty. Now, it's after eleven."

"I know, but it took longer than I thought. I tried to call you when I was leaving the parking lot, but you didn't answer."

"Answer for what? I figured it was you, but it was already too late for you to be calling here with some lie you finally came up with. You were screwing that bastard, and that's all there is to it."

"I was not," she spoke loudly.

Phillip grabbed her by her neck and shoved her against the wall. She tried to move away from him, begging him to stop the same as always. "Phillip, I swear, I really was working, and that's all."

Phillip slapped Gina across the side of her face and

slung her to the floor. "Why do you keep making me do this, Gina?" he asked like she'd requested a beating from him.

Gina lay on the floor crying, and the twins stood at the top of the stairs doing the same.

"Daddy, don't, don't, don't," Carl said, jumping up and down hysterically. Phillip looked up at his son, but didn't say anything. Caitlin screamed at the top of her lungs when she saw her father turning toward their mother again.

"I ought to kill you right now," he said.

But he walked away from her and went into the family room instead. Just like nothing had happened.

He was crazy. There was no question about it, and Gina knew she was going to have to get away from him, one way or the other. The twins rushed down the stairs, still screaming and crying, and Gina embraced both of them. They each sat on the floor sobbing as a threesome.

"Everything is all right now," Gina tried to convince them. "You two have to get back to bed. Mom is fine."

"Why is Daddy always trying to hurt you, Mom?" Caitlin asked between sniffles.

"He doesn't mean it," Gina lied.

"I really don't mean it," Phillip said, walking back toward where they were sitting. He gazed at Gina and the twins and the red bruise on Gina's face and burst into tears.

"I'm so sorry, baby. I didn't mean it," he said, kneeling on the floor beside his family.

He pulled the twins into his arms and held them tight. Then he released them and rested his head on Gina's lap, crying like a two-year-old child.

"I'm sorry. I don't know what's wrong with me. I promise you I didn't mean it," he repeated.

Carl and Caitlin looked on in silence, and finally Gina spoke.

"Phillip, it's late, so let me put the children to bed, okay?"

Phillip raised his head and turned to the children. "Daddy didn't mean to hurt Mommy," he said. "I promise I didn't."

Carl and Caitlin were speechless.

Gina rose to her feet, walked the children up to their rooms, and tucked them in. She wished she could sleep in Caitlin's other twin bed, because the last thing she wanted to do now was go deal with Phillip. His tears didn't mean a thing to her, and she had no sympathy for whatever remorse he might possibly be feeling. She'd had enough. But she had to admit, however, that she was afraid of him, because it wasn't a good sign when someone as violent and possessive as Phillip sat down on a floor and cried like a baby. It was almost like he was losing his mind, and she didn't know how she'd be able to pack her bags and leave him. She knew it wasn't going to happen overnight, but she knew she had to start planning her and the children's escape. She didn't want to leave the Chicago area, but she didn't see where she had a choice, since Phillip had almost guaranteed her that he would kill her if she ever tried to leave him. She didn't know for sure if he would or not, but she had a feeling he was very capable of it, and it wasn't worth chancing. She didn't want to leave her mother, Sydney, or Rick, but she feared that if Phillip knew how to get to her, she would never, ever be safe. She had to think all of this through. She had to plan every little detail. But most importantly, she had to make him believe that everything was business as usual, and do everything in her power to make him understand that they could and would work things out.

Gina forced herself to leave Caitlin's bedroom and walked into her own. Phillip was sitting on the bed in his usual spot staring at her. He really did look as though he was sorry for what he'd done, but he'd looked that way many times before, and for the first time ever, Gina wasn't buying into it.

"Baby, I don't know what's wrong with me. It's like, in my mind, I can actually see you having sex with other men."

Gina walked toward the walk-in closet and removed her clothing.

"Gina, are you listening to me?"

"Yes."

"I guess it's just that I love you so much, and I'm afraid that somebody is going to take you away from me."

Gina slipped on her nightgown. "Phillip, when we were dating, how many times did you tell me about your parents, and how your father used to come home and beat your mother for no reason at all."

"I know, I know," he said in frustration.

"And how many times did you promise that you would never do that to me? That you would never put your hands on me?"

"Baby, I'm sorry. I won't do it again. No matter what happens, I promise I won't do it again."

Gina stepped closer to her side of the bed, and sat down on it. Phillip moved closer to her. "You hear me, baby?"

"Yeah, Phillip, I hear you," she said unimpressively.

"I'm serious, Gina. I'm not going to hurt you anymore."

Gina listened and pretended that she was interested and that she believed him. It was what he expected her to do, and she didn't see any reason to do any different. It was what she had to do until she figured out the best time and best way to leave him for good. She was even willing to change her and the twins' names if she had to. She was willing to do anything to take her children out of this dysfunctional environment.

She couldn't wait for this all to be over with.

Chapter 6

Sydney plopped down in the royal blue easy chair in the family room, opened the novel she'd purchased at Afrocentric Bookstore down on State Street a couple of weeks ago, and turned to the first page. She, Wesley, Victoria, and Delores had all gone to church this morning, then to Red Lobster for dinner, but now Wesley was taking a nap, and Victoria was down the street at one of her girlfriend's. It was a peaceful Sunday afternoon, and Sydney couldn't remember the last time she'd actually found the time to read for entertainment. Usually, she had to read articles and magazines for work, and it was nice to slip into someone else's world for a change.

She read for a while, until she saw Wesley on the sofa stretching his arms toward the ceiling. It looked as though he was waking up, and Sydney didn't know if she liked that idea or not. They'd made love last evening, and to be honest, their lovemaking over the last two weeks hadn't left Wesley any room to complain. He was getting what he wanted, and he'd seemed more satisfied than he had been in a very long time. She'd really gone out of her way to put forth the extra effort, and they hadn't had even the tiniest argument about sex or the lack there of.

. Wesley rustled from side to side, and then looked back at Sydney. She could see him through her peripheral vision, but she continued reading like she hadn't noticed that he was awake. She loved her husband. She really did. But it was just that she really wanted to relax and read her book. She wasn't in the mood, and she was hoping that Wesley wasn't going to try and coax her into the bedroom.

"Where's Victoria?" he asked.

Sydney hated that he was asking her that, because she knew why he wanted to know. "She's still down to Marlene's," she said, not moving her eyes away from her book.

"Oh really," he said in a smiling voice.

Sydney sighed quietly and repositioned her body in the chair. She wasn't up to this, but at the same time, she didn't want to ruin this wonderful roll that they were on either. She didn't want to go through their usual bickering over him wanting it, and her unwillingness to "give it up." Wesley never used that phrase, but whenever he begged for sex, it always reminded her of what the boys back in high school used to say to girls when they were trying to lure them into bed. It sounded almost like a woman was being forced to hand over some sort of object, instead of a sacred part of her body.

"Think I can have some?" he asked, still lying on the sofa but looking over at her.

"Why don't we wait until tonight, because you know Victoria might come in here at any time."

"Now, Sydney, when have you ever known for that girl to come home from Marlene's house without you having to call down there. So, that's the least of our worries."

Unfortunately, he was right, and now she didn't know what other excuse she was going to be able to conjure up. It was Sunday, and while she was sort of exhausted, she knew Wesley wasn't going to understand anything like that. He wanted what he wanted, and that was that. As a matter of fact, she didn't see how he could be so fired up when it hadn't even been twenty-four hours since the last time. But he'd told her before that days and hours had no meaning when it came to his sexual organs, and she knew he was trying to make up for all the times he wouldn't be able to when she said no in the future. She was in a very awkward situation, but the bottom line was, she just wasn't in the mood to make love. Point blank.

"It'll just be our luck that she'll show up as soon as we darken the bedroom doorway. Plus, I just want to read a little bit more of this novel, if that's okay. But I promise we'll do it tonight," she said, taking a chance that he would agree.

"I'm telling you the truth," he said, standing to his feet. "You haven't worked all day, I haven't worked all weekend, Victoria is down the street, and you're still using some stupid book as an excuse."

She'd known this was going to happen, and now she wished she'd just stripped her clothes and counted backward from one hundred until he was finished. It usually took longer than that, but when it did, she started over again as often as she needed to with a brand new set of numbers. One hundred, ninety-nine, ninety-eight . . . all the way down to one and then back to a hundred again when necessary. If Wesley only knew that she sometimes did that, he would practically lose his mind. He'd go through the roof, and as serious as he took their sexual relationship, he'd probably file for a divorce.

It wasn't that she didn't desire him, because she did. But just not every day of the week. She had much more on her mind, too many other responsibilities, and rarely did she get any time to herself to read or do whatever she wanted on her own. Couldn't he understand that? Couldn't he understand that it simply wasn't normal for a man to be turned on every time he thought about having sex?

"I'm not using this book as an excuse," she finally said. "I just wanted to relax for a little while. That's all. I'm not saying that I don't want to make love, I'm just asking if we can do it a little later."

"And take the chance on you coming up with some other reason why we can't? When you were looking through the newspaper this morning, you were already talking about watching *The Ten Commandments*. So, what time does that come on?"

"Six o'clock," she said, shocked that he was already thinking ahead of her.

"And if I had to guess, I'll bet it's going to be on until ten-thirty or eleven. Right?" he said with his arms folded.

"Probably, but what's wrong with that?"

"What's wrong with it? What's wrong with it is that you're *really* going to be stretching and yawning by that time. You'll be putting on a straight-up performance like you always do, hoping that I'm going to turn over and go to sleep. But I'll tell you what," he said, slipping on his gym shoes. "If you don't want to make love to me, then I don't want it. Now, if I was the type of man who was out getting it from somewhere else, then you'd have a serious problem with it, but as long as I keep begging for it the way I do, then you don't care one way or the other."

"Okay, fine, Wesley. Let's do it now," she said in a huff.

"Uh-uh. I don't want you doing anything just for the sake of doing it, because I don't want you lying there like some corpse. That's a total turnoff and it's not even worth it," he said, grabbing his nylon sweat jacket and keys.

"Why can't you understand that I have to do everything around here. Clean up behind you and Victoria, take care of the finances, and just about anything else I can think of. This house runs smoothly almost three hundred and sixty-five days a year, and I know you don't think it's doing it on its own. And on top of that, I work every day just like you do."

Wesley pulled his jacket on. "I'm going out for a while."

"To where?" she said angrily.

"I don't know. Maybe over to my brother's. All I know is that I need to get out of here and give you your space."

"I never said I needed space."

"You said you wanted to read your book, so I'm going to give you all the time you need to do it. And I'll tell you another thing—I'm not going to keep hounding you for something that's yours," he said and walked outside.

Sydney closed her eyes, trying to calm herself. He was so unreasonable, and he made her so angry when he stormed out of the house like this. He acted like a child throwing a temper tantrum, and she wished he would grow up.

She turned her book facedown on her lap and leaned her head back. Why couldn't she have forced herself into the mood? It wasn't like she'd really tried, because she'd already adopted a negative attitude as soon as she saw him waking up. She didn't know why she was like this. Frigid almost. Maybe there really was something wrong with her. Maybe she needed to make an appointment with her doctor sooner than she'd planned to. She felt bad about putting Wesley off for tonight, and she wished she had at least tried to go along with what he was requesting. She was his wife, and while she wasn't obligated to have sex every time he wanted her to, she did have a responsibility to her husband. It was her responsibility to satisfy him in every way possible, and she didn't know what she would do if he did in fact start looking to have his needs fulfilled elsewhere. She couldn't stand that, and as close as they were, she knew Wesley was as human as the next man who needed sex and couldn't get it. She wasn't a fool, and she knew she had to work harder than she had since their last argument over this.

She wanted to call him on his cell phone, but decided that it was better to let him cool off. She would wait until he arrived home, and then go out of her way to let him know how sorry she was for depriving him.

Sydney read for another couple of hours, and realized that it was time for *The Ten Commandments* to come on. She watched it every year around Easter time, and it always felt like she hadn't seen it before. It told the story of Moses with much more clarity than when you read about him in the Bible, and that was one reason she enjoyed the movie so much.

She phoned down to Marlene's, asked Marlene's mother to send Victoria home, and switched on the television. The movie was just about to start, so Sydney adjusted the volume to her liking and coiled her body into the corner of the love seat. She watched the beginning, and heard Victoria coming through the garage door during the first commercial break.

"Mom, where's Daddy?" she asked, opening the refrigerator and pulling out a gallon of milk.

"He went out for a while. Did you have a good time down to Marlene's?"

"Yep, and she wants to know if I can spend the night with her next Saturday."

"I don't know. We'll see."

"Mommm. Why?"

"Victoria, I didn't say no, I just said, we'll see," Sydney said, frowning.

"We don't have anything else we have to do," Victoria thought she'd better tell her.

"I know, but you can't do whatever you want every time you get ready to."

Victoria blew her breath like she had an attitude. "Dog," she said in a muzzled tone.

"What did you say?" Sydney said, turning toward her and squinting her eyes.

"Nothing," Victoria said, picking up her glass of milk and preparing to leave the kitchen.

"That's what I thought, because you'll be keeping your little behind right here all weekend long if you keep it up," Sydney said, turning her attention back to the movie which was back on the screen.

Victoria didn't say anything else, and headed up to her bedroom.

Sydney wondered how long she was going to have to deal with this preteen I'm-positively-sure-I-know-more-than-you-Mom attitude. Victoria could be the sweetest daughter in the world, but when she wasn't, Sydney felt like ringing her little neck. It was the infamous mother-daughter conflict. Every friend she knew who had a daughter between the ages of eleven and eighteen had major issues and struggles to contend with. It was enough to drive any normal mother insane, and it was, at times like these, that Sydney longed for her daughter's high school graduation. Because as soon as it happened, she and Wesley would be free to ship her off to someone's college. Preferably on the West Coast, and sometimes, she didn't even know if two thousand miles would be far enough.

But Sydney knew she only felt that way when she was angry, and that deep down, she really didn't want her baby, her only child, going any farther than Illinois State University in Bloomington or the University of Illinois in Champaign. Which would mean she could drive home on weekends and holidays or whenever she wanted.

Victoria came back downstairs about an hour later to fix a ham sandwich, but didn't say more than "Good night, Mom" before she left the kitchen again. Sydney continued watching the movie, and right when Charlton Heston removed the tablets that God had scribed the Ten Commandments on and prepared to take them down to the Hebrews, Wesley walked through the door. It was just past ten-thirty. Sydney had wondered where he was, and had wanted to call him several times throughout the evening, but she hadn't thought it was worth causing an argument with him all over again. She'd told herself that it was better to wait for him to return home before she tried to discuss this situation again. She'd wondered if maybe he was out looking for someone else, but she'd quickly dismissed that whole idea when she thought about the love and trust they'd always had between them. More than a few times, she'd heard her grandmother say that there was always a first Sunday in every month, and that even iron eventually wore out, but she was counting on Wesley staying dedicated to her through all of this.

He set his keys on the counter, and pulled out a handful of cookies from the Oreo bag sitting on the breakfast table. Then he walked into the family room. "So, was the movie good?" he asked, obviously trying to break the ice between them.

He didn't seem to be upset anymore, and Sydney felt relieved already. "Yeah, it was good. Where did you go?" she asked.

"Over to William and Tracy's," he said, referring to his brother and sister-in-law.

"What were they up to?" Sydney asked, making small talk.

"Not much. We sat around talking and watching some movie on Starz, but that was about it."

"So, are you still upset with me?" she asked him and looked toward the TV waiting for his answer.

"No. I'm all right now, and I'm sorry I blew up like I did. I want what I want when I want it, and when it feels like you don't desire me, I get upset. And you're right when you say you do a lot around here, so I know you are really tired sometimes, and that you have a lot on your plate when it comes to your work."

"Sweetie, I don't want us to keep going through this. I'm not saying that we can make love every single night of the week, but I am saying that it should be more often than what it is. I'm going to make an appointment with my doctor to see what she has to say. Maybe she can run some tests. And if that's not it, then I'm going to call your Employee Assistance Program at work to see if they can refer me to a psychologist or sex therapist."

"You think it's that serious?"

"I don't know, but something isn't right. I could see it if I wasn't in love with you or if I wasn't attracted to you, but the fact that I am makes me wonder what's wrong with me."

Wesley slid behind Sydney, and she leaned her body against his chest. He wrapped his arms around her and kissed her on her neck. Not in a lustful way, but in a loving, caring manner. The movie ended after Moses gave Joshua his robe and staff.

"I don't like it when we're like this, baby," he said. "It ties my stomach up in knots."

"I don't either, but it seems like we are into it all the time over this, and that's why something has to give."

"I'll do whatever you need me to do. Even if it means going to the doctor with you or to a therapist if you end up doing that. This isn't just your problem by yourself. I know I get angry about all of this, but I'm always going to be here for you," he said, embracing her tightly.

Funny thing was, she really did feel like making love to him now. It was something about lying in his arms and talking with him. Maybe what they needed was more romance, more holding at first instead of going straight for the gusto. Maybe what Sydney needed was to feel loved first and not like some sex object that Wesley couldn't wait to get in bed with. She knew he didn't love her any less, but sometimes he seemed so rushed when it came to them making love. Although when she'd mentioned that to him before, he'd told her that he didn't mean to, but that it was hard not to get overly excited because she always made him wait so long from one time to the next.

They engaged in romantic foreplay until Wesley pressed the off button on the television. Then he led his wife by her hand into their master bedroom suite. Wesley closed the door and pulled his wife into his arms. V103 was playing a love song, and they slow-danced to it.

Sydney tried to hold back tears, but they flowed freely against Wesley's chest. She loved her husband more than anything, and it was obvious that he loved her just as much. Once again, she vowed to make things right in their marriage, no matter what it meant she had to do.

Chapter 7

"Man, I don't know why Samantha is trippin' out on me like this," Rick said to his boy Brent, his best friend of twenty years and now coworker. They were sitting at Olive Garden during the noon hour eating salad and waiting for their main entrées.

"She wants to tie you down with that leash, is what it is," Brent said, laughing.

"Man, shit. First she wanted to get engaged, so I finally broke down and bought her a ring, then she kept pressing me about moving in, so I gave in to that, too. And now she's still not satisfied. Women," Rick said, shaking his head in confusion.

"These women nowadays want complete control and all the financial security they can get. See, it's not enough for them to just live with you anymore, they want to make sure they're getting the 401K, life insurance, and alimony too, if it comes down to it. And they only have to be married to your ass for ten years to collect your social security benefits."

"I don't think Samantha is thinking about money, she just wants to get married, because she thinks it will legitimize everything in our relationship. I keep telling her that I don't want anybody else, and that she's the only woman I want to be with, but she's not hearing it. We've been fussin' and cussin' around that condo every other day, and I don't know how much more of it I can take. Samantha is a good woman, and I don't want to be without her, but I'm not allowing any woman to push me into getting married before I'm ready to."

"I hear you, man. I wouldn't let her push me, either," Brent boasted, and Rick wondered if he should be listening to Brent or not. Especially since Brent had recently been kicked to the curb by his live-in girlfriend of three years for practically the same reason. She'd told him to commit or get out, and Brent had chosen the latter. He pretended like it hadn't bothered him one bit, but Rick knew better, because whether he admitted it or not, Brent loved Adriana. She was the best thing that had ever happened to him, but he'd allowed his pride to take control of the situation, and now he was living with his brother and spending his time with scrappy women who really didn't care about him. He'd made a terrible move by ending his relationship with the one woman who truly loved him, and it was obvious that Brent was still hurt by it.

"I don't know what's going to happen with us," Rick said as the young waitress sat his order of spaghetti down in front of him, and Brent's ravioli on the other side of the table.

"Is there anything else I can get for you?" she asked.

"No, I think we have everything," Rick replied.

"Enjoy your meals," she said and walked away.

Brent sprinkled parmesan cheese over his entrée

and Rick twirled a forkful of spaghetti around on his plate.

"Maybe she'll get off of this marriage trip once she sees you're not going for it. Although Adriana never did, and you see what happened."

"Yeah, man, but admit it," Rick said, wanting to hear him tell the truth. "You miss her, don't you?"

"Hell no, I don't miss her," he said but Rick knew he was lying at an all-time high.

"C'mon, B, tell the truth," Rick insisted.

"What? I don't. That relationship is history, and I'm just sorry I wasted all that time with her in the first place," he said, eating his ravioli and acting as if Adriana had never been a big deal to him. He'd always been that way, even when they were twelve and in junior high school. He always pretended that nothing bothered him and that nothing was worth feeling any pain over. Even when he was overweight, and the boys in the neighborhood made daily fat jokes about him, he would laugh right along with them, like his feelings weren't actually hurt. But Rick had followed him into the boys' bathroom one morning after the bell rang, and he'd heard Brent in one of the stalls crying like a baby. Instead of mentioning it to him, though, Rick left the bathroom and went to class without ever bringing that crying incident to his attention. Even to this day, he never brought it up to him, because he knew Brent was still very self-conscious about being on the stocky side when he was a child. He hadn't been overweight as an adult, but was still very self-conscious, nevertheless.

"If you say so," Rick said. "But I'm not going to sit here and tell you that I don't care whether Samantha leaves or not. If it doesn't work out, then I'll just have to deal with it, but I do care about her."

"What you need to do is tell her how things are going to be and that's that. If she's cool with it, then everything will be kosher, but if not, then she'll pack her bags and move on, and so will you."

Rick drank his raspberry lemonade, but didn't say anything. He heard what Brent was saying, and while he didn't agree with most of Brent's overall philosophy on relationships, he did agree that it was time to tell Samantha what the deal was once and for all. She'd said she was going to leave him, but it was probably only because she was so sure that he'd change his mind and marry her. But if she saw that he was serious about not jumping into holy matrimony, she would probably shed a few tears, and eventually find satisfaction with the way the relationship was already going. Which, in his book, was great and the reason he didn't see why they needed to make any changes. Change could be a good thing, but sometimes change made things worse, and left a person wishing they had left things the way they were to begin with.

They finished eating, enclosed money for the bill and gratuity inside the miniature American Express leather portfolio, and headed out to Rick's SUV.

"I am not in the mood for going back to work," Brent said. "It must be eighty degrees today, and it's only April."

"Yeah, it is a beautiful day," Rick agreed. "But it's not like I could've taken vacation this afternoon, anyway, since George asked me to chair two of his inventory meetings," he said, referring to his boss.

"Well, at least somebody was smart enough to take the afternoon off," Brent added.

"No doubt," Rick said and suddenly wondered what Samantha was doing for lunch. They hadn't spoken as much during working hours, as they usually did, now that things weren't that great between them, and as much as Rick hated to think about it, he missed that. She would call him a couple of times per day, and they even went to lunch together whenever they were able to take long lunch hours. Which they always had to do since they worked so far away from each other.

"So, what you got up for this weekend?" Brent asked.

"Nothing, man. What's up with you?"

"I was thinking about going to that new club. I can't think of the name, but you know the one the fellas have been talking about at work. They keep saying there're some fine women there every time they go. So, I'm thinking about checking it out, if you want to go."

"I don't know. I'll see," Rick said, wondering if he and Samantha were going to get things right before then. Which is really what he was counting on.

"Gotta see if you can disconnect that ball and chain, don't you?" Brent said, laughing loudly at his own joke.

"Man, get outta here," Rick said, laughing with him.

Rick couldn't wait to get home from work. He couldn't believe how pleasant Samantha had sounded when she'd phoned him to say that she was cooking dinner for the two of them. It was almost as if she'd given up the battle and was calling a much-needed truce. Maybe he wouldn't have to set her straight after all, because it seemed like she was probably content with waiting until the time was right. She had to be if she was calling him with this newfound attitude of hers.

He continued his drive home, and as soon as he entered the condo, Samantha looked over at him from the kitchen and smiled the way she used to when they were happy. He walked over and hugged her, and they held each other in silence, until Samantha spoke up.

"Look. I love you, and I don't want us arguing the

way we have been anymore. I don't like it, and I'm tired of leaving this house angry almost every morning."

"I don't like it either, because I love you, too."

"We're both adults," she said, pulling back and looking straight into his eyes, "and I know we can work this out in a civil and understanding manner."

"I agree," Rick said, wanting to jump for joy because she'd finally come to her senses about this whole ordeal.

"The lasagna will be ready in a minute, so you can relax in the living room if you want," she said, pecking him on his lips.

He'd just eaten Italian food for lunch, but he wasn't about to disappoint her or sound ungrateful. As a matter of fact, he was going to eat that lasagna like he hadn't had Italian food in the last couple of months; like it was the best food he'd had an opportunity to eat in a very long time.

He kicked off his shoes, removed his navy linen blazer, and did the same with his tie. Then he relaxed on the sofa and enjoyed the jazz that was playing on the stereo system. He felt like he was in heaven, and it was such a relief to know that Samantha now realized that his way was the best way to continue their relationship. He didn't know why she'd had such a sudden change of heart, but he was glad to have everything back to normal. Maybe she'd even be willing to make love to him tonight, something she hadn't been doing, since she decided that this was a great way to punish him.

He watched her set the table and couldn't keep his eyes from her perfectly sculpted body. She wasn't wearing anything fancy, but her sleeveless black knit top and black jeans fit her in a tailor-made sort of fashion. She was so beautiful, and he couldn't imagine another man being with her.

He kept his attention fixed on her every move until

she finally told him that dinner was ready. They sat down at the table, passed a couple of dishes so they could fix their plates, and Rick smiled at her.

"What's the matter with you?" she asked him.

"Nothing. There's nothing wrong with me admiring the woman I love, is it?"

"No, I guess not," she told him, smiling back at him.

"It feels so good to be sitting here with you having dinner, and my mind feels so at ease."

"Mine does, too. As a matter of fact, I've been okay ever since last night when I realized that we weren't getting anywhere with all that arguing. So I sat down and really thought about the situation from every angle."

"I'm glad to hear you say that, because for a minute there, I was afraid we were never going to see eye to eye."

"Well, I don't know if we see eye to eye or not, but what I do know is that I'm not angry with you anymore, and to a certain extent, I even understand what you've been saying," she said contentedly.

Yes! He knew Samantha was too sensible and realistic not to see where he was coming from, and he was glad things hadn't gotten so far out of hand that they'd lost the love they had for each other.

"Baby, I'm glad you finally came around, because I didn't know what else to say or do to get you to see what I was saying," he said, biting a piece of buttered bread.

Samantha lifted her glass and sipped some water from it. "Oh, I see now what you're saying, and I respect it. And what I finally realized was that everyone is different and that no two people think exactly alike. As a matter of fact, it was wrong for me to try and force you to do something you weren't ready to do."

Rick felt like turning a few cartwheels right in the middle of the floor. There really was a God somewhere. There had to be, because only He could cause this complete turnaround with Samantha. It was so amazing how things just sort of worked themselves out when you least expected it.

"So, this is the deal," she continued. "You don't have to marry me, but if we haven't set a date by June first, then I'm packing all of my things, and I'm moving out. And I won't be angry with you, because I finally figured out that if being engaged for two years isn't enough time for you to know whether you want to marry me or not, then we're really not meant to be together. It doesn't mean either one of us is right or wrong, it just means we're not right for each other. It happens all the time, and I want to apologize for pressuring you the way I have been. Every person on this earth has a right to do what they want to, and if you know for sure that you don't love me enough to commit to me for the rest of your life, then I'm okay with that," she said, staring straight at him.

Rick couldn't believe what he was hearing, and the killing part of it all was that she wasn't upset; and with the way she'd explained it to him, he couldn't be upset with her either. He didn't like this. Here he'd planned on giving her an ultimatum, but now she'd given him one in a way that sounded almost like she was going to be fine whether he married her or not. He'd been sure that she'd come to her senses, but now he knew that she'd planned this whole dinner just to tell him to either step up to the plate or leave the baseball field. And she'd done it in such a calm, nonchalant manner. He looked at her, searched within himself for a response, but didn't know what to say.

Samantha spoke for him. "Rick, never ever did I want it to come to this, but there's no way I can spend the rest of my life shacking up with you. I want to start building the life that I've always dreamed of, and I can't do that with the way things are between us. But please believe me when I say that I really will respect whatever your decision is. Sometimes people want different things in life, and I don't blame you for that. But I do want you to know that I love you with all my heart, and that a part of me will always love you no matter what."

"So, that's it? If we don't set a wedding date by June first, then you're going to move out?" he asked.

"Yes."

"Well, I don't know what to say. You caught me totally off guard with all of this. I mean, here I am thinking this dinner was sort of your way of putting all of this behind us, and now you're telling me that you're going to leave if I don't do what you want me to?" he said, reaching for words he couldn't find. It was easy to argue with Samantha, but it was hard to talk to her about any of this now that she was being so cordial and calm.

"I'm not pressuring you, I'm just saying that I'll understand, whatever your decision is."

"So, what'll we do in the meantime?"

"I'm still here for you like I've always been, and the only thing different is that you're going to have to decide what you want. And if you decide before June, then that's fine, too. I know this isn't what you want to hear, but we can't go on like the way we have been."

He did have to agree with her on that, because all the arguing and silent treatments between them weren't getting them anywhere. In actuality, they were driving them further and further apart.

"So, you're sure about this?" he finally asked her.

"Yeah. I am," she said in a sad tone.

"Well, I'm not that hungry anymore, so if you don't mind, I'm going upstairs."

"Okay," she said, leaning back in her chair.

Rick left the table and wondered how their relationship was going to play out over the next few weeks. But more importantly, he wondered how he was going to make it without her when she was gone. Because even when everything was all said and done, he still wasn't planning to get married.

Chapter 8

Sydney drove onto Wabash Avenue, located a multi-leveled parking ramp, and left her vehicle with the attendant. She was meeting Gina for lunch so they could discuss their mother's retirement celebration. Gina hadn't wanted to, but Sydney had more or less insisted, since the dinner was just around the corner. They needed to finalize the plans, and Sydney had decided that she wasn't going to take the responsibility for everything all on her own.

Gina had given her excuse after excuse over the last few weeks, but when Sydney had spoken with her yesterday afternoon, she'd told her that she wasn't taking no for an answer, and that she'd see her at noon today. It was obvious that Gina wasn't too willing to meet her, and Sydney hoped it wasn't because of something going on between her and Phillip. Gina always kept her distance from the rest of the family whenever things weren't going quite right at home, and Sydney couldn't help but wonder what was happening now.

She pulled the glass door open, stepped inside, and searched for her sister. She looked toward the back of the establishment, saw her gazing through the window, and walked in that direction.

"Hey, Gina," Sydney said, smiling and hugging her sister.

"How's it going?" Gina said without much enthusiasm.

Something was definitely wrong, and Sydney wasn't leaving this restaurant until she found out exactly what was going on.

"Everything's good," Sydney replied. "Wesley is fine. He's working a lot of hours, but he's okay. Victoria is fine as well. How are the twins?"

"They're fine."

"And Phillip?" Sydney asked out of consideration for her sister, because in actuality, she couldn't really care less how he was doing.

"He's okay," Gina said, looking toward the window again.

Sydney didn't like the way Gina was acting, and she didn't like how tired and run-down she looked either. Her sister was a beautiful woman who'd just turned thirty-four, but she resembled someone well into their forties. Almost the way people look when they're worried to death about something on a daily basis. Sydney didn't know how this next conversation was going to sit with Gina, but she needed to know what was going on, and didn't know any other way to find out other than by asking her.

"Gina, is everything okay with you?"

"What do you mean?" Gina asked, hoping Sydney wasn't going to press her about her marital issues.

"I mean, is everything fine between you and Phillip?"

"Why wouldn't it be?" Gina answered, pretending that everything was great.

"Look, Gina. Mom's worried about you. I'm worried about you, and no matter what you say, I know when something's not right with you. You're my sister, for God's sake."

"Didn't you say that you wanted us to meet so we could discuss Mom's dinner?" Gina said irritably and looked up at the waitress, who was ready to take their orders.

They each ordered ham, turkey, and salami sandwiches with chips and a Sprite. The waitress left the table and Sydney was glad because she was anxious to continue her and Gina's conversation.

"Yeah, I do want to talk about that, too, but your well-being is more important to me at the moment."

Gina sighed deeply. "Look, Sydney, I told you that nothing is wrong, so why do you keep on insisting that something is?"

"Because you don't look the same, you don't even have the same smile anymore. You always seem sad or like you don't want to be bothered with any of us, and I'm sick of worrying about it."

"It's not my fault that you're worrying about nothing," Gina said, still trying to cover.

Sydney was getting upset. "Why are you always pretending like everything is just perfect? I could see it if I was some stranger off the street, but I'm your sister. A sister who loves you."

Gina hated this. She hated sitting face to face with Sydney, and she hated that she couldn't tell her about all of the physical abuse Phillip was inflicting upon her. She wanted to tell her, because she loved her, too, but she just couldn't do it. She couldn't tell a soul until she figured out a way to get out of this situation.

"Sydney, why can't you just believe what I'm telling you and let that do?"

"Because I know you're not telling me the truth.

And as much as I hate to ask this, has Phillip been putting his hands on you again?"

Gina was floored. "What?" she finally forced herself to say. "Why would you ask something like that?" she asked and was glad that the bruise on the side of her face had healed. Sydney didn't know it, but that was the real reason why Gina had put her off when it came to having this lunch date. She hadn't allowed any of them to see her until she'd known for sure that it had completely disappeared. It was bad enough having to see the suspicious, curious looks on the faces of her coworkers over the last couple of weeks. She'd tried to conceal it as best as she could, but it hadn't made a whole lot of difference. This was such a taboo subject, and it was better to leave well enough alone when it came to discussing it.

"Because I know he has a history of doing so?" Sydney said, staring at Gina.

"You know, Sydney, not everybody can have the perfect life like you, and I resent you bringing up things that have gone on between my husband and me."

"My life *isn't* perfect. Wesley and I have problems just like anybody else, but what I do know is that he's never raised his hand to me, no matter how angry he gets."

Gina didn't say anything.

Sydney reached across the table and lifted Gina's hand into hers. "Gina, I didn't come here to argue with you, and I'm not trying to be in your business. And the only reason I'm asking you all of this is because I'm concerned. How can you expect me to act like I don't care about my own sister? If I was going through something, I would expect you to do the same thing. That's what sisters are for. If you can't turn to me, then who can you turn to? And I can't help but worry about my niece and nephew either."

Tears rolled down Gina's face, and she squeezed

Sydney's hand. She wanted so terribly to confide in her sister, but no matter how hard she tried, the words just wouldn't come out. There was no way she could tell her that Phillip was beating her on the drop of a dime these days, and that his jealousy and possessiveness had risen to an infinite level. She was going to handle the situation soon enough, and there was no reason to get the entire family riled up until everything was over between her and Phillip. She knew Sydney was only trying to help, but it was better to leave things as is for now. It was better to keep things to herself for the time being.

"Gina, tell me what's wrong."

"Okay. Phillip and I are having some problems, but it's not what you're thinking. We've been having some disagreements about me taking this promotion that I'm up for, and that's all," she said, mentally asking God to forgive her for all the lies she was telling.

Sydney didn't believe her, though, and Gina knew it.

"And that's it?" Sydney asked.

"That's it. We're working it out, so there's nothing for you, Mom, or Rick to be worrying about."

"Well, I'm here for you, Gina. You hear me," Sydney said, still holding Gina's right hand across the table and grabbing the other. "I don't care what time it is or how bad it is, I want you to call me whenever you need me."

Gina smiled at Sydney as much as she could, and worked hard to keep from crying all over again. She knew her sister meant well, but she didn't want her thinking lowly of her either. She didn't want her wondering how she could stay in such a horrifying marriage. She wouldn't understand, and her experience over the years told her that no one ever understood why women stayed with men like Phillip regardless of how bad things got. As a teenager, she'd always said never. Not ever would she allow any man to pound on her under any circumstances. But now she was deeply reminded of the phrase "Never say never." People just didn't know how they'd handle a situation until they'd actually been in it themselves. It was easy to be an outsider looking in, but it was another thing to actually experience what another person was really going through. It was no different from when drug addicts lost family, spouses, jobs, but still weren't able to stop getting high. Or even when people knew they needed to lose a certain amount of weight because of serious health problems, and still couldn't find the will to do it. Not even when their physician had practically guaranteed that they would die if they didn't. It was wrong for anyone to judge or look down on another person for any reason, but it was simply the way society was. It was, unfortunately, the American way, and the reason why Gina wasn't about to spill her issues at home with anyone. She couldn't bear the humiliation, and it was better to keep things locked inside her household.

"If I need you, I'll call you," Gina told her. "I promise."

Sydney reached into her black nylon Donna Karan tote, and removed two sheets of tissue.

"Now, wipe your face, so we can talk about Mom's retirement," Sydney said, passing them to her.

Gina smiled at her sister. "Thanks."

Sydney pulled out a two-pocket folder and opened it.

"Now, I think everything is pretty much set for the dinner, but we still need to check on the delivery time for the cake, make sure that the DJ is there on time, because you know we had a problem with that when we had Rick's thirtieth birthday party two years ago. Then we need to decide who's going to pick Aunt Susan up from the airport that morning," Sydney said, scanning down her list.

"Mom is going to be so surprised when she sees her baby sister."

"I know. She thinks Aunt Susan can't make it, and I can't wait to see her face."

"And is the caterer all set?" Gina asked.

"Yeah, she's all ready to go."

"Well, we can split up any phone calls that still need to be made, so just let me know," Gina offered as the waitress set their lunch on the table.

"You know," Sydney said, "I really wish Daddy was still alive so he could be here to see Mom retire. He would be so proud of her, and it would make Mom so happy. Working thirty years is a real accomplishment; especially when a person can retire before they're too old to enjoy life."

"I know. I wish Daddy was here, too. Sometimes I miss him so much, and it's still hard to believe that he died so young."

"Never even saw his fifty-first birthday. But when it's your time, I guess there's nothing anyone can do to change it."

"That's for sure. But I'll tell you, Sydney, I can't imagine how things would be without Mom. I know the doctors keep saying that her tumor is benign and that it's not growing, but it still bothers me."

"Well, the last couple of times she had an MRI, her neurosurgeon said that she's probably had it for years, maybe even since birth, and that it may never grow any bigger than it already is."

"I pray every day that it doesn't, because I don't know what we'd do without her. Mom is the tie to this family, and she's such a good person."

"Well, let's not talk about that," Sydney suggested because she knew if they kept this conversation going, it was only a matter of time before she broke into tears herself. She didn't want to think about the possibility of her mother leaving her, and it was better to talk about something else.

They both bit into their sandwiches and looked over at the unruly child who'd just screamed like he was losing his mind.

"Johnny, please stop doing that," the twenty-something mother begged her child, who looked to be three or four years old.

"No!" Johnny yelled at her.

He was smearing food across the table, and his mother was acting as if she didn't know how to stop him.

"Okay, if you don't stop it, I'm taking you home to take a nap," she rattled off unconvincingly.

"Noooo," he told her, reminding her that he was the one running things this afternoon.

"Well, then stop it," she said, cleaning the food from the table as best as she could.

Johnny lifted the ketchup bottle and squirted it across the table, laughing like nobody's business.

"Okay, that's it. You put that ketchup down right now, or I mean, you're going to get it when we get home," she said, and Sydney and Gina looked at each other with raised eyebrows, because it was obvious that Johnny wasn't ceasing anything until he got good and ready to.

Johnny squeezed the plastic bottle again, and this time, part of it landed on his mother's shirt. She grabbed the bottle away from him, wiped herself, and dragged him by his hand out of the booth. They proceeded toward the counter with Johnny kicking and screaming.

"I'm telling Daddy," he said, threatening her. "And he's gonna whip your ugly face."

Sydney inhaled loudly. Gina snickered before she knew it. They couldn't believe what they'd just heard little Johnny say to his mother. It was sad on one hand, and hilarious on the other, because she should have had better control than that.

"Let's go, Johnny," the woman said, pretending she hadn't heard what he'd said to her. Johnny ignored her and ran back to the table where they'd been sitting. He folded his arms and his mother dropped her face in disgust, clearly not knowing how she was going to get him out of the restaurant.

"One," she began, counting.

Johnny swung his legs back and forth like he didn't have a care in the world.

"Two," she continued.

"Oh, my God," Sydney said, staring at them the same as everyone else sitting in the restaurant.

Johnny ignored her and picked up the ketchup bottle again. She rushed over to him, jerked the bottle from his hand, set it on the table, and forced him through the door leading out to the street.

"Can you believe that?" Sydney asked Gina.

"No," she said, laughing. "I wish Carl or Caitlin *would* embarrass me like that in public. But they know better than to even try some mess like that with me."

"I know that's right. I taught Victoria at a very young age that she'd better not even think about talking back to me like I'm some child. She's not running anything in our household, and when she gets to the point where she wants to, then she may as well start looking for another place to stay. She tries to debate me from time to time when she doesn't like what I'm telling her, but I don't hesitate to stop her right in her tracks. I'm not putting up with that. I'm telling you, nowadays you can't tell who's got the control, the parents or the children."

"Well, I know who's in charge in Johnny's household," Gina added. "And it sounds like, to me, his father allows him to talk to his mother that way. For all we know, that's probably where he got that 'ugly face' remark from," Gina said, and for whatever reason, couldn't help but wonder if Johnny's mother was living in an abusive environment the same as she was.

"Johnny is a natural trip," Sydney said, shaking her head, "and it's a good thing he doesn't belong to me."

They both laughed.

"Well, I guess I need to get ready to go back to work," Gina said, removing her wallet from her purse.

"How long are you going to be working downtown?" Sydney asked.

"Only a few more days. They asked me to work on a project at this office, since I worked on one similar to it last year."

"Oh, okay."

Gina left enough to cover the entire bill and tip, and they walked out onto the sidewalk.

"I'll check with you tomorrow to see if there's anything else we need to do before the dinner next weekend," Gina offered.

"That's fine," Sydney said, hugging her sister. "And girl. You take care of yourself, okay? And don't forget what I said, because I'm always here."

"I know you are, and I love you for it."

"I love you too," Sydney said and walked in a different direction from Gina.

She walked half a block and then turned to look back at her sister. She watched her for a few seconds and prayed that Gina would find the will to leave Phillip before it was way too late. Sydney didn't have any proof of what was going on, and couldn't be one hundred percent sure that he was hurting her, but her gut feeling told her that he was. She was worried sick, but she knew there wasn't anything she could do until Gina felt comfortable enough to open up about all of this. She prayed that God would keep her safe until she finally had the courage to do so.

Chapter 9

Why was it that she never seemed to have any time for herself? Sydney thought as she drove into the parking lot of Victoria's junior high school. Normally, Victoria rode the bus home, but today she'd stayed after watching a track meet, and Sydney had told her that she'd pick her up when it was over. She didn't mind chauffeuring her daughter around when it came to her education and extracurricular activities, but sometimes it seemed like it was all too much. She wondered if every other mother in America was feeling the same way, or if this was just a personal thing with her. She felt like she was being pulled in a thousand different directions, and there were times when she honestly felt like getting in her car and driving for as many miles as she could, without ever looking back. She knew it was a cruel thing to think, but it was the way Victoria, Wesley, and those doggoned magazine editors made her feel sometimes. Victoria needed her mother, Wesley needed his wife, and her editors needed her to meet very tight deadlines. Which, of course, meant there was never time for her to do any of the things she wanted. Like going to the bookstore, spending hours browsing through all of the new fiction and reference books on how to get published. Like going to a full-service salon and spending the entire day getting the works. Like watching movies based on novels written by Danielle Steel on The Lifetime Channel. She wasn't asking for a lot, just a little time for herself was all. She didn't want to seem selfish, but it was so amazing how Victoria and Wesley never even noticed all that she did, both career-wise and around the house. It was almost like they didn't realize how hard she worked, since she worked from her home office. As a matter of fact, her friends and family members didn't respect her working situation either. She couldn't count how many times people called her in the middle of the day because they needed her to do something for them or simply wanted to drop by for a visit. Which was the reason she'd started monitoring her Caller-ID box much more frequently, and was now being a lot more selective when she answered her phone.

But aside from her writing schedule, there were her many household duties. Picking up after Wesley and Victoria, who seemed like they migrated to the rooms that were clean, just so they could mess them up. Writing out the weekly bills. Taking care of the grocery shopping. Washing all of their clothing. Making sure they had all the necessities, such as toilet paper, dish detergent, washing detergent, and cleaning products in general. Not to mention, preparing dinner for them or going out to pick up something when she wasn't in the mood to cook.

It was obvious that they really didn't have a clue about everything she was doing, but she didn't know how much longer she was going to be able to keep up this ridiculous pace. She wasn't the only person living in the household, and it was time that her husband and daughter started acting like it.

Victoria opened the door to the Jeep and hopped inside. "Hi, Mom."

"Hi, honey," she said, reaching to hug her. "How was school today?"

"It was fine. We won the track meet, too."

"Good. Is there anyone else riding home with us?"

"No, Marlene had to leave early for a dentist appointment, and Sabrina didn't stay."

Sydney pulled off, and headed down the street.

"So, what do you want to pick up to eat?"

"I don't know. What about a pizza?"

"Sounds good to me, but your dad is going to have a fit."

Victoria laughed, because she'd heard her father complain a number of times about them having pizza too often.

"But tonight he's just going to have to get over it, because after I drop you off and get a bite to eat, I'm going over to your grandmother's."

"Why, is Granny okay?" Victoria asked, trying to figure out what was wrong.

"She's fine, but I'm going because I need a break. I haven't spent time alone with Mom in a long time. So, is that okay with you?" she asked, teasing Victoria.

"Yeah, it's fine with me."

"Thanks," she said, smiling at her daughter and then looked back toward the road.

"We should call the pizza in, so we won't have to wait," Victoria suggested.

"Use my cell phone, and remember to get half of it with bacon for your father. And get the sixteen-inch instead of the fourteen."

Victoria knew the phone number by heart, and dialed it. She ordered the size her mother told her to, and requested mushrooms, sausage, and double cheese on it the way she and Sydney liked it. They never liked the bacon like Wesley, thinking it was too salty.

They picked up the pizza, and when they arrived home, Wesley was relaxing on the sofa. He worked as a CNC operator at a top manufacturer, and it was obvious that he'd had a hectic and very stressful day.

"Hey, sweetheart," Sydney said.

"Hey, Daddy," Victoria added.

"How're my two favorite ladies?" he asked, standing up. His shoes were in front of the love seat. His jacket was sprawled across the sofa, and he already had two drinking glasses on the coffee table. Sydney didn't want to get upset before going over to her mother's, though, and decided not to say anything.

He walked up the two stairs from the family room into the kitchen. "Pizza? I know we're not having that again?"

Victoria giggled and looked at her mother.

"I didn't have time to cook anything, and Victoria said she wanted pizza."

"Mom!" Victoria complained.

"Well, you did," Sydney said, laughing.

"Yeah, but you were right there with her, and I'll bet you wanted pizza, too," Wesley told her. "Shoot, it really doesn't matter today, though, because I'm too tired and too hungry to care what I eat. Anything will do at this point."

Sydney was glad to hear it, because all she wanted to do was eat and head over to her mother's.

"I'm going over to Mom's in a little while."

"That's fine. I was thinking about going to the health club, but I don't think I'm going to make it," he said.

"I need to get back to working out myself, because it's almost like we're donating money to them every month for nothing."

"We should start going together when I get off work."

"Yeah, that could work. Maybe we can start next week."

"So, how was the track meet?" Wesley asked Victoria while scooping four pieces of pizza on his plate.

"We won. Covington Park has been doing good at every meet. They have a good team this year."

"That's good to hear. You should have been running yourself," he said.

"I know, but I didn't feel like doing all that practicing every day, and it would have interfered with my dance classes."

Sydney was proud of Victoria for taking the classes even if they did have to pay through the nose for her to do so, but she wondered how long it was going to be before dance had become boring and Victoria wanted to try something new. It was always like that with her—and most other children as well, based on what she'd heard from other parents.

They finished eating their dinner, and Wesley stretched out on the sofa. Victoria went up to her room, Sydney threw a load of sheets in the washer, and told Victoria to place them in the dryer when the wash cycle was finished. Then she left for her mother's.

Delores didn't live more than fifteen minutes away, and before long, Sydney pulled into her driveway. She hadn't told Delores she was coming, and now she was hoping that her mother was home.

She rang the doorbell, and shortly thereafter, Delores opened the door.

"Hey," Delores said, smiling, and it was almost as if she expected Sydney's visit.

"Hey, Mom. How are you?" she asked, stepping through the doorway.

"I'm fine. And how's my granddaughter and son-in-law doing?"

"They're fine."

"Come on in my bedroom. I was just sitting in here

sorting some old clothes. I'm tired of taking up space in every closet in this house. Some of this stuff, I haven't worn in the last five years. Some in ten or fifteen."

"I know what you mean. I need to get rid of a bunch of things myself. I thought about having a garage sale last year, but then I figured it would be better to just give it to the church for someone who needs it."

"That's what I'm planning to do as soon as I have it all packed up."

Sydney leaned back against her mother's backrest. "So, you getting ready for the big day?"

"Yep, I guess so. Friday is only three days away, and I can't believe it came so fast. It seems like it was just a little while ago when I finally decided to retire."

"You've been at the post office for a long time, and you've worked hard all your life. It's time for you to spend your time taking care of *you.*"

"I just wish your father was still here," she said sadly.

"I know. Gina and I talked about that earlier today."

"He just didn't seem like the type of man who would have a heart attack," Delores said, folding a pair of pants. "But I do have to admit, he didn't eat the most healthy foods. And I didn't either until that happened to him."

"That's true."

"So, you say you talked to Gina?"

"Yeah, believe it or not, we met for lunch. I told her that we needed to go over some things for your retirement dinner. I've been asking her for the last three weeks or so, and she finally agreed to come."

"So, did you find out what's going on with her?" Delores wanted to know.

"Not really, but I definitely think something's not right with her and Phillip. I don't know if he's fighting her or what, but she looks so exhausted. She says that he's upset because she might be getting a promotion, but I don't believe that's all there is to it."

"Why would he be upset about that, anyway?" Delores said, frowning.

"You know Phillip. He's jealous of everything Gina does."

"I don't know why that girl puts up with that mess. She should have gotten rid of that man a long time ago."

"She denies that he's jumping on her physically, but I have a feeling he is. And it sickens me to think that those babies are there watching every bit of it. If Gina doesn't care about herself, that's one thing, but she should at least think about what her children are going through. You can tell that they are being affected by something, because they act completely different when he's around. Almost like they're afraid to say anything unless somebody gives them permission to. But then, they talk nonstop when he's not around."

"If Rick knew Phillip was beatin' on his sister, he'd try to kill him."

"I know, and that's why I don't even discuss that with him," Sydney said, glancing at the shampoo commercial on television. "I know I've got my problems with Wesley, but there's no way I could live with a man like Phillip," she continued.

"What do you mean, your problems with Wesley?" Delores said, turning to give her daughter her fullest attention.

"Don't get upset," Sydney said, smiling. "It's nothing serious. Or at least I hope not, anyway."

"Well, what's the problem?"

"Sex. Or I guess I should say not enough of it."

"On whose part?"

"His."

"Why?"

Sydney was turning thirty-six on May tenth, one day

before her mother was turning fifty-six on the eleventh, which was only a week away, but she still didn't feel comfortable discussing her sex life with her. It felt sort of embarrassing, but it was obvious that her mother didn't see a thing wrong with it.

"I'm too tired to have sex with Wesley every night. I have a thousand things to do every day, and all he thinks I'm doing is sitting around the house waiting for him to get home."

Delores pulled a couple of dresses from her closet, and didn't say anything at first. Then she spoke.

"Girl, you'd better make time for your husband, before somebody else does."

"It's not that serious, Mom," she said, knowing that she'd become more and more worried that her husband would in fact end up in another woman's arms.

"I do make time for him, but I just don't have the energy or the desire to have sex as often as he wants me to. I can't help the way I feel, and I don't know what to do about it. It's been better these last two weeks, but I've had to muster everything in me just to go through the motions."

"Do you love him?" Delores asked, staring at her.

"Of course, I do. I love him more than ever before. But love isn't based on sex. There's a lot more to our relationship, and that's why we've been happily married for as long as we have."

"It's not based on sex, but the two things do go together. And you're not going to make any man see otherwise."

"I'm trying. I mean, I'm really going out of my way, but it's not like I really want to."

"It hasn't always been like this, has it?"

"No, but over the last couple of years, I've been feeling this way. I work a lot of hours on my writing, and by the time I do everything else, I don't want to do anything except lie down and go to sleep. At first, it wasn't that big of a deal to him, because he realized I was working hard to meet my deadlines, but these past few months have been terrible. We've been arguing on and off every week about all of this."

Delores looked away from her, and Sydney knew she was about to get serious on her.

"Now you know I don't like to get in my children's business, but it seems like to me, you need to talk to someone. A psychologist, your medical doctor, somebody. Because maybe there's something physically or mentally wrong that you can't see."

"I told Wesley the same thing, but I just haven't taken the time to make an appointment. I keep putting if off for some reason."

"Well, I suggest you do it soon, because you have a husband who really loves you. Not every woman has been blessed with a man like Wesley, and it would kill you if you lost him. I can't tell you what to do, baby, but I hope you try to take care of this, before things go too far."

Sydney sighed. "I know."

"And if it's all the work you're doing, then you need to slow down on some of those writing assignments. Nobody wants to see you succeed with your career more than I do, but I don't want to see your marriage fall apart either. And what good is work and money if you don't have somebody you love to share it with? Because you definitely don't want to end up like me."

Sydney wondered what she was getting at. "How is that?"

"Working myself to death for thirty years, when I could have retired in twenty. Now, I've got this brain tumor and don't know when it might start growing or causing me all kinds of medical problems."

"I'm not worried about it, because the doctors keep saying that it may never grow for the rest of your life."

Sydney had just made basically the same statement

to Gina earlier, and now she realized that she kept saying it as a way to convince herself that it was true. That her mother was going to be perfectly fine from here on out.

"But we don't have any guarantees that it won't, because no matter how you look at it, that tumor is still inside my head."

Sydney hated when her mother talked about this growth that a CAT scan had discovered by accident when they were checking to see why her mother didn't sleep much. She had never slept more than two to three hours per night over the last ten years or so, and her doctor thought they should do some tests to see if they could somehow find the culprit. But instead, what they'd found was a brain tumor. One that was housed in an inoperable area of the right frontal lobe, and they'd all agreed that it was best not to try and correct it. And since she'd been fine for over a year and a half, there really wasn't anything to be alarmed about. However, Sydney did understand her mother's concern, and rightfully so, especially since there was something lodged in her head that wasn't supposed to be there.

"You are going to be just fine."

"Oh, I know I will. God will take care of me whether this tumor grows or not, and even if it is His will to take me from this earth, I'm okay with that, too. But all I'm saying is that it's not worth working all your life and saving every dime you make, if you're not going to be able to enjoy it anyhow."

"I hear you, Mom, and I promise I'll make an appointment with my doctor before the end of the week."

"Now make sure you do, because I know how you can keep putting things off when you get busy."

"No. Seriously. I'm going to make an appointment. I don't want things to continue the way they are either."

Sydney sat around and talked with her mother for three hours. Something she couldn't remember doing in the last twelve months, and it was good to spend so much time with her. Her mother was her mother when she needed her to be, but she was more like her best friend. They were as close as a mother and daughter could be, and she didn't know what she would do if something were to happen to her. As far as Sydney was concerned, the sun rose and set on Delores Mathis, and not a day went by when she didn't thank God for giving her the best mother ever.

Chapter 10

"Phillip, did you decide whether you're going to Mom's retirement celebration this weekend?" Gina asked, hoping he wasn't going to cause any trouble.

But all he did was grunt, and she couldn't tell whether he was agreeing to go or whether he wasn't. He'd been in a halfway decent mood over the last couple of days, but it mostly had to do with the fact that she'd agreed with everything he said or wanted to do to her—including having sex in ways she didn't care to think about. He'd been wanting it every night, and it was almost as if he was using sex as a means to punish her. He'd asked her about the promotion at the end of last week, and when she'd told him that she was probably going to get it, he hadn't said one word. He'd acted as though he was happy with the whole idea of it. That is, until later that evening, when he'd forced himself inside her so roughly that tears seeped through her eyes, even though they were tightly closed together.

He'd promised her that he wouldn't hit her anymore, but the sexual abuse he was imposing on her was just as bad or worse, depending on how a person looked at it.

Then there was last evening, when he'd asked her what she did for lunch. She'd explained to him as calmly and carefully as she could that she'd met Sydney to discuss the plans for their mother's dinner. He'd pretended like he was fine with that, too, but eventually showed his disapproval by practically shoving his manhood down her throat. She'd gagged a few times, but Phillip never even acknowledged her pain and suffering. He looked at her like she was getting what she deserved.

She hated him so much now that it was becoming harder and harder to put on a happy face as if everything was okay. She still hadn't come up with a rock-solid plan, but it was just a matter of time before she left him. Before it was too late. Before she wouldn't be able to leave him while she was still alive.

She wanted to ask him to tell her yes or no about the retirement dinner, but she didn't want to piss him off in front of the children, who were sitting on the floor watching The Cartoon Network. She'd decided that she and the twins were going whether he went or not, and she would just have to deal with the consequences after the fact. Phillip kept her from seeing her family all the time, but she wasn't going to stand for it this time around.

She switched her eyes in the direction of the television, and as soon as she did, Phillip spoke.

"Hey, little ones," he called out to Carl and Caitlin.

"Yes," they turned and answered him together.

"You two want to go to your grandmother's retirement party?"

"Yes," they said with no enthusiasm because they knew their input didn't mean that much in terms of their father's decision making.

"You do, huh? Well, I guess we'll go then."

Gina was relieved, and took a deep breath. But it pissed her off whenever he asked the kids what they wanted to do, making it seem like he wasn't doing her any favors and that his approval was strictly to satisfy them.

"But I'm telling you," he said, pointing his finger at her. "Your family better treat me with some respect, or we'll be leaving as soon as we get there. I'm not putting up with their comments or their attitudes, so I suggest you talk to all of them before we get there."

"Honey, everything will be fine," she assured him. "I'm just glad you're going, so we can go as a family," she said as excitedly as she could. Because in reality, she wished he would drop dead. She wished something very bad would happen to him, so bad that she and the children never had to see him ever again.

They watched a movie on The Family Channel, and when it was over, they all paraded upstairs. Phillip went into their bedroom, and Gina waited for the children to slip into their pajamas so she could tuck them in. Carl came into Caitlin's room so they could say their prayers first, though.

"Dear God," Caitlin began, "thank you for Mom, Dad, Granny, Aunt Sydney, Uncle Wesley, Uncle Rick, Samantha, and Victoria. And thank you for all the kids in my school, too. I even thank you for Briana, who butted me in the lunch line today. And please God, make our family happy like the families on TV. Amen," she said and kept her eyes closed, waiting for her brother to say his prayer.

"God, please take care of our whole family, and help me to pass my math test tomorrow morning. And like my sister said, please let us all be happy. Amen."

Caitlin climbed into bed, and Carl headed toward his own bedroom next door. It was all Gina could do to keep from wailing. She'd known for a long time that the twins weren't as happy as children deserve to be, but now they were praying for things to change. They wanted to be happy, and now she knew that their unhappiness was all her fault. She was their mother, and a mother was supposed to protect her children at all cost. She wanted to pack them up and leave right now, but she knew she had to be smarter than that. She'd been stupid for what seemed like a hundred years, and now it was time for her to use her head and not be hasty. She was going to get them out of this mess, but unfortunately, it wasn't going to happen as quickly as she wanted.

It seemed easy enough to simply walk out and start fresh with just her and the children, but there was one thing that kept her from making such a rash decision: Phillip had promised that he would kill her if she did. It was easy to believe that he'd never do such a thing, but with everything else that he'd done over the years, she knew he wasn't playing games with her. He said what he meant, and usually meant what he said. She had to keep in mind that she wasn't dealing with a very stable individual, and that it would take time to escape him without bodily harm.

Gina left Carl's room last, and dreaded going into her own. She wished she could concoct some disappearing act, so she wouldn't have to lie next to this nightmare she'd been married to for almost a decade.

She removed her clothing and reached for her nightgown.

"You won't be needing that," Phillip told her.

She never even bothered picking it up, because she knew Phillip wasn't taking no for an answer. She didn't want him huffing, puffing, and sweating all over her, and she didn't feel like experiencing any more pain. She was still having horrible flashbacks from last night, and she didn't know how she was going to get through this one.

"Don't worry, I'll go easy on you tonight," he said as if he was doing her a favor.

Gina didn't comment, but slid into bed next to him. He kissed her wildly and it made her want to vomit. She closed her eyes and prayed that he would hurry to get this over with. He absorbed her breasts into his mouth so harshly, that her nipples went numb.

"Phillip, the children aren't asleep yet," Gina pleaded.

But Phillip paid no attention to her. Instead, he raised his body from hers, flipped her over on her stomach, pulled her buttocks upward, and pushed himself inside her with all the force he had. She hoped he wasn't planning to penetrate her anally, because she would never be able to stand that. He'd done it on a regular basis a year ago, but had finally stopped after her doctor diagnosed her with very severe hemorrhoids. But it always made her nervous whenever he entered her from behind.

He breathed heavily, motioning in and out, and he continued pushing and pulling in and out of her in a very rapid manner. But finally his body stiffened when he climaxed.

"That . . . was so . . . good," he said, trying to catch his breath.

Gina flattened her body and turned her head in the opposite direction. She couldn't bear to look at him, and she couldn't wait for him to drop off to sleep. Which didn't take very long, because he was now slightly snoring.

She felt so violated and, as much as she hated to admit it, like an idiot. What woman in her right mind would put up with all of this? It just didn't seem right, and she wondered what was wrong with her. She hadn't asked to meet a man like Phillip, and she certainly hadn't asked to fall in love with him, but it had happened just the same. She'd had a couple of serious boyfriends while she was in high school, and they'd slapped her around a couple of times as well. It seemed almost like she was drawn to men who pretended that they loved her so much that they couldn't stand to see her talking with another man or doing anything without including them. She was ashamed to say that she and one of her girlfriends, who was going through the same thing with her boyfriend, sort of thought it was cute. They'd actually been dumb enough to believe that physical abuse from a seventeen-year-old boy was proof that he really was in love with you. It didn't make any sense, but at least it was more fathomable when a person was young and dumb. But she was in her thirties.

So what was her excuse now? What reason could she possibly have for staying with a lunatic like Phillip? She thought about it for a long time, trying to weigh everything out, but it wasn't long before she arrived back at the same thing she'd been worried about all along. Her life, and if Phillip was going to end it. She couldn't even be sure that he wouldn't hurt the children either. She kept reminding herself that he'd never done so in the past, but she still couldn't trust that he never would. He might even do it just to spite her, for all she knew.

Maybe something was wrong with her, and not Phillip, because it was hard to believe that she was so well equipped educationally, yet so foolish when it came to life and common sense. How could anyone in their right mind love someone like Phillip, because whether she wanted to own up to it or not, it had only been recently that she'd begun hating him. That she'd begun thinking that she didn't want to be with him any longer. It had taken years of mental, physical, and sexual abuse for her to realize that this wasn't the way marriage was supposed to be. That the way Phillip treated her was as wrong as committing murder. She felt like she was being punished. Maybe she'd done some unforgivable thing a long time ago, and couldn't remember what it was.

But really, why did things like this have to happen? Why was it that some people traveled through life with no real problems at all, while others seemed to come here with misgivings and illnesses the very day they were born? And why was it that some people were smart enough to get out of an abusive situation from the start of a relationship, and others like her stayed for as long as they could take it? Why were there skinny people, and at the same time, there were overweight individuals who couldn't lose weight if someone paid them ten million dollars? Or at least if they did, they wouldn't be able to maintain it for very long. Why were some people blessed with all the right facial features, while others were not so enjoyable to look at? Why were some people filthy rich, with no financial problems, while others were barely making ends meet or able to feed their children?

Because it wasn't like anyone wanted to weigh three hundred pounds. It wasn't like anyone wanted to have dreadful facial features. It certainly wasn't like anyone wanted to be dirt poor. And Lord knows, Gina didn't want to have her brains beaten out whenever her husband wasn't happy with her.

She kept asking herself these questions all the time, because none of it made any sense to her. She didn't want to be stupid when it came to Phillip, but he was almost like an illness that she didn't know how to get rid of.

She tossed hundreds of thoughts over the next few hours, while Phillip slept peacefully. But the last thing she thought about before dropping off to sleep was that she wished she had the courage to boil a huge pot of grits and plaster Phillip's entire body with them.

Chapter 11

Rick pulled his black-and-gold tie securely in place, and then slipped on his black, three-button suit jacket. Samantha was in the bathroom finishing up her makeup, and as soon as she was dressed, they were heading out to his mother's dinner. He smiled when he thought about his childhood years, and how loving and caring his mother had been when he and his sisters were growing up. She was always there for them, a little more for Sydney in his opinion than for him and Gina, but she was there nevertheless. She was a good mother, and he couldn't complain about the way they were raised one bit. She'd done the very best that she could do, and their father had done the same. He missed his father something terrible, and although years had now passed since the day he passed away, Rick still found himself shedding tears with no warning. A father wasn't something that a son could ever replace, and he'd been taken from him much too quickly. He'd had a very hard time with his death, because there were so many things he still wanted to tell him, and so many things he still wanted to do with him. He remembered putting his father off every time he'd asked Rick to go fishing with him, and now Rick regretted it. He wasn't a huge fan of the sport, but now he realized that it would have been a good time just because his father loved it. His father was such a mild-mannered, understanding man, and Rick wished he could talk to him about this situation with Samantha. He had a feeling that his father, being the person that he was, would tell him to commit, but somehow it wasn't the same without actually being able to hear him say it. He wondered if his father would understand where he was coming from, and would see why he wasn't ready to get married. Why he needed to wait on this, and why he didn't think it was a good thing to rush to the altar without being one hundred percent sure about doing it. If only Samantha would see things his way, she'd realize in no time that he was right about all of this.

Rick smoothed out his eyebrows with both hands, and Samantha stepped out of the bathroom. She pulled on her sleeveless black crepe dress, and turned her back to him.

"Can you zip this for me?"

"Sure," he said, moving closer to her.

She slipped on her shoes, and glanced at herself in the mirror one final time.

"You look beautiful in that dress," he complimented her.

"Thanks, and you look good as well."

They hadn't argued since the news-breaking dinner she'd fixed for him, but things were still sort of on the chilly side, and it was almost like they were picking and choosing what words they could and should say to each other. But Rick didn't want to feel that way this evening. He wanted them to have a good time at the dinner. He wanted them to feel the way they used to whenever they went out somewhere together.

"Sweetheart, I know things haven't been the best between us, but I want to thank you for agreeing to go to Mom's dinner."

"Now, Rick, you know I wouldn't have missed your mom's celebration for the world. She means a lot to me, and she's always treated me like a daughter. And regardless of what happens, I will always care about her."

He kissed her on the cheek, she smiled at him, and they left for the banquet facility.

Sydney couldn't believe how beautiful the room actually looked. The decorators that she'd hired had done a breathtaking job, and she was very content with the colors she'd chosen. Black, silver, and royal blue. Everything looked immaculate from the balloons in the ceiling, to the elegant foiled-paper centerpieces on each of the round tables of eight. The silver-trimmed china and delicate crystal that the facility provided were gorgeous, and the music the DJ played was just as mellow and relaxing as she had hoped for.

The preparation had been as time-consuming and hectic as it was when she'd planned her own wedding, but as she gazed across the room and saw the huge smile on her mother's face, she knew it was all well worth it. Delores looked stunning in a black tailored suit, and the full-length skirt added even more class to it. Sydney had gone shopping with her when she'd purchased it, and as soon as they'd spotted it, they'd known immediately that it was practically made for her. She even liked her own outfit, which was a black floor-length, fitted dress that made her look a whole size smaller. Wesley had smiled at her in a hungry sort of way as soon as he saw her in it, and had made it clear that he couldn't wait until they arrived back home. She liked the way she looked in this outfit so much that, believe it or not, she was feeling a bit sexual herself.

She did a thumbs-up motion to Rick, who was looking rather sharp in what seemed to be a new suit. They'd all agreed to wear black, and Rick was looking exceptionally handsome in his. Samantha looked striking as always.

Sydney loved Gina's outfit as well. She looked gorgeous, and while it really didn't matter what she wore, since she looked good in just about anything, the black evening gown she was wearing tonight was ravishing on her.

But then there was Phillip. Sydney's attitude went sour as she watched Gina catering to that fool. She'd heard her ask him if he needed anything as soon as they walked in an hour ago. Now she was walking toward the bar, preparing to order him a drink. Why couldn't he get his own drink? Why couldn't Gina spend this time with her mother, the children, or mingle with the rest of the guests for that matter? Sydney shook her head slightly and decided that she couldn't worry about any of that now. This was her mother's night, and that was what she needed to be thinking about.

Delores strolled through the crowd of at least three hundred people, shook their hands, and thanked them for coming. She posed with each of her children as the photographer shot memorable photos. She posed with her supervisor, coworkers, and some of her family members as well. This was one of the happiest moments of her life, and Sydney knew her mother wasn't thinking it could get any better. That is, until Delores saw her sister, Susan, walk in.

Delores covered her mouth, and tears filled her eyes. "Oh my God," she said, moving toward her.

"Hey, there," her sister said in a delightful voice.

"It's so good to see you," Delores said, hugging her sister like she hadn't seen her in years. It had only been a short while, but it seemed like forever.

"It's good to see you, too," Susan said, smiling and holding her sister's hands.

"I thought you weren't going to be able to make it."

"I know you did. I slipped up on you, though, didn't I?"

Delores looked at all three of her children, when she realized that they were the guilty parties. They'd gone out of their way to convince her that Aunt Susan wasn't going to be there. She hadn't thought her sister would miss such an important time in her life, but she really had believed her when she'd called to express her apologies for not being able to attend.

Sydney, Gina, and Rick hugged their favorite aunt, and laughed.

"We got you this time, didn't we?" Sydney teased her mother.

"Yeah, you really did," Delores admitted.

Aunt Susan embraced her great-nieces and great-nephew, chatted with Wesley, and spoke to Phillip, who actually held a conversation with her. For some odd reason, he'd always liked Aunt Susan, and she was really the only family member he gave the utmost respect to. Maybe it was because he didn't have to see her as often as the rest of his in-laws, and she wasn't aware of how terrible he was treating her niece. Delores had confided to her that she didn't think Gina was happy in her marriage, but she hadn't gone into any specific details.

Another half-hour passed, and everyone finally took their seats. Delores, her supervisor, Tom Powell, her minister, Pastor Joseph, his wife, Sydney, Wesley, Gina, Phillip, Rick, and Samantha took their seats at the head table. Sydney stood, stepped in front of the podium, and positioned the microphone where she wanted it.

"Good evening, everyone. This is a very special evening, not just for my mother, but for our entire family. We are all so very proud of her, and we appreciate each of you taking the time out to share this joyous occasion with us. Mom has worked very hard these last thirty years, and she raised her children to be the best that they could be in the process. What I think about most is how she did everything she could to instill confidence in us, and it is because of her that I've always believed that the sky is the limit in terms of what I can do. And I just want to say, thank you, Mom, for always being there, and for being the best mother we could have ever possibly hoped for," Sydney said, fighting back tears.

Delores smiled, and everyone applauded.

"Now, Pastor Joseph, if you would come lead us in prayer, the servers will begin bringing out dinner."

Sydney took her seat, and Pastor Joseph delivered the invocation. The servers brought out bread and salad initially, and then a tasty grilled chicken pasta dish with white sauce. It was almost as good as the meal she'd eaten at Maxine's Restaurant on Warren Street in Trenton, New Jersey. She'd had an opportunity to go there during one of her business trips, and she hadn't been able to forget how well the food tasted. They served everything from soul food to international cuisine, and she'd never eaten anywhere since then that could compare to it. Which was the reason why she would never go back to Trenton without having dinner there again.

As the crowd began eating the strawberry cheesecake that the servers had just set on the tables, Sydney stood at the podium again.

"I do hope everyone enjoyed their entrée, because I sure did."

Everyone mumbled in agreement and laughed.

"Good. Then, what we'd like to do now is have Mr. Powell come up and say a few words."

Everyone applauded, and Tom stepped in front of the microphone.

"Well, all I can say is that we couldn't be here celebrating the retirement of a more dedicated, caring woman than Delores Mathis. She has worked for me for the last fifteen years, and I must say, she's the only employee I've had who has never been late and who has had more years of perfect attendance than most of us can even imagine. Even when she was sick, she was right at the post office. And when she had to take a few hours off for a doctor's appointment, she was never happy about it. She always wanted them to give her an appointment after her normal working hours, and I always knew when they hadn't, because she'd be walking around talking about it," he said, chuckling. The guests laughed as well.

"But seriously," he continued. "She was the model worker and friend, and from the moment you meet Delores, you understand immediately why everyone loves her from the very beginning. She always has a smile on her face, regardless of what is going on. Even if she's had a bad day or doesn't feel very well, she doesn't take it out on anyone else, and that particular quality is hard to find in people. She has the best personality in the world, and I'm just happy that I was able to work with her for as long as I have. So tonight, Delores Mathis," Tom said, picking up his champagne glass. "We honor you in the highest capacity, and wish nothing but great things for you as you begin your new life of leisure," he said, and everyone stood and sipped from their glasses in unison. They applauded her and remained standing until Delores hugged Tom and prepared to speak.

When the room had quieted down, Delores opened

her mouth to begin, but couldn't because of the tears rolling down her face. She was so happy, and it took her a moment to gain her composure.

"Who could ask for anything more than this? I've always tried to do the best I could with everything. My family, my job. I've even tried to be there for anyone I know in need, and I've tried to be a friend to everyone. Tom is right when he said I was never tardy, and that there were years when I didn't miss a single day from work, and I am very proud of that. Some people didn't see why I was so dedicated, but it's just the way my parents raised me, and I didn't know any other way to be. My daughter Sydney, who's never late, but likes to arrive right on the dot to everything, knows firsthand that I become a nervous wreck when I have to stand in the door waiting for her to pick me up. And I know she's aware of it, because she's always turning my street corner on two wheels before she pulls into my driveway," she said, looking at Sydney, and everyone laughed with both of them.

"But don't get me wrong, she is a wonderful daughter, and I have no complaints. She's my best friend, and I guess it's because she's the oldest. And then there's my beautiful daughter Gina, who is one of the most intelligent young women in the computer world today. I saw great potential in her at the age of five when she began choosing books over watching TV programs. And then there's my baby, Rick, who has grown up to be a handsome, caring young man. I may not tell you often enough, but I am filled with happiness every time I see you. It seems like it was only yesterday that you were wearing diapers and your sisters were doing things they shouldn't and then blaming them on you, because you didn't know any better.

"Your father would be so proud of all of you if he was still here with us. I miss him terribly sometimes, but I do know that he is with me in spirit. And I want you to know that the three of you, my three grandchildren, my son-in-laws, my sister, and Samantha, my son's fiancée, are the reason my life is so full and so satisfying. I love all of you from the bottom of my heart, and no matter what, I want you to remember that always. And I want to thank all of my friends, coworkers, and the rest of my family for all the love and support you have given me."

There was barely a dry eye in the room.

Delores turned and looked at Sydney, preparing to walk back to her seat, but before she could, she stared at her in a daze, then her eyes rolled toward the back of her head and she collapsed onto the floor.

"Mom!" Sydney screamed, falling to the floor near her mother.

"Oh my God," Gina yelled, dropping down on the other side of her.

"Someone call 911," Rick yelled.

The guests spoke among themselves a thousand miles a minute, and some stretched their necks, trying to see what was going on.

Why was this happening? Sydney thought. She didn't know what was wrong with her mother, but she had a strong feeling that this emergency situation was definitely related to the brain tumor. The doctors had all come to a consensus that it probably wasn't going to grow any more than it already had. It wasn't cancerous—at least the doctors didn't think so—therefore, Sydney hadn't been as worried about it as her mother.

Victoria pushed her way through the crowd which was huddling around the commotion. "Mom," she said hysterically. "What's wrong with Granny?"

Wesley grabbed his daughter to console her, and when he saw that Delores's sister Susan looked as though she was in a state of shock, he pulled her near him as well. Phillip stood back with his arms around the twins, looking on, but didn't make one attempt to show any support to Gina.

Sydney called out to her mother, trying to bring her around, but she didn't budge. Gina held her mother's hand, crying uncontrollably. Rick called out to his mother over and over, but there was still no response.

Pastor Joseph raised his hands above his head and prayed for Delores and the entire family, and soon after, the paramedics cleared the way up to the head table. They made sure she was still breathing, checked her pulse rate, and started oxygen almost immediately. They had to ask Sydney and Gina to move back so they could lift Delores onto the gurney. Sydney was a complete mess, Gina acted as though her whole world had just tumbled down around her, and Rick hugged Samantha tightly while staring at his unconscious mother.

He wondered how such a wonderful celebration could end on a note like this, and why on earth everything that mattered to him was falling apart.

Chapter 12

They'd been waiting for almost three hours now. Some of the family members and close friends paced the floor back and forth, some sat silently in prayer. Others flipped through magazines or tried to hold conversations about anything that came to mind. It was almost as if this wasn't really happening.

At least in Sydney's eyes anyway, because her mother had been completely fine before this evening. She hadn't complained about any headaches or any difficulties with her right eye. She'd known since the discovery of the growth that the tumor was intertwined with her main right optic nerves, but so far Delores hadn't experienced any problems with her vision. But it was almost as if Delores knew something wasn't quite right, because she'd made that comment about being okay with whatever her fate was. She'd said loud and clear that even if it was her time to leave this earth, she was okay with it. But Sydney had more or less dismissed all that sort of talk, believing that her mother was going to remain healthy and be here with them for many, many years to come.

Oh, how things never worked out the way we wanted them, though. No matter how well things could be going in general, there was always some unthinkable situation to remind the human race that they weren't in control of anything. They wanted to be, but Sydney had learned a long time ago that it just wasn't possible.

Sydney looked over at Rick, who was holding Samantha in his arms. She was glad that her brother had someone to lean on. Samantha was a good woman, and whichever way this all played out with their mother, she knew he was going to need someone to be there for him. He was a strong, independent young man, but Sydney didn't know how their mother's illness was going to affect him.

Gina sat quietly stroking Caitlin's hair, while Carl read one of the children's books he'd picked up from one of the tables. When Gina looked over at Phillip, he pursed his lips, leaned forward, and placed his head inside the palm of his hands. It made Gina cringe. It was so obvious that he didn't want to be there, but he had better hope that her mother was going to survive whatever she was going through or she was never going to forgive him. Not for the way he was blowing off this entire situation or for all the years he'd prevented her from spending time with her.

"Why won't they come out and tell us something," Gina said to Sydney without even thinking about it.

"I don't know, but the nurses keep saying that the doctor will be out as soon as he has something to tell us."

"It's been over three hours," Rick added.

"They have a lot of tests to run, and it will probably take some time," Sydney tried to explain to them. She'd gone through all of the MRIs, CT scans, blood work, and physical exams with her mother, and she knew how time-consuming some of it could be. But Gina and Rick had never gone to the University of Wisconsin Hospital in Madison one single time. They'd had plenty of opportunities, but hadn't thought it was necessary. Madison was a hundred and fifty-eight miles from her mother's home, but her neurosurgeon, Dr. Rogers, in Covington Park, had informed them that Delores's brain tumor was inoperable and that it was way over his or his local colleagues' heads. He had immediately called in a special referral to her HMO, and she and Sydney had gone to Madison to consult with Dr. Kumar, one of the top neurosurgeons in the country. They'd driven back and forth a few times for her MRI testing to ensure that the tumor hadn't grown, and so far it hadn't.

They waited awhile longer, and finally, Dr. Rogers came out to talk to them.

"How are you, Sydney?" he asked, shaking her hand.

"As well as can be expected," she answered. "Everyone, this is Dr. Rogers, Mom's neurosurgeon here in the area."

"How's everyone doing?" he said. "You have two other siblings, right?" he asked Sydney.

"Yes. Rick and Gina," she said, pointing to them.

Rick walked over and shook the doctor's hand, and Gina moved closer to Sydney and did the same. Everyone else waited for the news in silence.

"Okay. What we're dealing with is a slight stroke. Your mother is conscious, and although she's not completely coherent, she does know who I am, where she's at, how many children she has, and so on. We did an MRI, and for the first time, we can see that the tumor has started to grow. And unfortunately, it's no longer just a matter of it causing problems with her vision, but it is now growing toward the brain stem, which means we now have to worry about loss of life."

Sydney's head felt like it was going to explode. Gina

couldn't tell if she was dreaming or if this was all really happening, and Rick gazed at Dr. Rogers like he hadn't heard a word he said.

"So, the only option left at this point is to try to remove it," Dr. Rogers continued. "And as you know, Sydney, Dr. Kumar in Madison is the best neurosurgeon to handle this. I've already phoned him, and he's prepared to resect the tumor as early as Monday or Tuesday."

"Can she wait two or three days?" Sydney asked fearfully.

"Yes, she's stable enough to withstand the transfer from here to Wisconsin and to go through whatever presurgical procedures they need to perform when she gets there."

"Now, I know the tumor is in the right frontal lobe, sinus cavity area, and that it's intertwined with her right optic nerves, but with the exception of her having some short-term memory loss, is there a chance that she could end up blind in her right eye?"

Everyone looked as if they couldn't believe how knowledgeable Sydney was about her mother's condition. Gina and Rick didn't have the slightest idea what she was talking about.

"I can't say for sure, but there is a very strong possibility that could happen. But as I said, her vision is not the main concern as it was, say, a week ago, because now we're talking about a life-and-death situation. It's mine and Dr. Kumar's opinion that her best option now is surgery. But since you have power-of-attorney, the final decision has to be left up to you."

"When did Mom give us power-of-attorney?" Rick asked, sounding surprised.

"She gave me power-of-attorney for her health care right after she found out about the tumor," Sydney said. "I didn't think it was necessary, but she insisted on having her attorney draw the papers up."

Rick didn't seem too happy about what he'd just learned, and Sydney didn't even want to think about how he was going to react when he found out that she also had her financial power-of-attorney, and was the executor of her will. She hadn't asked to play any of those roles, but Delores had thought that Gina had too many issues at home to deal with any decision making and that Rick might not be strong enough to act if something happened to her.

Gina didn't seem to have a problem with it one way or the other, and Aunt Susan didn't see anything wrong with it either. Although she would probably be livid if she knew Delores had granted Sydney the health care power-of-attorney so that the rest of the family wouldn't give her any trouble if the hospital wanted to use life support, feeding tubes, etc. Delores had decided that she didn't want any of those things or her life prolonged in any manner, if Sydney realized that she wasn't going to get any better. She'd been sure that her sister, Susan, would be the first one to suggest that they keep Delores alive no matter what.

It was funny how Sydney hadn't seen where it was needed, but she was glad her mother had been responsible enough and wise enough to plan and look ahead. Not enough people thought about doing that, and when they did, it was usually too late. Not to mention people who thought they were going to live forever, and never thought it was necessary to purchase adequate life insurance.

"What are her chances of surviving this surgery?" Rick asked.

"The survival rate is pretty high, but with any brain surgery there is a chance that the patient can experience a massive stroke, paralysis, and other medical problems."

"But there's a good chance she'll pull through the surgery, though, right?" Gina interrupted.

"Yeah, but what good is the surgery if she's going to have to suffer for the rest of her life?" Rick said irritably.

Sydney looked at him and then at Dr. Rogers. "Is Mom conscious enough for us to ask her what she wants to do?"

"She may be. We can go in and try to talk to her, but the ultimate decision will still have to lie with you, and you'll have to sign the authorization for us to move her up to Madison."

"I'd feel better doing that," Sydney said.

"Let me check with intensive care to see if they have her situated, and I'll have one of the nurses come out to get you when you can go in," Dr. Rogers said and stood up. "I'm sorry I don't have better news, and that I had to meet all of you under these sort of circumstances, but I want to assure you that she's going to be in the best hands possible if you decide to send her up to Dr. Kumar. He comes highly recommended from neuro-surgeons all over the country. I'll see you up in intensive care in a little while," he said, smiling, then he walked through the automatic double doors.

"So, what do you guys think?" Sydney asked Rick, Gina, and Aunt Susan.

"You're the one with the power-of-attorney, so it's not up to us anyway," Rick said, sitting back down next to Samantha, obviously teed off.

"Rick, don't start," Gina told him. "Sydney, I think we should ask Mom like you said, because I think she would choose to have the surgery. But even if she's not able to tell us what to do, I think we should go ahead with it anyway. The doctors think so, and I feel comfortable with that."

"I agree, but I'm hoping Mom is awake enough to make the decision herself. I don't mind signing the paperwork, but I want it to come from her."

"I think she'd want to have the surgery, too, if she knew it was a matter of life or death," Aunt Susan finally said. "My sister is a strong woman with very strong faith in God, and she would never give up this quickly."

Some of the other family members agreed.

They waited another hour before Sydney, Gina, Rick, and Aunt Susan were escorted up to the neurological intensive care unit. They walked single-file and surrounded Delores's bed when they located it. Gina winced at all the tubes, IVs, and various machines that her mother was connected to. Aunt Susan gently massaged her back and whispered to her to be strong.

"Mom," Sydney called out to her. She wanted to release all of the pent-up tension and tears that she'd been holding back, trying to be strong for the rest of the family, but she didn't know how much more of this strength she was going to be able to show. "Mom, can you hear me?" she asked.

Delores opened her eyes and tried to smile. But she didn't say anything.

Sydney held her mother's hand. "Gina, Rick, and Aunt Susan are here, too," she said and Delores slowly but surely moved her eyes and looked at each of them.

"Mom, Dr. Rogers said that your tumor is growing, and that you need to have surgery. But we don't want to tell them yes or no until you tell us what you want to do. There are some risks involved, but he feels pretty good about you pulling through the surgery, and that they can remove most of it, if not all of it."

Delores nodded her head affirmatively, but no one knew if she was trying to say she wanted the surgery or if she was simply acknowledging what Sydney said.

"Mom, do you want to have the surgery?" Rick asked her directly.

Delores slightly turned her head in his direction, and nodded agreeably again.

"Are you sure, because we don't want to do anything that you don't agree with," Sydney assured her.

She looked at Sydney, smiled, squeezed her hand, and spoke in a hoarse, barely audible voice. "God will bring me through it."

Sydney smiled at her mother as warm teardrops rolled down her face. Gina hugged her Aunt Susan, and Rick looked away, batting his eyes rapidly. It was an emotional time for everyone involved, but Delores was strong-willed, knew what she wanted, and that's what they were going to go with.

Somehow the problems they were having in their personal lives didn't seem to matter, and were menial in comparison to what their mother was dealing with. Let alone the life-threatening surgery she was about to endure. It was very obvious that the issues they'd all been arguing and complaining about were now the very least of their worries.

It was now well after midnight, and everyone except the immediate family members had gone home. Sydney had decided that she wasn't leaving, and had asked Wesley to go to the house to pick her up a sweat suit, socks, and a pair of athletic shoes. He was now walking back in to drop off her clothing, and Sydney tried to wake Victoria, so she could go back home with him.

"Are you ready?" Phillip asked Gina.

"Phillip, I told you, I don't feel comfortable leaving just yet."

"What about the twins? They need to get home so they can go to bed."

Gina had told him two hours ago to take the children and go, but he'd insisted on waiting for her instead. She'd told him that she didn't know when she was leaving, and that she'd call him at home when she was ready. He hadn't bought into her suggestion, though, and was now trying to force her to leave all over again.

Rick had listened to his sister's conversation with Phillip, but he'd had just about all he could take of him. Sydney could tell by the way Rick stared at Phillip, and she hoped there wasn't going to be a big blow-up.

"We can drive up to Madison to see her tomorrow when she gets there."

Gina wondered who he thought he was fooling, because everyone and their mother knew Phillip wasn't driving anywhere long distance to see his mother-in-law or anyone else who didn't mean anything to him. He was only saying all of this so he wouldn't piss everyone off, but it wasn't working.

"Phil, man," Rick jumped in. "Didn't you hear my sister say that she's not leaving this hospital?"

Phillip ignored him and kept pressing Gina. "Baby, you know it's not right to keep the kids up this late, so why are you being so difficult?" he said and Gina wished he spoke this calmly and considerately when they were at home. He was putting up the front of a lifetime, and she could barely stomach him.

"Oh, you're just going to ignore me, huh?" Rick said to Phillip and stood up.

"Rick. Don't," Aunt Susan and Sydney said simultaneously.

"No, I'm sick of this fool trippin' all the time with my sister. Mom is in there fighting for her life, and he's trying to make Gina go home so she can be stuck up under him? But I don't think so. Because Gina is staying right here, and if you have a problem with that, then you can deal with me," he said, pointing at his brother-in-law.

"Man, why don't you mind your own business," Phillip said and turned his head away from him.

"When it comes to my sister and my mother, it is my business."

"Will you two stop it, before those babies wake up and hear you?" Sydney demanded.

"Look, Gina. Are you coming or not?" Phillip asked as an ultimatum.

She knew she was going to regret it, and that he was going to punish her gravely for not leaving with him, but she wasn't giving in on this. Her mother needed her. Her family as a whole needed her, and she wasn't going to abandon them.

"All right," Phillip said, laughing sarcastically, and no one could tell if it was from humiliation or because he was letting Gina know that she was going to suffer for disobeying his wishes.

He woke the children, they hugged their mother good-bye, and she told them that she'd see them in a few hours. Phillip grabbed the children's hands, and walked out without saying a word.

"You need to check that fool, Gina," Rick said.

Gina just looked at him.

"Rick, honey, don't do this," Samantha pleaded. It was obvious that she didn't want to become involved, but Rick seemed to be getting angrier by the minute.

"He's gone, and that's all that matters," Sydney added.

"I don't care if he's gone or not, because now Gina is gonna have to deal with that asshole when she gets home. I swear, girl, I don't know what's wrong with you," he said, turning his attention to the younger of his sisters.

Gina broke down in tears, and Sydney moved over to the sofa she was sitting on to console her. This wasn't the time for this, and while she did understand Rick's frustration, she wished he would leave this Phillip issue alone. At least for the time being anyway.

Rick looked at her and sighed. "I'm going home to change clothes," he said. "Sam, are you ready?"

"Whenever you are," she answered.

"I'm on my way back out, too, if I can keep Victoria awake long enough to walk out to the car," Wesley said. "Oh, and Gina, I brought you one of Sydney's sweat suits, some socks, and a pair of her gym shoes."

Gina smiled and then thanked him. She was happy that her brother-in-law had looked out for her, but she knew Sydney had probably suggested that he bring something for her, knowing that Phillip wasn't going to.

"I think I'll ride with you, Wesley, since that's where my luggage is anyway," Aunt Susan said.

"Sounds good," he said.

"Honey, I'll call you when I'm ready to come home," Sydney said to her husband. "Because I need to pack enough clothing so I can stay in Madison for the week."

"Just let me know when you're ready, and I'll be here," he said and kissed her good-bye. Victoria kissed her mother as well, and they all headed out to the parking lot.

Sydney and Gina headed toward the rest room, changed their clothing, and went to look in on Delores again.

Chapter 13

"*Phillip, stop it!*" Gina screamed as he shoved her against the wall. Wesley and Sydney had just dropped her off at home, but now Gina wished she hadn't convinced them that she was going to be fine, and that it wasn't necessary for them to escort her inside the house. She was trying diligently to put together some clothing so she could spend the week in Wisconsin with her mother, but she could already tell that Phillip wasn't having it.

"Bitch, don't you ever disrespect me again like you did at that hospital," he said, squeezing her throat with his hand.

Gina was afraid to breathe for fear that he was going to strike her again, and she didn't make a sound.

"I'm your husband, and when I say it's time for us to go, that's exactly what the hell I mean," he said, releasing her.

"Phillip, you know how sick my mom is, so why would you want me to leave her?"

"I told you we would go see her today up in Madison, didn't I?"

"I know, but I just didn't feel comfortable leaving her so soon after she had that stroke. She's my mother, Phillip."

"We can go see your mother as a family or not at all. And you can forget about going up to that hospital with your sister for the whole week, too, because I'm not taking care of your responsibilities around here. I guess I just don't fit into your schedule at all anymore, do I? Either it's that goddamn job or your crazy family trying to keep you away from here. And if you know what's good for you, you'd better talk to your brother, because he has one more time to stick his nose in my business. He's not paying any bills over here, so he doesn't have anything to say to me about anything."

"Phillip I want to be there for Mom's surgery," she pleaded. "I have to be there for her."

"Not for an entire week you don't."

"I have vacation time, so it's not like I won't get paid for being off."

"Who's gonna keep the twins when I work late at the construction site?"

"We can make some other arrangements. Your sister or your mother probably won't mind. If everything goes okay, I'll only be gone for a week."

"You can go up there on the day of the surgery, but I expect to see your ass back here as soon as it's over with," he said cold-bloodedly and walked out of the room.

Gina felt her heart drop into her stomach, and she couldn't believe that Phillip was so evil that he didn't want her spending time with her mother—a mother who was about to go through one of the most life-threatening surgeries that could be performed. This didn't make any sense, and she didn't know how she was going to explain any of this to Sydney. They'd stayed at the hospital until just an hour ago, it was now 9:30 A.M., and she'd told her that she was going to pack her things as quickly as possible so they could get on the road. But now Phillip had forbidden it. Wesley, Victoria, Rick, and Samantha were going to drive up together, and she, Sydney, and Aunt Susan were going to ride in Sydney's car, since they were all staying until the end of the week.

She just couldn't understand what was so wrong with her going to support her mother and the rest of her family. It was one thing when Phillip abused her and treated her like a slave, but it was another when it came to him keeping her away from her mother, who was facing this life-and-death situation. What if her mother pulled through the surgery, but turned for the worse and passed away the second day or even the following? She'd never be able to forgive herself or Phillip. The line had to be drawn somewhere, and while she'd wanted to plan her escape from him in a very careful manner, it was obvious that there wasn't going to be any time for that. She was going to have to put an end to this much sooner than she thought. She would obey his orders by only staying for one day when her mother had surgery, but she was going to put an end to this crazy marriage of theirs once and for all. Or she was at least going to begin the initial process. It wasn't going to be an easy state of affairs, but it was time for her to stand up for herself and her children. She'd talked about doing it, thought about doing it, and shed too many tears for far too long. She was just going to have to trust that he wouldn't try to kill her like he'd promised, that he would eventually move on and find a life without her. Deep down, she knew it wasn't going to be as easy as that, but at the same time, not much could be worse than living in the house with a man who could simply look at his wife and, for no reason, decide that she needed a little physical discipline. It was sick, and while she hadn't wanted to resort to this, she was going to have to inform her brother and sister of everything that had been going on over the last couple of years. They'd had their suspicions anyhow, but they didn't know the entire story. She felt like the women she saw in some of the Lifetime movies when they were afraid to leave their abusive husbands. They knew that they should, but were too afraid to actually go through with it; and what about the wives who did leave the way Gina was planning to and had to deal with being stalked and constant death threats? Even worse, what about the women who really did end up dead, even though they had an order of protection against their offenders? She was terrified of becoming a murder statistic, but she was going to have to take her chances. She knew her family would be there for her, and that's what she'd have to depend on. There just wasn't any other way out, except to leave him. She didn't know where she'd go or whom she'd live with, but she just had to trust that everything would work itself out in the long run.

It was 6:00 A.M. on Tuesday, and with the exception of Phillip, everyone else was standing around Delores's bed joined together in prayer, led by Aunt Susan. Sydney and Aunt Susan had met with Dr. Kumar yesterday afternoon, who had gone over the entire procedure with them. He'd informed them that it looked like he would successfully be able to remove seventy percent of the tumor. Sydney had wanted to know why they couldn't remove all of it, and he'd told her that if they tried to remove the other thirty percent, they'd have to make another incision toward the back of her head, and he didn't think it was safe to take her through another surgery. He did say, however, that she was a candidate for radiosurgery, and that they'd had success in the past with patients who had been diagnosed with meningiomas but couldn't withstand any further surgery. He told them that the surgery would begin around 7:00 A.M., and that it would probably take anywhere from twelve to fourteen hours to complete. He'd said that one of the surgical nurses would be out every two hours to give an update on Delores's condition.

Rick kissed his mother and told her that he loved her, everyone else followed suit, and two female members of the hospital staff wheeled her off to the operating room. It was going to be a long, intense day, but there was nothing any of them could do except wait, and pray for the best outcome.

"Hey, little ones," Aunt Susan said to the twins. "Why don't you guys come with me to get some breakfast from the cafeteria. And you too, Victoria."

"Okay," the twins said.

"Is anyone else hungry?" Aunt Susan asked.

The rest of them either said they weren't hungry or that they wanted to wait to hear the first report from the nurse before they went down to eat. Sydney didn't think it was a good idea for everyone to be gone at the same time anyway.

Aunt Susan and the children left the private waiting area. There was silence for a short while, but then Gina spoke.

"There's something that I need to talk to all of you about, and I don't know any better time than right now, when everyone is all together. I know we're dealing with Mom's illness, and I'm sorry for unloading my problems on all of you, but I don't know what else to do."

Sydney had a strong feeling that this was going to be about Phillip, and she hoped that Gina was finally opening up to them. "You don't have to apologize for anything. We're your family, and that's what we're here for."

"I know I'm not your sister-in-law legally, but I'm here for you, too, Gina, and I've always told you that," Samantha added.

Rick didn't know why the legality of their relationship had to be mentioned, but it wasn't worth getting into it with Samantha about it. He still hadn't changed his mind, but he couldn't imagine that she was still going to insist that he propose on or before June first now that all of this was going on with his mother. This was already the middle of May, and getting married was, quite honestly, the least of his worries.

"I know that, but what I have to say is not easy, especially because I've tried to hide it from all of you. But I just can't do this anymore," she said, tears welling up in her eyes. "I can't deal with Phillip or the abuse."

Everyone waited for her to continue, because it wasn't like they were shocked at what they were hearing. They'd known for years that it was going on, and the only things they didn't know were all the specifics.

Gina swallowed hard. "I have had bruises on practically every part of my body, and sometimes even on my face, if Phillip was angry enough. It was almost like he tried to hit me in areas where no one could tell, but sometimes he didn't care one way or the other. He's even gone as far as jumping on me in front of my babies, and even when he wasn't doing it in front of them, they had to listen to it, and have been ever since they were two years old. He didn't abuse me as badly when they were first born, but it eventually got worse as time went on. He's so jealous of everything I do, everyone I talk to, and sometimes he doesn't even want me to wear certain suits. Not because they look sleazy, but because he's worried that some other man might like the way I look in them. Sometimes . . ." She paused nervously.

"Sometimes he just looks at me and decides that I've slept with some man during my lunch hour, and then loses it. He doesn't want me gone for more than one hour without him, and then I have to explain everywhere I go. There have been times when I've stayed at the mall longer than I was supposed to, and I've had to pull out receipts with the time printed on them, just so I could prove that I hadn't been anywhere else. He doesn't even like me spending time with any of you, and to keep at least some peace in our house, I've had to go along with whatever he wanted."

"Somebody needs to knock that Negro down a couple of notches," Rick interrupted. "I promised him when you first got married, that if I caught him putting his hands on you again, he was going to have to deal with me. And I meant that."

"It's not worth all of that," Sydney told him.

"It is if I say it is, Ms. Power-of-Attorney," Rick lashed out at Sydney. "You might be making all the decisions when it comes to Mom, but you're not running anything when it comes to me."

"What are you talking about?" Sydney asked, frowning.

"Just let Gina finish talking," Rick said, dismissing his elder sister altogether.

Sydney shook her head in confusion, but it was obvious that her brother still wasn't sitting quite right with Delores's power-of-attorney designation. But what was Sydney supposed to do about it? She looked over at Wesley, but all he did was hunch his shoulders, clearly not wanting to become involved in this mess between his wife and her brother.

"Rick, please don't do this, okay?" Gina said. "We're already going through enough as it is."

"Whatever," he said. "Just finish saying what you need to say."

"I guess what I'm trying to say is that I have to leave

Phillip, and I can't do that without all of you. I'm going to need someone to help me move, and the children and I are going to need a place to stay until I can find another place for us to live."

"Whatever you need us to do, we'll do," Sydney said. Wesley seconded the motion, and Rick and Samantha did the same.

"I feel so bad for having to involve all of you in this mess, because it's not like Phillip is going to just lie down and play dead after we move out. He has threatened to kill me if I leave him, and I'm afraid that he really is capable of it. He's crazy, and there's no telling how he's going to react to all of this."

"You're going to have to file for a legal separation and for an order of protection against him," Samantha said. "I have a good friend from college who practices family law, and I know she'll be glad to help you. She went through something similar herself, and she goes out of her way to help wives going through domestic violence."

"I appreciate that," Gina said. "The kids and I are driving back after Mom comes out of recovery, but as soon as we find out when Mom will be coming home, I'll decide the best day to do this."

"I wish you didn't even have to wait that long," Sydney said. "And I don't think you should begin packing a single thing until the police or some of us are right there with you. Because as much as I hate to say it, I think you're right about the way he might act. He'll never just let you walk out without trying to stop you."

"I know. I wish I could get the order of protection before I move out, and it's my own fault that I don't have one, because there have been many incidents where I should have called the police and filed for one. I guess I was hoping to leave the area for good, and I wouldn't need it."

"What do you mean by that?" Sydney asked.

"I couldn't see any other way out except to move to another state, because Phillip keeps saying he's going to take my life if I leave. And it wasn't until he told me that I couldn't spend the week up here with Mom that I knew I had to get away from him. And I can't stop replaying the last time he beat me down and my babies saw him do it. I can still see them jumping up and down and screaming in terror."

"Damn, Gina," Rick complained. "How could you let that fool treat you like that?"

"I don't know," she said in humiliation. She wished Rick wouldn't make her feel so senseless. Because even though she did feel that way, she had no idea why she'd tolerated this lifestyle. She wished she did, and she'd asked herself a thousand times, but she just didn't have the answer. All she knew is that she wasn't going to take it anymore, because right now, her children were her main concern.

"You know, I could see it if you had grown up watching Dad abuse Mom or even if you were abused yourself. Or even if you were some dependent house-wife who had never worked and didn't have anywhere to go. But, girl, you make more money than Phillip and probably everyone else sitting in this waiting room. I'm not trying to make you feel bad, but I'm just trying to understand all of this."

Sydney was getting fed up with him and decided to interrupt what he was saying. "None of that even matters, because it's not like you're perfect either."

"Meaning what?" he asked.

"Meaning that nobody's asking you why you haven't married the best woman you've ever been with."

"That's none of your damn business, Sydney," he said angrily. "What goes on in my household is for me and Samantha to worry about. And the only reason I'm questioning Gina's marital situation is because she brought it up. But I haven't brought up anything that has to do with my life, so you need to keep your mouth shut. You talk too doggoned much anyway."

"You guys, please," Gina said. "I didn't mean for my problems with Phillip to cause all of this."

"Don't even worry about it," Sydney said, ignoring Rick. "We'll do whatever it takes to help you, and that's all that really matters."

"I'm going down to get something to eat," Rick said in a huff. "Samantha, you coming?"

Samantha sighed deeply and stood up. Then they walked toward the elevators and stepped onto the middle one when the doors opened.

"Sometimes Rick gets on my last nerve," Sydney complained. "He makes me so sick when he acts like that."

"I know," Gina said. "But I think it's worse today because he's so worried about Mom. He always tries to be so hard when something is bothering him, but deep down, I know this thing with Mom is killing him."

"No, what he's pissed about is Mom giving me power-of-attorney. What did he expect? Her to give it to him? Because we all know that he never acts rationally with anything when he's upset or angry like he is now."

"I know, but you know Rick has always thought Mom favors you over us."

"No, she doesn't," Sydney said defensively. "It's just that I talk to her every single day, sometimes more than once, and I spend time with her. And if Rick has a problem with that, then he should call her every day and go by there more often. Because not one person is trying to stop him from doing that. He's never going to make me feel guilty about my relationship with Mom, so he might as well get over it," Sydney said, sounding frustrated.

"He's just going through some things right now," Gina said.

"Honey," Wesley said to Sydney. "This is a tough time for all of us, so you're going to have to try to look over your brother right now."

"Well, I know one thing, Mom is my main concern, so he'd better get off my back," she said adamantly.

They sat and waited for another hour and a half. Aunt Susan and the children had come back from breakfast, as had Rick and Samantha. They all looked down the hallway when they saw two nurses dressed from head to toe in turquoise scrubs, walking toward them.

"Are you the Mathis family?" the young mocha-colored woman asked, smiling.

"Yes, we are," Sydney answered. "I'm her daughter, and this is my brother and sister," she said, pointing toward her siblings. Everyone else looked on, waiting for the news.

"Well, we just wanted to come out and give you a quick update on your mother. She's doing very well. Her heart rate is stable, her blood pressure is doing great, and Dr. Kumar is very happy with the way the procedure is going. We still have a long way to go, but everything is looking good so far."

"That's so good to hear," Sydney said, relieved.

"Did she say anything before you put her under?" Aunt Susan asked.

"As a matter of fact, she did," the forty-something, blond-haired nurse answered. "Dr. Kumar told her that he was going to do the very best he could, and that he was going to take very good care of her, and she told him that she wasn't worried, because she'd already asked God to guide his hands during the surgery."

Everyone smiled, because they all knew those were just the sort of comments Delores would make, no matter how dim a situation looked. She had very strong faith in God, and there wasn't anything anyone or anything on this earth could do to shake it.

"You're mom is an amazing woman," the nurse continued. "She's very strong, and it really does make a big difference when a patient has such a positive attitude like she does. And I don't know that I've seen anyone quite like her."

"She is amazing," Sydney agreed. "And if anyone can pull through this surgery, it will be her."

"We think so, too," the young nurse said. "Well, we'd better get back in the OR, but one of us will be out again in a couple of hours to let you know how things are going."

"Thank you so much," Sydney said. Everyone else thanked them as well, and the nurses walked back down the hall from which they'd come.

"Well, two hours down," Wesley said.

"Yep, but we've got a ton more to go," Rick added.

"But at least everything is going good so far," Gina said.

"Everything is going to be fine," Aunt Susan said. "We just have to trust in that."

Sydney didn't say anything, because even though everyone thought she was the strong one in the family, she still couldn't shake this idea of "what if?" What if her mother didn't pull through the surgery? What if she did, but was completely paralyzed? What if she had a stroke and died instantly? There were so many consequences to contend with, but she didn't dare bring up her negative thoughts to the rest of the family. She had faith just like her mother and everyone else, but she couldn't help but analyze the logic of the situation, the same as she did with everything else. She didn't want to, but she just couldn't help it. It was the Taurus in her, she guessed. But what she did know was that she was going to have to prepare herself for any possible outcome, because regardless of how things turned out, they were all going to expect her to handle whatever needed to be taken care of. Including Rick, who was acting like he had a serious problem with her and the authority Delores had given her.

Sydney leaned back on the sofa, against her husband, stroked her daughter's hair, and prayed that the hours would pass more quickly than normal. Then she thought about something that she hadn't thought about since early this morning. Today was her mother's birthday, yesterday was hers, and Victoria's was coming next week. What a way they'd been forced to celebrate.

Chapter 14

D r. Kumar strolled down the hallway, and Sydney breathed deeply. Everyone sat in silence, waiting to hear what he had to say. He sat down in the chair adjacent to the sofa Sydney, Wesley, and Victoria were sitting on, and clasped his hands together.

"Well, it's all over with, and they're closing her right now," he said in an East Indian accent. "She's doing very well, considering, and I am very satisfied with the outcome of the surgery. She lost quite a bit of blood, but we were able to replace it with her own, and that was good."

"How did you do that?" Rick wanted to know.

Dr. Kumar chuckled. "You're mother donated her own blood at the local blood bank where you live a good while ago."

"Why?" Rick asked. "Did she know something was wrong?"

"No, but she knew she had the tumor, and she told

Dr. Rogers a couple of months ago that she wanted to be prepared for whatever might happen. We always suggest that patients donate their own blood for their own use before the day of surgery, but we usually have weeks to plan it. So, it's a good thing your mother was thinking ahead of all of us."

Dr. Kumar had told her and Aunt Susan that yesterday when he'd spoken with them, and Sydney had forgotten to mention that to the rest of them today. She'd been shocked at first, but not for long when she remembered how organized her mother was with everything. She thought about things that no one else paid any attention to or didn't think they'd ever have to worry about. Sometimes she worried too much, but she always seemed to be prepared when things went wrong.

"But anyhow," Dr. Kumar continued. "The next few days will be trying for her. We have to watch for strokes, paralysis, motor skill problems, memory loss, and confusion issues. I can't say exactly what will happen, but we'll know soon enough as time goes on. They're going to do an MRI this evening, just so we know how things looked right after surgery, and then we'll be moving her into neuro ICU. She'll have a nurse assigned to her for the next couple of days, and if everything stays okay, then we'll be able to move her to a regular room."

"How soon do you think she can come home?" Sydney asked.

"It's still hard to say, but maybe by the end of the week or by this weekend. We'll have to play it by ear, but you do need to be thinking about her care at home, because she's not going to be able to live on her own right away. I don't know if all of you will be able to take care of her, or if you need me to write an order to admit her to a nursing home facility."

Sydney looked at Gina and Rick. They gazed back at her, but didn't say anything. She knew Gina was going through this thing with Phillip, but right now, that was beside the point. Rick, of course, didn't have an excuse, but it was already pretty obvious that he wasn't about to volunteer to bring their mother into his condo.

"No, there's no need for you to contact a nursing home," Sydney said. "There's three of us, and we can take care of her ourselves," she said, looking at Wesley for confirmation that she could bring Delores home with them.

"Sweetheart, you know your mother is welcome in our house anytime, and I will help you take care of her for as long as she needs us to," Wesley said without any thought.

Sydney smiled at him and squeezed his hand. She was so thankful for the loving relationship that had evolved between her mother and husband from the very beginning. Things didn't always turn out that way when in-laws were forced to come together, and she didn't know what she would have done if her mother and Wesley hadn't cared for each other. As a matter of fact, Delores was the primary person who told her that she needed to follow her heart when she'd decided to marry Wesley. Which wouldn't have been an issue, except that they'd only dated four months before entering holy matrimony. There had been all sorts of negative comments from everyone else, but Delores had given them her blessing without thinking twice about it. She saw something in Wesley that no one else could see, and she'd seen how he and Sydney were together, whenever she was in their presence.

"If you're sure you can take care of her," Dr. Kumar said.

"We're sure," Sydney said and wondered when Gina and Rick were going to grunt, yawn, stretch, or do something. They were sitting there like this wasn't their mother too, and Sydney was starting to become a little annoyed by their detachment from the conversation.

"She may be a little groggy, but you should be able to see her in a couple of hours. We've got her on pain medication, steroids to prevent swelling, and she'll be back on her blood pressure and cholesterol meds tomorrow morning," he said, sighing from exhaustion.

"You look tired, Doctor," Aunt Susan said.

"Yeah, it's been a long day, and I only stepped away from Delores a couple of times. I always have a team of doctors working with me, but I don't feel comfortable unless I do almost the entire surgery myself."

"So, do you still think she's a candidate for the radiosurgery you talked about yesterday?" Aunt Susan asked.

"Yes, I do. As I had suspected, we did have to leave thirty percent of the tumor, and I think there's a strong possibility that we can stop the growth of that portion of it. The one thing I do want to tell you, however, is that she may never see in her right eye again. We can't say for sure right now, but if I had to guess, I'd say that even if she has partial vision left in it now, over time, she'll probably end up losing it."

Everyone looked at him sadly, but in silence.

"But we agreed that the surgery was the best choice, because we're more concerned now about saving her life," the doctor continued.

"We understand, Doctor, and we appreciate everything you've done so far," Sydney said.

"You're mother is one of the best, and I wish we had more patients like her. Her attitude is so great, that she ends up making you feel better, when you should be trying to boost her spirits instead," he said, standing. "But if you don't have any other questions, I'm going to get changed and get ready to head home."

"No, I don't think we do," Sydney said, looking at the rest of the family for validation.

"Okay, then, I'll be in first thing tomorrow morning to see your mother, and we'll see how things go from there," he said and shook everyone's hand. Then he left the area.

"Well, I guess Wesley and I will have to bring Mom home with us," Sydney said, bringing up the caretaking issue again.

"Yeah, I guess so," Rick said with hesitation. "We all know that that's where she'd want to be, anyway."

"But that doesn't mean that you can't help out. You can still come over to do things with her and be there for her," Sydney said.

Rick just stared at her like he didn't know what she was talking about.

"Well, you know I would gladly bring Mom to our house if I weren't in this situation, and if I weren't getting ready to do what we discussed," Gina said, trying to be discreet in front of the twins.

Sydney understood what Gina was saying, but it wasn't making her feel any better about it. She'd never considered it before, but she couldn't believe that her brother and sister were acting as though this was all going to be her responsibility. It wasn't that she minded taking care of Delores, because she didn't. But she was their mother, too, and as far as Sydney was concerned, they should play a part in the caretaking as much as they could.

"You don't work anyway, Sydney, so it won't be as hard for you to adjust," Rick said.

"What do you mean, I don't work?" Sydney raised her voice.

"You don't. I mean, I know you do a little writing here and there, but it's not like you have a clock to punch or a time card to fill out every day."

"Just because my office is at home doesn't mean that I don't work all day. As a matter of fact, I probably work more hours than you do," she said.

Rick rolled his eyes toward the ceiling in disbelief. He wasn't hearing any of what Sydney was saying, and didn't know why she was making such a big deal about all of this.

"You have power-of-attorney, so to me that means that Mom expects you to handle everything. You like to be in charge anyway, so I don't see why we're even having this discussion."

"We're having this discussion, because Mom is your responsibility, too. And yours too, Gina," Sydney said, now looking at her.

"I'll do the best that I can, but you know it's not going to be that easy for me," Gina said nervously because she knew Sydney was becoming more and more upset with her and Rick.

"I'll fly in on any weekend you need me to until Delores gets better," Aunt Susan offered and Sydney couldn't believe her aunt was willing to do more than her mother's children; children who didn't live more than a few miles from her.

But it was all so typical. She'd heard people complaining about family members who didn't think they had to do anything, so long as one person seemed to be able to handle it. It was so unnerving to think that they didn't care about their mother's well-being. Yes, she was the eldest child, and yes, she was probably the closest to their mother, but that didn't mean they didn't have responsibility in all of this. She wanted to ask them what their problem was and how they'd somehow decided that they didn't have to help out when it was time for Delores to come home. She wanted to lose it, but she was too tired and emotional, and she didn't want to say anything that she might regret in the long run. Not to mention that this really wasn't the time or the place to argue with them. This was a hospital environment, and the children didn't need to hear any of this either.

"I appreciate that, Aunt Susan," Sydney said, smiling at her. Tears leaked down her face.

"I can only stay until the end of this week, but I'll do everything I can in the meantime," she said.

"I know you will," Sydney said.

Rick looked at his watch, as if he hadn't heard any of what they'd been saying.

Gina wanted to say something to make things right with Sydney, but she didn't know what she could say. She didn't understand her sister. Sydney had told her that she would be there for her through this whole Phillip ordeal, but now she was acting as if she didn't care whether she left him or not and almost like she wasn't going to help her in the least. She knew Sydney's mind was on Delores's recovery, but she didn't have to be so inconsiderate. Gina agreed that she and Rick had a responsibility, too, when it came to their mother, but Sydney should have understood that she couldn't take a leave of absence from work or go and come as she pleased as long as she lived under the same roof with Phillip. She'd been knowing it for a very long time, and she didn't know why, but all of a sudden, she was making it seem like Gina just didn't care. But it wasn't worth trying to explain it to her, because when Sydney started thinking the way she was now, there wasn't anything anyone could say to change it. No, Gina decided to keep her thoughts and opinions to herself. Especially since Sydney's attitude was going to be the least of her worries when she drove home in a few hours and had to deal with Phillip.

Chapter 15

"That was an awfully long surgery," Phillip said suspiciously.

"They started right at seven in the morning, and the doctor didn't come talk to us until almost eight at night. Then we didn't get to see her until after ten o'clock," she explained and wondered if he realized she had to drive over 150 miles after that, since they lived in the far south suburbs.

"*Mm*," he grunted as if he wasn't sure if she was telling the truth or not, but he obviously believed some of what she was saying, because he wasn't as angry as she'd expected him to be. Which didn't make a lot of sense, because he was always in an uproar whenever she was gone away from him for such a long time.

It was one-thirty in the morning, and the children had barely awakened when she'd slipped their clothing off and put on their pajamas. They were now fast asleep, and she couldn't wait to do the same thing herself.

She began undressing, and hoped like she always did that Phillip wasn't going to want to have sex with her. She didn't desire him, but even worse, she was far too exhausted.

She pulled on her satin pajamas and kneeled down on the side of the bed to say her prayers. When she'd finished, she climbed into bed and turned out the light on her nightstand. Phillip continued to lean against two plush pillows, and Gina wished he would turn his light out, too, so she could try to get some sleep.

She lay there for a few minutes, and it wasn't long before she started to drift off to sleep. But right at that moment, Phillip spoke.

"Gina, I lost my job today," he said without warning.

She opened her eyes wide, but didn't move.

"Gina? Did you hear me?" he said in the calmest voice she'd heard him use in years.

"I heard you," she finally said. "What happened?"

"I got sick of them telling me what to do and how I'm supposed to do it."

Gina couldn't believe she was hearing what she was hearing. Because what exactly did he think it meant to be an *employee* working for an *employer*? She didn't understand where all of this was coming from, but she knew this was going to make things even harder when it came time for her to leave him. He was going to be around, watching her every move, and she didn't know what she was going to do about it.

"I brought half a beer back to the site, and they made it seem like I'd killed somebody or something. They just wanted to let me go for no reason is what it was."

Gina didn't reply, because she knew if she said something he didn't like, he was going to take it the wrong way.

"Gina, don't you have anything to say? I mean, I'm trying to tell you that I just lost my job."

"Maybe you can talk to your boss, and work things out with him."

"What? I'm not kissin' his ass or anybody else's. Let 'em have that stupid job if they want it, because I was getting sick of it anyway."

Gina closed her eyes and exhaled. But not so loudly that Phillip would think that she was frustrated with him. "Well, I don't know what to say," she finally said.

"I sat here all day and thought about how I've been treating you, and I feel real bad about it. I'm sorry for everything, but I promise, it's not going to ever happen again. You and the twins mean everything in the world to me, and I would rather die than live without you. I couldn't stand it if you ever tried to leave me, Gina," he said in a deranged manner.

It was almost as if he'd heard her conversation with her family at the hospital. She didn't like the sound of any of this, and her stomach turned just thinking about what this was going to mean in terms of her leaving him.

"Gina, baby, I know you don't believe me, but I can change," he said, pulling her toward him.

His touch sickened her, and she hoped he wasn't going to force her to do anything she didn't want to.

"I love you, Gina," he said, hugging her tightly. "I love you and the kids, and I'm going to make this right. I'll look for another job starting tomorrow, and I promise things are going to be much better for all of us."

She felt numb. Almost as if she was having an out-of-body experience. She'd finally mustered the courage to spill her guts to Sydney and Rick, and now Phillip had lost his job and was acting as though he was going to become the best husband ever. She wished he'd taken this attitude months and months ago when she still loved him, because now, she didn't feel anything except hatred.

"Gina. I know I acted crazy about that promotion you're supposed to be getting, but I really think you should take it if they offer it to you," he said.

She couldn't believe he'd had such a change of heart. But she knew it didn't have anything to do with that, and that he was only telling her to take it because they were now going to need more money. He was actually putting on this whole act so he could use her financially. He didn't love her. All he cared about was himself and the lifestyle he'd become accustomed to. He was so pathetic, and she wished he would die in a plane crash or have some other fatal accident. He didn't deserve to live, and it would be so much easier if he was somehow wiped off the face of the earth.

"I don't know if I'm going to get it or not," she said, knowing that she was.

"You'll get it. Don't even worry about it," he said, sounding extremely supportive.

"Phillip. It's been a long day, so if it's okay, I really need to get some sleep so I can go in to work in the afternoon."

"I was thinking we could all drive back up to Madison to see your mother. Don't you wanna go see her?"

Wasn't he just full of surprises? She didn't know how to take him, but he was starting to scare her.

"I didn't think you wanted to go," she said.

"I do wanna go, and I was wrong for not driving you up there for the surgery. But I'm telling you, Gina, I'm not going to treat you like that anymore. You hear me, baby?" he said, gently pulling her face against his chest.

She hated driving such a long distance, but it had ended up being better going without him. She wouldn't have been able to speak freely to her family, and she would have had to dance on eggshells the entire time they were there. She never knew when Phillip was going to go off, not to mention his dislike for practically everyone she was related to. It wasn't worth the headache, and she wished he would just let her go back up to the hospital alone. It was better that way for everyone, but he was sounding as though he was going with her no matter what.

"Gina, I'm sorry, baby," he said and Gina felt tears dripping onto her forehead. What was he crying about? This couldn't have been the same man who'd beat her down so many times she didn't know which way to turn.

"Say something, baby," he requested, sobbing. "Tell me you love me, too."

She didn't want to, because she didn't want to confuse the situation. She didn't want him thinking that they were going to be together forever when they weren't. But she didn't want to see him switch into one of his furies either.

"Phillip, you know I love you," she said reluctantly.

"Promise me that you won't ever try to leave me."

"I won't," she lied.

"Baby, can I make love to you?" he asked and Gina cringed at the thought of it.

"Phillip, please, honey, I'm really tired from the drive, but I promise we'll make love tomorrow."

"No, I need you to make love to me now, so I'll know you understand about me losing my job."

"Phillip, let me just get a few hours' sleep, and I promise—"

"I'm not taking no for an answer," he said calmly, yet seriously.

She knew better than to argue with him about it, and while he was sounding like he'd turned over a completely new leaf with his attitude, she could still hear a twinge of violence in his voice. He was nice about the way he asked her to make love to him, but she could tell that he wasn't going to keep begging her either.

She knew that if she didn't give in to what he wanted, he was going to take what he wanted anyhow.

He removed her pajamas, and she tried hard to lift her soul from beneath him. He breathed heavily, and she wondered if he knew that it was a crime to rape any woman—even if that woman was his wife. She wondered how one man could turn the art of making love into something so terribly disgusting.

"I am so tired, I can't even think straight," Rick said to Samantha as he kicked off his shoes and dropped his keys on the kitchen cabinet. They'd left the hospital shortly after Gina and the kids, and had just arrived home a few minutes ago.

"I know, I am, too," Samantha agreed. "And I don't think I'm going to make it into work this morning either. Because even if I get to sleep in the next hour, I'll have to get right back up in less than four."

"No, I don't think I'm going either."

They both headed up to the bedroom, preparing to turn in.

"I sure hope Mom makes it through all of this without a lot of pain," Rick said.

"Yeah, I know what you mean. But you heard the doctor—she's a strong woman, and I don't think she is anywhere near ready to leave here."

"I guess I just never thought my mother would ever be sick. I always figured she'd be there for me for as long as I needed her. I was the last one at home, and all I ever remember is her picking up all the pieces for everyone else. I do sort of remember that she always used to have headaches, but she was always there when we needed her to be."

"We all have to get sick at some point, though," Samantha said, pushing her teddy down over her body. "There's just no getting around it."

"I know, but why did it have to happen to *my* mother?" he said sadly. "It just doesn't seem fair, and while she keeps talking about all this faith she has in God, I want somebody to tell me why God would do something like this to someone like her. I know I've had my issues with her, because she always makes it seem like everyone should be like Sydney, but she has always tried to be a good person, and she has a good heart, too."

"Sweetheart, everything happens for a reason. Even if it doesn't seem like it now, you'll eventually see what I mean."

They moved closer to each other at the center of the bed.

"You know, it's amazing how life can be going great, and then just like that, it can all change without you having any say-so one way or the other."

"That's the way life is, and when things like this happen, it reminds us that life is too short not to enjoy it. That's why I want to be married, because tomorrow isn't promised to anyone."

Rick didn't know whether to take Samantha's comment the wrong way or not, but he hoped she wasn't about to bring this same, tired conversation up. She'd tried to bring it up a couple of times on the way home, but he hadn't allowed her to do it.

"Marriage should be something that both parties are ready for," he said for the umpteenth time.

"Oh, I realize that, and don't misunderstand what I'm saying. Because what I said was that's why *I* wanted to get married. I told you I'm not pushing you to do anything, and I meant it when I said that I won't be angry with you if you decide you're not going to set a date."

She made him sick with this I'm-going-to-be-okay-with-or-without-you business, and he wished she would leave now if it was that big of a deal to her. June first was less than a month away, and if he'd said it once, he'd said it five hundred times, he wasn't marrying Samantha or anyone else until he was good and ready to. He'd thought she would give him more time with everything that was going on, but she was actually sounding like she was still going to leave him, whether his mother was sick, well, dead, or whatever. It didn't seem to make a difference to her, and he almost wanted to tell her to pack her things and get the hell out before this day was over with.

But he decided not to say anything. He decided that he needed to get some sleep so he could drive back up to Madison later that afternoon to see his mother.

Chapter 16

It was Monday afternoon, six days since the surgery, and Dr. Kumar finally released Delores from the hospital. It seemed like it was much too soon, but Sydney had to admit that her mother was able to talk, walk, and do things that she really hadn't expected her to do so soon. Aunt Susan had been thrilled when she saw her sister's progress, and had flown back home yesterday evening somewhat content. Now, Wesley had driven to Madison to pick Sydney and her mother up.

The doctor prescribed a list of medications, and the attending nurse had gone over each of them with Sydney a couple of hours earlier. Prednisone and Dexamethasone, two steroids for brain swelling; Dilantin, to prevent possible seizures; Tylenol with codeine for pain; Doc-Q-Lace, for the constipation that the mixture of medications was already causing; Nystatin, to prevent fungus in the mouth that would probably appear as a result of taking such a high dose of steroids; and Ranitidine, to prevent ulcers, which might occur because of all the different medications going into her stomach. She'd never seen any one person take so many different pills in one day, and most of the medications had to be taken more than once—some up to four times per day.

Sydney saw her mother looking out of the car window. It was a very warm day, and Delores seemed to enjoy the sun that was shining in her face. She'd always loved the sunshine for as along as Sydney could remember, and even though she was a tad confused, it didn't seem to make a difference when it came to that.

They were on their way home, and Sydney was glad that the last couple of days had come and gone, because she'd been devastated when she realized that her mother didn't know who she was. Delores had recognized her half-sister, Paulette, and her husband, Dave, when they'd come to visit her on Saturday, four members of the church who came on Sunday, and every other relative she could think of. She'd known everyone she'd laid eyes on except Sydney, and it just didn't make any sense. Especially since Sydney was the one who was with her most of the time.

Aunt Susan had taken a room at a hotel which offered special rates for visitors of patients at the hospital, but Sydney had slept in a geriatric chair next to her mother's bed for the duration. She'd thought that her mother kept looking at her strangely, but it never dawned on her that she didn't know who she was. However, it was more than obvious when Delores finally asked Aunt Susan to call Sydney to tell her where she was—even though Sydney was sitting right next to her. She'd said that if Sydney knew where she was, she would have come to see her by now. It took all of Sydney's strength not to burst into tears in front of her. She hadn't known what to do until her friend, Terry, suggested that Sydney take her hair down from the French roll she was wearing, because Delores was probably seeing herself. Sydney was the spitting image of her mother, and they usually wore their hair the same way. And just as expected, her mother recognized her immediately after she'd combed her hair down around her shoulders. It was almost as if Delores's mind was playing tricks on her, and the doctor had told Sydney that this was all a result of brain swelling, and the short-term memory loss that he'd talked about before the surgery. Important brain cells had been depleted, and there was no way getting around these particular symptoms.

They still had a couple of hours to go before they'd arrive back in Covington Park, so Sydney wondered if her mother was comfortable. She was sitting in the front seat with Wesley, and she was sort of fidgeting from side to side. "Mom, are you okay?" she asked.

"Honey, I'm fine," Delores said, laughing a bit louder than usual.

"Are you hungry?"

"I'm always hungry, and I could eat anything you sit in front of me right about now," she said, laughing again like Richard Pryor had just told one of his wittiest and funniest jokes. It was hard seeing her mother this way, but the doctor had cautioned her about all of this, and she knew it could get worse before it got better.

Wesley took the next available exit, and they pulled through a McDonald's drive-thru. Sydney loved McDonald's fries, and Delores loved their hot fudge sundaes, which they ordered along with three Big Mac Value Meals, and they parked in the parking lot so they could eat. Sydney had thought about going to a much nicer restaurant, so they could enjoy a sit-down meal, but she wasn't sure her mother could handle it. She was talking at a much higher volume than was probably acceptable in a public environment, so it was better for the three of them to eat their food in private.

"Mom, how's the food?" Sydney asked, making conversation.

"Good," Delores said, barely acknowledging the question.

Her mom was never this way, and Sydney was beginning to feel weak. She didn't know how she was going to continue handling her mother's illness, but she knew she had to be strong for her.

"I know you're glad to be out of that hospital," Wesley said to his mother-in-law.

"I sure am. They don't give you enough food when they bring you dinner," she said.

Sydney sort of smiled, because her mother had always been very health-conscious when it came to her eating habits, and she was more than particular about her weight and the way she looked in general. This wasn't her normal appetite, but Dr. Kumar had already warned them about the effects that the steroids would eventually have on her desire for food; and if it wasn't because of that, then it was because her brain still wasn't functioning properly.

They finished their food, and headed back out to the highway. Sydney had thought Delores was going to fall asleep with all the medication she was taking, but she'd stayed awake for the entire trip home. It was good to finally arrive into their subdivision, but Delores didn't seem too happy about it.

"Wesley, honey, how come you didn't take me to my house first?" Delores asked.

"Mom, remember, the doctors want you to stay with us for a while until you recover from your surgery," Sydney answered for him.

"Oh, I'm doing just fine," she said cheerfully. "So, there's no need for you all to be bothered with having me stay at your house."

"Mom," Wesley said to his mother-in-law. "You know

you're never a bother to us, and we want you to stay with us until you're better."

"I just want to go home and get in my own bed," Delores continued.

Sydney didn't know what she was going to do if her mother didn't accept her new place of residence, but she hoped her mother would eventually become satisfied with it.

Wesley drove into the driveway, parked, and he and Sydney stepped out onto the pavement. Then, Sydney opened the front passenger door, so her mother could exit as well.

"I'll stay here tonight, but you can take me home after that," Delores said and started walking toward the garage, which was now open.

Sydney looked at Wesley, and he grabbed Delores's arm and walked side by side with her. "Baby, I'll bring those overnight bags in later," he said.

"That's fine," Sydney said, pulling out the plastic wash basin and miniature toiletries they'd given her mother at the hospital.

When they'd all entered the house, Delores sat at the kitchen table.

"Mom, do you want to lie down and get some rest?"

"Yeah," she said, sounding as though she wasn't sure. "I guess so."

"Okay," Sydney said and was glad Wesley had changed the sheets in the guest bedroom on the first floor. They never used the extra room, but Sydney had wanted the sheets to be fresh when her mother retired on them.

She led Delores into the room, helped her change into a nightgown, and before Sydney could hang her sweat suit, she'd already dropped off to sleep. Sydney gazed at her mother for a long time, and while she hadn't paid as much attention to her mother's face while they were in Madison, the severe swelling was now very obvious to her. Her right eye was closed shut, and even though the doctor said that it might eventually open, she knew that there was a strong chance it wouldn't. Her mother looked so peaceful, and it was still hard to believe that she had been diagnosed with this horrendous condition. Not that she was too good for it to happen to her, but because it just didn't seem right at the age of fifty-six. She knew that age was often not a factor when it came to illness, but somehow it always seemed worse when a person had barely retired and even worse when it happened to children.

Sydney continued staring at her mother in deep thought, and the more she thought about all the good times she and her mother had shared, the more her eyes filled with tears. Until finally, her face became soaking wet. She wanted to understand, but didn't. Her mother had explained life to her in every way possible, but now it didn't seem to matter. It didn't matter, because she had a feeling that everything wasn't going to be all right in the long run. She prayed that it would, but there was just this feeling that she couldn't seem to shake.

Her stomach moved rapidly, and tears continued to roll down her face.

Wesley came into the room, pulled her into his arms, and led her out of the bedroom.

"Honey, your mother is going to be okay, and you have to be strong for her."

"I know," she said, still weeping. "But . . . it's so hard for me to see her going through this."

"But look how well she pulled through the surgery. Not many people would be in high spirits like she is after having a brain tumor removed."

"But they still left thirty percent, and she's still not talking quite right. You know Mom would never have said she was fine and wanted to go home, if she realized what type of surgery she'd just been through."

"Yeah, but when you called me last night, you said

that the doctor told you that it might be this way until the swelling left."

Sydney sighed. "I know, I know. I guess I'm just having a hard time with it right now. I'll be fine."

"I know you will. You're a strong person just like your mother, and we're going to get through this."

"Wesley, I want to thank you for driving back and forth to the hospital this past week, and for saying it was okay for Mom to come stay with us for a while," she said, holding his hands and gazing into his eyes.

"You want to thank me?" he said, obviously offended. "Baby, I want you to understand something right now, so that we don't ever need to have this conversation again. Your mother has been one of the most instrumental people in my life, and I love her like she was my own mother. And it's like I told you before, she can stay here for as long as she needs to."

"I know how you feel, but I just want you to know how much I appreciate you for being the person that you are. A lot of men would be upset if they thought their mother-in-law was going to interrupt their daily lives, because you know I'm going to have to spend a lot of time with her."

"So what you're saying is that we're *really* about to go into drought season when it comes to our sex life again, huh?"

Sydney didn't know whether to laugh or take him seriously, because she knew this was still a very touchy subject. So she chose to stay neutral, and didn't say anything one way or the other.

"You're not taking me serious, are you?" he asked, laughing.

"I don't know," she said, looking away from him.

"Now, you know I'm just kidding. You know my theory is that—" he started.

"I want what I want when I want it," Sydney finished his sentence for him.

"Exactly," he said, smiling. "But right now, I know your priority has to be with your mother. And I would be upset with you if it wasn't."

"I love you so much," she said with much emotion.

"Not as much as I love you," he said and they stood in the middle of their bedroom holding each other. Sydney was relieved to know that she at least had her husband to lean on during all of this. She knew Gina really did want to be there to help, but something hadn't seemed quite right when she, Phillip, and the twins had come up to the hospital for a visit yesterday evening. She couldn't put her finger on it, but Sydney hoped she hadn't changed her mind about leaving him. She'd seemed so sure when she'd told them all about it a week ago, but there was no telling what Phillip had said or done to make her see things differently.

Sydney thought about her sister for a while longer, and she even thought about the way her brother had been acting toward her. But it wasn't long before she and Wesley realized their exhaustion and lay across the bed. Before long, they were fast asleep like Delores.

Victoria had arrived home from school a few hours ago, Sydney had just returned from the pharmacy having her mother's prescriptions filled, Wesley had just stepped outside to mow the lawn now that she was back, and Delores was now asleep in her room. She'd gotten up for an hour or so, but had seemed so tired that Sydney had suggested she lie back down again.

There were so many different medications that had to be kept track of, that Sydney had purchased a plastic pill holder which contained four slots for all seven days of the week. But now that she had figured out the schedule, she realized that she needed even more slots than that, because she needed to give Delores her medication at 3 A.M., 8 A.M., 10 A.M., 1 P.M., 4 P.M., 6 P.M., and 10 P.M. A lot of it had to do with the heavy dosage of steroids, but at least she'd be able to start tapering those down every few days until she was weaned off them completely.

She wrote a note to remind herself about making a follow-up appointment with Dr. Kumar, and also an initial appointment with Dr. Mishra, the radiation oncologist in Madison who was going to consult with them about the radiosurgery for the remaining portion of the tumor. They weren't planning to perform the procedure until six months from now, but he wanted to talk with them during their next visit to the hospital. Then there was physical rehabilitation that the doctor had ordered to take place right there in Chicago to help rebuild Delores's strength and to help with the motor skill problems in her left hand. The tumor had been removed from the right side, which meant the left part of her body was at risk. Delores, who was left-handed, had dropped her food and utensils a few times at the hospital and in the car when they'd stopped to eat on the way back from Madison, and she'd dropped a glass of Sprite not too long ago just before going back to bed. She didn't have any control over it, and it was almost like she was holding the glass one minute, and like someone had laid fifty pounds on her arm and forced it down instantly. She'd tried to eat some baked beans as well, and while she continuously dropped her fork over and over, she never stopped trying to make it work. Sydney had seen her struggling with it, and had told her that maybe it might be better if she tried to use her right hand to eat, just until her nerves began to heal. But Delores had told her that her left hand was never going to get better if she didn't keep trying to use it. She was determined, and Sydney decided that she wouldn't try to prevent her from doing what she felt she had to do.

Sydney was scanning through her mother's HMO

manual, reviewing her coverage information, when she heard the phone ringing. She'd thought Victoria was going to answer it, but after the third ring, she knew she was probably listening to her CD player through the headphones and hadn't heard it.

"Hello?" Sydney answered.

"Hey," Gina said. "So, you guys are back, huh?"

"Yeah, we've been back for hours. We've taken a nap, Mom has already been up and gone back to bed, and I'm sitting here now going through the orders from the doctor."

"So, is she doing okay?"

"Yeah, as well as can be expected. Her short-term memory is still not quite back to normal, and her motor skills are somewhat off, but she's doing okay."

"That's good to hear. Was she okay with staying with you guys?"

"Not at first, but she finally said that she would spend one night," Sydney said, chuckling.

"She's so independent, you should have known she was going to want to go home," Gina said, laughing with her.

"So are you coming by?" Sydney asked.

"Well, maybe not tonight," Gina said, sounding squirrelly. "I was, but I think we'll just let Mom get some rest and come tomorrow instead."

Sydney tried to think before speaking, because she couldn't believe that Gina was now only minutes away from her mother and was already making excuses for not coming over. She'd been worried about the Phillip situation anyhow, and she wanted to ask her what was going on with it. But she'd be willing to bet that he was probably standing watch over her right now like some tree dog, and she wouldn't be able to answer any questions that Sydney had anyway.

"Well, whatever," Sydney said. "She's here when you want to come see her."

"I know, and we'll come tomorrow after I leave work and pick the children up from aftercare."

Sydney changed her mind about not asking any questions. "So, are you still planning to do what we talked about at the hospital last week?"

"Well, tell Mom I called when she wakes up, that I love her, and that I'll see her tomorrow," Gina said, disregarding Sydney's inquiry.

"I take it you can't talk."

"No, but I'll see you tomorrow evening."

"See you later," Sydney said and hung up the phone. She couldn't believe Gina. She knew she was going through pure hell with her husband, but didn't she realize that this was her mother—the mother who had just come home from the hospital? Didn't she understand that some things came before Phillip and her job? She knew Gina had vacation time, because she'd told her that she was going to use it last week when Delores had her surgery. But of course, it was Phillip who had brought that idea to a screeching halt.

She couldn't worry about Gina and her problems right now, though. She wanted to, but her priorities were with her mother, and she wasn't going to allow other people's issues to distract her from the most important matter at hand.

She went to place the cordless phone back on the base, and it rang again.

"Hello?"

"Hey, how's it going?" Rick asked.

"I'm good. How's it going with you?"

"I'm makin' it. And how's Mom?"

"She's been resting pretty well since we got in," she answered and was surprised that Rick didn't sound like he still had an attitude.

"That's good. Is she still having problems with her left hand?" he asked.

"Yeah, she is, but I think it will get better with time."

"Yeah, I think so, too," he said and paused.

Sydney didn't know what else to say, so she waited for him to finally speak.

"Hey, I shouldn't have said some of the things I said to you last week, and I want to apologize. I know you're doing everything you can for Mom, and whether you realize it or not, I do appreciate that. I'm just under a lot of stress because of this whole thing, I guess, and I've been going off on everybody for no reason."

"It happens," she said. "But the best thing for us to do is stick together. For Mom's sake if nothing else. You and I have had our differences, but this isn't the time for us to be at each other's throats."

"You're right, and that's why I wanted to call you before I drop by."

"I'm glad you did, because Mom is who we need to be focusing our attention on. She's going to need all three of us to get through this."

"I know," he said and paused again. The conversation was awkward between them, and it was almost like they barely knew each other.

"Well, I guess I'll see you when you get here."

"All right. Oh, and does Mom need anything?"

"You can bring her another twelve-pack of Sprite, because she loves to drink those. But I'll be going to the grocery store tomorrow to get everything else."

"I'll pick it up on the way, and I'll see you in a minute," he said.

"See ya."

Sydney was glad that she and her brother were speaking cordially again, and she hoped that he and Gina really were going to be there for their mother. She hoped they weren't going to be like so many other adult children in America who decided that the care-giving of a parent should reside with only one person.

They hadn't been there for their mother when their father had passed, at least not the way Sydney thought they should have, but she hoped it was going to be different this time around. Because if it wasn't, she knew there were going to be major problems between them.

Chapter 17

Gina drove the children to their bus stop, waited for them to get on, and then headed off to work. She didn't know what she was going to do now that Phillip wasn't working. He'd been going through these bouts of anger and frustration ever since he'd told her about being fired, and she didn't know what he was going to do or say next. It had been that way for a very long time, but now it was actually worse. He'd said that he was going to begin looking for other employment right away, but every evening when she'd arrived home from work, he'd told her that he hadn't felt like it, and that he was going to start looking "tomorrow." But of course, tomorrow had never come, and it had now been one whole week. He'd said he was going to apply for unemployment since he was fired and not laid off, but so far he hadn't even bothered to do that. He'd seemed to have lost his motivation to work, and when she'd told him yesterday that her promotion was official, he'd told her that was good, because he really needed a break from this whole work thing anyway.

She'd planned on picking up take-out, so she could drive over to Sydney's to see her mother, but Phillip told her that he wanted her to cook him a real dinner for a change, because he was sick of eating out. She'd told him that she needed to go see her mother, but he'd told her that he was tired of her putting "outsiders" first. He was so wishy-washy, because he'd actually suggested that they go to Madison on two different occasions, and hadn't complained about it afterward.

Even worse, he was drinking just a little more every day. She could smell it on him as soon as she entered the house, and it was obvious that instead of looking for a job, he was planning to hold these pity parties on a daily basis.

She felt trapped, and while she didn't know how to tell Sydney or Rick, she didn't think this was the best time to be leaving. Phillip didn't have a single thing to lose, and the risk of him taking her through more changes had increased. Things were so bad, that she would actually be better off dead than to stay with him, but she had to think about her children. She had to think about whether they were going to be harmed or left in this world without a mother. She knew her brother and sister would never understand, and that Rick was going to lose his mind over her decision to stay with Phillip for a while longer, but she didn't care what they thought. She didn't care what anyone thought, because her children had to be considered and no one was going to make her see this any differently.

When Gina arrived at work, she fixed herself a cup of coffee, went into her office, and shut the door. She sat down at her shiny wooden desk and kicked her shoes off. She didn't feel like working today, but her new position wasn't going to allow any downtime. She could tell that it was going to be hectic making the transition from her previous position to this one, and it didn't help that she always had to make sure she left the office at a decent time. She needed to work ten- and eleven-hour days until she settled into this new director's position, but she knew she would have to fuss and fight with Phillip if she did it too frequently. She was so caught up, and it was a wonder she hadn't had a nervous breakdown.

She sighed deeply, trying to relieve some of the mental stress she was feeling, but just when she did, the phone rang.

"Gina Harris," she answered.

"Did you know that there isn't any bread here?" the voice on the other end said, and all she could do was close her eyes, trying to gather her thoughts.

"No, honey, I didn't. But I'll pick some up on the way home."

"Well, that's not gonna help me right now, is it?"

"All I can say is that I'm sorry," she said because she could tell that he'd already been drinking.

"Yeah, Gina, you are sorry. You can't even take care of petty shit like making sure bread is in the household."

She didn't even bother responding.

"All you want to do is run your ass over to that job all day, and then hang out with your family all evening. But I'm telling you this now, until you can take care of things here, I don't want to hear one thing about you going over to your sister's."

"Honey, I—" she started.

But he slammed the phone down before she could finish her sentence. Her hand shook as she laid the phone on its base and she wondered how she was going to explain her absence all over again. She'd lied to Sydney and told her that she wasn't coming to see her mother last evening because she wanted her to get some rest. But if she came up with a new reason as to why she wasn't coming, Sydney was going to lose her patience. But it didn't matter how angry Sydney was going to be; it still didn't change the fact that Phillip was the one calling the shots with everything she did, and there wasn't anything anyone could do right now to change it.

Gina picked up the phone to call him back, but changed her mind when she realized she might make bad matters worse if she tried to reason with him. She was an emotional mess, and she had to try to pull herself together for the MIS meeting she'd called with her new staff members. This was all too much for her to handle, and now she wished they hadn't offered her the promotion and that she hadn't considered taking it. This wasn't the sort of position that could be taken lightly, and with everything that was going wrong in her personal life, she didn't know how she was going to run an entire department—one of the most important departments in the company.

She just didn't see any way out of this, and she was starting to understand more and more why people committed suicide when things didn't seem to be getting any better. They were getting worse for her, and she didn't know how she was going to continue juggling her husband, her job, and her family members. She was trying to satisfy everyone, but it didn't seem like anyone was paying attention to it. No one cared about what she thought, what she wanted, or what they could do for her, and she was starting to see where none of this was worth it. None of this was worth living for. She couldn't stay with Phillip, but she knew he was going to kill her if she didn't. She'd debated this so many times over the last few weeks, she didn't know why it hadn't happened already. She'd decided that her children needed their mother, but maybe they'd be better off if she was dead. Phillip would certainly be sent to prison, and then Sydney would end up raising the niece and nephew she loved with all her heart. The more she considered her alternatives, the more she understood that this was the best-case scenario. It was the most sensible thing she'd come up with since the day she'd made the mistake of marrying her husband.

"I think we should all pat ourselves on the back for completing the Sales Database Project in such a timely manner," Gina said as an opening statement. She was sitting in an elegant conference room with all ten of her employees situated around the cherry wood table and was now portraying a strong, intelligent role of authority. She was no longer the helpless, battered wife the way she'd been while speaking to Phillip on the phone, and the way she switched personalities at a moment's notice was fascinating. She led this double life on a daily basis, and no matter how hideous things were at home, she was always able to smile and feign this independent, career-oriented personality. She'd learned to do it well, and while her coworkers had seen questionable bruises and obviously knew what was going on, no stranger would ever suspect that she was a victim of severe domestic violence—not if they'd seen her within her work environment.

"You were the major player," Michael Wilson said. "We were simply following your lead."

"I can't take all the credit," Gina added. "All of you worked very hard and we did it as a team."

"I'm glad it's over, because I think my husband was beginning to wonder if he still had a wife," Jessica, a senior programmer, said. "It was getting to the point where I was dreaming about that database project in my sleep."

Everyone laughed and agreed.

"Well, I appreciate everyone's time and effort, and it won't go unnoticed when it's time for raises and promotions," Gina promised.

Then she passed copies of the meeting agenda to Ken, who was sitting to her immediate right. He took one and passed the stack to the person sitting next to him. Gina waited until everyone had a copy and then she continued.

"Purchasing is the next department we have to work with. Their project is something we'll have to work on daily, but we won't have to work tons of overtime to complete it. They've tested various software, and they think they've decided on which one they want us to implement. I've looked at each of them, and it looks like they've chosen the best one in the bunch. It will make all of their jobs a lot easier, and it doesn't seem to have a lot of glitches that we'll have to be concerned with once it's up and running."

"Don't tell me we're going to have to work one-on-one with funk-pot Jim," Jessica complained.

Everyone snickered at her comment.

"I know he's not the easiest person to work with," Gina agreed diplomatically. "But we really don't have a choice. And he's one reason why we want to get this project completed as quickly and as competently as we can. I'll make sure he knows that he should come to me whenever he has questions or problems, and that way his interaction with all of you can be kept down to a minimum. You'll have to deal with him at times, but at least it won't be on a frequent basis."

"Thank God for that," Michael said. "Because I think old Jim is terrified of soap and water."

The entire room broke into laughter, and it was all Gina could do not to join in. "Okay," she said, slightly chuckling. "Let's move on to the next item." She knew they were right, because Jim really did carry a monstrous odor, but she wasn't going to condone the fun they were having with it. Management had approached him in the past, and while he claimed he had some sort of skin disease, no one in the company believed him. Gina didn't know one way or the other, but she did have to admit that it was sort of strange how every now and then he did smell like a normal person. But who was to say and what difference did it actually make? Especially since he ran the purchasing department in an award-winning manner.

Everyone settled down and Gina leaned back in her chair.

"We've sort of been having a problem with taking more than an hour for lunch," she stated reluctantly. She knew enforcing company policies was part of her job description, but she wasn't fond of doing it. "I'm not saying that I expect all of you to run in here right on the dot every single day, but in some cases, we've been coming back twenty and thirty minutes late," Gina said, scanning the room. She never came back that late herself, but the word "we've" sounded a lot less authoritative. "I know you all work very hard and that it's not always possible to do what you need to do within an hour, but at the same time, we don't want Dennis coming down on us about this," she said, referring to her boss. "Right now he's pretty flexible when it comes to our working hours, and I don't think any of us want to see that change."

Everyone was silent at first, then Michael finally spoke.

"Crackin' that whip already, aren't you?" he joked and everyone laughed.

Gina shook her head and laughed with them, because she knew his comment was all in fun.

They discussed the rest of the agenda, and finally the meeting adjourned. Gina walked back to her office, closed the door, and sat behind her desk. She was happy that the meeting had gone as well as it had and she was thrilled that the members of her department were such team players. It made all the difference in the world, and no director could ask for a better group of employees. She felt like she was on top of the world—at least for now. Because once she arrived home, she'd have no choice except to reenter the battered wife syndrome.

"It's so hard for me to look at Mom with her face swollen the way it is," Rick said to Samantha as they sat on the patio eating cereal and drinking pink grapefruit juice. Rick was skimming through the *Chicago Sun-Times,* and Samantha was flipping through one of her accounting magazines. When they discovered that they couldn't go another day without making love to one another, they'd both called into work stating they were going to be late. They'd been too tired on the evenings they'd taken the long drives to Madison, and before that they really hadn't been on the best of terms because of the ultimatum Samantha had given him. But now there was less arguing, and they were spending more time with each other the way they used to. Nothing had been resolved as far as the marriage proposal, but they each believed that everything would work out in the end. Rick believed that Samantha would eventually see things his way, and Samantha was sure that she was only days away from setting their wedding date.

"I know it is, but you're going to have to get past that," she said.

"I don't know how I can. It pains me to see her that way, and it was all I could do not to break down like some little five-year-old boy."

"Well, all I know is that your mother needs you, Rick. She may be staying with Sydney, but she still needs to see you and talk to you, too. It's important that you spend as much time with her as you can while she's recovering."

Rick turned the page of his newspaper, but didn't respond because he really couldn't stand to see his mother that way. He couldn't remember ever feeling so helpless and so weak until he'd seen his mother the day before. She didn't seem herself, and it was almost like he didn't really know what to say to her. Sydney seemed to be handling everything fine, but he wasn't surprised about that, because Sydney never shed too many tears about anything. She'd been that way even when they were children, and while he hated to admit it, that was probably the reason his mother had given her legal control over her finances and health care. It bothered him that his mother hadn't consulted with him and Gina, but it wasn't worth losing any sleep over. What had been done was done, and he wasn't going to worry about it.

"You know, Rick," Samantha said, sipping her juice. "It's like I said before, everything happens for a reason. I know you don't see it now, but even your mother's illness will eventually bring about something good. I don't know what, but I really do believe that."

"What good could possibly come from my mother having a brain tumor?" he said irritably.

"I can't say right now, but there's always something. For one thing, it's causing you to think about your family and life in general a lot more than you ever have."

"Maybe, but I'd rather have my mother well, and worry about life later."

"Sometimes things happen so that you will realize that tomorrow isn't promised to you."

"Damn, Samantha. How many times are you going to keep repeating that same thing over and over again?"

She squinted her eyes and gazed at him. "I'll repeat it as often as I feel like repeating it, because it's true."

"Well, I hope you're not trying to throw any hints."

"Hints for what?" she asked and it pissed him off because he knew she was trying to be funny.

Rick tossed the paper onto the table. "I should have known it was too much for us to wake up, make love, and then sit down to a peaceful breakfast together. You just can't let this shit rest, and if you want to know the truth, I'm really getting sick and tired of it. You know what I'm going through with my mom, and you're acting like it doesn't make any difference."

"Don't even try it," she said, staring straight at him. "I'm fully aware of how ill your mother is, and you know I'll care about her and her well-being no matter what. But if you think that I'm going to let you use your mother's surgery as a scapegoat, you can forget it."

"Oh, so what are you saying? That your ultimatum still stands? And that you don't care whether my mother lives or dies?"

"What I'm saying is that we're either going to get married or not."

"Well, if you still feel so strongly about it, then what was that this morning? Because if my memory serves me correctly, you were all over me, like you couldn't get enough."

"My feelings for you are very real, but I will not continue this relationship without a permanent commitment."

"Well, then you may as well start packing right now, because I'm not changing my mind by June first or any other first day of the month."

"You mean that?"

"More than I've ever meant anything," he said harshly.

"Fine. I'll start putting my things together this evening," she said. Then she gathered her dishes and walked inside the condo.

Rick snatched his glass from the table and slammed it against the pavement.

* * *

"Hey, what's up?" Rick said to Brent. He'd left the condo right after Samantha, and now he was talking to his best friend on his cellular phone. He knew he was going to see Brent when he arrived at work, but he was so pissed off that he couldn't wait to tell him what happened.

"Not much, man. What's up with you? And why did you call to say you were going to be late? Your mother is okay, isn't she?"

"My mom is doing fairly well, but the problem is with Samantha. She laid up in bed with me this morning, acting like she couldn't live without me, and right after that she started going on and on about getting married."

"Oh, shoot," Brent said, laughing.

"Man, this isn't funny," Rick said seriously. "I told her that she may as well pack her things, because I wasn't setting a date."

"I feel you. So, what did she say?"

"She told me fine, and that she would start putting her things together this evening."

"Man, get out. I guess she was as serious as a heart attack about tying you down."

"Whatever. But what I'm calling you for is to see if you ever found out the name of that club you wanted to go to."

"Yeah, I did. It's called Club 111. Why? You wantin' to hang out after work?" Brent said ecstatically.

"Might as well, because I'm not about to go straight home."

"Hey, you know I'm game, so let's just plan on it."

"All right, man. I'll see you in a minute."

"Later," Brent said and hung up.

Rick didn't know who Samantha thought she was. God's gift to every eligible bachelor, he guessed. But he wasn't having it. He wasn't going to play her game of chance. He'd been doing just fine before he met her, so it wasn't like he wouldn't be able to live without her. If she was so eager to leave, then she wasn't all that in love with him in the first place. What she was in love with was the *idea* of being married. It probably didn't matter who she walked down the aisle with either. Any man with the right credentials would have probably suited her just fine.

To think that she had the nerve to make an ultimatum in this day and age, when the ratio of men to women seemed almost infinite. She had to be crazy, trying to force his hand the way she had. There were too many available women who would quickly trade places with her, and she wasn't even aware of it. But she would eventually see it when it was too late—when he'd found someone else, settled down, and moved on to greener pastures. He didn't see why she was so discontent, and the more he thought about it, they lived the same as or better than most married couples. But all Samantha concerned herself with was a measly piece of paper, issued by some city or county office.

Rick drove a few more miles and then pressed on his brake when he approached a stoplight. He sat there waiting for it to change, and then he thought, "Two whole years we spent building a relationship, and now this. What a waste."

"Kelli, can you get me a status report for last week's shipments?" Rick asked his secretary. He'd been putting out fires ever since he'd walked into his office, and now he knew this hadn't been the day to come in late.

"Sure. Do you want it for all locations?" she asked.

"Eventually, but right now, I need reports for Rockford and Dundee. I've been on the phone for the last hour with stores from both cities, and it sounds like a couple of their orders for women's apparel weren't shipped, or for whatever reason, haven't been delivered yet."

"I'll run them right now," she said, walking back out to her cubicle.

Rick scrolled through the distribution menu on his computer, selected current shipments, and scanned the listing. He'd studied this same listing a half-hour ago, and even though he hadn't found the problem, he wanted to check it again just to be safe. But he still didn't see anything out of the ordinary. The items were showing as shipped, but unfortunately, there was no guarantee that they actually had. Especially since they'd been having quite a few problems ever since they switched over to a new tracking software a few weeks ago.

He prepared to search another file, but just as he pressed the enter key, his manager walked into his office.

"Any luck with those missing shipments?" George, a tall, slender middle-aged man, asked Rick.

"So, now they're calling you, too," Rick said, shaking his head in disbelief.

George laughed. "You know how hyped some of those buyers get when they don't get their orders on time. Especially Theresa over in Rockford."

"Yeah, tell me about it," Rick agreed. "And you know I'm not her favorite person anyway, so it's always right up her alley to try and go over my head."

"Hey, don't even worry about it. I know you're working your behind off to solve this situation, but I just wanted to let you know that she's on her usual rampage."

"I'll get it taken care of, even if I have to send her a duplicate shipment."

"Sounds good," George said, turning toward the doorway. "Oh, and hey, how is your mother doing?"

"About as well as can be expected, but she's hanging in there."

"I know this is a hard time for you, and it's like I told you before, don't ever hesitate to let me know when you need time off. I've been there, and I know what it's like dealing with family issues and work all at the same time."

"Yeah, it is difficult, and I appreciate your offer," Rick said.

"No problem. You're one of the most dedicated supervisors I have, and that's the least I can do."

"Thanks," Rick said.

"I'd better get back over to my office," George said, glancing at his watch. "I have a performance review to do, but I'll see you later this afternoon."

"See ya," Rick said, and George left down the corridor.

It was good to know that George realized his employees had a life on the outside. A lot of managers were slave drivers and, in some cases, didn't even care if a person had a death in their family, let alone a sick mother. But George wasn't like that, and that was the reason Rick worked as hard as he did to keep his particular department running smoothly.

He wished his relationship with Samantha had been running on the same wavelength.

Chapter 18

It was five o'clock on the dot, and Brent was rearing to go. However, Rick wasn't nearly as excited as he had been this morning. He'd been teed off until shortly after lunch, but then he'd started thinking about all the good times he and Samantha had shared. If only she'd been able to go with the flow and hadn't wanted to disrupt the good thing they already had going.

"Let's go, man," Brent said, heading toward the exit.

Rick grabbed his blazer and followed behind him.

"I hope this Club 111 is as nice as you keep hearing," Rick said, pressing the alarm gadget on his key ring.

"It will be. Some of the fellas were talkin' about it again this afternoon, and they swear you've never seen so many women. Intelligent ones, too. Why? You havin' second thoughts about goin'?" Brent said, entering Rick's SUV.

"No," he lied. "I'm just hoping it's worth the ride and the cover charge is all."

"Mmm-hmm," Brent joked. "You've got your mind on Samantha."

"No, I don't," he insisted and wondered how many more lies he was going to have to tell over the next few hours.

"Yeah, right."

"Can we talk about something else?" Rick asked.

"Don't tear my head off just because you and your girl called it quits. Because like I told you before, it was probably the best thing for you."

Rick loved Brent like a brother, but it was at times like these that he wished he didn't know him. He sounded as though he was thrilled about him and Samantha breaking up, and it just went to show that misery really did love company. It really didn't matter who the company was, so long as there wasn't any happiness involved.

As soon as they had arrived in front of the club, they saw one person going in after another. Happy hour must have been a very popular time. They drove a short distance down the street, parked, and then walked back up to the entrance.

They paid the cover, and as soon as they stepped inside, they looked around and had to agree that the women were out of this world. There were, of course, a few unattractive females, but the rest were definitely worth looking into.

"Man, they were right," Brent bragged.

Rick laughed at him.

"Shoot, I should have come here a long time ago, because this is the place to be. And this is only a week-night."

Rick shook his head at him, because Brent always became excited whenever he was in the presence of beautiful women. Only thing was, they didn't usually feel the same way when they saw him. It wasn't that he didn't look good enough to meet a nice-looking woman, because he did, but he always came off in a too-cool, and sometimes desperate fashion. Almost like he hadn't had one date with any woman his whole adult life.

"I need to take a leak," Brent said.

"Go ahead, I'll be here."

Rick stood against the wall with his arms folded, slightly bobbing his head to the music. He scanned the room, and although he hadn't thought about it, he realized that he hadn't approached another woman with dating interest since he'd started seeing Samantha. He hadn't even danced with more than a couple of women since then either.

He looked to his right, and saw a tall woman with black shoulder-length hair smiling and walking toward him.

"I hope this doesn't sound too forward, but would you like to dance?" she asked.

"Sure, why not," Rick answered, but what he'd wanted to say was no, and that he was waiting on his friend to return from the rest room. It would have sounded too juvenile, though, so it was better to agree with her request. It wasn't like it was a slow song, so at least he wouldn't have to get too close.

They danced until the song was over, she thanked him, and then went on her way. Rick was glad.

"Getting your freak on already, I see," Brent said as soon as Rick walked back over to where they were originally standing.

"Please. It was only a dance, and that's it."

"Yeah, but I've had many, many dances wake up in my bed the next morning."

Rick laughed. Brent never ceased to amaze him. He needed to find some moral values and could stand to grow up a tiny bit, but he was fun to hang out with. He always had been, and right now Rick needed someone to make him laugh. He was having very mixed feelings about this thing with Samantha, and he didn't know how it was going to feel living alone again. He'd loved his space prior to her moving in, but now he'd gotten used to her being there. It had become routine for him—them waking up side by side seven days a week, and now he couldn't help but wonder if he was going to feel lonely. But he was just going to have to get used to it, whether he liked it or not, because he knew she really was going to leave him.

"Wanna get a beer?" Brent asked.

"Yeah, why not. I'll take a Bud," Rick said because he needed something to help him relax.

Brent went over to the bar.

Rick saw another young woman standing a few feet away from him, smiling. He hated to be the bearer of bad news, but he wasn't interested. He wasn't all that interested in being there, but he was trying to make the best of it. Especially since it was better for him to stay away from the condo while Samantha was packing. She wouldn't be able to find a place right away, but he still didn't want to go home until he knew she was already in bed. He was planning to sleep in the guest bedroom anyway, but he didn't want to argue with her. They'd argued far too long as it was, and he couldn't do that anymore.

Brent returned with two bottles of beer, passed one to Rick, and took a drink from his. "I needed that," he said.

"Yeah, I did, too," Rick admitted.

"But as soon as I finish this, I'm plannin' to *stay* on the dance floor."

"Go for it," Rick encouraged him.

Brent finished his drink then walked across the room and asked a young woman who didn't look to be more than five foot four to dance. She agreed, and Brent pulled her out on the floor.

Rick watched Brent dance to one song after another, and he was still partnered with the same woman. Rick, on the other hand, was ready to go. He'd tried to enjoy the scene, but it wasn't working. Maybe he'd been in an exclusive relationship much too long, and it was going to take time for him to find interest in other women. He wanted to believe that that was the reason, but deep down, he feared that time didn't have a thing to do with the way he was feeling. He had a feeling that the reason he felt so out of sorts was because he really wanted to be with Samantha.

Rick finally found a seat after about an hour. Brent had come over to the table for a hot minute, but he'd quickly gone back on the dance floor with his new acquaintance, and had stayed there ever since. It was going on eight o'clock, and the place was packed. Rick cracked up when he saw a man out on the dance floor dressed like he owned a thousand prostitutes. It was obvious that he thought he was sharp in his red suit, red shoes, and matching Boston-lean hat. But best of all was the hoochie-mama he was dancing with who must have been one of his top-selling employees, because she looked as though she'd just stepped off a street corner. But for the most part, Rick had to admit that Club 111 was a decent place to go if a person was in the mood for going out, because ninety percent of the crowd did seem respectable.

He gazed around the club and wondered about his mother. With everything that had gone on with him this morning, he hadn't taken the time to see how she was doing. He'd had a couple of opportunities at work, but he hadn't taken them. But he wasn't that worried, because he knew Sydney would have called him if something was wrong. He hadn't heard from Gina in a couple of days either, and he was going to be upset if she'd changed her mind about leaving that jerk she was married to. He'd told her that he would help her, and if that wasn't enough for her, then he was going to wash his hands of the situation. If she wanted to keep getting her brains beaten out, then that was her business, because he was tired of begging her to get out of a terrible situation. He didn't understand women who voluntarily took abuse from any man, and for the life of him, he couldn't see how Gina ended up with someone like Phillip. Sydney certainly would never have married a man unless he relinquished at least sixty percent of control in his own household, so he didn't know how Gina had turned out so differently. She was weak and very insecure for some reason, but he didn't have the slightest idea why. He had complaints about both of his sisters, but he couldn't tell grown people what to do or how to do it. It was better to let them live their own lives the best way they knew how.

Rick ordered four more beers before Brent finally came back over to the table to tell him that he was ready to go.

"Man, I hate to do this, but Matrice invited me over to her place," he said.

"Hey," Rick said. "Don't feel bad on my account."

"You are okay with driving home, aren't you? Because it looks like you had quite a few beers since we got here."

"I'm cool. Don't worry about it."

"I don't know, man. I can drive you home, and have Matrice pick me up there if you want."

"B, it's not like I'm drunk."

"All right, then, if you say so."

"Seriously, I'm fine."

"I'll see you tomorrow at work then," Brent said, hesitating at first, but then he grabbed his date's hand and left.

Rick stood, left a tip for the waitress, and walked out of Club 111. He felt a little woozy, and maybe he had drunk too many beers back to back. Maybe he should have allowed Brent to drive him like he wanted to.

He walked to his vehicle, sat inside, and closed the door. Then he started the engine. He debated as to whether he should drive himself home or not, but it wasn't like there was anyone else who could do it for him, and he wasn't about to call a cab and leave his Expedition down in the Loop. He sat there for a few minutes until he heard someone knocking on the window. He laughed when he saw Brent and Matrice standing there, and rolled down his window.

"Man, get out," Brent said, cracking up.

Rick didn't argue with him, because he knew he needed someone to take the wheel before he killed himself and maybe a few others. Now he really did feel drunk, and as soon as Brent pulled off, Rick didn't remember anything else until they arrived in front of his condo, and Brent woke him up.

"Rick, man, look," Brent said, shaking his shoulder. "Your girl is moving her stuff out."

Rick sobered up quicker than the blinking of an eyelid. He couldn't believe she was doing this so soon and so late in the evening. It was almost eleven o'clock.

"Here're your keys, and I'd better get going," Brent said, glancing over at Matrice, who was waiting for him.

"All right, B, thanks for driving me home," Rick said, trying to figure out how his heart had ended up outside of his body and why he was feeling so nervous.

Brent and Matrice pulled off, and Rick walked inside the condo.

Samantha walked passed him again with another box and out to her car, but she didn't acknowledge him. She walked back and forth three more times until, finally, Rick decided to say something.

"So, you're really leaving?"

"That's what you wanted, isn't it?"

"You know it wasn't as simple as that," he tried to explain.

"Well, it was for me. We want very different things in life, and I told you weeks ago that I respect the way you feel. I don't agree with it, but I do respect it," she said, walking back out to the car. Then she came back in again.

"My sister and I have already taken most of my clothing over to her house, but I'll be back tomorrow or the next day to get everything else."

"And that's it? Just like that?"

"I guess so. I do want you to know one thing, though," she said, pulling her purse onto her shoulder. "I've loved you from the very beginning, and even though things turned out the way they did, a part of me will always love you. And I hope we can be friends as time goes on."

Rick was speechless. She'd summed up two years in two sentences, and it all seemed so final. He wanted to say something. He even wanted to beg her to give him another chance, but he knew it would boil down to the same thing all over again. She'd still be adamant about getting married.

"I hope you find what you're looking for, and I'm just sorry it wasn't me," she said. Then she walked outside, entered her car, and left the subdivision.

Rick sat quietly on the sofa for a couple of minutes, then he broke into tears. The same as he had the day his father passed away.

Chapter 19

Rick twisted his body with his arms stretched above his head, and squinted his eyes, trying to adjust them to the sunlight. It was beaming through the vertical blinds which he hadn't bothered to close before going to bed, and now he was awake because of it. He felt hung over, and his head pounded like nobody's business. He closed his eyes and held his head with both hands, trying to relieve the pain, but it didn't help. Now he wished he hadn't decided to drink as many beers as he had, but he just couldn't seem to help it. Brent had spent all of his time with his latest flavor of the month, and Rick had been left alone for most of the evening. He'd had a very boring time, and while he'd been excited about going out with Brent yesterday afternoon, the thrill had completely worn off as soon as he realized he wasn't interested in dancing or in any of the women who were there.

He'd been so angry at Samantha when he left for

work, and he'd wanted to prove that he didn't need her, that the world didn't revolve around her, and that there were plenty of other women he could be with. But he hadn't been attracted to even the most attractive women at the club. It hadn't been that way before he met Samantha, but it was almost like he no longer knew how to be with another woman. He didn't know what to say to them, and in all honesty, he didn't want to be bothered with them. If only he'd been able to convince Samantha to hang in there for a little while longer, just until he was actually ready to commit for life. He'd known that he was in love with her, but now he knew for sure that he loved her more than any woman that he'd been with. So, he didn't know why he was against the idea of marriage. He wasn't planning on being with anyone else, but getting married seemed so everlasting, and he was afraid of feeling tied down.

But now his heart ached for her. He yearned for her more than he'd ever yearned for anything or anybody. He wanted her there beside him, and he wanted to make love to her in a way that she'd never experienced before. He'd really messed up this time, and he knew it. He'd dated a few other women in the past that he thought he might have a future with, but when the relationship had ended, it hadn't phased him one bit. But this thing with Samantha was one hundred percent different, because he was starting to feel like he couldn't live without her. He'd wanted to chase her car down the street last night, begging her to come back. But his pride hadn't allowed him to move one inch. He wanted to tell her that he was sorry, and that he loved her with everything he had, but the words hadn't come out.

Now he was all alone. He didn't feel like going to work, so he reached for the phone to call his boss. He dialed his direct number, but his voice mail box answered instead. Rick pressed zero so he could speak with his secretary.

"Lisa, I'm not feeling very well today, so will you let Ken know that I won't be in, but that I'll be there tomorrow?"

"Sure," she answered. "No problem."

"Thanks a lot."

"You take care of yourself."

"I will," he said, and they hung up.

He thought about calling Sydney to see how his mother was doing, but he wasn't in the mood for talking to Sydney or anyone else who might figure out that something wasn't right with him. His elder sister picked up on everything, and the last thing he wanted to do was tell her that Samantha had left him. He'd never hear the end of it, and she would go on and on about how Samantha was the best thing that had ever happened to him. He couldn't deal with her right now, and it was better to call when he could tolerate all of her questions. His mom was probably resting anyway, and it didn't make sense to wake her.

He lay in the bed staring at the ceiling fan gyrating round and round. He watched it for so long that he felt almost hypnotized. It was so relaxing, and he wished he could go to sleep, wake up, and find that this was all just a dream, that Samantha hadn't even considered leaving him. But he knew it wasn't a dream, and that she really had moved out and was now living with her sister. He wanted to call her to see how she was doing. Maybe she was feeling as lost as he was, and had decided that her moving out hadn't been the right thing to do.

Rick jerked when he heard Tom Joyner's voice blasting on the radio. Which was what he used as his alarm signal instead of the traditional buzzer. Tom's show was syndicated through V103, and Rick and Samantha loved listening to him and the rest of his crew. They were hilarious, but even they couldn't lift Rick's spirits on this particular morning, so he turned it off. He was depressed, and he never wanted to leave his condo again.

He couldn't believe Samantha had left him so quickly and so easily. Like she already had another man lined up to take his place. She claimed she loved him, but she wouldn't have walked out of that front door if she had. But then she was no different from any other woman who forced an ultimatum on a man when she couldn't get what she wanted.

He wanted to be angry with her, but the pain he was feeling was too strong to muster any other emotion. He wanted to know when he was going to feel better about all of this and when he'd be able to forget about Samantha and get on with his life again.

He wanted to go into the bathroom, so he could take some over-the-counter pain medication, but he couldn't will himself out of the bed. He'd never felt so down in all his life, and now he knew for sure that a woman really was every man's weakness. He'd never understood it before now, but the song was right. There really was a very thin line between love and hate. He loved Samantha, but he hated her for not being patient and for leaving him so abruptly.

Women. Couldn't live with them and couldn't live without them. This was all too complicated for him, and he wished someone would explain what he'd done that was so wrong. Wasn't he entitled to his opinion? Didn't Samantha want him to be honest with her? Because clearly, she didn't want him marrying her when he wasn't ready. It wouldn't have made any sense, because if he did, they'd probably end up in divorce court before the ink was dry on the marriage license.

He wanted to go back to sleep, but his mind was racing in too many directions. He didn't feel like going out anywhere, but maybe it would help if he went downstairs. The bedroom reminded him of Samantha, and he couldn't stand lying in a bed that they'd slept in as a couple for over a year. He didn't want to admit it to himself or anyone else, but he missed her something terrible. When he'd told her that she may as well start packing, he hadn't expected for it to feel this bad. His ego had fooled him into jumping the gun, and she'd called his bluff as soon as he'd offered it to her. His grandfather was dead and gone, but he could hear him now, saying, "Boy, you've done shitted, and then stepped in it."

Which was exactly what Rick had done.

Chapter 20

Sydney strolled down the hallway to her mother's room and walked inside. Delores was still sleeping, and as much as Sydney hated to wake her, it was time for her eight o'clock medication. She was tired herself, and she hadn't had more than a couple hours of sleep since the last dose she'd given her. But the six o'clock rising hadn't been nearly as hard as the one at 3 A.M. Sydney had never been a morning person, and while this had gone on for only four days, she was starting to feel completely exhausted. Everything she did revolved around her mother's schedule, and she was trying her best to keep up with it.

"Mom," Sydney said, gently rubbing her mother's arm. *"Mommm,"* she sang. "It's time for your medicine."

"Huh?" Delores said without moving her lips.

"It's time for your medicine, and I have some orange juice for you to take it with."

Delores opened her left eye, and for the first time,

Sydney saw her right eye partially cracked. The doctor had said it could be weeks before she would be able to open it, but her mother was already making progress.

"Ooh, I hate to even raise up," Delores said.

She'd become more and more fatigued as the days passed, but Sydney knew this was all part of the process. She'd even gone out and bought a shower bench, so her mother could sit down when she showered, and a toilet riser, so she wouldn't have to stoop so low when she used the rest room. Every time Delores needed to leave the room, Sydney had to pull her up from the bed with both her hands. Her mother would sit for a few minutes, and then she finally stood up. But it was a very difficult task for her. The exhaustion was similar to chronic fatigue syndrome, and Sydney wished there was something she could do to alleviate it. She'd scheduled the initial physical rehab appointment for next week, and she hoped they'd be able to help strengthen her muscles.

"You can do it," Sydney said, trying to encourage her.

"Okay," Delores said, taking a deep breath. Then she reached her hands toward her daughter so they could execute their daily routine.

Sydney pulled her up and handed her three round, white tablets, and one rose-colored octagon. Delores looked at them and pushed all of them into her mouth at the same time with the palm of her hand. Then she drank the orange juice to chase them down.

"Are you ready to eat breakfast?" Sydney asked.

"Well, I could eat a little something, but I'm not really all that hungry."

"I guess not, since you had me warming up all that food that Aunt Paulette brought over here yesterday," Sydney said, laughing. Paulette was Delores's half-sister, but they didn't refer to each other that way. They were born from different mothers, but they loved each other no different than two children who shared a mother together.

"Yeah, but that was a long time ago," Delores said.

"It wasn't that long ago, because you got up and ate right after I gave you your three o'clock medicine." Sydney smiled at her.

"Did I?" Delores asked. "Shoot, you know how my memory is."

"It'll get better," Sydney said, hoping that it would. But she did have to admit that her thought patterns and conversation were improving. She'd gotten up on her own the second night she'd stayed with them, walked down the hall to Sydney and Wesley's bedroom, and called out Sydney's name. She spoke loudly. "Sydney, I want something to eat." Sydney had looked over at the clock and saw that it was only two o'clock in the morning. She knew for sure her mother couldn't help the way she was acting, because she never would have disturbed Wesley's sleep, knowing that he had to be up at four. As a matter of fact, she never would have gotten Sydney up either. But it had happened only one time, and yesterday she'd been more like herself, and even more so today. Her state of confusion was almost nonexistent, and Sydney was happy to finally have her real mother back.

"Maybe we should get you a shower before I fix you some breakfast," Sydney suggested.

"I don't feel like that either," Delores responded.

"I know it's hard, but we have to do this," Sydney said, sympathizing with her.

"Okay," she said the way people do when they know something is difficult, but for their own good.

Sydney helped her pull her nightgown over her head, assisted her with putting on her robe and shower cap, and then she went into the bathroom to turn on the shower. When she adjusted the temperature to her liking, she went back to get her mother, and they slowly strolled out of the bedroom. When they entered the bathroom, Sydney pulled off her mother's robe, and helped her step into the shower. She stood for only a few seconds, and then she sat down on the bench. One of the physical therapists in Madison had told Sydney that certain equipment could really make a difference, and she could see where it really was.

Her mother washed her face and arms, but that was all she could muster. Sydney washed the rest of her body for her. She wasn't glad her mother was sick, but taking care of her like this gave Sydney a warm feeling. She was so glad that she was able to be there for her, and it was so ironic how she'd decided to leave corporate America to begin a freelance writing career. She hadn't wanted to write professionally prior to a few years ago, and it had all happened sort of unexpectedly. But now she knew that everything happened for a reason. Because right now, she needed the flexibility of choosing her own working hours or the choice not to work at all on certain days if necessary. She couldn't imagine what she would have done if she'd still been working a normal nine to five. Her mother needed someone with her around the clock, and there was no way she could care for herself. Especially since it wasn't like Sydney could depend on anyone else. Her Aunt Paulette worked, her Aunt Susan lived in Texas, and both Gina and Rick had been by only once. Gina called every day, but Sydney wasn't appreciating all these phone calls and no visits. But then Rick wasn't even doing that. She knew Gina was being held hostage by her crazy husband the same as always, but she didn't know what her brother's problem was. Not that she was excusing Gina, because she wasn't, but it was just that Rick was free to go and come as he pleased. She'd known they would eventually slack with their visits and phone calls, but she hadn't expected them to neglect their mother so soon after the surgery.

She wasn't fully recovered, and it just seemed that they would be a bit more concerned than they were. Wesley was doing more for his mother-in-law than the two of them put together and it wasn't right. Even their neighbors and various members of the church had called wanting to know when they could cook dinner and bring it over for them.

Sydney tried not to think about her siblings and their absence, but it was becoming more and more difficult for her to ignore them. It wasn't like she needed them to do anything in particular, although it would have been nice if they at least offered. But Delores had asked about both of them last night, wanting to know when Sydney had last spoken with them. She'd even wanted to know where Samantha was, and while she wasn't Delores's daughter, Sydney had also thought it was rather strange that they hadn't heard from her either. But maybe she was just busy with work.

After Delores stepped out of the shower, Sydney dried her body, saturated it with lotion, and helped her slip on a T-Shirt and a pair of shorts. Then they went into the kitchen.

Sydney microwaved a packet of instant oatmeal, toasted two pieces of wheat bread, scrambled two eggs in margarine, and poured her mother another glass of orange juice.

Delores spooned up a helping of cereal as soon as Sydney placed it in front of her. She was hungry again, and Sydney hoped she'd be off the steroids soon, because her mother wasn't going to be happy if she started gaining weight.

"If you want, we can sit out on the patio for a while when you finish eating," Sydney said, trying to get her mother to stay up for as long as she could.

"That sounds good. You know I like being outside in the springtime."

"I know. I think Wesley is going to throw some meat

on the grill when he gets home from work, so maybe I'll make some potato salad."

"I haven't had potato salad in a while, so that sounds good, too," Delores said, raising a forkful of eggs toward her mouth.

Sydney sat down in the chair adjacent to her mother and leaned back in it. She hadn't done any writing over the last few days, but she hadn't forgotten about the two major magazine pieces that were going to be due in a couple of weeks. Taking care of her mother hadn't allowed her any time to start writing them, and even when her mother was asleep, Sydney washed, cleaned, and took care of personal business for her household and her mother's too. She even entertained her mother's visitors—not to mention trying to spend at least some quality time with Wesley and Victoria. But even when she had a few moments of down time, she didn't have a mind to do any work. She was too emotionally drained to think about it, and she couldn't concentrate well enough to write the articles the way they needed to be written.

Her mother was her priority, and she didn't see how she could change that anytime soon. Delores had taken care of her, Gina, and Rick when they were children, raised them up to the best of her ability, and now it was time for them to return the favor. Which is exactly what Sydney was going to continue doing.

They moved out onto the patio, pulling two beige and brown striped patio chairs a few steps away from the table. The warm air felt good, and Sydney could have stayed out there for hours. Delores enjoyed it too, but she enjoyed it so well that she dropped off to sleep.

Sydney stared at her and smiled, because her mother looked so peaceful. She had a very serious illness, but no one could tell just by looking at her. Sure, she had a small bald area on the top right side that had been shaved down to her scalp and some visible stitches, but she still looked like there was nothing wrong with her. She had such an upbeat attitude, and even after all that she'd been through, she still had a smile on her face whenever she spoke to anyone. She was such an inspiration to Sydney, and she wondered why every daughter couldn't and didn't feel the same way she did about their mother. But then, she knew not every mother had been there for their children 365 days of every year, taught them right from wrong, taught them the importance of family values, spent quality time with them, worked long hours to make sure they had food, clothing, and a roof over their heads, or sat up with them in the middle of the night when they were sick. Delores had done all of the above and a long list of other motherly duties Sydney could think of. She wasn't perfect, because no one was, but Sydney always believed that her mother was the closest thing to it.

Sydney noticed her mother's head leaning forward and wondered if it would be better for her to lie down in bed. She'd probably be a lot more comfortable if she did. But just when Sydney went to wake her, the door-bell rang. She wondered who it could be, and she hoped it wasn't anyone coming for a visit this early in the morning.

She walked inside the house, through the living room, and opened the front door. It was Gina.

"Hey," Gina said, walking into the foyer.

"Hey," Sydney said, wondering why her sister wasn't at work, especially since she was dressed in a business suit.

"Is Mom up?"

"Yeah, but after we went out on the patio, she fell asleep. I was just about to wake her so she can go get into bed."

"Oh."

"You must have the day off?" Sydney asked, wanting to know what was going on.

"No, but I decided to go in late so I could come by here first."

Sydney wanted to ask her why it had taken her so long and how she'd managed to sneak over there without Phillip knowing it. But then, maybe since he was at work, she had a little leeway.

"Well, I wanna get Mom inside, so you may as well come out here with me."

"All right," Gina said and followed her sister out to the patio.

Sydney felt her heart pounding when she saw her mother slumped over on the glass table.

"Mom," she called out, rushing to her side.

"Huh?" Delores answered in a low, groggy tone.

"Mom, are you okay?" she asked, kneeling down and looking in her mother's face.

"Uh-huh," Delores answered and opened her left eye.

"Oh. You scared me lying across the table like that," Sydney said, holding her chest and taking deep breaths.

"I just wanted to take a rest is all," Delores said and straightened her body to an upright position.

Gina was still standing in front of the patio doors trying to recover from shock. She hadn't moved, and Sydney could tell that she'd thought their mother had either passed out or passed away as well. They didn't know what to expect, but they knew anything was possible whenever the medical profession made an attempt to fix the brain or heart. Technology had come a long way, but those were two very critical parts of human existence, and they couldn't be taken lightly. Sydney had been on pins and needles all week. She watched the way her mother breathed, she paid close attention to everything she did. Every single day.

"She's okay," Sydney said to Gina. "So, come on out."

Gina proceeded toward the table and kissed Delores. "Hi, Mom."

"Well, hi, baby. How are you?" Delores was elated to see her other daughter.

"I'm fine, and the twins are, too. They're at school, but they wanted me to tell you that they love you."

"*Ohhhh.* Tell them that I love them, too. And how's Phillip?"

"He's fine," Gina said, and Sydney wondered what was going on between them, because she still hadn't mentioned anything about moving. She hadn't talked about much of anything come to think of it. She was hiding something. Sydney was sure of it.

"Tell him I said hello, and that he *could* come and see about me," Delores said. "You can tell your brother the same thing when you talk to him too."

Sydney didn't comment, but now she knew her mother's mental capability was back to normal. She was well aware of who'd been over to see her, and who hadn't, and she wasn't biting her tongue when it came to bringing it to Gina's attention. Gina was part of that same crowd, but Sydney knew Delores would never ask Gina why she had only been over once before now herself, because she didn't want to hurt her feelings.

"I will," was all Gina said.

She looked down and out, and Sydney wanted to have another talk with her. But she didn't want to do it in front of Delores, because she didn't want her mother worrying about any family problems.

"Mom, I think you might feel a little more comfortable in your bedroom."

"I was thinking the same thing, because I'm feeling a little tired again."

"Well, if you're ready, we can go inside," Sydney said, grasping her mother's arm and assisting her with standing up. They entered the house and then the bedroom, and as soon as Delores was settled, she drifted off to sleep.

Gina kissed her on the cheek, and she and Sydney left the room.

"Why don't you sit down for a minute," Sydney told her.

"No, I'd better get going. I don't want to get to work too late."

"Are you okay?"

"I'm fine," Gina said.

"Have you decided what day you're going to move?"

"No, and it might take a little longer than I thought."

"Why?"

"With Mom sick, I don't want to take you and Wesley away for a whole day helping me move."

"Victoria is old enough to stay with Mom, so that's not a problem."

"I know, but I'm gonna wait awhile. Not for very long, but just until I have everything figured out."

Sydney didn't know what she was talking about. She didn't know what she could possibly be waiting on, when all she needed to do was call the police, so they could protect her.

"Gina, I know this isn't my business, but don't let Phillip scare you into changing your mind. You *can* get out of this. I know it's hard and that you're worried about what he might do, but we're all going to be here to help you. Just like we said we would."

"I know that, and I appreciate it. I am going to leave, but it's not going to be as quick as I had planned. I know you don't understand, but I have to handle this in a different way. But I promise you, I am leaving."

She seemed so calm, and Sydney didn't know if she liked the way she was sounding or not. Something still wasn't right, but Sydney didn't have the slightest idea of what was going on.

"Well, I'd better get going," Gina said, picking up the purse she'd laid on the kitchen island just before going out to the patio.

"Okay. Give me a call later from work if you have a chance," Sydney said, but she knew Gina wasn't going to call, because she didn't want to answer any questions about Phillip.

"See you later," Gina said and went to her car.

Sydney watched her sister drive out of sight, and prayed that she would end her sick relationship with Phillip once and for all.

Chapter 21

Sydney had experienced everything imaginable over the last three weeks. She'd struggled and met her deadlines with both *Essence* and *Redbook* magazines, and she'd driven her mother to Madison on four different occasions—once for her initial follow-up and to discuss the radiation treatment, once because her fatigue seemed to be getting worse instead of better, another time because she was having severe pain in her right temple area, and the last visit was due to severe pain in her right ear. It had been one thing after another, but Dr. Kumar explained that these symptoms were all very common. He'd said that her fatigue would eventually begin to improve, and now that she'd been going to physical therapy three times per week, Sydney was finally seeing some progress. Her mother had been so tired that Sydney had started dressing her without her mother's help, the same as a person would a newborn baby. She'd even put on her socks and tennis shoes, which she tied for her. She'd tried to get her mother to do as much as she could for herself, but it had been hard watching her struggle just to raise her hand to her face, trying to wash it. Everything she did was such a great task, and Sydney felt sorry for her. So sorry that she decided that it was better and quicker just to go ahead and do everything for her mother. But two days ago, her physical therapist had informed her that she was doing Delores a major injustice. Sydney could still hear the conversation now.

"Okay," Kristen said. "Tell me everything that Delores is doing for herself, and then tell me everything you and your family are doing for her."

Sydney had had to think about it first, then she answered. "Well, she's really too tired to do much of anything. She does feed herself, though. Sometimes, she washes her face and her arms when she's in the shower, but that's about it."

"What about dressing herself and combing her hair?"

"No, I pretty much do all of that for her."

Kristen continued jotting down notes on the piece of paper in front of her.

"It's so hard for her," Sydney continued. "I try to encourage her to do things for herself, but it's too tiring for her."

"Well, the thing is this," Kristen said. "I think it's time for us to start preparing your mom to go back to her own home. Sometimes it's better when brain tumor patients are living back in their own environment. It may not seem like it, but it really can make a huge difference."

Sydney didn't know if she was comfortable with what Kristen was saying or not. She knew Kristen was the professional here, but she couldn't imagine her mother going back home all alone.

"I don't know about that," Sydney commented. "She lives alone, and even if I stayed with her during the day,

I don't think it's a good idea for her to be there at night all by herself."

"I understand that, and I'm not saying she should go home immediately, but that we should start planning for it. She's really beginning to get stronger, and she's moving around a lot quicker than she was three weeks ago."

Sydney did have to admit that she was, but she still felt uncomfortable with this. She'd become comfortable with the current arrangement, because she didn't have to wonder how her mother was doing or try to figure out what was going on. She always knew firsthand, and it gave her a sense of contentment.

But she'd taken these last couple of days to seriously think about Kristen's advice, and as much as she hated to acknowledge it, she knew she actually was doing way too much for her mother. She was almost crippling her, because it had gotten to the point where she didn't even ask her if she needed her help, Sydney just automatically did what she thought needed to be done. Her mother was capable of doing things for herself much more so than she had, and since the brain swelling had consistently gone down, she was back to her normal self from a cognitive perspective. She didn't want to, but she had to let her mother go, the way mothers had to leave their children at day-care facilities or baby-sitters only weeks after giving birth to them. It seemed so cruel, and while she knew it was going to be painful, she knew she had to succumb to what was right.

"Victoria, I want you to clean up that room of yours before you leave out of this house," Sydney yelled up the stairs to her daughter. Summer break had just begun last week, and Sydney was already counting the days until the start of the next school year. It seemed like Victoria had become lazier and messier than she'd ever been before.

"Victoria, do you hear me?" she asked again when her daughter didn't respond.

"Yeah," she said with an attitude.

"What did you say?" Sydney said, walking closer to the stairway.

"I said, 'Yes, Mom.'" Victoria repeated her response the way she knew she'd better, but in a sarcastic tone.

"No, that's not what you said at all. And since you have such a smart mouth, you can forget about going anywhere for the rest of the week," Sydney said angrily.

"Dang!" Victoria said, stomping across the second floor.

"Victoria, get your behind down here right now," Sydney yelled.

Victoria walked down the stairway and looked at her mother.

"Have you lost your mind?"

"No," Victoria answered like Sydney didn't phase her one bit.

"I don't like your little attitude, and if you keep playing with me, I'll keep your butt in this house for the rest of the summer. I'm running around here doing a thousand things, and you're acting like it's a crime to keep your room clean. I'm sick of you thinking you can just run out of here without doing anything."

"Well, I'm sick of you yelling at me all the time," Victoria said and regretted it immediately.

Sydney grabbed her daughter's shirt sleeve and yanked her so close that they were now face to face. "I've had just about enough of your mouth. And I mean I don't want to hear another word. Do you hear me?" Sydney said, breathing heavily.

Victoria was speechless with tears streaming down her face.

"I said, 'Do you hear me?'" Sydney said, grasping Victoria's arm in a forceful manner.

"Sydney," Delores called out, walking toward her daughter and granddaughter. "That's enough."

Sydney rolled her eyes at Victoria and then released her. "You'd better get out of my sight," she said, and Victoria rushed back up the stairs crying loudly.

"I know you're under a lot of stress," Delores said to Sydney. "Taking care of me, taking care of your own household and your business. But you've got to try and relax."

"Sometimes, that girl gets on my nerves." Sydney sighed deeply and then walked toward the kitchen counter.

"You mean the same way you and Gina got on mine when you were about Victoria's age? You both thought you knew everything, and *you* were the worst one of all."

Sydney was still furious, but had to smile, because she remembered those days very well. When she was in junior high school, she saw her mother as the enemy. She hadn't understood why her mother felt so compelled to tell her what to do all the time, and there were days when she couldn't stand her.

"You're right," Sydney agreed. "So I guess I'm getting paid back for all of that."

"No," Delores said. "I just think it's something every mother and daughter have to go through when they're so much alike. Victoria has the same exact personality as you do, and you know both of you can be real stubborn when you want to," Delores said, sitting back down in the family room in front of the mustard greens she'd been picking before the fiasco.

"Well, I'll be glad when this mother-daughter thing is over, because I am not enjoying it."

"Neither did I, but look how close you and I have been since the day you left for college. It's only a phase, and when it's over, you and Victoria will be able to laugh about it just like you and I are now."

"I guess," Sydney said pessimistically.

"I pray I'm not overstepping my boundaries, but I

have to tell you that you were wrong for grabbing Victoria the way you did."

"I know, I know, I know," Sydney said, feeling guilty now that she was beginning to calm down. "Sometimes, Mom, I feel like screaming, and I know it's wrong to take the way I'm feeling out on everyone else. I've been short with Wesley too, but I can't seem to help it."

"It's understandable. You're angry about my illness, and because of everything else you have to do, and no one can blame you for that. But you're going to have to find some time for yourself and your family."

"I am stressed, but Mom, please don't think you're a burden on me, because you know that's not the case."

"I know it's not, but all I'm saying is that you're going to have to deal with all of this a little differently."

Sydney agreed with her mother, but she didn't know how she was going to alleviate this stressful feeling. She'd always been in control, but now she felt like she didn't have a handle on anything.

They were both silent for a few seconds until Sydney finally spoke.

"Now, Mom, if you start to feel tired, you don't have to do those greens. I can pick them and wash them right before I cook them."

"No, I want to do this, because it's time for me to start getting back to my normal routine. I know you mean well, but that therapist was right about it being better for me to go back home."

Sydney hadn't told her the entire conversation, but she had told her mother that they thought she should go back to her own environment. She was glad that Delores had brought it up, because it made her feel better knowing that she didn't have a problem with it. For some reason, Sydney had been worried that her mother would feel like they were kicking her out, but now she knew Delores wanted to go home.

"Well, you know I hate to see you go, but I do see that your recovery will happen a lot quicker if you do."

"Of course it will. You've been doing everything for me, and I've been letting you. I really didn't have any energy, but I needed to at least try to do some of those things on my own. Even if it took longer than usual."

"I know, and I'm sorry for making you so dependent on me."

"There's nothing for you to be sorry about, because you are the one who kept me going. Lord knows, if I hadn't had you pushing me to take a shower and get dressed every day and to go to all of my therapy appointments, I don't know what I would have done. You are the best daughter, Sydney, and I want you to always remember how much I love and appreciate you. You are what every parent dreams of when they are sick or getting old."

Sydney looked at her mother and smiled, but she turned away quickly so she wouldn't see her eyes watering.

"You know I would do anything for you, Mom," she said, trying to gain her composure. "Anything at all."

"I know it, and everybody else does, too. You take care of me the way I took care of my mother, and I'm so very proud of you for doing that."

Tears rolled down Sydney's face. It seemed like she was crying all the time now when it came to her mother, and it always seemed even worse when she had conversations like these with her.

Sydney sniffled and swallowed hard when she thought about how terribly she'd treated Victoria. So, she called her to come downstairs again.

Victoria strolled down the stairs and into the kitchen, and when she saw her mother weeping, she looked over at her grandmother.

"She's just having a moment," Delores told her. "She'll be fine."

Victoria stood there looking at her mother, but it was obvious that she didn't know what to say or do. Sydney reached out her arms to her. Victoria embraced her mother willingly, both of them now in tears.

"Baby, I am so sorry," Sydney apologized to her daughter. "I'm going through so much right now, but I shouldn't have grabbed you the way I did. I was wrong, and it won't happen again."

"I'm sorry too, Mom," Victoria said, and they continued holding each other.

There was a short silence, and then Delores spoke. "Now that's what I like to see."

"Weren't you talking about going to the mall?" Sydney asked Victoria as an additional peace offering.

"Yeah, Marlene and I were wanting to go today," Victoria said, wiping her face with her hands.

"So, what are you planning to buy?" Delores asked her granddaughter when she realized Sydney was going to let her go.

"I don't know yet," she answered.

"Do you have any money?"

"Yes, I still have fifty dollars from my birthday money."

"Is that enough?" Delores asked.

"I can always use some more," Victoria said, smiling.

"Why don't you go in my room and get my purse," Delores told her.

"Okay," Victoria said in a hurry and followed her grandmother's instructions.

"You've got her so spoiled," Sydney said to her mother.

"No worse than how Mama and Daddy had you," Delores said, chuckling.

"I guess you're right about that, because they did have me caught up," Sydney agreed and laughed.

"I remember one time when you were about three,

and Mama and I went to the store and left you home with Daddy. But when we came back, he had moved every what-not piece from the coffee table and both end tables. Talkin' about all that stuff was in his baby's way. Mama had a fit, and told him that she wanted all of her little ceramic pieces and ashtrays put right back where they were supposed to be, and that if you were meddling with them, then he should have spanked your little hands. Especially since you never did that when we were there. From the day you were born, you had him wrapped around your little finger. And you could fool him into letting you do just about anything you wanted."

They both laughed, and Sydney knew her mother was telling the truth. Delores had already divorced Sydney's father before she turned one, and Delores had lived with her parents until she married her second husband, John. Sydney was almost three when she married him, and since her biological father had never laid eyes on her until she was twenty-two, that was the only father Sydney knew.

"Granddad didn't like to see me crying, I do know that," Sydney said.

"No, he didn't. He loved all of his grandchildren, but I think the reason he was so attached to you was because you were the first one he brought to his own home from the hospital. Mama was the same way. I remember when John and I rented our first apartment, and you kept saying that you wanted to go home. I used to get so upset with you, and I would tell you that you *were* at home. And of course, Daddy couldn't wait for me to call and tell him that you wanted to come spend the night, because he and Mama would come flying over there to get you. They didn't care what time it was, and sometimes Mama drove over with him and still had her robe on."

Sydney had heard her mother and grandparents talk

about her relationship with them on more than one occasion, but it always made her smile every time she heard it. She missed her grandparents so much, and while her grandfather had been deceased for twenty years, and her grandmother for ten, she sometimes missed them like they'd just passed away yesterday.

Victoria returned with her grandmother's purse and passed it to her. Delores pulled out fifty dollars and handed it to her. "Now, don't blow it. I want you to get something nice."

"I will, because now I have a hundred dollars." She was so excited.

Sydney shook her head. "How are you guys getting there?" she asked Victoria.

"Marlene's mother is on vacation this afternoon, and she's going to drop us off. And I'm supposed to ask you if you can pick us up."

"That's fine, and if I can't, then your daddy will. And you be careful at that mall," Sydney warned her.

"I will, Mom," she said and headed back up to her room. After she finished cleaning it, she left for Marlene's.

Delores finished the greens, then Sydney added them to the pot of water and sat down in the family room with her mother. "I'm beat," Sydney said.

"You've been cleaning up all morning, so I can only imagine. I'm a little tired myself, and I'm going to go lie down in a few minutes."

"That's what I feel like doing, too, but I still need to fry the chicken and bake the corn bread. You know Wesley loves to have fried chicken with his greens."

"Yeah, but you need to be giving him a little more than some food."

"Mom!" Sydney winced.

"I'm not talking about that. Well, not exactly anyway, but I'm talking about giving him your time. You've been spending so much time taking care of me that you haven't been paying hardly any attention to him."

"But he understands that, and he doesn't have a problem with it."

"I know he doesn't, but you still need to spend more time with him. You've been stuck in this house ever since I came here, and Wesley has been having to stay here too or go places by himself."

"The only place he goes is fishing, and he would be doing that whether you were staying here or not."

"I know, but you and him used to go to the movies and out to restaurants all the time. And I haven't heard you say anything about making an appointment with your doctor. Remember when we had that conversation right before the party?"

"I know, but I haven't had time."

"You better make time, because if I know you, you're probably telling him you're too tired more than you were before." Delores giggled.

Sydney was in fact telling him that, but it was mostly because she didn't feel comfortable having sex with her mother in the house. It was awkward enough when Victoria was there, but at least Victoria's bedroom was on the upper level. However, Delores's quarters were only a few doors down the hallway. They'd managed to make love a few times in a very quiet manner, but Sydney hadn't felt comfortable with it. She'd been worried that her mother would hear them, and it hadn't been very enjoyable. Wesley was sort of frustrated, but he insisted that he understood how she felt.

"Wesley really does understand."

"Well, I'm going back home in a few days and definitely by next week, because you have more than me that you're responsible for. Wesley needs his wife, and Victoria needs her mother," Delores said, standing up.

"I'm telling you, everything is fine," Sydney tried to convince her.

"I'm sure it is, but we want to make sure that it stays that way. Now, I'm going to take a nap."

"Okay, let me know if you need anything," Sydney offered and Delores went into her room.

Sydney thought about what her mother said, and she knew she was right. But what she didn't tell her was that she'd been having some very disturbing flashbacks again, regarding her childhood. She'd been having them for quite some time, but she'd been trying to push them out of her mind—the same as she'd done five years ago when she'd remembered them for the first time as an adult. Except the more she tried to ignore them, the more frequently the memories seemed to be coming. She hadn't told a soul, and she really didn't know if it had anything to do with her sporadic desire to have sex with her husband or not. There were so many possibilities in terms of what could be wrong, so she really couldn't be sure. She'd wanted to call her internal medicine physician or her gynecologist, but she didn't know that they could do anything for her or not. She didn't think they could, but she knew if this situation started to get worse again with her and Wesley, she was in fact going to have to do something.

Chapter 22

"Bitch, didn't you just hear what I said," Phillip yelled after Gina asked him the same question again, but in a different manner. "You're not spending the night anywhere except here. You married me, not your sister and your mother."

"But Sydney can't do this all by herself. Mom is going home in a few days, and somebody's gotta stay with her at night until she can stay on her own."

"Don't ask me this shit again, Gina. I'm telling you now," he said, holding his finger close to her nose, pointing at her.

Gina's body shook like a leaf on a tree. She hoped he wasn't going to strike her, and now she wished she'd kept her mouth shut. But he had been so tranquil all evening. He still hadn't gone to look for a job, but he hadn't been angry with her about anything. She'd even had sex with him a short while ago and done all the things he wanted her to. She could tell he was pleased, and she'd decided that this was the best time to ask him if she and the twins could spend a couple nights with her mother. She'd debated all day as to whether she should, but Sydney had told her in no uncertain terms that she and Rick were going to have to help out when their mother went home.

But now Phillip was in a rage over all of this, and she didn't know what was going to happen next. She didn't want him waking the children, so she had to figure out a way to calm him down.

"Phillip, honey, I'm sorry. Please don't be upset. I'll do anything to make this up to you," she said. Her own voice sickened her.

Phillip looked at her and rolled his eyes angrily.

"I didn't mean to get you upset," she continued. "But Sydney is putting so much pressure on me about Mom. She's been taking care of her since she had the surgery, and she needs to start back doing more of her work."

"Work?" Phillip said, pursing his lips together. "How does a person do any work when they never have to leave the house?"

"She writes from her home office."

"Ha. Yeah, right. Your sister might have all of the rest of y'all fooled, but not me. All that writing she's talking about is nothing more than a hobby."

Gina didn't want to argue with him, so she didn't respond to what he'd just said. But she wanted to tell him that Sydney sometimes earned twenty-five hundred dollars for a single article. Even smaller pieces with the major magazines sometimes earned her a thousand, and it was to the point where editors called her, instead of her having to court them.

"Why can't Victoria stay with her grandmother? She's out of school for the summer anyway. And what about that brother of yours? It's not like he's married, so let him do something for a change."

"I just thought—"

"Well, you thought wrong," he interrupted. "Because your place is here, and there is more than enough around here for you to do without you going to take care of someone else."

Gina hated him. She was tired of cowering to Phillip, and more and more she was starting to see that there really was only one way out of this craziness. It was so drastic, and she didn't know if she actually could take her own life, but she could see where it really was worth trying. Phillip had pretty much assured her that she was never going to have a normal life—whether she stayed with him or whether she left him. Leaving seemed easy enough, and everyone kept telling her that that was what she should do, but she didn't see how dealing with death threats and him stalking her was better. Because at least now, she knew how to dance by his music well enough to calm him down. She was successful at it every time she tried, but still there were times like now, when she couldn't talk him down from one of his rages.

"Okay, I'll tell Sydney that I can't stay with Mom."

"You do that," he said, looking over at her. "And just so I can feel better about this, you can suck my dick again, too."

No. She didn't want to do that. She'd told him that she would do anything to make this up to him, but she'd hoped that he wouldn't take her up on her offer. She wanted to tell him no, but she knew better than to even think it.

"C'mon," he insisted.

She pulled the sheet back and lifted him into her mouth. He was limp at first, but she could feel him swelling with every second. She wanted this to end as quickly as possible, but just as she increased the speed of her movement, he pushed her head away and stood up.

"Get on your knees, so you can suck this like a pro," he ordered her.

She still had carpet burns from before, and she didn't see any reason why they couldn't remain in bed. Oral sex was oral sex, regardless of what position he was lying or standing in. He was doing this out of spite, and to remind her that he was in complete control; that he could make her do whatever he wanted, no matter how terrible it was.

She moved down onto the floor, pulled him into her mouth again, and decided that this was going to be the very last time she allowed him to sexually abuse her. She'd told herself that more than once before, but this time, she really did mean it.

Gina was glad that her mother-in-law had called Phillip to give her a ride to work, because it had allowed her an opportunity to think as well as an opportunity to call Sydney. She was dreading this whole conversation with her sister, but she knew it was better to tell her now instead of later.

It was still very early, but she dialed Sydney's phone number.

"Hello?" Sydney answered.

"Hey, how's it going?"

"Fine. How are you?"

"Okay, I guess."

Gina wished she could hang up the phone, because she knew this idea of her not being able to stay with her mother was going to drive a very thick wedge between them. But she didn't have a choice.

"I told Phillip about spending the night with Mom for a few nights, and he's not going for it."

Sydney sat up in her bed. "What do you mean, *he's* not going for it?"

"He really got upset, and Sydney I don't want to piss him off any more than I already have, because it will make it that much harder for me to leave."

"Well, when exactly are you planning to leave, Gina? Weeks have passed by, and from what I can see, you're still there."

"Look, I don't want to argue with you, and you're just going to have to understand."

"No, you *look*. This is your mother we're talking about, too, and I'm sick and tired of you and Rick acting like I'm an only child. I don't mind doing everything I can, but you and Rick have just as much of an obligation to her as I do. What if I took the same I-don't-care attitude like the two of you? I guess Mom would just have to be SOL, wouldn't she?"

"I do care about her, but what do you expect me to do when you know how Phillip is?" Gina pleaded with her sister.

"What the hell do you think I expect?" Sydney screamed and stood up. "I expect you to have enough sense to take your children and leave Phillip's crazy ass. That's what I expect."

Gina didn't speak. She knew this wasn't going to go over well with Sydney, but she couldn't remember her ever being this upset before.

"You need to start acting like a woman. And what kind of mother would keep her children in such an abusive situation when she earns over seventy thousand dollars a year? For a long time, I've tried to understand what you're going through. Even when you kept lying to us about what was going on, I still tried to keep an open mind, but now I'm tired of tap-dancing around when I talk to you. I'm sick of hearing this same old excuse about Phillip, and I'm sick and tired of you being stupid. Hell, there's not that much love in the whole world, let alone between two people," Sydney said, pacing back and forth.

"Sydney, what's going on in here?" Delores asked, walking into her daughter's bedroom.

"Mom, I'm sick of Gina and Rick," she answered.

"Sydney, all I can say is that I'm sorry," Gina said.

"Sorry isn't going to cut it this time. Because, I'm through with both you and Rick," Sydney said, and Gina heard the phone click.

Gina paused for a moment and tried to calm herself. Everyone was so against her. First it was Phillip, and now it was her sister—the sister who was supposed to love her unconditionally. She didn't understand Sydney. She was usually so level-headed when it came to every other situation, so she couldn't understand why this was so different. Didn't she know that it wasn't possible to simply leave an abusive marriage without any repercussions?

She needed to talk to her brother. She knew it was still early, but he'd told her a couple of months ago that he was going to be working summer hours starting the first week in June. So, that meant his work hours would begin at six-thirty in the morning. She dialed his number. But when the secretary answered, she told Gina that he'd taken the day off again. She wondered what the secretary meant when she said "again," so she hung up and called him at home.

"Yeah," he answered his phone after the second ring.

"Rick? What are you doing at home?" she asked.

"Because I don't feel like going to work," he said sarcastically.

"Why? Are you feeling sick?"

"No, I just don't feel like dealing with anybody today," he said, and it sounded like he was referring to her, too.

"Well, I needed to talk to you, so that's why I'm calling. Sydney just hung up on me, because I told her that I couldn't come stay with Mom."

"Yeah, she called over here last night, too. And the conversation was going fine until she started sticking her nose in my business."

"About what?"

"She wanted to know why I hadn't been over there and how come they hadn't seen or heard from Samantha. And then of course, when I told her that Samantha had moved out, she started trippin'. And I wasn't trying to hear that mess from Sydney, so I hung up on her. She makes me sick, always trying to run everything. Sometimes I think she forgets that she's my sister and not my mother."

"Well, I hope you don't get upset with me for asking, but when did Samantha move out?"

"Over three weeks ago."

Gina wondered why he hadn't told anyone. She hadn't seen him, but she had spoken to him quite a few times at work during the period of time he was speaking of.

"Why didn't you tell me?"

"Because I don't feel like talking about it to anybody. She left, and that's all there is to it."

"Have you been to work this week?" she asked, worried that he hadn't, since today was already Wednesday.

"I went Monday, but not yesterday. Why? Did they make some scrappy comment when you called?"

"No," Gina lied because she was afraid he might go off about that, too.

"Well, if I were you, I wouldn't worry about Sydney. She's just under a lot of pressure, but believe me, she'll be okay. She always is, let Mom tell it. Because for as long as I can remember, Sydney has been perfect in Mom's eyesight. That's who Mom wants to take care of her anyway. And it's not that I don't want to go over there, because I even called a truce with Sydney the first day Mom came home from the hospital, but I get sick of Sydney telling me what I should be doing. I'm grown, and I don't need her telling me when to come see my own mother. I can't be running over there all the time anyway, so she needs to get over it."

"Well, I don't think she expects that, but I know you

and I haven't gone over there as much as we should have."

"I've got my own issues to deal with right now, so if Sydney doesn't understand that, then it's just too bad."

"I hate to hear that you and Samantha broke up. You know we loved her like she was part of the family."

"She shouldn't have kept pressing me about getting married, after I told her I wasn't ready," he said.

Gina wanted to ask him the full details of the break-up, but after he told her that Sydney was in his business, she decided against it. But then, Rick did usually confide in her from time to time when it came to his personal life. She didn't know why, but he always had.

"Maybe you guys just need some space for a while."

"I don't know," he said, sounding more relaxed. "I've only talked to her two times since she left, and it was mostly small talk even then."

"She'll come around, and you will, too, if you guys really love each other. You do love her, don't you?"

"I guess. No, I do. But I'm just not sure about this marriage thing. It's too permanent for me, and the last thing I want is to be going through divorce court."

"My marriage is the worst thing that ever happened to me, but it can be good if two people love and respect each other," Gina said, realizing that she wasn't in any position to give out any advice when it came to relationships.

"But *you* can get out of your marriage anytime you want. I've told you so many times, that I would take care of Phillip. All you have to do is say the word."

"That's not the way. Although I am going to put an end to all of this and soon. But I don't want you getting involved, because Phillip isn't worth you losing your freedom over."

"I don't know how you do it, but my offer still stands," he told her.

"Hey, I better get off of here, before he gets back, and plus I have to get the twins up so they can get ready for day camp."

"What do you mean before he gets back? Isn't Phillip working?"

Gina could kick herself for letting this information slip from her mouth. She hadn't wanted anyone in her family to know about Phillip losing his job, because she knew they'd come down on her even worse for staying with him. She didn't know whether to lie about his not working or to go ahead and tell Rick. She paused for a moment.

"Well," Rick said. "Is he?"

"No. He got fired."

"I know you're not telling me that you're letting that jerk beat on you and use you at the same time, are you?"

"No, I'm not telling you that at all."

Rick laughed, but she could tell he didn't think it was funny.

"Girl, girl, girl. I don't know what to say about you," he said.

"Rick, don't start, okay. I'm going through enough as it is."

"Hey, that's you if you want to keep going around in circles."

"Talk to you later," she said, ignoring him.

"Oh, so now you've got an attitude."

"No, but I'm tired of everybody talking to me like I'm some child. You don't know what my situation is and neither does anyone else, but everybody keeps giving me all this free advice. It's easy to be on the outside looking in, but it's a different story when you're really going through it."

"Yeah, but there's *some* things you just don't put up with," he said.

"Oh, you mean like Samantha not wanting to shack with you anymore?" Gina shot back at him before she realized it.

"My relationship with Samantha doesn't even compare to what you've been taking for all these years, Gina, so don't even try it."

"I'm just trying to make a point, because every time I turn around, everybody is always trying to point their finger at me," she said irately. "And I'm getting sick of it. As a matter of fact, I'm sick of life in general. All of this just isn't worth it."

Rick was quiet, and she knew it was because he wasn't used to her speaking to him in such a hostile manner.

"I'm gonna let you go, okay," she said abruptly.

"Bye," he said like he couldn't care less.

Gina couldn't believe the way Sydney and Rick were treating her. She'd tried to reach out to them, but they weren't paying her the slightest bit of attention. They saw what they wanted to see, and they didn't seem to care about how she was feeling. She tried to tell them that she was fed up, and that she'd taken all she could take in one lifetime. No one was listening to her, though.

But then, no one ever did, until it was too late.

Chapter 23

Rick wondered what Gina meant when she'd said that she was sick of life in general and that none of this was worth it. He hadn't been very cordial to her, and now he wished they hadn't ended their conversation the way they had. He hoped she wasn't thinking about doing something crazy. He couldn't imagine that things had gotten that bad for her, but maybe they really had. Maybe he and Sydney *had* been pointing their fingers at her for so long that they hadn't paid attention to the actual damage Phillip had done to their sister.

He lay there thinking about Gina, and then he thought about his mother. He wanted to see her, but he just couldn't face them now with Samantha gone. They'd ask him too many questions, he'd become angry, and it wasn't worth going through all of that.

He thought about Samantha, and while he hadn't heard from her since their talk last week, he'd been thinking about her for what seemed like every moment of the day. He tried to put up this front for Brent when he was at work, and he tried to do the same thing a few minutes ago when he was talking to Gina, but deep down he wanted to call her and beg her to forgive him. He wanted to beg her to come back to him. He'd been trying to figure out how he could make his case with her, but he hadn't come up with anything. He had a feeling that she still loved him, but he knew there was only one way she would have a relationship with him again. He didn't know why he was so dead-set against getting married. He kept telling himself and everyone else that he didn't want to feel tied down, that marriage was too permanent, that he didn't want to take the chance of having to muddle through a divorce. He kept trying to see things Samantha's way, but every time he did, all he saw was her trying to force him to marry her. It was almost like he didn't have a choice in the matter, and he didn't like her telling him what he had better do or else. A part of him wanted to know who she thought she was, but another part of him wondered why he wouldn't just give in and go along with the program.

He debated as to whether he should call her. He wanted to, but he didn't want to sound like he was desperate. He flipped on the television instead, but it wasn't long before he flipped it back off, because nothing he wanted to see was on. He tried to go back to sleep, but all he did was toss and turn.

When he became tired of that, he went downstairs and opened the refrigerator. There wasn't much to choose from, but he did see some sparkling water pushed way in the back. He pulled it out, removed the top, and turned it up. He thought about making himself a sandwich, but changed his mind when he realized he really didn't have an appetite. He lay across the sofa with his legs propped on the arm of it and stared at the painted portrait above the fireplace of him and Samantha. They'd had it done not even six months ago, and she'd hardly been able to wait for him to help her hang it. She was so beautiful.

He stared at the painting for a long time, and finally decided to swallow his pride and call her.

"This is Samantha speaking," she answered.

"Hey, what's going on?" he said, not knowing how to begin the conversation.

"Just working. How are you?"

"I'm here. What about you?"

"I'm fine. I've been putting in a lot of hours here at work, but I'm doing okay."

"Just okay?" he asked, hoping she was missing him as much as he was missing her.

"Actually, I can't complain," she answered, disappointing him.

"Well, that's good to hear."

"How's work?"

"It's the same, I guess. I didn't go in today or yesterday."

"Why? You're not sick, are you?"

"Not medically, but I guess you could say I'm lovesick," he admitted.

She didn't respond.

"Did you hear me?"

"Yes."

"But you don't have anything to say about that, though, right?"

"What do you want me to say? I mean, you've always told me that you love me, but you never loved me enough to make me your wife. And I don't understand that. It wasn't like I was trying to trap you or tie you down. I wanted to marry you because I loved you more than I have ever loved any man. And to me, that was reason enough for us to get married."

"But Samantha, it wasn't like I wasn't ever planning to marry you, it was just that I wanted to wait."

"And I told you before I moved out, that I would respect your decision, regardless of what it was. And I'm not angry with you because of it."

"Then why haven't you called?"

"You haven't called either. And to be honest, I don't know what we have to talk about. We see things so differently when it comes to relationships, and if I can't be with you the right way, then I'd rather not be with you at all. Don't get me wrong, I do still love you, but the only way I'm going to get past this is to get on with my life."

"So, you don't want me to call you anymore?" he asked.

"I think it's best that you don't because when we do talk, it makes the rest of my day feel so lonely. It's not that easy living without someone when you were so sure that you were going to be with that person forever."

Rick felt bad and he wished he could say something to make things better. But he was speechless.

"You know what I'm saying?" she continued.

"I guess, but at the same time, I don't know how you can just walk away from what we had without looking back."

"I didn't want things to turn out like this, and I did everything I could to try and make you happy. But it wasn't enough."

"It was enough, because ever since I met you, I haven't wanted to be with any other woman," he explained.

"But it wasn't enough for you to marry me, Rick."

They always kept coming back to that same statement, which always brought them to a standstill.

"Well, maybe if we keep seeing each other, things will work out."

"I don't think so," she said. "Because the last thing I want to do is start dating a man that I was once engaged to. It doesn't make a whole lot of sense, because as long as you feel the way you do, and I feel the way I do, we're going to end up in the same boat all over again. And if we keep disagreeing on something as serious as this, we're going to end up hating each other."

"So, are you planning to see other men?" he asked, hoping she wasn't.

"I'm not looking for anyone, because I'm still trying to deal with our separation, but eventually you and I both know it will happen. And you'll start seeing other women, too."

"No, I don't think so. At least not for a very long time, anyway."

There was silence for a noticeable period of time.

"Hey, I'm not trying to change the subject on purpose, but how is your mom?"

"She's doing okay. She's moving back to her house in a few days."

"That's wonderful. She must be recovering very well."

"Yeah, I guess. I haven't seen her in a few days, but Sydney was asking why they haven't heard from you."

"I know. I feel so guilty. I guess I didn't want to have to tell them about us breaking up. I think your mom wanted us to get married almost as much as I did. But I am going to call her, and if I leave here at a decent hour, I'm going over to see her this evening."

"She would like that, and it would be nice if you came to visit me, too," he said, trying hard to change her mind about them seeing each other.

"Rick, please don't do this."

"C'mon, baby. I miss you so much. And all I want to do is talk to you."

"We're talking now," she said.

"But I want to see you. Ever since you left, I haven't been able to think, sleep, or do anything I should be doing. Baby, this split between us is taking a toll on me," he confessed. He hadn't wanted to go this far, but he didn't know what else to do to make her see how much he was hurting.

"But after we see each other, then what?"

"Then we take it one day at a time. And I won't pressure you about anything."

"I don't know," she said, sounding confused, and he knew he was finally making some headway with her.

"I promise, all we'll do is talk."

"I just don't think we should see each other until more time has passed."

"What time are you going to be here?" he said, reaching for any chance he could grab hold of.

"Rick, I just don't know about this."

"Okay, if you're not comfortable with that, then what about I meet you over to Sydney's. You said you were going to see Mom anyway, right?"

"Yeah, if I get off in time."

"Okay, then I'll see you over there."

"Bye, Rick," she said.

"Bye, sweetheart," he said, smiling for the first time since this whole ordeal began.

Wesley heard the doorbell ringing, and walked through the hallway to see who it was. When he saw that it was his brother-in-law, he opened the door.

"Hey, what's up?" Wesley said.

"Not much, man. What about you?" Rick asked, stepping inside.

"Just hangin' in there."

"So, where's everybody at?"

"Sydney's painting your mom's fingernails out on the patio."

"She's probably gonna be pissed off when she sees me."

"Who? Your mother or Sydney?" Wesley asked as they walked toward the kitchen.

"Sydney. We had some words yesterday, and you know how long she can hold a grudge."

Wesley laughed. "Yeah, you know I know her better than anyone. She told me that you hung up on her. And I don't have to tell you how through she was with you."

"Guess I better go out there and kiss-up, huh?"

"If I were you, I would. And hey, what's this about you and Samantha, anyway?"

"Man, I don't know. She wants to get married, but I'm just not ready."

"I can understand that, but if you love her, you'd better to make sure you're doing the right thing by letting her go."

"Yeah, I know. I've been thinking about nothing else ever since she left. But she's supposed to drop by here after work to see Mom, so I'm hoping I can talk to her then."

"Well, I will say this," Wesley said, moving toward the patio doors. "You are my brother-in-law, and I love you, man, but at some point you're going to have to settle down, or you'll end up regretting it for the rest of your life. You and Samantha seemed good together, and it's not that easy to find the perfect woman more than once."

"I hear you," Rick said.

"But the question is, are you really paying attention?" Wesley said.

They both laughed.

"No, seriously, man. I hear you."

"All right, because I don't want to see you laying on the side of the road like some wounded duck when you realize she's gone for good."

"I know that's right," Rick agreed, and then they walked outside.

"Hi, Mom," Rick said, hugging his mother.

"Hi, sweetheart."

"Hey, Sydney," Rick said to his sister.

"Hey," Sydney said without looking up from her mother's fingers. He'd seen her look at him when he first walked out onto the patio, but it was obvious that she didn't have anything to say and was planning to ignore him.

"So, that's all you have to say?" he asked.

"What else do you want me to say?" she said, frowning. "Because if you wanted to talk to me, you wouldn't have thrown the phone on the hook last night."

"I shouldn't have done that, and I'm sorry. But, girl, why do you always have to stress your opinion when it comes to my business?"

"If you didn't want me to know your business, then you shouldn't have told me. And if you're mad because I said that you won't ever find another Samantha, then I'm sorry. But I still meant it. And if I didn't care about you, I wouldn't care what happened to your relationship with her or anyone else. And the same thing goes for Gina when I tell her stuff about her marriage and she doesn't want to hear it. All I want is for you and Gina to be happy. And whether you like it or not, you're going to be miserable if you don't marry Samantha, and Gina is going to stay miserable if she doesn't leave Phillip."

Rick had to agree with her on both accounts, but he wasn't going to tell her. "But Sydney, it's the way you say things. Sometimes you can be so self-righteous."

"Whatever, Rick," she said and refocused her attention on her mother's nails.

"You two, cut it out," Delores said. "You all are brother and sister, and I'm tired of hearing all this arguing between the two of you."

"That's Rick," Sydney said.

"Why is everything always me?" Rick asked.

"Because it is," Sydney said, looking at him. Then she forced a smile on her face and glanced at her mother, who was shaking her head.

"You're a trip," Rick said, smiling back at her.

"So, are you staying for dinner?" Wesley interrupted.

"Yeah, if your wife doesn't throw me out," Rick said, looking at his sister.

"When have I ever thrown you out of our house? You might get on my last nerve sometimes, but that doesn't mean I don't love you."

"Oh, isn't that sweet," he said, grabbing his sister from behind and kissing her on the cheek.

"Boy, leave me alone. You play too much," she said, pretending like she didn't want him touching her.

"Boy? Girl, I'm thirty-two years old," he said, laughing.

"You're always going to be a boy to me," she said. "I don't care if you're fifty."

They all laughed, and Rick was relieved that he was on decent terms with Sydney. He didn't like having issues with her, but they'd always had these problems with each other since they were children. She always knew everything, and he always resented it. His mother always praised her, and he always resented that, too. He wanted to get past those feelings, but every time Sydney tried to tell him what to do, he lost it. Although he did feel a stronger sense of respect every time he saw her with his mother, because Sydney really was going out of her way to take care of her. Although it saddened him to know that his mother was still having problems with her coordination, because if she wasn't, she'd be polishing her own nails.

"So what are you planning on cooking?" Rick asked Wesley.

"Sydney made some spaghetti, and I'm getting ready to grill some Italian sausage, bratwursts, and some chicken legs. Shoot, it seems like I've been grilling every night for the last week, but you know Mom loves her meat grilled," Wesley said.

"That's right, son-in-law, and I appreciate you doing

it. Rick, this man works all day long, and as soon as he comes through that door, he asks me what I want him to grill for me or where can he take me. He's been rolling out the red carpet the whole time I've been staying here, and that's why it's time for me to go home before I gain a hundred pounds," she said, chuckling.

Rick laughed, but he felt bad at the same time. He was Delores's son, and he knew he should have been the one asking her those questions. He hadn't been very supportive, but this thing with Samantha had caused him to withdraw from everything and everybody. He vowed to do better from here on out, though, no matter what was going on.

"So, how come I haven't seen Samantha?"

"Sydney didn't tell you about us separating?" he asked, knowing his sister had told her as soon as he'd hung up on her.

"She told me. But what does that have to do with her not coming to see me? Because you know my feelings for Samantha are going to be the same whether you and her stay together or not."

"I know, and now that you brought it up, she's supposed to be coming over to see you this evening."

Sydney looked at him and Rick knew what she was thinking: that this was the only reason he'd come over to see his mother. But that wasn't it at all. Maybe it had helped him show up a bit sooner, but he'd planned on coming to see his mother today or tomorrow, anyway.

"Oh, really. Well, I can't wait to see her, because you know that's my girl," Delores said elatedly.

"You like her that much?" Rick asked.

"Boy, you know I do," Delores said.

"There's that 'boy' word again," he said, laughing.

"Well, shoot, I guess Sydney and I just can't help it, can we?"

"I'm just teasing you. I'm used to it now," he said.

"But yeah, I love Samantha. She's a smart girl, and

she loves you. And that's the most important thing to me."

"So, I guess you think I should marry her like everybody else."

"It doesn't matter what I think. This is something you have to decide on your own."

Now, that was one of the things he loved about his mother. She may have disagreed with some of the decisions he made or felt very strongly about some of the things he did, but she never judged him or made him feel like he had to do something he wasn't ready to. She gave him advice in a subtle way, which was why it was easier taking it from her than from his sister.

"I don't know what's going to happen, but I am going to have a long discussion with her."

"I think you should," Delores agreed.

"See. Told you," Sydney said, smiling at him.

"Girl, shut up," Rick said, pushing her shoulder playfully. Then he walked inside to help Wesley bring out the meat.

They all sat around talking for an hour, and now Victoria and Marlene had come from her house so they could get something to eat. Rick wondered what was taking Samantha so long, but he remembered she'd said that she might be working late again and figured she'd be there eventually.

"So, have you talked to Gina lately?" Delores asked Rick.

"Yeah, I talked to her this morning."

"Was she okay?" Delores asked.

"You know Gina. You can't really tell what's going on with her, because she always pretends like things are better than what they are. She did tell me something that I'll bet you guys don't know, though. Phillip lost his job."

"He what?" Sydney said.

"Lord have mercy," Delores said. "What is my child going to have to go through next?"

"How did he lose his job?" Sydney wanted to know.

"She didn't say, and I didn't even ask her, but what I do know is that she's still beating around the bush about moving out."

"Yeah, I noticed the same thing," Sydney said. "And I don't know what else we can do to get her to leave."

Rick wanted to tell Sydney the comments Gina had made about being sick of life in general, but he didn't want to upset his mother or say it in front of Victoria and Marlene. He still wondered what she meant, and he was going to call her from work tomorrow morning to see if she would give him clarification on it.

Wesley told everyone that the meat was ready, but just when he did, the phone rang. Sydney reached across the patio table and picked up the cordless.

"Hello?" she said.

"Sydney? How are you?"

"Hey, Samantha. I'm fine. How's it going with you?"

Rick felt a warm sensation running through his body, and couldn't wait to speak to her.

"I'm fine. Just working hard."

"I know what you mean. So, what time do you think you're going to be here? Wes just finished grilling, and we're getting ready to eat."

"Well, unfortunately, I don't think I'm going to make it. I wanted to see your mom, but I'm thinking I may have to wait until this weekend when I'm off."

"Oh, okay. Well, did you want to speak to Rick?"

"Yeah, but put your mom on first."

"Okay, and you take care," Sydney said and passed her mother the phone.

"Hi, baby. How are you doing?" Delores said cheerfully.

"I'm fine, Mom, and I know you're going to kill me for not coming to see you."

"No, I know how it can be when you're working and just trying to take care of yourself."

"That's still not an excuse, and I wanted to apologize to you. I promise you, though, I will see you before Sunday is over."

"Whenever you can get here is fine," Delores said, smiling.

"Okay, well, I won't hold you, and could you put Rick on the phone?"

"Sure, he's right here. Love you."

"I love you, too," Samantha said, and then Delores handed Rick the phone.

Rick took it and walked into the house. "Hey."

"Hi. I know you're wondering why I'm not there yet."

"Yeah, but I figured you were still working."

"I am," she said, pausing like she didn't know how to tell him whatever it was she was about to say, and he didn't like the way she was sounding. "But even if I'd gotten off at a decent time, I had already decided that I wasn't coming by."

"Why not?" he asked disappointedly.

She sighed. "Because I don't think we should see each other anymore. At least not until we've both moved on and come to the realization that we are not going to be together. Or at least that's what I feel I need to do anyway."

"Samantha, why are you doing this? All I wanted was for us to sit down and talk. So how is that going to hurt anything?" he said, becoming upset.

"Because you know that if we see each other, one thing is going to lead to another. I left because I knew I had to, but as long as I'm still in love with you, there is no way I can see you and not want to hold you or make love to you. This is all very hard for me, and I hope you understand what I'm trying to say."

"What I understand is that you just don't want to see me, and that it's pretty obvious that you've already moved on," he said in an adverse tone.

"Rick, you know it's not like that. But I don't want to keep repeating the same thing over and over again. You keep trying to convince me that we should wait to get married, and I keep trying to convince you that we shouldn't. We're never going to see eye to eye on this, and I don't want to keep going through all this pain."

"Fine. Then don't come."

"See, that's why I didn't want to agree to this in the first place, because look how angry you are."

"What do you expect when you told me one thing and now you're doing another?"

"I'm sorry. And you're right, I never should have said I was coming. But you wouldn't stop pressing me about it."

"Well, excuse me for wanting to see you. But hey, if you don't want to see me, then I guess I'll just have to accept that."

"But I don't want us to be enemies."

"Yeah, whatever."

"Rick, I'm serious. I don't want you to start hating me, just because we have different opinions."

Rick was losing his patience. "I want you to understand this right now. If we're not going to try to work this out, then I don't have anything else left to say to you."

"It shouldn't have to be that way."

"Well, that's the way it's going to be. And since you're so busy, I'll let you get back to work."

"Rick . . ." he heard her say, but he pressed the off button on the cordless phone. His heart was aching the same as it had been before he called her this morning, and he despised feeling this way. He felt like some little punk who couldn't get a grip on life. He hated going through this, but what he dreaded even more was going back out on the patio to face his family members.

Chapter 24

Sydney saw Wesley bringing the last bag of groceries inside her mother's house, so she went into the kitchen to start unpacking it. They'd driven Delores home a couple of hours ago, Wesley and Victoria had gone to the store to buy her a few breakfast items, and Sydney had stayed with her mother to help her get situated. She really was doing much better as the days went on, but Sydney still didn't feel comfortable leaving her all alone. At least not for a few days anyway. She knew she would eventually have to, but she needed to make sure that her mother could do at least the bare necessities like showering, putting on her clothing, and warming up food to eat. Not to mention taking her medication at the times it was scheduled. She'd been doing okay, as long as Sydney kept the pill box filled with the proper time slots and told her what day of the week it was, and she was planning to continue doing it for as long as her mother needed her to. She'd been doing pretty well with it over the last couple of weeks, but Sydney wanted to make sure that her progress continued, now that she was back at home. The therapist kept insisting that it would be even better, but Sydney needed to see for herself.

"Ohhh, it feels so good being back in my own house again," Delores said, walking through her dining room.

"So, what are you saying? That our house wasn't good enough?" Wesley teased her.

"Honey, no," she said, taking him seriously. "You know better than that. I really enjoyed staying with you, but you knew I couldn't stay forever. You all have your own lives to live, and so do I."

"Well, I think you moved back too early," Wesley said matter-of-factly.

Sydney smiled, because Wesley had been ranting and raving ever since he found out the rehab people thought it was better for her mother to go back home. He didn't understand it, and as far as he was concerned, those people at that hospital didn't know what was best for his mother-in-law anyway.

But even if she'd stayed with them another six months, Wesley would still have the same opinion. He loved having Delores in the household, and he'd made it clear that she never had to leave their home ever again, if she didn't want to.

"Granny, *Young and the Restless* is getting ready to come on," Victoria said, flipping the channel from BET. She'd been watching videos, but now she was ready to watch her favorite soap opera. Sydney wasn't too thrilled about her watching it, but ever since the school year had ended, she and her grandmother hadn't missed more than one episode. Sydney was usually working in her office during that time of the day, so she really hadn't tried that hard to stop her daughter from seeing it. Not to mention the fact that she used to watch *One Life to Live, General Hospital*, and even *The Edge of Night* herself with her grandmother. *The Edge of Night* had eventually been canceled, but she could still remember dreading the start of the school year, because she didn't want to miss what was going on with the Buchanans, the Quatermaines, Luke and Laura, and the rest of the characters.

Sydney thought the soaps had too much adult content for Victoria, and while her mother had thought the same thing about her when she was Victoria's age, she didn't seem to have one problem with Victoria watching them. Which just went to show, grandchildren really did get away with murder. Delores was so much more lenient with her three grandchildren than she had been with Sydney, Gina, and Rick, but now that she was ill, Sydney didn't mind it, because she knew that it was important for her to spend quality time with them, doing some of the things they wanted to do.

"Oooh, Shemar Moore is so fine," Victoria said when she saw *Y&R*'s Malcolm character walk into his brother's office.

"Victoria," Sydney warned her.

"I'm sorry, Mom, but he is."

Delores got a kick out of her granddaughter's infatuation with Mr. Moore, so she cracked up laughing.

Sydney shook her head, and Wesley smiled like he thought it was cute, too. But then Victoria had him wrapped around her finger as well.

"Look at old Victor," Delores said. "Lookin' handsome as usual in all that black he's got on." She was just as bad as Victoria.

"Uh-huh," Victoria agreed, which seemed odd to Sydney, because most thirteen-year-old girls could care less about the looks of a middle-aged man.

"Mom, do you want me to put your pop in the refrigerator or in the pantry?" Sydney asked.

"You can put it in the pantry, because I always drink it with ice anyway."

"All right," Sydney said.

"So, do you need me to do anything else?" Wesley asked Sydney.

"No, I think that's about it. Why? You getting ready to go somewhere?"

"Yeah, I think I'm going over to the health club to work out after the noon rush hour is over with."

"Good it's you, because I wouldn't spend my vacation day working out anywhere," Sydney said.

"See, that's the difference between you and me, I don't look for excuses to keep from working out," he said, grabbing her in a gentle head-lock.

"I guess that's true," she acknowledged.

He kissed her on the lips. "I'll see you when I get back, okay?"

"See ya," she said.

"And I'll see you two soap queens later, too."

Delores and Victoria said their good-byes, but never looked at him.

Wesley grabbed his keys and whispered, "So, are you going to be ready for me tonight?"

Sydney frowned, fearing that her mother and daughter were going to hear him.

"They can't hear me," he whispered again.

She waved her hand, dismissing what he'd said.

"So, are you?"

"Bye, Wesley," she said, blushing.

"I'll take that as a yes," he said and winked at her. Then he left.

Sydney didn't know if she was going to be in the mood or not, but she knew she'd better get into one, because too much time had passed since the last time they'd made love. It had been at least seven days, and she didn't want to think about the fact that it was likely even more. They were going to stay with Delores through the weekend, and then Victoria was going to continue staying with her for the rest of the summer, or until

Delores was fully recovered. So, Sydney didn't know how making love would be in her mother's house. They were married adults, but it just didn't seem like it would be right. Almost like it would feel too awkward. But there was no sense in her trying to figure it out, because she could already tell by the way Wesley had looked at her that he wasn't going to be able to keep his hands off her.

Sydney called and listened to her voice mail messages for both her business and personal phone lines. There was a message from an editor at *Upscale* magazine, saying that they liked the piece she was proposing on sexual abuse and the lifelong effects. She'd submitted three different proposals, but she was glad they were interested in this one, because she really wanted to do some in-depth research. She wanted to talk to adults who had survived childhood sexual abuse, and women who were being sexually abused by their husbands or boyfriends. The magazine wasn't planning to run it for six or seven months, so she had plenty of time to contact and speak with a couple of psychologists.

Next, she listened to her personal messages and heard a message from Marlene, who was calling to tell Victoria that she already missed her and was wondering if it was okay for her to come spend the night at Delores's. Then there was a message from Madison confirming Delores's appointment for next Monday.

When she pressed seven to erase it, she heard the call waiting signal, and pressed the flash button to answer it.

"Hello?"

"Hi, Sydney," Gina said. "How's Mom?"

"Mom, Gina wants to talk to you," Sydney said, taking the phone over to her mother without saying a word to her sister. She was still upset with Gina for not taking any responsibility when it came to her mother, and she didn't see where they had anything at all to talk about.

She heard her mother say a few words, and then she heard her say that she would see her in the morning. Sydney raised her eyebrows, wondering why Gina was lying. Especially since tomorrow was another workday, and there was no way she could take a day off without Phillip going off the deep end.

She heard her mother telling her to kiss the twins, and then she saw her press the off button.

"Gina said you can go do whatever you have to do tomorrow, because she's spending the whole day over here."

"Hmmph," was all Sydney said, not believing one word of it.

"She said she already took the day off, and that she's bringing the twins with her."

This, Sydney had to see, but she wasn't going to say anything negative, because she could tell that her mother already had her hopes up. She loved seeing Gina and her grandchildren, and for that reason alone, Sydney prayed that they really were going to spend the day with her.

"Oh. Well, that's good," Sydney finally said.

"Yeah, it is. She sounded a little down, so I'm glad she's coming so I can really get a chance to talk to her. I haven't done that in a long time."

Sydney was upset with Gina, but she had to admit that she wanted to talk to her sister, the same as Delores. She was so angry with her for staying in that abusive situation, but at the same time, she did feel somewhat sorry for her. She rode this emotional roller coaster when it came to Gina all the time, but it had become much worse since the day her mother had her surgery. One minute she wanted to grab her and shake some sense into her, because she didn't understand how anyone could be so caught up with a man like Phillip, and the next minute, she wanted to hold her like she used to do when she was two and Gina was just an infant. She didn't actually remember holding her sister, but she'd seen the photos that their father had taken of them. She wanted to understand, but she couldn't—no matter how hard she tried. She'd even read a few articles on the subject, and while she'd read that it really wasn't that easy for any woman to walk away from her abuser, she still couldn't see her sister tolerating something like this. Although there was one article that she'd read that talked about middle children, and how they usually ended up with very low self-esteem and very serious emotional problems. The oldest child received lots of attention and was authorized a variety of privileges simply because they were firstborn. The baby of the family was showered with loads of affection, because everyone in the household usually went out of their way to spoil them. But the middle child, according to the article, never seemed to get much attention from anyone, specifically from the parents. It wasn't like it was intentional, but for some reason, middle children always found themselves competing unsuccessfully with the oldest and the youngest in every way shape or form.

Sydney hadn't thought Gina was neglected by their parents in any way, but who could say for sure, except her. Maybe she had experienced some things in her childhood that made her feel less than adequate. Sydney hadn't thought about it much before, but she knew herself that it certainly was possible to block out deep, dark secrets and pretend that life was peaches and cream. Only problem was, those horrifying, yet shameful memories always forced their way back to the forefront. Then the victim either dealt with them head on, or struggled daily to keep them hidden.

Sydney wondered which method was going to be better for herself in the long run.

Chapter 25

"Honey, is there anything you want me to bring you after I leave work this evening?"

"No," Phillip said, pulling on his jeans. Gina couldn't believe it, but a north suburban employment agency had actually called him two days ago for a temp-to-hire position at a paper manufacturing company. He hadn't been overly thrilled about it, but he'd told them he was interested. Today was his first day, and he was already getting dressed, since he needed to be there by 7 A.M.

"Do you want anything special for dinner?" Gina asked, being extra nice to him. Unlike in the past, she wanted him to become suspicious, and she hoped she was laying her cheerfulness on thick enough to initiate it. Because if he didn't start to suspect something, he wouldn't check up on her, and her plan wasn't going to work the way it was supposed to. The twins weren't going to camp today, she wasn't going to work, and she needed him to find out about it.

"Make whatever you want," he said, looking at her strangely.

"But I want to make something you really like," she said, wrapping her arms around his neck.

"What's the matter with you?" he asked. "And if you think all this lovey-dovey stuff is going to win you an overnight ticket to your mother's house, you can just forget it."

"It's nothing like that," she said. "You said I couldn't go, and I'm not going."

Phillip tightened his leather belt around his waist and inserted the end of it inside the buckle, all the while staring at her.

"You do love me, don't you, Phillip?" she asked, still holding on to him.

"Gina, just stop it, because you're really about to get on my nerves," he said, moving her arms away from him.

How inconsiderate. She was finally being the attentive wife that he wanted, and still, he wasn't satisfied. Shame on him, she thought, and then she cracked up laughing.

Phillip looked confused. "You are one crazy bitch," he said and walked out of the room.

Maybe. But she'd come to her senses very quickly two days ago, only hours after she'd ended her conversations with Sydney and Rick. Luckily, Phillip hadn't found out, but she'd taken that afternoon off and spent the whole time thinking about what it was she was doing to herself and her children. Sydney had yelled and screamed at her, but there was one thing that she'd said that Gina hadn't been able to shake: How could she keep her children in such an abusive situation when she earned over seventy thousand dollars a year? She'd asked herself that before, but it was something about the way Sydney said it to her. Then, there was the comment Rick had made about her not only allowing

Phillip to beat on her, but now she was letting him use her for money. She'd thought about all of those things from every possible angle, and she'd finally decided that taking her life was clearly not the right decision. She'd been sure that her children would be much better off with Sydney and Wesley, but when she'd dropped them off at camp that very morning and watched them walk up to the door, something had come over her. It was almost like she was seeing them for the first time in her life. They looked so innocent and so helpless, and it was at that very moment that she realized how crucial it was for her to raise them herself. She'd kept them in what was worse than a prison environment, and it was up to her to get them out of it, so she could give them a better life. She had to take a stand on this, and while it had taken her all afternoon and most of the night, she'd finally discovered a way to bring this all to an end. It was going to be a very rough time over the next few weeks for everyone involved, but in the end, it was all going to be worth it.

She heard Phillip calling her name, and she wondered what he wanted.

"Yes," she answered in a passionate tone, walking toward the top of the stairway to look down at him.

"You better not be up to anything, or I promise you, you're going to regret it. You hear me?" he said, obviously trying to figure out what was going on with her.

"Why would I be up to anything, Phillip? You know me better than that," she said, smiling.

"Okay, Gina, when I get on that ass, don't say you weren't warned."

She stood there in silence, and he finally walked out of the house and drove off to his new job.

It was so amazing how love really could turn to hate, but the scariest part of all was that she had no idea that hatred could start to feel so satisfying.

* * *

"Mom, how come you didn't go to work today?" Carl asked Gina.

"I wanted us to spend the day with Granny. We haven't been over to her house since she went back home."

"I thought she was still at Aunt Sydney's house," Caitlin said.

"No, you didn't," Carl reminded his sister. "Remember when I told you last week that she was going home?"

"Oh, yeah," Caitlin remembered.

"How did you know she was going back home?" Gina asked her son. Then she looked through the rearview mirror and saw him look at his sister with a funny expression on his face.

"Well?" Gina said, wanting to know where he'd gotten his information.

"I heard you tell Aunt Sydney that Daddy said you couldn't spend the night with Granny when she moved back to her house."

Gina continued looking straight ahead, and wondered what else he'd heard. Her door had been shut that morning when Phillip had gone to give his mother a ride to work, and she'd thought for sure that the children were asleep.

"Mom, how come Daddy doesn't like us to see Granny and Aunt Sydney, and how come we don't get to spend the night with them that much?" Carl asked.

Gina didn't know how to answer her son's question. It was a legitimate inquiry, but she knew whatever reason she gave him wasn't going to make a whole lot of sense. She tried to explain it as best as she could, though.

"It's not that he doesn't like us to see them, he just likes for us to spend a lot of time together at home," she said, feeling guilty for lying to him.

Gina gazed through the rearview mirror again, and saw Carl and Caitlin looking at each other. It was obvious that they weren't buying into what she was saying. They were only eight, but they were far from being that naïve.

"But you get to spend the whole day with Granny today, though," she said, trying to lift their spirits.

"I miss seeing Granny," Caitlin said.

"So do I, and I'll bet Granny misses us, too," Carl added.

It pained Gina to hear her children speak so openly about seeing their grandmother. She hadn't known that they felt so strongly about it, because they'd never talked about it before. At least not to her. But, then, it probably had something to do with the fact that they were never able to speak their minds in front of their father. He was like a dictator, and they had learned to speak only when spoken to while in his presence. The lifestyle they lived was so unfair, and hearing them voice their concerns made her feel even better about this newly created plan she was preparing to execute.

They pulled into Delores's driveway, left the car, and went inside.

"Hi, Granny," the twins said simultaneously and ran toward their grandmother, who was sitting on the sofa in the family room.

"Hi, babies," she said, reaching out to both of them and hugging them at the same time.

"We really missed you, Granny," Caitlin told her.

"Well, I missed both of you, too."

"How are you, Mom?" Gina said, kissing her mother.

"I'm doing fine. How are you, sweetheart?" Delores asked.

"I'm doing okay, too," Gina answered. "So, where is everyone?"

"Wesley left for work already, and Sydney went

home to get her laptop computer and to make a few business calls. Victoria is upstairs."

"They all spent the night with you?" Gina felt somewhat envious.

"Honey, you know Wesley isn't going to spend too many nights without Sydney if he doesn't have to, and you know he feels right at home when he's at my house, anyway. He's more like a son than a son-in-law, and I don't know what I would have done without him."

"Wesley has always been a good man," Gina said, wishing she'd married a man with even twenty percent of her brother-in-law's personality.

"Mom, we're going upstairs to see Victoria," Carl interrupted, and he and Caitlin dashed toward the stairway.

"Slow down," Gina ordered them.

"So, how are things with you?" Delores asked.

"Hmmph. I really don't know where to begin, Mom. My life is such a mess right now, and things won't be right until I get the twins and me out of this situation."

"Well then, baby, that's what you need to do. I'm not trying to tell you how to live your life, but you need to leave Phillip if he's not treating you with all the love and respect that I know you deserve. I've stayed quiet about your marriage for a very long time, but when I start to see it affecting you the way it is right now, I have to say something. You are a smart, ambitious young woman, and the last thing I want is to see you just as miserable in your thirties as you were in your twenties. And all of these problems with Phillip can't be good for the twins either."

Gina glanced at the television, trying not to become emotional.

"I don't mean to pry, Gina, but is Phillip abusing you again?"

Gina wanted to deny it, but she didn't know why, because this was all going to be over with very shortly.

"Mom, I don't think we should talk about this. Anyway, I came over to see how you were doing," she said, changing the conversation.

"Gina. Look at me. Is Phillip putting his hands on you again?"

"Yes. He does it all the time, and things are getting worse than they've ever been before. He's so angry all the time, and nothing I do is right with him."

"Honey, I know you love your husband, but men like that usually don't change. When they hit you once, they'll always do it again. And I've never seen it any different."

"Mom, I'm not in love with him anymore. There was a time when I loved him more than I loved myself, but now I hate him so much, I wish he would just die."

"I hate to hear you saying that, but I do understand how you feel. You've been putting up with this for a very long time, and I can only imagine what it's been like."

"I am so sorry for not being here for you, like I should have been," Gina said, holding her mother's hands with tears streaming down her face. "I am so, so sorry."

"Baby, you don't have to apologize for anything. I know you would have been here if you could have, and we can't look back on any of that."

"He wouldn't let me come stay with you in Madison, and he won't let me come stay with you a few days now. I know Sydney thinks I'm putting him before you, but I'm not. Phillip is so violent, and it's better to just go along with what he wants just to try and keep things right between us. And sometimes that doesn't work, because there are times that he goes off for no reason at all."

"He's got a serious problem, Gina, and you've got to get away from him as soon as you can. No time is going to be the right time, so you just have to do it."

Gina didn't want to tell her mother, but she'd already begun the process when she'd gone out of her way to filter suspicion in Phillip's mind this morning. She was pretty sure it had worked, because of the way he'd threatened her just before leaving the house. By now, she was willing to bet he'd already tried to call her at work and that her secretary had told him that she'd taken the day off. He was probably going insane at this very moment, and she knew holy hell was going to break loose as soon as she arrived home. It always did whenever she disobeyed him, but this time, she wanted it to happen.

"I am going to put an end to all of this, and it won't be much longer," Gina said.

"I'm glad to hear it, and I want you to know that as long as I have a place to live, so do you and my grand-babies."

"I know that now, but believe it or not, there were times when Phillip had me thinking I didn't have any-where to go, and that my family didn't care anything about me."

"We have always loved you, and don't you ever let anyone make you think any different," Delores said, and Gina could tell that her mother was angry.

"I know, but you have no idea how much control Phillip has had over me all these years. I feel so stupid, but I couldn't help it. I loved him so much, and I be-lieved everything he said for a long time. It was almost like a sickness, and I would have done anything he told me, no matter how bad it was. But when he kept me away from you while you were sick these last few weeks, it really made me see how cruel he actually was. Then, I really started paying attention to what Carl and Caitlin have been going through. I've always known that they were suffering, but this week I decided that enough was enough."

"Honey, I've been praying day and night for God to speak to you. For Him to deliver you from all of this."

"It's not going to be easy when I leave, but I know that I have to do this."

"Everything will be just fine," Delores said, hugging her daughter. "It may not seem like it now, but it will be with time."

Gina sighed. "I love you, Mom, and thank you for always understanding and for not judging me like everyone else."

"Baby, I'm your mother. And that's all I need to say about that."

Gina felt so secure, and she was happy that she'd finally found the courage and strength to come visit with her mother. She didn't know how terrible things were going to become from here on out, and she wanted to spend some quality time with her. She wanted to spend some time talking to her alone. She hoped Sydney would be able to forgive her, too, once this thing with Phillip was over, and that they could find the closeness they had once shared as sisters. She hoped they could find a common bond with Rick as well, because she wanted them to be the family that they should be. She wanted them to make up for all the times they'd been at each other's throats and for all the times she'd had to miss celebrating holidays and family get-togethers with them. She wanted Carl and Caitlin to experience unconditional love from their family on a frequent basis. She owed them that, and the sacrifice she was about to make was going to make a decent down payment.

Chapter 26

Gina turned the corner two blocks away from her mother's house and felt a nervous churning in her stomach. There was no doubt in her mind that this was the only way to handle her marital situation, but she still couldn't seem to shake this frightful feeling. She'd mentally plotted the entire plan from beginning to end, but now that it was time for her to execute it, she was starting to have second thoughts. She'd left the children with her mother so that they wouldn't have to witness this terrible thing that was about to happen between her and their father. She kept telling herself that this was the appropriate action to take, because if she didn't, she and the children would be forced to live in bondage for the rest of their days.

She drove into the driveway, spied Phillip's automobile, and shut her vehicle off. Then she closed her eyes and took a deep breath. She couldn't believe she'd had the courage even to imagine something like this let alone follow through with it, because she knew she was about to receive the beating of a lifetime—and this time, she'd done everything she could to provoke it.

She spoke a silent prayer, and then stepped out of the car. She walked slowly but diligently inside the garage, then the house, and as soon as she pushed the door shut, Phillip walked toward her.

"Where have you been all day?" he screamed. "I've been calling your ass at work, and everywhere else I can think of."

"I was at Mom's," she said with no facial expression.

"You lying bitch," he said, moving closer to her. "I called your mother's house, and the phone just rang."

Gina knew he was telling the truth, because they'd purposely not answered when they saw his work number flash across the Caller-ID screen.

"Why are you lying?" he continued.

Gina just stared at him without responding.

"And where are the twins?" he roared.

She continued to gaze at him in silence.

"I told you this morning that you better not be up to anything, didn't I?" he asked, shoving her against the wall by her throat.

She squirmed, but she never took her eyes off him. She was determined to see this beating through until the end.

"Oh, so you're not going to say anything, I see," he said, obviously not knowing what was going on with her.

She blinked a couple of times, but showed no sign of movement.

Phillip breathed more and more rapidly, becoming more and more angry with every second.

"Where are my kids?" he asked again as a final warning.

He was holding her neck fairly tight, and she wanted

to beg him to let her go. But she gazed into his eyes and refused to say one word.

Phillip released her, pulled back his fist, and blasted her in her right eye. She grabbed it with both hands, but he jerked her away from the wall, stuck his foot behind both of her legs, and tripped her onto the floor.

He lunged on top of her, throwing blow after blow. Until finally he'd thrown so many blows that Gina tasted her own blood, and felt her face going numb. She didn't know whether she was completely conscious or not, but she didn't have the strength to say anything. Not that there was anything to say in the first place.

"I told your crazy ass that I wasn't playing games with you," he said, pointing his finger at her, breathing in and out in a deep manner. "You always make me do this shit to you."

Gina moaned quietly in pain and moved her head slightly to one side. Her head pounded wildly, and she was sure it was going to explode at any moment.

"Get up," Phillip said, standing up himself. "I said, get up and stop acting like you can't move. You're not hurt that bad, so stop faking."

Gina opened her eyes, but she felt a dizzy spell approaching and closed them.

"I'm gonna ask you one more time, Gina," he yelled, still panting from all the commotion. "Where have you been all day?"

Gina didn't say anything, and she wished he would get this over with. She wished he would kill her dead or leave her lying there so she could call the police.

"I said, where have you been all day?" he bellowed and kicked her in her side as hard as he could.

She shrieked with pain and tears rolled down her face.

"Huh? Where have you been?" he said, swinging his leg back and kicking her again in the same place.

This time she screamed for his mercy. "Phillip, please."

"Then tell me where you've been," he said, lifting his knee, preparing to jolt her again.

"Okay," she cried. "Okay. I was at my mother's, and that's where the twins are."

"Why are you lying to me again?" he asked with his eyes bucked like a maniac.

"I'm not lying to you, Phillip. That's where we were all day. We just didn't answer the phone."

"You little whore. You dropped those kids off at your mother's so you could go screw some bastard all afternoon, didn't you?"

"No," she said, begging him to believe her.

"Why do you keep pushing me, Gina?" he said, pressing his foot onto her chest.

She swallowed hard and moved her lips in prayer.

"There's not a prayer in the world that can help you get away from me, so you might as well stop all of that mumbling."

Gina opened her eyes. "Why don't you just go ahead and kill me," she yelled out.

"What?" he said, squinting his eyes in confusion.

"Just kill me and get it over with."

Phillip laughed loudly and moved his foot back to the floor. "Kill you?"

Gina sniffled but didn't speak.

"No, that's too easy for a whore like you. So, what I'm gonna do now is go pick up Carl and Caitlin, and when I come back, I want you to have dinner started," he said. "And do something about your face while I'm gone, because you look like a complete mess."

Gina watched him grab his keys and walk outside. He was so calm all of a sudden, and she wondered if he had actually snapped. She had to call the police, and she had to warn her mother not to let Phillip into her house when he arrived. She sat up very slowly but grabbed her side when she felt tremendous pain flowing through it. She willed herself to her knees, took a deep breath, and stood up. Her right eye felt severely swollen, and it was difficult for her to see from it, but she walked over to the phone and dialed 911. The party answered on the first ring.

"911, what's your emergency?" the man said on the other end.

"My husband just assaulted me, and I need someone to come out to arrest him."

"Where is he now?"

"He just left to go get our children from my mother's."

"Are you Mrs. Harris?"

"Yes."

"Your first name?"

"Gina."

"Are you—"

"I need to phone my mother to warn her about Phillip," Gina interrupted.

"I understand that, but we need to verify your address so we can dispatch a car to your location."

Gina told him that the address he was showing was correct.

"Okay, an officer should be there—"

"Please tell them to hurry before my husband comes back," Gina said and hung up the phone. She didn't mean to be rude, but she had to call her mother.

"Hello?" Sydney answered.

"Sydney, Phillip is on his way over there to get the twins, but whatever you do, don't let him in and don't let him take them," Gina said in desperation.

"What's going on?" Sydney said with concern. "And why is he coming over here?"

"Because he just jumped on me, and I had no choice but to tell him where they were. I've already called the police, though, and as soon as they get here, I'm going to have him arrested."

"Are you going to be okay by yourself until they get there?"

"I don't know," Gina said, sniffling again.

"Look. Wesley just got in, so I'm on my way, okay?"

"Yes, and Sydney, please don't tell Mom about what Phillip just did to me."

"I won't. Everything is going to be fine, you just hang in there," Sydney said and hung up the phone.

Gina hung up hers as well. She sighed deeply and struggled over to the kitchen chair. Her side ached in an excruciating way, and her face felt like a tight balloon. She couldn't believe Phillip had beaten and kicked her to the extent that he had. He'd beat her numerous times before, but never with such force or anger as a few minutes ago. She'd wanted and needed for the beating to happen, but she hadn't planned on him beating her in her face or her head like she was a complete stranger. Then there was this thing of him acting as though everything was normal. He'd acted this way every other time, but he seemed so emotionally unstable this time around, and it made her nervous. Everything about this whole idea of hers made her feel a bit uneasy, and she hoped she'd decided to do the right thing. She hoped that phase two was going to run much more smoothly.

She looked outside the window when she saw her sister pulling up. She dragged her body through the hallway and over to the front door, then opened it.

"Oh, my God," Sydney wailed as soon as she laid eyes on Gina and all the bruises plastered across her face. Not to mention her right eye, which was swollen so badly, it was barely even open.

Gina didn't say anything.

"Gina, what's wrong with Phillip? Oh, my God. I am so sorry," she said, reaching for her sister.

"Are Carl and Caitlin okay?" Gina asked.

"Yes. Wesley is there with them, and Mom and Victoria are there too, so you don't have to worry."

"What if he gets in?" Gina said hysterically. "What if Wesley can't stop him from taking my babies with him?"

"Gina, calm down. Wesley would never let him take those children. I promise you that," Sydney said and heard the doorbell ringing. "It's about time," she said and opened the door.

"We're here about a domestic violence situation," the first officer began.

"Please come in," Sydney welcomed two of them and wanted to ask why she'd arrived at Gina's before them.

"Thank you," the second officer said after the first.

"So, are you Gina Harris?" the first officer inquired.

"Yes," Gina said and wondered who else she could be with all of the evidence painted on her body.

"And you are?" he asked Sydney.

"I'm her sister, Sydney Taylor."

Then he turned his attention back to Gina. "And your husband is the one who did this to you?"

"Yes," Gina answered.

"Where is he now?"

"He left to go over to my mother's house to get our kids."

"Is your mother aware of what's going on?"

"Yes, and my brother-in-law is there with them."

"Is that your husband?" he asked Sydney.

"Yes, it is," she answered.

"How did all this start?" the first officer began his routine questioning.

"I came home from my mother's, and he asked me where I had been and where the children were."

"Uh-huh," the officer acknowledged.

"I told him where I was, but he said I was lying. Then he started beating on me."

"Have there been any other occurrences like this in the past?"

Gina hesitated. "Yes. He abuses me all the time," she said.

"Have you reported these incidents before?"

"No."

"Have there been any witnesses to these incidents?"

"No. Well, just my children," she answered sadly.

"But the rest of us have always known that it was going on," Sydney chimed in.

"Did you ever see any bruises or signs that your sister was being abused?"

"No, but it was always obvious," Sydney responded.

"If we go to your mother's, do you think he'll still be there?" the second officer asked his first question.

"I don't know. Maybe. They're not going to let him in, so I don't know if he'll keep trying to get in, or if he'll just come back here."

"Well, I think we'll go over there to see, and if not, a warrant will be placed for his arrest," the second officer informed her.

"Do you think you need medical attention?" the first officer asked as he watched Gina holding her side.

"No, I think I'm okay."

"It might be a good idea for you to go anyway, just so you can have your injuries documented," the second officer suggested.

"I agree," Sydney commented.

"I will, but not until I know my babies are safe."

"Do you need us to arrange for transportation to the hospital?"

"No," Gina answered. "I'll have my sister take me."

"Sounds good. Now, what is your mother's address?" the first officer inquired.

"It's 2317 Rosemont Circle," Sydney told him.

"Okay," the officer said, jotting the information down.

"We're going over there, and we'll let you know if he's there or not."

"Thank you, officers," Gina said. Sydney opened the front door, and the officers walked out.

"I'd better call over to Mom's to see what's going on," Sydney said, walking toward the kitchen to pick up the phone. Then she dialed the number.

"Mom, is everything okay over there?"

"Honey, Phillip is over here showing his natural behind. He's outside on the lawn yelling in here for us to send these babies out."

"Where's Wesley?" Sydney asked.

"He's in the living room looking out the window at Phillip. He already told him that he wasn't sending the children out, and Phillip keeps saying that he's not leaving without his kids. I'm telling you, this doesn't make any sense at all," Delores said.

"Well, the police are on their way over there to arrest Phillip now, so it shouldn't be that much longer," Sydney assured her mother.

"I hope so, because pretty soon, that man is going to be trying to burst his way into this house."

"What's going on?" Gina asked Sydney.

"He's outside clownin' on the front lawn, but everyone else is inside, and the twins are fine."

"Please tell Mom to keep them away from the window, because I don't want them seeing their father being arrested," Gina instructed Sydney.

"Mom, Gina doesn't want Carl and Caitlin to see the officers arresting Phillip, so if you can, try to keep them away from the window."

"I will," Delores acknowledged. "Because Lord knows those children have been through enough as it is.

"Oh, my. He's trying to beat the door down," Delores added.

"He's trying to tear the door down," Sydney reiterated to Gina.

"I don't believe this is happening," Gina said worriedly. "I wasn't counting on him going over to Mom's to get the children, and I should have never told him where they were."

"Where are those police?" Sydney said, changing the phone from one ear to the other.

"I think I just heard the siren shut off," Delores said. "Victoria, get those babies back in this family room," Sydney heard her mother telling her granddaughter.

"Wesley just went outside," Delores said. "So, I'll call you back when they've picked Phillip up."

"Okay, Mom," Sydney said and hung up.

"Are you Phillip Harris?" the second officer asked, moving toward him with his partner.

"Yeah. And?" Phillip said in a cocky tone.

"You're under arrest," the officer said, forcing Phillip's body toward the door. Then he pulled both of Phillip's hands behind his back and enclosed them in handcuffs.

"Under arrest for what?" Phillip asked, trying to resist.

"For assaulting your wife," the officer answered and then recited the Miranda statement. "You have the right to remain silent. Anything you say can and will be used against you in a court of law. You have the right to talk to an attorney and have him present with you while being questioned. If you cannot afford to hire an attorney, one will be appointed for you. You may also waive your right to counsel and your right to remain silent, and you may answer any question or make any statement you wish. If you decide to answer questions, you may stop answering at any time to consult with an attorney. Do you understand what I have told you?"

"What do you mean, assaulting my wife?" Phillip said, waiving his right to be silent. "Take these cuffs off of me," he demanded, twisting his arms back and forth.

"Sir," the second officer said to Wesley. "Your sister-in-law is waiting to hear from us, but if you would, please call and let her know that we have her husband, and that she should go to the hospital to get examined as soon as possible."

"Sure thing, officer," Wesley affirmed.

"You tell that bitch, that I'm gonna kill her the next time I see her," Phillip told Wesley, but Wesley just shook his head at him.

"And you got an ass whippin' comin' too for keeping my kids locked inside that house," he threatened Wesley.

"I'll be waiting for it," Wesley said, smiling, but it was obvious that none of this was amusing to him.

The officers dragged Phillip over to the squad car, and pushed him inside.

Chapter 27

"I should kill that asshole for doing this to you," Rick told Gina as he examined her facial features. He'd just dropped by her house to see her after coming from the health club with Wesley. Carl and Caitlin had spent the night at Delores's, and she was planning to leave them there until her face began looking a bit more presentable. She didn't want them to see her that way, and she hoped a few coats of foundation would disguise her bruises a few days from now.

"I told you if you didn't get out of that situation, something bad was going to happen," he continued.

"Yeah, well, Phillip is behind bars, and that's all that matters," Gina said, wishing he would change the conversation.

"But for how long?"

"I don't know, but I'm going to court first thing Monday morning to request an order of protection, and

I'm going to ask the judge if he will order Phillip to live somewhere else until the divorce is final."

"So you're actually going to end this for good?" Rick said, sounding as if he didn't believe his sister.

"There's no doubt in my mind."

"Well, I'm glad to hear it, because Phillip doesn't mean you any good."

"I know he doesn't, and the worst part of all is that I know he's not going to take this order of protection lying down. And it'll be even worse once I file for the divorce and request sole custody of the children."

"Do you have an attorney in mind?"

"No, but I need you to get me Samantha's phone number so I can ask her about her friend that she mentioned when we were in Madison."

"Let's not even talk about her."

"Why? You guys still aren't speaking?"

"No. She called me once and left a message, but I didn't even bother calling her back."

"Why not?" Gina said, stroking her hair toward the back of her head.

"Because all she called for was to see if I was still mad at her or not. She keeps talking this crap about us being friends and how she doesn't want us to be enemies, but I don't need to hear that," he said, throwing his leg across the arm of the leather chair.

Gina looked at him and then glanced over at the television.

"Oh, so you think I should talk to her, right?" he asked.

"I'm not saying anything," Gina said, still looking away from him.

"No, I want you to say whatever you're thinking, because maybe I'm missing something."

"I'm not saying anything, because whenever I say something that you don't agree with, then you get pissed off, and right now, I can't handle that. I'm going through enough problems on my own, and I don't need any attitudes between you and me."

"Just say it, girl," Rick said, wanting to know how his sister felt about his relationship with Samantha.

"Fine. Then, let me ask you this. Do you love Samantha?"

"Yeah, I guess," he said, raising an eyebrow.

"Yes or no. Because either you do or you don't." Rick blew a sigh of disgust. "Yes."

"Is there someone else you want to be with besides her?"

"No."

"Does she make you happy when you're with her?"

"Yeah."

"When you're not with her, do you feel like a part of you is missing? You know, like you can't even function without her?"

"As much as I hate to admit it, yeah. I do."

"So why is it that you're willing to give her up, just because she wants to get married?"

"Because I'm not ready, that's why."

"But why, though?" Gina asked, leaning her elbow against the back of the sofa.

"Because I don't want to be tied down like that."

"If you think that marrying Samantha is going to tie you down, then you're not in love with her."

"I am in love with her, but that doesn't mean we have to rush into marriage."

"That's fine, but it's not right for you to be upset with her because she wants to settle down."

"We *were* settled down until she moved out."

"You guys weren't settled down, Rick. And no matter how you look at it, you didn't have a real commitment to her. You want her to be there for you, but you want the freedom of being able to put her out or leave her whenever you get ready."

"No, I don't," he said defensively.

"See, that's why I didn't want to discuss this, because I knew you were going to get an attitude."

"I'm not upset with you, and all I'm trying to say is that I'm not running after Samantha, and I don't see a reason for us to be friends either."

"Well, I think you're making a big mistake, but as long as you know you don't want to marry her, then there's nothing else I can say."

"I keep telling you, it's not that I don't want to marry her. I just don't want to marry her right now."

"Then you shouldn't, but you shouldn't be angry with her for wanting to either."

"Yeah, whatever," Rick said, sounding frustrated.

They sat silently for a few minutes.

"I guess I'd better call to check on the twins," Gina finally said. "All of this is going to be so hard on them."

"They'll get through it. Mom and Sydney are going to be there for you and them, and so am I."

"I know. You don't know how relieved I was when Sydney walked through that door yesterday evening after Phillip jumped on me. I needed her to be here with me, and I don't know if I could have gone to the hospital and faced all of those people if she hadn't been there. I know she can be controlling and extremely opinionated sometimes, but the one thing I can say about her is that I can always depend on her."

"Yeah, I'll give her that," Rick had to agree.

"She's always there for you, too, whether you want to admit it or not."

"Oh, I never said she wasn't there for me, I just don't like some of the things she says and does."

"Well, I will say this," Gina said. "She does have a reason to be upset with us about Mom, because we really haven't been there for her the way we should have been. I know I blamed my absence on Phillip, but deep down, I automatically assumed that Sydney would handle it. I've always expected her to handle everything for as long as I can remember."

"But she wants it that way. She likes to be in charge, so I let her."

"Yeah, but it's not right, because she has a life to live just like the rest of us. She and Mom are real close, but we need to be there as much as we can, too."

"It's hard for me to see Mom dropping everything she picks up, and it's hard to see her head shaved on one side like it is."

"I know, but what if Sydney felt the same way? Then, there wouldn't be anybody to help take care of her."

"Well, it seems like she's doing a lot better," Rick said, trying to convince himself and Gina.

"Yeah, she is. But she's still not completely out of the woods, and you can tell that her short-term memory is still not all that great."

"But it's hard seeing her like that," Rick repeated, and Gina could see his eyes filling with water.

"I know it is, but she needs us more now than she's ever needed us in her life, and being there for her is the least we can do."

Rick took a deep breath and looked toward the ceiling.

"Staying away isn't helping her. Mom will probably never say anything about it, but when she doesn't see us, I know it destroys her inside. I know it would me, if Carl and Caitlin deserted me because I was sick."

"But everybody doesn't deal with sickness and death in the same way. I love Mom, but it's too hard for me to see her the way she is. It might not be right, but I just can't help it."

Gina could tell that she wasn't making any headway with her brother, so she decided that it was time to end their discussion concerning it. She didn't know what she could say or do to make him see the mistake he was making with both his mother and his ex-fiancée, but she hoped he would eventually come around before he regretted it.

She didn't say anything else, and Rick stood up and went into the kitchen. "I think we should just agree that we disagree and end this conversation," he said and then pulled a bottle of sparkling water from the refrigerator.

"Fine," Gina said.

"So, when is Phillip's hearing?" Rick asked, walking back to his seat.

"Not until Monday, since it happened on a Friday night and the courts are closed all weekend. I know he can't get out, but it makes me nervous wondering what's going to happen two days from now when he does go before the judge."

"As much as I hate to say it," Rick said, sitting his water on the floor, "if he doesn't have any priors, the judge is probably going to let him out on bail."

"Yeah, I know. And I don't know how he's going to react to being put out of here."

"Well, I'll come stay here with you if you want, because there's no telling what that fool will do. Wesley told me this morning that he was acting like he'd lost his mind when the police handcuffed him."

"I'm afraid, but I'm not going to live in fear for the rest of my life."

"Then you're going to have to take care of Phillip once and for all," Rick said, gazing at his sister. "I told you that before, and I'm telling you, if you don't, Phillip is going to trip as soon as he gets out. And no order of protection is going to stop him."

Gina was ahead of her brother's thinking. She'd thought about all of that when she sat down and decided that she had to provoke him in a manner like she never had before, so that she'd have enough bruises. Proof to show the police. She'd known that it was the only way they would arrest him, and the only way she'd be able to file for an order of protection without a whole lot of questions. She wanted to tell Rick that this was just the beginning, and that she was going to take care of Phillip once and for all. But she couldn't, because there was a chance that he might not understand, and she couldn't take the risk that he wouldn't. She truly did want to tell someone, though. Sydney, a friend, anyone who could fathom where she was coming from, but she knew it was better to keep her thoughts and decisions to herself. It was better just to bide her time quietly.

Rick tossed this thing with Samantha through his mind, back and forth, over and over again, and finally he decided that maybe Gina was right. Maybe he *was* taking this thing about marriage too far, and maybe he was making a huge mistake by feeling all this anger toward Samantha.

He'd tried to push her completely out of his mind, but after going to visit his mother, and running a few errands, he'd arrived back at home feeling lonely. It was almost like he didn't know what to do with himself on a sunny Saturday afternoon, and he didn't like this idea of spending all of his time with just himself. Brent usually made somewhat decent company whenever Rick was feeling this way, but to his surprise, Brent and that girl he'd met at the club were still seeing each other. He didn't know if the relationship was getting serious or not, but Brent didn't seem to want to hang out as much anymore, unless it was with her.

He lay across his bed, debating whether he should call Samantha, or if he should simply buy a dozen roses and show up on her sister's doorstep. She loved flowers and she loved surprises, and he was starting to think that this was the best way to approach her. He lay there for a few more minutes until he heard WGCI playing Eric Benet's "Spend My Life with You," featuring Tamia. Samantha melted every time she heard it, and he had to admit that it made him feel a bit sentimental whenever he heard it as well. It made him think of her and how he didn't know if he really could live his life without her. He listened to Eric and Tamia until the song ended, and he decided at that moment that he had to see Samantha. He had to tell her how wrong he'd been, that he didn't want to lose her, and that if marrying her would make things right between them, that he was willing to do it.

He ran down to the flower shop and purchased a dozen red roses saturated with baby's breath and brought them back to his condo. Then he showered, threw on a pair of khaki shorts and a black polo shirt, and headed out the door. Samantha's sister didn't live more than ten miles away, and he drove in front of her apartment building before he knew it. He saw both their cars parked outside, picked up the vase of roses, and stepped out of his vehicle. When he had pushed the door shut, he turned and saw Samantha walking toward a two-seater red Mercedes which was parked next to hers. It looked like that arrogant Negro she used to date before she met him a couple of years ago. Rick could feel his blood boiling, because he'd known all along that there had to be someone else as soon as she'd moved out as quickly as she had.

He wanted to get back in his car and drive off with some dignity, but he decided instead to let her know why he'd come there armed with roses and the proposal she claimed she wanted so badly. That Negro she was about to go out with would never marry her, and Rick wanted her to know just what she was missing out on.

"So, is this why you wanted to move out?" he asked Samantha, walking toward the Mercedes.

Samantha turned toward him quickly, and he could tell he'd caught them both completely off guard.

"Rick, what are you doing here?" she asked.

"What the hell is *that* Negro doing here? Hell, we've been engaged for the last two years, and you want me to explain why I'm here to see you?"

"Rick, this isn't the time for this," she said, sounding as though she didn't know how to deal with his presence.

"Well, when will it be the right time? After you go out on your little date with this little stuck-up Negro, right here?"

"My name is Ron, and I would prefer for you to keep me out of this."

"I don't give a damn what you prefer, and if you don't like it, I suggest you take your happy ass somewhere else," Rick said.

"Rick, you are so wrong for doing this," Samantha said, sounding disgusted. "Ron, let's go," she said, and Ron opened the passenger door and waited for her to slide in.

"Oh, so you're just going to ignore me, huh?"

"I can't talk to you when you're like this, and I told you before that this is not the time, and it's certainly not the place."

"Yeah, all right. So, I guess these were just a waste of money," he said and smashed the glass vase against the brick building. A mixture of roses, water, and glass landed everywhere.

Samantha took cover, trying to avoid any flying glass. Ron stepped behind his car, trying to do the same thing.

"To think I came over here to propose to you. I must have been out of my freakin' mind," Rick said and walked back toward his truck.

Chapter 28

It had been one week since Phillip's arrest, and as expected, he was released on bail that same Monday after the hearing. But the good thing was, the judge had issued an order of protection for six months and Phillip hadn't tried to contact Gina since the day he'd come with the police to pack his clothing. He'd moved in with his mother, but Gina still couldn't believe he wasn't harassing her. Hadn't even tried to contact her by phone. Although something told her that this quiet attitude of his was the calm before the gigantic storm, because with Phillip, nothing was as easy as it seemed.

She'd taken a leave of absence from work because of the black eye and all the bruises she possessed, but her boss had informed her that he couldn't guarantee her position as director of MIS because they needed someone in that slot to carry on the department. She'd been crushed when he'd told her, but she did understand his predicament. He did tell her, though, to take all the time she needed, and that her old position would be waiting for her when she returned. She was thankful just to hear him say that, given the situation, but the thought of all the hard work she'd performed in an effort to climb her company's career ladder made her sick to her stomach. It made her loathe Phillip more than ever before.

Gina packed enough clothing for her and the children to last two days, since Sydney and Wesley were going to Lake Geneva for an overnight stay at one of the resorts. Delores seemed to be doing much better this past week, but they'd decided that it was still a good idea for someone to stay with her for a few more days. Gina was happy that she could finally help look after her, but Rick still wasn't coming around as often as he should. He'd been sort of withdrawn since he'd come by her house last Saturday, and she didn't know what was going on with him. She'd wanted to ask him when she'd called him at work two days ago, but he'd rushed her off the phone much too quickly.

"Mom, is Daddy ever coming back to live with us?" Caitlin asked, walking into her mother's room.

Gina didn't know how to answer her, because she'd already told her that he wasn't on three other occasions. Caitlin was having a very hard time dealing with her father's absence, and Gina could only hope that things would get better for her with time. Carl, on the other hand, seemed livelier and much happier, and she was glad that he, at least, was benefiting from this separation.

"Mom, is he?" Caitlin asked again.

"No, sweetheart. He's not. Mommy and Daddy can't live together anymore, so he's going to live in his own house, and you, Carl, and me are going to live here."

"But why won't he come see us?"

"We have to work some grown-up things out first, and then we'll see after that."

"Well, I want to see him," Caitlin said with tear-filled eyes.

Gina grabbed her daughter, hugged her, and they both sat down on Gina's bed. "I know you do, honey, and I'm sorry that you have to be without him."

"Be without who?" Carl asked, entering the room and zooming his toy airplane through the air like he was on top of the world.

"Be without Daddy," Caitlin whined to him.

"Because he doesn't treat Mom right," Carl told her. "I explained that to you last night, remember?" he said, obviously trying to figure out why his sister didn't get it.

"I know, but he said he didn't mean to hit Mom," Caitlin reminded him.

"Yeah, but then he always did it again," Carl reminded her.

Gina sat and listened, and while she wanted to comment, her eight-year-old son had summed it all up in a nutshell. She was amazed at how well he was dealing with the matter at hand, and he sounded more like he was eighteen instead of eight. She wished her daughter could see things the way he did as well.

"I'll bet he wouldn't do it again if you let him come back, Mom," Caitlin said, and Gina knew she wasn't going to let up. "Because when you punish me for doing bad things, I never do them again. And I don't think Daddy would either."

Gina sympathized with her daughter, and she wished there was something she could do to make things turn out the way she wanted, but it just wasn't possible. She and Phillip could never work, and it had taken her far too long to get out of this abusive situation ever to think about going back to it. She couldn't go back—not even for her heartbroken daughter.

"Honey, I know this is hard, but this is the way things have to be for us," Gina said, stroking Caitlin's hair.

"You said you wanted us to be happy, Caitlin, and now I'm real happy," Carl informed her.

"Well, I'm not," she told him.

"We just have to get used to all of this, and it will feel much better as time goes on," Gina assured her.

Caitlin didn't look too impressed, but she didn't say anything else.

Gina loaded their overnight bags into the car, and went back inside the house. The twins stepped into the garage, shut the door leading to the kitchen, and waited for her to set the alarm. She'd changed the security code a few days ago, and had to keep reminding herself of the new one every time she set it or had to disarm it. She debated whether she should have the locks on the outside doors changed as well, and she finally decided to do that, too. Just in case Phillip decided that he wanted to pay her a visit in the middle of the night while she was sleeping.

She reached her hand up to set the alarm, but stopped when she heard the phone ringing. She noticed her mother-in-law's phone number on the screen.

"Hello?" Gina answered.

"Yeah, Gina. This is Phillip's mother," Ms. Harris said, and Gina cringed at the sound of her voice. Her mother-in-law had never liked her very much, and it still irked Gina whenever she thought about the time her mother-in-law tried to justify Phillip's abusive behavior. She'd told Gina that Phillip would never have slapped her if she hadn't deserved it, and that she'd made that same mistake a number of times herself with his father—a father who Phillip hadn't heard from in over fifteen years. The woman was sick, and Gina was sorry that she'd allowed herself to become equally afflicted during the course of her marriage to Phillip.

"How are you?" Gina tried to be cordial.

"Fine. I'm callin' because Phillip is over here cryin'

his eyes out because you done put him out his house. And I wasn't gone just sit back and watch my baby in pain like this without callin' to tell you about yourself. You ought to be ashamed, and your mama should have raised you better than this."

Gina was going to hang up until she heard this woman mention her mother. "Look, Ms. Harris, I don't know what Phillip has told you, but you don't know the half of what your son has been doing to me, and I would appreciate it if you would leave my mother out of this conversation."

"Phillip ain't done nothin' to you that you ain't brought on yourself, so I don't wanna hear *nothin'* about what he been doin'."

"Ms. Harris," Gina said, trying to calm herself. "I don't want to argue with you, and I don't want to disrespect you, but I'm hanging up now."

"I wish you *would* hang up on me," Ms. Harris bellowed.

Gina threw the cordless phone on the base. That woman really got under her skin, and she couldn't believe she actually had the nerve to call her, trying to defend her terrible son. It was one thing for a mother to love her child unconditionally, but this was plain ridiculous.

Gina reached to set the alarm a second time, but the phone rang again.

"Hello?" she said, losing her patience.

"I know you think you're going to get away with this, but I've got news for you," Phillip said, and Gina had known it was just a matter of time before he called her or showed up in person.

"Phillip, you're not supposed to be calling here," she reminded him.

"What? Says who? Because I know you don't think that order of protection is going to keep me away from you. You belong to me, and you can get all the orders of protection and divorce papers you want, but in the eye-sight of God, you will always be my wife."

She wondered where he got that from, because for as long as she'd known him, he never read the Bible, and with the exception of his children's christenings, and baptisms, he'd never stepped foot inside a church. But he was no different than anyone else who finally decided to call on God when they were in trouble or wanted something very badly.

"Phillip, I'm hanging up now," she said and was proud that she was able to stand up to him.

"You already hung up on my mother, and I suggest you think twice before hanging up again. Because you're about to piss me off."

"Good-bye, Phillip," Gina said and rested the phone on the base again.

She had to admit that he did worry her to a certain extent, but she wasn't going to let him ruin the time she was getting ready to spend with her mother and children. She'd allowed him to do that on so many other occasions, and she wasn't going to do that any longer.

She set the alarm successfully this time, and headed out the door.

"It's so good to finally get away," Sydney said to Wesley as she unpacked her black garment bag. They'd just settled into their room in Lake Geneva and she wanted to hang her clothing before they left the room to go strolling around on the premises.

"Yeah, it is good to be here, because we are definitely long overdue."

"This thing with Mom has me so worried all the time, and I hate leaving her."

"That's understandable, and you don't have to feel bad about it."

"Well, at least Gina is able to be there with her now, and I'm glad Aunt Susan came this weekend, because I don't know if I would have felt comfortable leaving Victoria there with Mom by herself. It's one thing when we're only a few minutes away, but it's a little different being all the way up here. Because even though we're not that far away, it still would have made me nervous."

"Your mother is going to be fine. She's made some great improvements over the last couple of weeks, and she's doing almost everything for herself again."

"I know, but no matter how many times those doctors keep saying she's doing well, I still can't shake this feeling I keep telling you about. And then there's this thing with Gina. Phillip hasn't been bothering her yet, but as sure as I'm standing here, I know he's not going to just move on and live happily ever after without her. Not someone who's crazy like he is."

"I don't think he's going to leave it like this either, but if he violates that order of protection, they'll throw him in jail."

"Yeah, but I guess it bothers me, because I've really been trying to read more and more articles about women who have gone through what Gina's been dealing with. A lot of men end up killing their wives or girlfriends when they leave them, and now I understand why Gina was so afraid to leave Phillip. I never did before, but I've been surfing the Internet looking for information every day," Sydney said, pulling a document from her overnight bag. "This one I printed out, and it says that nearly one-fourth of all relationships include violence; that wife beating is the most common but least reported crime in the U.S., and that over forty percent of the women are killed by their husbands or partners, usually after having been abused by them for years," she said, scanning down the list. "And get this, up to one-half of all wives are beaten at least once by their husbands, and the violence usually becomes more frequent and severe over time."

"Really?" Wesley said, reaching for the document Sydney was reading from.

"It also says that it happens to people of all races, income, and educational levels, and that the victim may be silent because of embarrassment or shame," Sydney continued from memory. "And that's the thing that bothers me the most, because I was always pressing Gina to talk about it, and I used to get angry at her for not telling me what was going on, and you know I've told her more than once that I didn't understand how she could stay with Phillip with all the money she earns."

"Well, now you know," Wesley said and passed the document back to her.

Sydney tucked it inside the bag she'd taken it from, and sat down on the bed.

"What's wrong?" he asked her, sounding concerned.

"Nothing. I'm fine," she said, standing and walking into the bathroom, then closing the door behind her.

She covered her face with both hands and then moved them outward to the sides of her head, gazing into the mirror. She couldn't believe she'd gone all these years pretending like she'd had the perfect childhood, the same as every other fairy-tale daughter on TV. She really hadn't remembered for the first time until five years ago, and now she knew that it was in fact possible to repress terrible childhood events once they were over with. At least for a period of time, anyway. Most people didn't believe it was possible to forget such horrifying events, but she was now a living victim and truthfully hadn't remembered any of what had happened until right after her thirty-first birthday. But it was society's disbelief that had forced her to keep her secret to herself, because she knew she would never be able to bear any criticism or blame that might evolve from her family members or friends. It was one thing to endure such trauma, but to have someone insinuate that she was somehow at fault would be far too much to handle.

"Syd, what's wrong?" Wesley asked, opening the door to the bathroom.

Sydney turned to look at him, all the while sobbing and shaking her head. Then she slid down the side of the vanity onto the floor like a helpless child, emotionally torn apart.

"Baby, what's wrong?" Wesley said, pulling her back up to her feet and leading her out to the bed.

She hadn't planned on telling Wesley this weekend about the things she'd been remembering, but it just didn't seem fair to keep it from him any longer. She wanted them to enjoy their getaway at the resort, but he deserved to know what was bothering her. He deserved to know why her frigidness was putting a major damper on their sex life. She wasn't positively sure, but after interviewing that psychologist yesterday morning for the article she was preparing to write, she had a feeling she'd found the culprit, and she hadn't been able to think about much else ever since. She'd even spent a few hours on the Internet last night, searching for any and everything she could find on the subject, and the information she'd come across had confirmed what she was already thinking.

This was the most difficult thing she'd ever had to deal with, the worst thing she'd ever had to tell her husband, and the one and only thing she would never be able to tell her mother. Not because she wouldn't understand, but because it would kill her if she knew that the man she loved and married had fondled her oldest daughter every chance he got. She'd wondered about this a thousand times now, but she *still* couldn't believe it had taken her so long to remember it, even though everything she read insisted that adults who were sexually abused as children almost always blocked out those experiences, and that they usually blamed themselves even though they were never at fault.

"Talk to me, Sydney," Wesley said, caressing her back, trying to comfort her.

Sydney shook her head and held her hand on the side of her face in deep thought.

"Baby, you're making me nervous, now tell me what's going on," he asked her.

"This is so hard, and I'm so sorry for bringing this up," she said, staring at him, but then she looked away from him, feeling embarrassed.

Wesley didn't say anything, and she knew he wasn't going to press her about it anymore if she didn't want to tell him. It wasn't his style, and she knew that the best thing for her to do was spit it out before she lost the courage.

"My stepfather sexually abused me when I was a little girl," she said and felt her heart surpassing the normal beats per minute.

"What?" Wesley asked in total shock.

"You heard me. He sexually abused me, and all of a sudden I've been remembering all of it."

"Damn, Sydney. Baby, I am so sorry," he said, pulling her into his arms. "I am so, so sorry."

She hated shedding all of these tears, but it was sort of a relief, because until now, she hadn't been able to cry about any of this. She'd felt sad, angry, dirty, and unworthy, but she hadn't felt like crying. It seemed as though she should have, but she'd always felt more of a numbness than anything else.

Sydney breathed deeply. "I think that's why I feel the way I do about sex. I haven't been to a doctor, but when I interviewed that psychologist yesterday, she told me some of the possible reactions that come from adults who have gone through what I have, and not wanting sex is one of them. You know how sometimes when you touch me, I pull away?"

"Yeah."

"Well, sometimes when you do that, it makes my skin crawl. Not because I don't want you touching me, but because it makes me feel like you're trying to touch me in places that you shouldn't be. But then there are times when I love having you touch me, and I enjoy making love with you. I know it's confusing, but do you understand what I'm trying to say?"

"Yeah, I guess. Sort of," he said, and Sydney knew he was flabbergasted.

"I didn't want to have to tell you about this, but this thing with our sex life is getting progressively worse, and I had to."

"I know this is hard for you, but I have to know," he said.

"What?"

"Did he actually have sexual intercourse with you?"

"No. Not that I can remember, anyway. He would stick his hand down in my underwear and say that he was tickling me. We lived in a really big house, and I hated being in a room with him when nobody was around, or when Mom wasn't home. He used to make Gina and Rick go play when she would be gone, and he would tell me that I shouldn't tell anyone about what we did, because nobody would understand, and it would only cause a whole lot of problems for our family."

"That bastard," Wesley said angrily.

"I loved my father, too, because he was the only father that I ever really knew, and I can't believe he did that to me.

"I've often wondered if the same thing ever happened to Gina, but she's never talked about it before."

"Yeah, but you never talked about it before now either."

"I know, but maybe he did it to me because I wasn't his blood daughter."

"It doesn't matter, Sydney. You were still a child and that's all that matters. And I'm telling you, if your father was still alive, I would probably tear his head off," Wesley told her. "Because it takes a very sick individual to mess with children in that way."

"It's so hard to believe he did that to me, and I feel so ashamed," Sydney said, closing her eyes.

"Baby, you don't have to feel ashamed about anything. You didn't make him do that to you, and it wasn't your fault."

"It doesn't matter. I still feel like I did something terrible, and that's why I feel so bad about coming down on Gina all those times. Because I know how it feels to be violated and then feel all this shame."

"Are you going to tell your mother?"

"No. There's no way I could ever do that. She's going through so much, and it would only cause her a major setback."

"Yeah, I agree with you on that. But I am glad you told me."

"I'm going to make an appointment with the psychologist I interviewed, so I can go and talk with her."

"You should, because maybe it will help you get through this. And baby," he said apologetically. "I'm really sorry for getting so upset with you all the time, but I didn't know. I honestly thought that you just didn't have a desire to make love to me."

"You don't have anything to be sorry about either, because you had every right to think what you were thinking. It's not normal for a woman to love her husband as much as I love you, and not want to have sex. I knew something wasn't right, but I was thinking that maybe it was more of a medical problem instead of a mental one."

"You know I'll help you in any way I can."

"I know that, and I'm glad because, Wesley, I'm going to need you now more than ever before."

With the exception of his underwear, Wesley removed all of his clothing, and slid under the covers.

Sydney looked at him. "I'm sorry for ruining our trip."

"You didn't. Now come here," he said, reaching for her.

She slipped out of her sleeveless dress and climbed in next to him. Then she removed her underwear once she was under the sheet and comforter.

"What are you doing?" Wesley asked her.

"You know."

Wesley smiled at her. "That's not why I wanted you to get into bed. All I want to do is hold you."

"I thought we were going for a walk and then to get something to eat."

"Maybe later. But for now, let's just lie here."

Sydney leaned her head inside his arm and before long they both fell into a deep sleep.

Chapter 29

Gina dropped the children off at day camp two hours ago, and returned home so she could wash a few loads of clothes. She hadn't engaged in much housework over the last couple of weeks, but it had taken her that long just to try and adjust to her new lifestyle. Things were different now that Phillip was gone. It wasn't like he helped out around the house or like he brought great joy to her or the children, but it was different, because she no longer had to ask him how high whenever he told her to jump. She didn't have to answer to his every beck and call, and she didn't have to glance at her watch every minute, making sure she wasn't going to be late coming home. She could do what she wanted when she wanted, and it was a wonderful feeling. She felt so free, and her only regret was that she hadn't been able to leave Phillip before now.

She started the wash cycle, waited for the water to fill, poured in bleach and liquid Tide, and threw in a bunch of white garments. She walked out of the first-floor laundry room and sat down at the kitchen table to pay some bills. She was so glad that Phillip had at least allowed her to handle their finances. She didn't know why he'd given her control over something so important, but she suspected that it had a lot to do with the fact that he wasn't all that good with numbers, and she wasn't even sure he could write a personal check in the proper manner, because she'd never seen him do it. She'd suggested that he take a personal check to pay for his brake repair a few years ago, but he'd become angry and told her that he wanted her to go to the ATM machine to withdraw the cash instead.

They didn't have a ton of bills, but there was the mortgage, utilities, insurance, their car payments, two major credit cards, and cell phone usage that had to be paid for. Although, whether Phillip knew it or not, she wasn't making any more payments toward his BMW or his cell phone.

She scanned through her checking account register to make sure she'd transferred enough money from her personal savings account. She'd gone to the bank and withdrawn every dime from their joint accounts and then opened two brand new ones in her name only. She was sure that Phillip was going to flip over that as well, and while she knew she'd probably end up having to give him his share of it, she wasn't planning to do so until the judge ordered it. He'd told her that she was stupid on a more than frequent basis, but when it came to her financial stability, he was now going to see a different side of her. The side that looked out for herself and her children, but not too much else.

She pulled out a pad of paper and wrote the first item on her to-do list, which was to phone Sydney's hair stylist to see if she had availability. She'd never gone to a salon on a regular basis to get her hair done, because Phillip didn't see a reason for it. But now, she was planning to make a weekly, standing appointment. She'd decided to start having her nails manicured as well, and she made a note to schedule an appointment for that, too. She was completely on a roll, and it was a relief to know that she could finally live at least somewhat of a normal life. Whatever that was.

After the wash cycle had finished, she threw the load of clothes into the dryer, and came back to the kitchen to wash the dishes. They owned a dishwasher, but for some reason, she never liked using it. Just didn't feel as natural as washing them manually, she guessed. Her mother was the same way, and she knew that was probably who she'd inherited that idea from.

She wondered how her mother was doing. She'd called to check on her early this morning, and she was going to go visit her as soon as the clothes finished drying. She knew she could leave them there, but there were always fewer wrinkles to contend with whenever she hung her garments up as soon as the buzzer sounded.

She did a couple of other domestic chores, and after hanging the clothes, she took a shower, threw on a pair of jean shorts and a T-shirt, and headed out the door. But when she backed her car out of the driveway, she saw Phillip parked down the street watching her. Stalking her was more like it, and she didn't know whether she should drive away as planned or go back inside to call the police. She'd hoped the order of protection was going to keep him away from her, but he'd already violated it a couple of times with phone calls. That first time when he'd told her that they would always be married in the eyesight of God, and then this past weekend when he'd told her that he had no fear and no problem with going to jail on a charge of first-degree murder. She'd wanted to call the police then, but she knew she had to hold out until he did something in person. She didn't want to take the chance of allowing him to kill her, but she knew that his phone calls wouldn't be enough to put him away for life. She debated whether she should report his whereabouts now, but she knew he'd probably drive away before the police could get there. He was playing games with her, and she couldn't help but wonder when those games were going to become serious situations.

She decided to drive out of the subdivision in a different direction than where he was sitting. She glanced through her rearview mirror to see if he was following, but she never saw him move. She drove until she reached her mother's house, and when she arrived, she wondered why Phillip wasn't at work. But knowing him, he'd quit his job just so he could continue keeping tabs on her. If he had, she knew things were about to get out of hand, and it would finally be time to end all of this. For good.

"So, has Phillip been trying to contact you?" Sydney asked Gina. They were sitting in the family room with their mother, visiting, and Sydney was refilling her mother's pill container.

"He's called me a couple of times, but that's about it," she said, not wanting them to know that she'd just seen him parked barely a block from her house.

"Did you report it?" Delores asked.

"No, but if he calls again, I will."

"You should call them every time he calls or tries to come near you," Delores suggested.

"I know. I listed my address, yours, Sydney's, Rick's, and my employer's and he's not supposed to come near any of those places. He's not supposed to call any of the numbers I listed either," Gina said.

"How are the children doing?" Delores asked.

"Fine. Caitlin still misses her father, but Carl is happy that he's gone and never brings his name up."

"Caitlin will be okay," Delores told her.

"That's what I keep telling myself, and I hope she gets over this."

"So how long are you planning to be off work?" Sydney asked Gina.

"I don't know. I'm thinking maybe another month or so. I really need this time off to adjust and so that I can spend some time with myself. I haven't been able to do that in such a long time, and it feels really good."

"I can only imagine, and if I were you, I would take off as much time as I could," Delores said. "Because I'm telling you, whatever it is you want to do, you should go ahead and do it, before you end up like me."

Sydney looked at her mother and then back down toward her lap where the pill box was, but Gina spoke.

"Mom, why are you saying that? You're doing so much better now."

"Yeah, honey, but when they start messing around in your head, I don't think you can ever be completely right again. And don't get me wrong, I thank God for bringing me as far with this as He has, and I still believe that He can heal me if He wants to, but if it's not His will, then it's not going to be."

"But Mom, you shouldn't lose faith," Sydney finally said. "You've always had the strongest faith I've ever known."

"And I still do. I know what God can do, and I believe in Him more than ever before, but what I'm trying to get the two of you to understand is that it's not always what *we* want, but what *He* wants instead. Sometimes God has to move people who have their lives right, out of the way, so that He can bring others closer to Him. Leaving this world seems sad, but it's not a bad thing. And while I'm not saying that I'm getting ready to die next week, I want you to see that you have to enjoy life to the fullest, because you don't know if you'll be up or down by tomorrow evening."

Sydney and Gina were speechless.

"You don't have to be sad, because I'm ready for whatever His decision might be. I used to talk to God often, and I've always had a relationship with Him, but when He laid me flat on my back these last few weeks, I was able to talk to Him all day and all night. And He allowed me the chance to really get things right with my spirituality. It might sound funny, but my illness was a blessing. Everyone keeps saying, 'Why you?' and I keep telling them, 'Why not me?' Because what makes me so special that I shouldn't have to go through trials and tribulations? Then everyone wants to know why this happened to me at such a young age, and all I can do is smile and ask them if they'd rather I leave here now with my life right or stay here, get sidetracked, and take the chance of losing my soul at eighty?"

Sydney didn't know why her mother was telling them all of this. She was content with the fact that her mother was satisfied with living or dying, but she didn't know why she'd decided to have this conversation with them now. It was almost like she was trying to prepare them for the worst, and Sydney didn't like what she was hearing.

No one spoke, so Delores continued.

"I don't mean to depress you, but I needed to tell you girls how I feel. Because even if you can't see it now, one day all of this will help you stay strong. It will make all the difference in the world."

"Mom, you're going to be just fine," Gina said and walked over to the television like her mother didn't know what she was talking about. "They removed the majority of your tumor, it's not cancerous, and in a few months they're going to kill the rest of it with radiation."

"That's what we'll keep praying for," Delores told her.

"And that's what's going to happen," Gina said, and Sydney knew at that very moment that her sister was in straight denial. It happened all the time, and if something did happen to her mother, she knew Gina was going to be extremely devastated, because Phillip had kept her away from their mother the entire time they'd been married. Here she'd finally secured her freedom, and now their mother was talking as if she wasn't going to be with them for too much longer. Sydney couldn't say one way or the other, but the one thing she did know was that she'd just told Wesley this past weekend about this strange feeling she kept having regarding her mother's illness. Which wasn't a good sign, given the fact that she and her mother always thought on the same wavelength. She wasn't having any problems, and the doctors were still more than satisfied with her prognosis, but Sydney had learned a long time ago that this didn't mean anything.

She didn't want to think about any of this, because when she did, she found herself becoming angry with God. Her mother had taught her never to feel that way, but she couldn't help herself. She wanted to know why this had to happen to her mother, and she wanted God to give her some answers at this very moment. She wasn't in denial like Gina, but she didn't want her mother to pass away either. They did so many things together, and she wondered who she was going to watch *Lifetime* movies with on the phone, because it had become routine for one of them to call the other, and then remain on the phone for two hours until the movie was over with, talking only during commercial breaks. Although they did make a few comments during the movie if something dramatic happened, but that was about it. Who was going to cook huge, tasteful Thanksgiving and Christmas dinners? Who was going to shop with her at the mall when she needed to find a specific suit for one of her writing assignments? Who was going to become the peacemaker in the family? But most of all, who was going to love her unconditionally without an ounce of judgment? She knew that Wesley loved her, and that her daughter did, too, but the love she received from her mother was something very different. Something that no other love could ever compare to, and couldn't even come close.

"So, where's Victoria?" Gina asked, trying to change the subject.

"She and some of her school friends went over to the water park for the day," Sydney answered.

"Sounds like a good idea, because it must be ninety degrees already."

"It used to be that August was the hottest month, but now July is just as bad," Sydney said.

"You can't tell spring from summer from fall from winter anymore," Delores commented.

"No, you really can't," Gina agreed and heard her cell phone ringing. "I wonder who that could be," she said, frowning.

"Hello?"

"Hey, I picked the kids up early from day camp, and they're sitting outside with me in front of your mother's house right now," Phillip boasted.

Gina felt like she was going to pass out. Especially since she'd informed the camp coordinators about the order of protection against Phillip and had told them to phone her if he showed up there. "You what? Why?" she spoke loudly.

Sydney and Delores stared at her with much concern on their faces.

"Why?" He laughed sarcastically. "Because I felt like it, that's why."

"Phillip, why are you doing this?"

"Why am I doing what?"

"Why are you involving the children in this?"

"You involved them as soon as you decided to have me arrested," he said, sounding upset.

"Just let them come in the house," Gina pleaded.

"I'll do whatever you want, but I'm begging you, please let them out of the car."

"Maybe. But maybe I'll just take them with me far away from here, and you'll never get to see them again."

"Phillip, no. Please don't do that. Please," she said, walking into the living room to look outside her mother's window. But she didn't see his car. Sydney and Delores followed behind her.

"Where are you at, Phillip, because I don't see you," she asked.

Phillip laughed wildly. "I got your ass good, didn't I? Huh?" he said and wasn't laughing any longer. "Carl and Caitlin are fine, but I just thought I'd let you know that you're not runnin' anything, and if you even think about filing for a divorce, I'll make damn sure that you never hear from or see those twins ever again. Now, if you think this is a joke, just try me."

Gina hung up the phone.

"What did he want?" Sydney asked her sister. "And why were you looking out of the window?"

"He said that he'd picked the twins up, and that he had them outside in the car. But then he told me that he didn't, and that I'd better not try to divorce him," Gina said, dialing the park district so she could speak to one of the day camp coordinators.

"Hello, this is Gina Harris, and I just wanted to let you know that we have a family emergency, and that I'm on my way to pick up Carl and Caitlin," Gina said nervously.

"No problem, we'll have them ready to go when you get here," the woman on the other end told her.

Gina hung up, grabbed her keys and purse, and headed toward the door.

"Gina, you've got to do something about Phillip, and if I were you, I'd call the police as soon as you pick those children up," Sydney said.

"Lord, Lord, Lord," Delores said. "Please help my

child get out of this mess," she prayed and walked through the hallway to her bedroom.

"I'll see you later, Sydney, and tell Mom I'm sorry about all of this," Gina said.

"You just go get those children, and call the police," Sydney said. "And you call me if you need anything."

"I will," Gina said and walked out the door.

Chapter 30

R ick walked into his condo and fell across the sofa. The central air felt good, and he couldn't believe it was after seven-thirty and the temperature outside was still right at eighty. He'd stopped by the health club to work out, and now he was completely exhausted. He'd been working out every single day since that night he'd caught Samantha with her ex-boyfriend, trying to burn off his many frustrations. She'd been calling and leaving messages on a daily basis, but he hadn't bothered to answer even one of them. He despised her for treating him the way she had, and he could still kick himself for actually buying her flowers and making the decision to ask her to marry him. Not to mention the fact that he'd told her all about it right in front of that Negro, Ron. They'd probably laughed at him for the rest of the evening, because he made the mistake of letting them know just how hurt he was. He didn't know why he'd reacted the way he had, because the last thing he wanted to do was punk out in front of another man. Especially a man who had taken the love of his life away from him. He hadn't even known that Samantha and Ron still communicated, but it just went to show that women were straight-up sneaky with their shit, and that if they wanted to get away with something, they were certainly crafty enough to do it. Here he'd been thinking that Samantha loved him more than life itself, and now she was seeing another man like their relationship hadn't mattered to her one bit.

He hated women, and he was never going to allow himself to fall in love with any others. Samantha had ruined everything for him and any other woman he would date in the future, because now he wasn't going to show any dedication to anyone except himself.

He lifted his body from the sofa, and went into the kitchen to see if he had any voice mail messages, and he did.

He entered his pin number and the computer-generated voice told him that he had three messages. He played the first one.

"Hey, Rick, man, you won't believe this shit, but I think that bitch Matrice gave me somethin', because every time I take a leak, I feel like screamin'. Give me a ring when you get in. Damn," Brent said and hung up. Rick couldn't help but laugh, and now he knew why Brent hadn't been at work today.

Rick deleted the first message and waited to hear the second.

"Rick, call me when you get in," Sydney said. "Something has to be done about Phillip, because now he's threatening to take those children away from Gina. She looked like she really thought he would do it, too, and we can't take any chances with that. I'll be up late, so call me as soon as you can. Bye."

Damn. Rick couldn't believe that Phillip was still acting a complete fool, and he was willing to bet that Gina hadn't called the police to report these phone calls a single time. He'd had about as much of this as he could take, and tomorrow he was going to confront Phillip face to face. Even if it meant going over to his mother's house and calling him outside.

Rick deleted Sydney's message too, and played the third one.

"Rick, honey. Why won't you return my phone calls? I really need to talk to you about last Saturday night. It wasn't what you thought, and all I'm asking is that you give me a chance to explain. I've been leaving messages for you at work, and I know you've been getting them. I'll be home for the rest of the evening, and I hope you'll give me a call. And Rick, regardless of what you think, I do still love you," Samantha said and hung up.

Rick played the message again, and then saved it. He didn't know why really, because he wasn't about to call her back. She'd made her decision to see someone else, had gotten caught, and now she wanted him to pretend like none of this had happened. He loved her too, but this thing they'd had between them was over with.

He ran upstairs, turned on the water, and took a shower. Then he dried himself off, and threw on a pair of shorts. He thought about calling Brent, but he decided to call Sydney first.

"Hello?" Wesley answered.

"Hey, man, what's goin' on?" Rick asked him.

"Not much, man. What's up with you?"

"Work, and that's about it."

"I hear you. You lookin' for Sydney?"

"Yeah, I'm returning her call."

"Hold on a second," Wesley said and Rick heard him calling her. Then he heard him tell her who was on the phone.

"Hey, Rick," Sydney greeted him.

"Hey, what's up?"

"What isn't? Phillip is acting crazy again, and I'm afraid he's going to do something stupid."

"Where's Gina now? She's at home, but you know I'm worried to death about what Phillip might try to do. He's like a time bomb waiting to go off, and I don't think Gina is taking any of it all that serious."

"She just doesn't get it, does she?" Rick complained.

"No, I don't think she does, but I was wondering if maybe you could go spend the night with her and the twins?"

"Yeah, it's probably best if I do, because I guarantee you, if he sees my truck in the driveway, he won't try to mess with her."

"That's what I was thinking, because Phillip is no different than any other wife beater. He has no problem beating a woman, but he's all talk when it comes to dealing with a man."

"He's a trip," Rick said.

"Tell me about it. He called her on her cell phone while we were sitting over at Mom's and told her that he had picked the children up early from day camp, and that they were sitting outside with him in the car. But when she went to look, he wasn't there. He was just playing head games with her, but he did tell her that if she tries to divorce him, that she will never see those twins again."

"I wish he *would* take those kids away from here," Rick said matter-of-factly. "See the problem is that we've all stood by and let this go on for too long, and Phillip thinks he can get away with whatever he wants."

"Well, at least he's finally out of the house," Sydney said.

"But he's not going to leave her alone until somebody gives him the ass-kickin' of a lifetime."

"I think you're right about that, but I don't want you to get into trouble."

"Don't even worry about it, there're ways to take care of Phillip, and I won't even have to touch him," Rick said confidently.

"You be careful," Sydney said worriedly. "Because we've got enough going on with Mom and Gina. The last thing I need is to be worried about you, too."

"I told you not to worry. I'm not talking about killing him, I just want to make sure he ends up with just as many bruises as he gave Gina. And I can think of a few high school friends who would be glad to take care of it."

"I don't know, Rick," Sydney said, wondering if she'd made a mistake by calling him. She'd been so upset this afternoon, but now that she'd had some time to calm down, she was thinking much more rationally.

"Hey, how is Mom?" he said, switching the conversation.

"She's doing okay. When Gina and I were over there, she was saying how we'd better do some of the things we want to do before we end up like her, and then she talked about how she's got her life right with God, and how she will accept whatever His will is."

Rick was silent for a moment. "Why was she talking like that?"

"I don't know, but if you can, you need to go and see her, Rick. I know you don't like me telling you what to do, but I don't think it's a good thing that she's talking this way."

"Nothing has happened since the last time you took her up to Madison, has it?"

"No, but for some reason she brought that conversation up. So, I don't know," Sydney said, sighing.

"I'll go see her tomorrow as soon as I leave work," Rick said, and for the first time he didn't feel like Sydney was trying to control him. She sounded more concerned than he'd heard her sound since the day their mother had passed out at the party and then had to have surgery a few days later. He didn't want to think about any of this right now, though, and it was time for him to hang up.

"Hey, sis. Let me get dressed so I can get out of here and head over to Gina's."

"Are you going to call her to let her know that you're coming?"

"No, because you know she's going to tell me that I don't need to come."

"That's true. Well, call me if you need to," Sydney said, "and maybe I'll see you over at Mom's tomorrow."

"See you then," he said.

He brushed his hair, threw on a T-shirt and a pair of rubber slides. Then he tossed a few toiletries into an overnight bag. That way, he could shower at Gina's and then all he'd have to do in the morning was run home real quick to get dressed for work.

He walked downstairs, but just as he went to grab his keys, the doorbell rang. He opened the door and was surprised to see Samantha standing on his doorstep.

"Can I come in?" she asked.

He wanted to tell her no, but he figured it was better to get this conversation over with, so he dropped his bag on the floor and moved to the side, so she could walk in.

"Did I catch you at a bad time?" she said, dropping her purse down on the table, and looking at his nylon bag.

"As a matter of fact, I was on my way out," he said and didn't see a reason to tell her that he was on his way over to his sister's.

"Well, this won't take that long, so can we sit down for a minute?"

"Talk," Rick told her unenthusiastically. Then he sat

down at the opposite end of the sofa from where she was standing.

She sat down and locked her fingers together. "I know you're upset with me, but it's like I told you in the message, it's not what you think," she said, and he could tell she was waiting for him to respond, but he didn't.

"I saw Ron when my sister and I went out, he asked if he could call me sometime, and I told him yes. And when he called, he asked me out to dinner," she said, pausing, and Rick couldn't believe she still expected him to say something. When he didn't, she continued.

"There's nothing going on with Ron and me. We went out, and that was it."

Rick looked at her and then at his watch.

"Rick, why are you acting like this? And why won't you say anything?"

"There's nothing *to* say," he finally said. "You are your own woman, and you don't have to explain anything to me. You have a right to date whomever you want to, and I wish you all the best."

"You're blowing this whole thing out of proportion," she said.

"I'm not blowing anything out of anywhere, because I didn't see you telling Ron to leave when I came over there, and I definitely don't remember you trying to explain the situation to me the way you are right now."

"Because it wasn't right for you to come over there going off like you were."

"Whatever," Rick said and looked away from her.

"So, that's all you have to say?" she asked.

"What do you want to hear?" he said angrily. "That I'm in love with you? That I can't live without you? And that I was jealous as hell because you went out with another man?"

"It would be a start," she said, smirking.

"You think this shit is funny, don't you?" he said,

standing up and walking over to the kitchen as if he had a reason to go in there.

"No, I don't, but I'm just trying to get you to see that I don't want Ron. I've always loved *you,* and there's not another man on this earth who can change that."

He hated when she told him that she loved him, because it always made him weak. He'd felt this same way when he'd heard her say it on the message, which was why he'd played it a second time. But it was always worse when she said it in person.

"Did you mean what you said when you came over that night?" she asked.

"Did I mean what?"

"You know, when you said you were going to ask me to marry you?"

"It really doesn't matter," he said, walking over to the love seat, because he could tell that even though he'd been sitting at the opposite end of her on the sofa, it was still too close for comfort.

"It matters to me," she said, "because marriage is the reason why we split up in the first place."

"If it mattered so much, then why did you go out on a date so quickly?"

"I was hurt, Rick. And I was tired of sitting at home all alone hoping that you would change your mind and set a wedding date. You never did. You wanted us to see each other like we were dating again, and I couldn't do that. But deep down, you have to know how much I wanted to be with you."

"Yeah, but you couldn't even come to my sister's house to see my mom like you said."

"Because, Rick, I knew that one thing was going to lead to another, and then we were going to end up back at your place. I wasn't strong enough to see you on a platonic basis, and I knew you were counting on that."

He had to admit that he had been, but there was no reason to reveal his thinking to her.

"Well, what's done is done," he said. "And it's like I said before, I wish you all the best with whomever you end up being with."

"I don't believe this," she said. "All because I went out on one little date?"

"No, it's not just that," Rick said. "Girl, I came over there ready to pour my heart out to you with flowers and a proposal, and all you did was tell me that that wasn't the time or the place. I don't know if you were just trying to put on a show in front of that Negro or not, but I didn't appreciate the way you treated me."

"You're right, and I apologize for that. But you seemed so angry."

"Damn right I was angry. Hell, how do you think I felt watching you get into someone else's car all dressed up like you were about to have the time of your life? If you'd seen me with someone, you would have had a fit, too, and you know it."

"Not if I knew for sure that you didn't care anything about her."

"Samantha, please. You can save that conversation for some knucklehead, because you know good and well if you'd seen me with another woman, you would have lost your natural mind."

She laughed.

Rick still didn't see anything funny, and he gave her a dirty look.

"Okay, okay, I'm sorry," she said, leaving her end of the sofa and moving over to where he was sitting. "But you know I love you, right?" she said, sitting on his lap.

"Whatever," he said, looking away from her.

"Sweetheart, don't be mad at me," she said, wrapping her arms around his neck.

He wished she hadn't sat on his lap this way, because it was becoming more and more difficult for him to stay angry with her. He felt his stomach fluttering, the same as he always did whenever she got to him emotionally. He'd wanted to brush her off and head over to Gina's, but he could already see how hard it was going to be.

"Rick. Baby. Look at me," she said, moving his face toward hers so that they made perfect eye contact. "I made a mistake, but I promise you, the whole time I was with him, I wanted to be with you. Look, I've never even taken off my ring—not even that night," she said, showing him the engagement ring he'd given her. "I guess I wanted to go out with anyone, hoping that it would take my mind off you, but it didn't work. I love you so much, and this separation between us has practically torn me apart. My heart aches every time I think of you, and moving my things out of here was the hardest thing I ever had to do."

"But you kept saying that you were going to be fine whether we stayed together or not. And to me, that sounded like you didn't care one way or the other."

"But I've always cared, and I never stopped. My love for you goes much deeper than you even realize," she said, caressing the side of his face.

Rick stared at her and she leaned forward to kiss him. Their lips met, and they kissed passionately, but in a very hungry sort of way. They kissed for a long while, and they were both completely out of breath when they finally stopped for air.

"Damn, girl. I missed you so much," he said, wiping tears from each of her cheeks with both his hands.

"I missed you, too," she said, wiping tears from his face as well.

"I don't ever want us to be apart again," he said, motioning for her to stand up. When she did, he moved from the sofa onto the floor and steadied himself on one knee.

"Girl, I love you more than anything in this world,

and if you still want to be my wife, then I'm asking you, right now, to marry me," he said, pulling her engagement ring from her finger and holding her hand.

She was too emotional to answer him, and her face was now soaking wet.

"C'mon, baby," he said, smiling at her. "You've wanted this for a long time, so what is it gonna be?"

Her body jerked with every sniffle, and she still couldn't speak.

"I'm waiting," he sang.

"Yes . . . yes . . . yes," she said finally, and Rick pushed the ring back on her finger, then stood up.

"It took you long enough," he said humorously and pulled her body close to his. She rested her head against his chest.

"Rick, I will be the best wife you could have ever hoped for, and I'll be dedicated to you until one of us leaves this earth."

"And I'm going to take care of you to the best of my ability, Samantha. I promise you that, and I will always be here for you."

They held each other close, enjoying the moment.

"Baby, I hate to break the mood, but I promised Sydney that I would go spend the night at Gina's, because Phillip has been threatening her again. That's where I was going when you stopped by."

"Do you want me to go with you?" she asked.

"If you don't mind, because I really want to spend some more time with you. What I really want to do is make love to you all night long, but I just can't leave my sister hanging like that," he said apologetically.

"And I don't want you to, so let's go," she said. "I'll drive my car over too, so I can leave from there to go home a little later," she said, walking over to pick up her purse.

"Come back here," Rick ordered her.

"What?" she answered, blushing.

He pulled her into his arms. "I must have been crazy to let a woman like you pack up and leave me."

"All that matters now is we're back together, and we're always going to be together."

"And rightfully so," he said.

Chapter 31

"Rick, are you up?" Gina asked, knocking on the door of the guest bedroom where her brother was sleeping. "It's five o'clock."

"Yeah, yeah, yeah," he groaned.

"Don't be complaining to me, because I didn't tell you to stay up until the wee hours of the morning," she said amusingly. "What time did Samantha leave anyway?"

"I don't know. I guess maybe about one or so."

"Well, no wonder you're so sleepy. But you had something real important to celebrate, I guess, huh?"

"Yeah, we did."

"I know I told you when you got here, but I'm really happy that you finally decided to marry Samantha."

Rick opened the door. "Yeah, I am, too. Because all I know is that life would never be right if she wasn't a part of it."

"Is this Rick Mathis I'm talking to?" Gina teased.

"Shut up, girl, and get out of my way, so I can go take my shower," he said, smiling, then yawning.

"You'd better hurry up if you still have to go home to get dressed."

"Yeah, I know," he said, walking toward the bathroom.

"Do you want me to fix you something to eat real quick?"

"No. I don't usually do breakfast, but thanks anyway."

"Well, I'll be downstairs if you need anything, and I already put you some towels out on the vanity."

"That'll work. And hey. You didn't get any phone calls last night, did you?" Rick asked.

"No, but there's no telling what will happen today, especially if he drove by and saw your truck here last night."

"If he does harass you again, you have got to call the police this time."

"I know, and I will. I promise," she said and walked down the stairway.

Rick shut the door, showered, and then went downstairs as well.

"Hey, you take care of yourself, okay, and you make sure you call me at work if you need me," Rick said, hugging his sister. Then he kissed her on the forehead.

"I will, and Rick, no matter what happens, I want you to know that I am so happy for you and Samantha, and that I love you so much," Gina said, hugging him again.

"Whoa. What's all this for?" he said, looking confused.

"I just want you to know how much I care about you, that's all," she said.

"You are okay, aren't you? Because I can call in to work if you need me to," he said.

"I'm fine," she told him. "Now get out of here before you end up being late."

"Okay, but promise me that you'll call the police if Phillip as much as dials this phone number and hangs up."

"I will. Now go," she said, smiling.

He left, and Gina shut the door behind him. She picked up a little around the house, and did a few other things that she'd been putting off, and then she woke the children up at seven.

"Mom, I don't want to wear these red shorts to day camp," Caitlin told her when she saw what her mother had laid out for her.

"You and Carl aren't going to camp today. You're going over to Granny's instead," Gina informed her.

"Yippy," Caitlin said, running out of her room and into her brother's. Gina could hear her telling him the news, and it was obvious that he was just as happy as she was.

Gina took a shower and got dressed, and drove the children over to her mother's. As always, her mother was elated to see them.

"Hey," Delores said when she opened the door.

"Hey, Mom," Gina said.

"Hi, Granny," Caitlin said and then Carl spoke to his grandmother as well.

"Is Victoria here?" Gina asked.

"Uh-huh. She's still asleep, though. I think she watched TV practically all night long."

"I'm sure she did. Well, if you don't need me to do anything, I'm going to head back home, so I can get a couple of things done."

"That's fine. I'm just glad you called last night and said you wanted the twins to stay over here today, because you know I love it when they stay over here. And I thought I would die when Rick and Samantha got on the phone and told me they were getting married. I'm so excited."

"I know, it's long overdue."

"That it is," Delores said happily.

"Well, you all have a good time," Gina said.

"We always have a good time with Granny," Carl let her know.

"Yep," Caitlin agreed.

"Give Mom a hug," she said, leaning forward to hug both of them at the same time. "I love both of you so much, and even though this has been a hard time for all of us, I want you to remember that Mom loves you, no matter what, okay?"

"Yes," they both said, and Gina kissed both of them on the cheek.

"And Mom, I love you, too. I know I haven't been here as often as I should, but I never loved you any less when I wasn't."

"Honey, I know that. Now go on and do what you have to do. Go shopping if you have some time. Enjoy yourself, because these children are going to be just fine," Delores said.

"Thanks, Mom, and I'll see you later." Gina hugged her mother and walked out to her car.

She'd barely been able to look her mother and children in their faces, but she'd managed to say good-bye in a very discreet manner. She had to make sure that they knew how much she loved them, and she needed to tell Sydney how much she loved her as well. She dialed her sister's number and fought back tears.

"Hello?" Sydney answered.

"Hey," Gina said.

"Are you okay?" Sydney said, sounding alarmed.

"Don't get upset. I'm fine. I just dropped the children off at Mom's so they can spend the day with her, and now I'm feeling a little sentimental is all."

"Oh. Did everything go okay last night?"

"Yes, it did. Samantha stayed over pretty late, and Rick left for work when he woke up this morning."

"I was so shocked when they called saying that they were finally getting married."

"I know. I think we all were caught off guard, but Samantha will be good for him."

"There's no doubt about it."

"Well, I just wanted to thank you for always being here for me and for standing by me that day when Phillip was arrested. I know I've told you this a couple of times already, but I don't know what I would have done without you that evening."

"And I've told you that you don't owe me anything for that. You're my sister, and I was supposed to be there for you."

"I know, but I just wanted to tell you how much I love you, and that your love has meant everything to me."

"You know I feel the same way," Sydney said.

"Well, I'm on my way home, but maybe I'll see you later on today."

"Yeah, I'll probably see you when you pick up Carl and Caitlin."

"Talk to you then," Gina said.

"See ya."

Gina drove by instinct, and before she realized it, she was pulling into her driveway. She'd found herself in deep thought the entire ride, but now she had no doubt that she was doing the right thing. She'd gone back and forth, trying to weigh her options, but now she was one hundred percent sure of what she had to do. It was dreadful, but it was the only way things could work out for her children. She'd wanted to put this day off for as long as she could, but now Phillip was threatening to take the children away, and she wasn't going to stand by and let him get away with it.

She entered the house, arranged things the way she needed them to be, and then she turned on the television. When she flipped to *The Today Show,* she sat the remote down on the sofa next to her. She watched portions of the show, then she turned the TV to a weight loss infomercial and finally to QVC to see what they were showcasing.

Then the phone rang as expected.

"Hello?" Gina answered.

"You think you're so smart, don't you?" Phillip said.

"I don't know what you're talking about," she said, playing dumb.

"I followed you all the way over to your mother's house, and if you think you can keep me away from my kids, you've got another thing coming."

"What do you want, Phillip?"

"Why, you got some company you need to tend to?"

"That's exactly what I've got, and if you're not calling for anything important, then I'm going to let you go."

"There's nobody there with you, Gina, so stop acting stupid," he said, but Gina knew she'd riled his attention.

"Believe what you want to."

"I watched you walk back in the house not too long ago, and I've been sitting down the street ever since. So, I don't know who you think you're fooling."

"I'm not trying to fool anybody. I left Michael here when I went to take the children over to my mother's," she said, telling the biggest lie yet.

"Please. So, now you're going to try and make me think that somebody spent the night with you. Yeah, right."

"Somebody did."

"Like who, your brother and his girlfriend?"

"Yeah, but Michael was here before they even got here."

"Stop playing with me, Gina," he said irately.

"I'm not playing. You've controlled my life ever since the day I met you," she said, raising her voice. "I've been tired of hiding my relationship with Michael for a long time, but guess what, now I don't have to hide it anymore."

"Michael who?"

"The same Michael who fronted you at that scholarship dinner a few months ago. That's who. Yeah, that's right," she boasted. "The Michael that I work with."

"You stupid ass, crazy ass, bitch," Phillip said in an uproar. "You better be lying, because if you're not, you won't live to see another day."

"Yeah, yeah, yeah, Phillip. Anything you say, but I'm not afraid of you anymore."

"Hmmph. You'd better be."

"Well, I'm not, and I'll tell you another thing. Every time you forced yourself on me, the only way I got through it was by pretending that you were Michael the entire time."

Gina heard a loud thud at the front door and pressed the flash button on her phone. Then she dialed 911.

"911, what's your emergency?"

"My husband is trying to break my front door down, and I have an order of protection against him."

"Can you get out of the house?"

"Oh, my God, *no*," Gina screamed when she heard glass shattering and dropped the phone.

"Bitch, I'm going to kill you," Phillip yelled when he saw her running toward the kitchen.

"Phillip, you're not supposed to be here," she told him, fumbling to open the cabinet drawer next to the refrigerator.

"This is my house, and if I can't live here, nobody will. I told you that I would see you dead before I see you with another man, and I meant that," he said, moving closer to her with fire in his eyes.

But she pulled the revolver out of the drawer and pointed it at him. "Don't come any closer, Phillip," she said, breathing hard and heavy and moving farther into the corner near the sink.

"You stupid bitch. I took the bullets out of that a long time ago," he said, pulling an enormous knife from the cutlery set on the counter. "And now, I'm going to slit your fucking throat for playing with me," he said, charging toward her.

Gina pressed the lever and fired the gun. Phillip bugged his eyes, and dropped the knife on the floor. Gina shot him again. She saw him make a step in her direction, so she shot him a third time. And then a fourth.

Until finally, Phillip fell to the ground in cold blood.

Gina stood there in a daze and didn't move. She didn't know how long she'd been standing there, but she felt the officer pulling the gun away from her hand.

She gazed down at Phillip and then back at the officers. She heard siren after siren, and it wasn't long before she saw a mob of people spreading throughout her house. They asked her question after question, but she didn't have any answers.

She didn't have any answers, because she didn't want to incriminate herself. Especially since everything had turned out exactly the way she'd planned it.

Not ever in Gina's wildest imagination did she think she'd end up sitting in a police department going through interrogations because she'd killed her own husband. The detectives hadn't arrested her, but they'd brought her down to the station for questioning nonetheless. They'd asked her the same questions over and over again, and there was a point when she'd started to think that they were going to book her on a murder charge.

However, when it was all said and done, they'd finally told her she could go, but that they might need to question her again in the near future.

But it wasn't like they didn't believe her story, and she knew they were only doing their jobs. And rightfully so, because a man was actually dead. What had saved her, though, was the fact that Phillip had beaten her to no end the night she'd had him arrested, she'd had Sydney take pictures of every bruise, and the hospital had documented every injury. Then, it had been a blessing that Phillip had told Wesley to "tell that bitch that I'm gonna kill her the next time I see her" right in the presence of the arresting officers. But nothing could compare to Phillip throwing a huge rock through the living room picture window, entering the house, and violating the order of protection that the judge had granted her. Then he'd ranted and raved a number of obscenities, vowed that he was going to kill her, and then yelled that he was going to do it by slitting her throat—all of which the police had confirmed when they listened to the 911 tape.

The police had wanted to know why he'd gone as far as breaking into the house, and she told them that he'd been stalking her for the last few days, and that somehow he'd fabricated this idea that she had a man in the house with her. Which was partially true, but what the police didn't know was that he hadn't fabricated a thing, and that the reason he'd thought a man was in the house was because Gina had insisted there was.

Then they'd asked her why she'd kept a loaded gun in the kitchen drawer, since it obviously wasn't a very smart thing to do when there were children in the household. But she told them that Phillip had threatened her so regularly, that she started keeping it in the kitchen during the day when Carl and Caitlin were gone, and that she kept it in her nightstand when she went to bed in the evening.

Which brought them to the question regarding her children's whereabouts, wanting to know where they usually went during the day, so she told them that they went to a day camp. But then they'd wanted to know why she'd taken them to her mother's house on this particular morning instead. She felt a bit uneasy, because it was the one track she hadn't thought to cover. But she told them about Phillip's call to her just the day before, claiming that he'd picked the children up and taken them away. She told the police how she'd been afraid he really would do just that, and she'd thought it was better to take the children over to her mother's, where they'd be safe.

But then, they'd wanted to know why she'd taken them over to her mother's so early if she was on a leave of absence from work, and that's when she was sure her story was going to fall apart. She couldn't think of a lie, so she had no choice but to tell them the truth, and hope for the best. She told them that her mother enjoyed spending time with the twins, but that Phillip hadn't allowed her or the children to visit her that often. She went on to tell them about her mother's brain tumor, and how she'd decided that she was going to take Carl and Caitlin to see their grandmother as often as she could from here on out, trying to make up for lost time. She explained how she always took them to day camp early in the morning, and when her mother had told her the night before that she was going to fix them breakfast—something she'd just started doing again—Gina had told her that she'd bring them over at the same time she usually took them to camp.

She hadn't been sure if they'd bought any of what she'd said or not, until the detective had apologized for everything she'd been through in her marriage, and then told her she could go.

Sydney, Wesley, Rick, and Samantha had been waiting outside for her, and the children and Victoria had stayed home with Delores. Now, Gina was there as well, resting in the guest bedroom. She'd sat down with the twins to tell them that their father was gone and that he wasn't coming back, but she wasn't sure if they really understood that he was dead. She knew she'd eventually have to explain his absence with more detail, but it was better to sit down with them tomorrow, when she was thinking more clearly, and hopefully when her head wouldn't be pounding so profusely.

She lay there thinking a thousand what-ifs. What if she hadn't dated Phillip? What if she hadn't married him? What if she'd gotten out before the beatings became so severe? What if she'd just moved away so he couldn't find them? What if there was another way she could have handled this without actually killing him? She tried to weigh everything out, but she knew there hadn't been any other way to deal with this, because if she hadn't killed him, he was certainly destined to kill her. He'd warned her on a continual basis, and the moment she'd seen him coming toward her with a butcher knife, she'd known for sure that he had no problem taking her life.

She thought about a few other what-ifs, until she thought about the greatest one of all: What if Phillip hadn't been bluffing, and he really had taken the bullets out of the gun?

She'd planned everything like a complete science, but it wasn't like she'd checked to see if the gun was actually loaded. She assumed that it was, when she pulled it from their bedroom closet and brought it down to the kitchen. But now she knew that her carelessness could have been her ultimate demise.

Because right now, she could have been a dead woman.

Chapter 32

"I never would have thought that it would come to anything like this," Sydney said to her mother. Everyone had finally gone home last night around eleven, it was now seven the next morning, and Sydney was already back at her mother's. Gina was still in bed upstairs, and the twins and Victoria were still sound asleep.

"I can't believe it myself," Delores said, preparing to drink the decaf coffee she'd just brewed.

"There was a time when I was worried about Gina committing suicide or Phillip killing *her,* but never did I think she'd end up killing *him.*"

"No, neither did I, but when there's a crazy person like Phillip involved, anything is possible," Delores said.

"First Gina spends all these years being abused, and now she has to live with this. I feel so sorry for her, and

I wish there was something I could have done to help her."

"There wasn't anything any of us could have done, because now we know that if she hadn't shot him, Phillip really did mean to kill her yesterday morning. There's no doubt in my mind at all."

"Yeah, but it's almost like she had a feeling something was going to happen, because out of the blue, she called me on the phone to thank me for being here for her and to tell me that she loved me," Sydney said, spreading cream cheese on her bagel. "And Rick was saying how he thought she was acting sort of funny when he left her house yesterday for work."

"Sometimes people can sense when something bad is going to happen, and maybe Gina just knew. She was so afraid of him, and I'm glad she had that gun where she could get to it," Delores said.

"I am, too. I'm not glad that she had to take his life, but if it had to be his or hers, I'm glad it turned out the way it did."

"I'm glad it's over with, so I can finally get some sleep at night, because Lord knows I've been worrying about my child every hour of the day."

"I just hope the twins won't have any problems behind this, and I'm worried about Gina, too, because she's not the type of person who would just up and kill someone, and even though it was self-defense, she might have a hard time dealing with this."

"We just have to be there for all three of them, and they'll get through it. It won't be easy, but they'll get past it."

Sydney looked over at the phone when she heard it ring. "That's probably Wesley calling from work," she said and picked it up.

"Hello?" she answered.

"Who is this?" the irate voice said on the other end and the caller was crying hysterically.

"This is Sydney. May I ask who's calling?"

"You tell that bitch, Gina, that she's gonna pay for killin' my son. You hear me?" Phillip's mother screamed at Sydney.

"Ms. Harris, I understand how you feel, and I'm really sorry about your loss."

"All of y'all ain't nothin' but a bunch of murderin' son-of-a-bitches, because I know y'all ain't did nothin' but plotted to kill my son."

"What are you talking about?" Sydney asked, starting to lose her patience.

"You know exactly what I'm talkin' about. If Gina hadn't provoked my baby, he never would have gone over there tryin' to talk to her. She just wouldn't be a good wife to him, and that's why he was always havin' to put her in line."

Now Sydney knew why Phillip was such a lunatic, because it was clear that he'd inherited every one of his psychotic traits from his mother. This woman was completely insane, and Sydney couldn't believe she had the audacity to call her mother's house this early in the morning with all this nonsense.

"Ms. Harris, I don't appreciate you calling here, and if you're finished, I'm going to hang up."

"Y'all are about the most hangin'-up bunch of bitches I ever met in my life," Phillip's mother said and wasn't crying as much as when she'd first called. "That sister of yours hung up on me the other day, and I'll be damned if I'm gonna keep gettin' hung up on when I still have shit I need to say."

"Good-bye, Ms. Harris," Sydney said.

"You tell that bitch that they won't release my baby's body to the funeral home until she goes over to that hospital, and I'm giving her till noon to do it. If she hasn't gone over there by then, there's gonna be some serious ass-kickin' goin' on. You hear me?"

Sydney pressed the off button on the cordless phone and laid it on the table.

"That woman is a trip," Sydney said.

"What did she want?" Delores asked.

"Was that Phillip's mother?" Gina asked, walking into the kitchen.

"Uh-huh. She's was going on and on about how we all plotted to kill Phillip."

"Please," Gina said. "That woman is crazy, and she never thought her son could do any wrong, no matter how terrible he was."

"I believe that, because she said you were always provoking him, and that you weren't a good wife."

Gina didn't say anything, because she knew she really had provoked him this time around, but she would never tell a soul what had actually happened. She was planning to take it to her grave.

"She also said that you need to go release the body from the hospital to the funeral home," Sydney continued.

Gina hadn't thought about that, and she wished she didn't have to go to the funeral let alone the hospital. But she knew she had to follow through with all of this to the end for the sake of her children. They had a right to see him one last time, and she couldn't deny them that opportunity.

"I know I have to do this, so if you have some time this morning—" Gina said.

Sydney interrupted. "Don't say another word. We can go over there in a couple of hours."

"How are you feeling?" Delores finally asked Gina.

"I don't know. I feel almost numb. I can't believe that any of this actually happened, and it's going to take me a very long time to come to terms with it," she answered.

"Just pray. That's all you can do, and that's all any of us can do when something like this happens."

Gina believed in prayer, but she wondered what the

power of prayer was going to do for her, since Phillip's murder was premeditated. She'd planned everything from the day she'd made him angry enough to beat her and she'd had to call the police, to the incident yesterday morning, when she'd finally pulled the trigger four times in a row.

Surely God wasn't going to forgive her for taking matters into her own hands like she had, but at the same time, it really had been a self-defense ordeal. Yes, she'd lured him there, and yes, she'd shot him dead, but it was only because she was positive that he really would kill her as soon as she'd tried to file for a divorce. She couldn't stand being married to him any longer, and there was no sense in trying to weigh this out any more than she already had, because the bottom line was: Phillip was dead, he was going to remain dead, and he was never, ever coming back. She'd made sure of it.

"I'm just worried about my babies," Gina finally said.

"They'll get through this. I was just telling Sydney that. It'll take time, but they'll get through it just the same."

Sydney drove up to the red light about two blocks away from the hospital and stopped.

"You know," Gina said, "I wish Daddy was here right now."

Sydney didn't know what to say. She wanted to agree with Gina the same way she always had whenever they discussed their father's absence, but she couldn't do that any longer.

"You know what I'm saying?" Gina asked, waiting for her sister to respond.

"Yeah, I guess," Sydney answered and leaned her head into the palm of her hand with her elbow resting on the edge of the car door.

"You guess? What's wrong with you?"

"Nothing," she said and pulled off when the light turned green.

"You seem like something's wrong," Gina prodded.

"Do I?" Sydney said, trying to decide whether she should tell Gina her problem or not. Her sister was already going through enough as it was, and she didn't know if it was a good thing to drop this new set of issues on the table.

"Yes. You do. So, what's going on?" Gina said, staring at her.

Sydney drove through the next light and turned into the hospital parking lot. She parked and turned the ignition off.

"Sydney, why won't you tell me what the problem is?"

"You've got enough on your plate, and my stuff is the least of your worries. Now let's go inside, so we can get this over with."

"No. We're not. Because I want to know why you're acting like this," Gina insisted.

"Fine. I've been wanting to tell you this for a while now, but I just couldn't bring myself to do it. I just told Wesley last weekend, and I don't even know how I was able to do that."

"You told him what?"

"Dear God, Gina," she said, pausing. "Daddy sexually molested me when I was a little girl."

Gina covered her mouth. "Sydney," she said with hesitation. "Please don't tell me that."

"I didn't want to, but it's true."

"Are you sure?" Gina asked, looking confused.

"I'm very sure. He used to stick his hand inside my underwear, and he told me that he was just tickling me."

"I can't believe I'm hearing this," Gina said, looking away from her sister.

"I know."

Gina turned back toward Sydney. "Couldn't you have done something to stop him? I mean, how could you let him do that to you?" Gina asked in a critical tone.

"What do you mean, how could I let him do that to me? I was only five when he started it."

"Yeah, but how could you keep letting him do that and not tell Mom?" Gina said accusingly.

Sydney had had enough. "The same reason you let Phillip pound on you for the last ten years and then did everything you could to pretend like it wasn't happening. And the only difference between you and me is that Daddy died—but you *murdered* Phillip," she said without taking her eyes away from her.

Gina sat silently and thought about what Sydney had just said, because she knew she was wrong for blaming her sister for her father's sick behavior. But it was just that Gina worshipped the ground the man walked on, and it was hard for her to understand why he would do something so demented. She didn't mean to accuse her sister of making him do it, but she was hurt over what she was hearing.

"Let's go in here and get this over with," Sydney said, opening her car door in disgust.

"Sydney," Gina said, pulling her sister's arm to stop her from getting out. "I'm sorry. I didn't mean what I said, but you have to understand how difficult this is for me. I loved my father, and you loved him, too."

"But that doesn't change the fact that he did what he did to me, Gina," she said sadly.

"I know it doesn't, but this is all too much for me to deal with. First, it was Mom's tumor, then this thing with Phillip, and now this. Our family is falling completely apart."

"It seems like that, but Gina, we have to stay close through all of this, because if we don't, the family really will fall apart. And we won't ever be able to put it back together again."

"Mom always says that God never places any more on you than you can bear, but I'm starting to think otherwise."

"We're just going through some really tough times right now," Sydney said.

"Have you told Mom about this?" Gina asked.

"No. And I'm not going to. I will never tell her about this, because she would really go downhill if she knew what Daddy did."

"She would never live that down, and knowing her, she'd find a way to blame herself."

"I know she would. Just like I keep blaming myself. And if I didn't have Wesley telling me over and over that this wasn't my fault, I don't know what I'd be thinking. Sometimes I feel like I'm a child all over again, and I feel so helpless."

"I'm so sorry that he did that to you, and I'm sorry for getting upset with you about it."

"It's a hard pill to swallow," Sydney admitted. "And now I'm glad I have an appointment with a therapist, because I really need to talk to someone about it in depth."

"I think that's a good idea. But what about Rick? Are you planning to tell him?"

"I've thought about that a hundred times, and I really don't think I can. Rick can sometimes be mad at the world for no reason, and there's no telling how he would take hearing something like this. He might be angry with Daddy or he might be angry with me, and I'm not taking any chances one way or the other. I took a chance just by telling you, but that's where it ends."

"You're probably right, but I don't know," Gina said.

"Promise that you won't tell anyone else," Sydney said.

"I promise. I wouldn't even know how to begin telling anyone else, anyway."

"I'm so ashamed," Sydney said.

"Now you know how I felt when Phillip was abusing me all the time. I felt so humiliated, and I actually used to think that if I could just learn to do the right things, he would never hit me again."

"This thing with Daddy was blocked completely out of my mind, and it wasn't until just a few months ago that it all started coming back. But ever since it has, I've been trying to figure out what I did wrong to deserve having him stick his fingers inside me like that. I want to know what made him do that."

"There's no sense in you trying to figure it out, because then you'd have to ask yourself why anyone does anything they do. I've been thinking about that question for a long time now, and I'm finally starting to see that there aren't any real answers and that it's just the way life is," Gina said.

"True. But it does make you wonder if it's all worth it."

"I don't know," Gina said, opening her car door. "But what I do know is that, slowly but surely, I'm starting to understand why Mom keeps saying that leaving this earth isn't so bad. I'm not saying I want to die, although at one time I did, but what I *am* saying is that even though it's great to be alive, there's so much pain and suffering we all have to deal with."

"So, what is a person to do?"

"I guess we just have to do what Grandma always used to tell us."

"What's that?" Sydney asked.

"Pray and go on, no matter what."

"And she was right. Because in the long run, I do think our problems make us stronger than we've ever been."

"I think so, too. Because I know I'm a lot stronger

since the day I filed those charges against Phillip. I had to go through a lot to get to that point, but I'm finally able to hold my head up now."

"Well, we'd better go in here, so we can get back home," Sydney said.

"Yeah, I guess we better," Gina agreed and they walked into the hospital.

Chapter 33

It had been only one month since Phillip's funeral, but his death had already officially been ruled self-defense and Gina felt completely relieved. Sydney was making wonderful progress with her psychologist, and her marriage to Wesley couldn't have been better. But the happiest news of all was that Rick and Samantha had set a September wedding date in Las Vegas and everyone in the family was attending, as well as most of Samantha's relatives. They'd wanted to have a large, traditional ceremony in a church, but quickly decided that it would take much too long to plan it.

Life simply couldn't have been better. That is, until two days ago, when Delores had called Sydney and informed her that something felt strange on the right side of her head. She was experiencing an unusual sort of pain in her right temple area and above her right eyebrow. Her hearing wasn't all that great on the right side either, and while she still had no vision in her right eye, she was starting to have problems with her left one.

Sydney had called Dr. Kumar's office to see if her mother could schedule an appointment, and he'd told them that he could see her today. Which was where they were right now, sitting in an examination room.

They'd taken an MRI scan when they'd arrived three hours ago, and they'd taken some blood samples shortly thereafter. Now Dr. Kumar and Dr. Mishra were reviewing the film, and Sydney was sitting on pins and needles waiting to hear the results. Her mother seemed fine as usual, and didn't seem like she was worried one way or the other.

"I wonder what's taking them so long," Sydney said.

"Something isn't right," Delores told her.

"I don't think that, but maybe the radiology department took longer than usual getting the film down here."

"What they're out there trying to figure out is how to tell us the results of that MRI I just had."

Sydney didn't know what else to say. She'd tried to stay positive, and she'd tried to make her mother see that everything was probably fine, but her mother wasn't listening to a thing she said. She had her mind made up for some reason, and it bothered Sydney, because her mother's wisdom and intuition were always so strong. Gina had asked her if she wanted her to take the day off and drive up with them, but Sydney had told her they'd be fine, and she hadn't thought it was necessary for Gina to miss work since she'd just gone back from her leave of absence. But now she wasn't so sure she'd made the right decision, because if those doctors came in and told her that her mother still wasn't making progress, she didn't know how she was going to deal with it. She knew she needed to be strong for her mother, but she was already starting to feel weak just from all the waiting. Her nerves felt shot, and she wished they'd come in there to tell them something. Anything. Anything at all would be better than all this waiting.

Sydney picked up an old issue of *Good Housekeeping,* and flipped through the pages, but she didn't see anything all that interesting, so she placed it back in the magazine rack.

Her mother sat with her eyes closed, and it was obvious that she'd become tired of all the waiting the same as Sydney. She looked so peaceful, yet so exhausted from everything she'd gone through, and it didn't seem right for a person to go through all of this only to hear more bad news. The family as a whole had dealt with enough problems as it was, and it just seemed so unfair for things to continue like they were.

Sydney sighed, but finally she saw the door opening.

"Good afternoon," Dr. Kumar and Dr. Mishra said almost simultaneously.

"Hello, Doctors," Delores greeted them.

"Hi, Dr. Kumar. Dr. Mishra," Sydney said.

"So, how are you feeling today, Delores?" Dr. Kumar asked.

"I still have quite a bit of pain, and I just don't feel quite right."

Dr. Kumar nodded his head in acknowledgment, took a deep breath, and then he spoke.

"Well, we looked at the MRI and it looks like the tumor is growing again back in the area we removed it from."

Sydney was sure her heart had missed a beat, and her body felt paralyzed.

"I figured that's what it was," Delores said softly.

"Sometimes this happens and sometimes it doesn't, but the thing with tumors is that they feed and survive from the blood supply, so when a surgery is performed, it's sort of like a, how do you say, a catch-22 situation, because you are removing the tumor and at the same time feeding it with lots and lots of blood."

"Well, what about the other thirty percent that you didn't remove?" Sydney finally asked.

"That's the strange thing. Because that part of it is unchanged, and has been since before surgery. It hasn't grown one bit."

"So, is there still a chance that we can try radiation?" Sydney asked.

"Yes, I think so, but I do have to say that I don't believe that another surgery would be feasible at this point."

"Will the radiation shrink it?" Delores wanted to know.

"It's hard to say, but there is a good chance that it will at least stop the growth."

"And you're still sure that this isn't cancerous?" Sydney asked.

"It's not cancerous. But even though it's benign, it's acting worse than a malignant one."

"Well, what's the next step?" Delores said, smiling.

"Dr. Mishra wants to map out a radiation plan and schedule and we want to get going with it fairly soon. We were contemplating what we call a one-shot radiation for the thirty percent we left, but now it's more crucial that we take care of the part that's growing back. You'll probably have to drive up here five days straight over five or six weeks, so if you want, we can try to make arrangements to have it done in the Chicago area."

"No," Sydney said in a hurry. "It's a long drive, but I'd feel much more comfortable if you can do it here. All of you know my mom's history, and I don't see a reason to have her go somewhere else."

"We feel the same way," Dr. Mishra said. "But we just want to make it convenient for you, if it's not possible for you to get her here."

"We'll be fine. I can drive her every day, and if there are a few times that I can't, there are a number of people in our church who will be glad to drive Mom up here."

"Yes, that won't be a problem," Delores added.

"Okay, then, we'll go over the scan, pinpoint the area exactly that we need to target, and then we'll have one of the secretaries give you a call with the schedule," Dr. Mishra said.

"I'm sorry we don't have better news than that," Dr. Kumar said, sounding sort of down.

"It's not your fault, Doctor. I know you're doing the best you can do, and that's all we expect," Delores said cheerfully. "My daughter doesn't think there's any other neurosurgeon in the country except you, so believe me, we have no complaints."

Dr. Kumar blushed at Delores's compliment. "Thanks."

"We'll let you ladies get out of here, and we'll be in touch tomorrow or the next day," Dr. Mishra said, and both of the doctors left.

"I told you something wasn't right," Delores said. "And I'm telling you, if it's not one thing, it's another all the time."

"Well, at least it sounds like the radiation will help," Sydney said for lack of anything else better to say.

"It might," Delores said, standing up, and then they walked through the hospital, up to the main floor, and then outside to the parking lot.

Then they headed through town and out to the highway.

"Susan is going to be so upset when she hears the news," Delores said, referring to her sister in Texas.

Sydney didn't comment. She'd been trying to think about something else, so she wouldn't fall apart at the wheel.

"See, this is why you have to be ready at all times, because you don't know when your time is coming to go home," Delores said.

"Yeah, I guess so," Sydney finally said because she didn't want her mother to think she was ignoring her.

"Play my song for me," Delores said, referring to Kirk Franklin's "Lean on Me," featuring R. Kelly, Mary J. Blige, and a few other very talented artists. Her mother wasn't all that fond of contemporary gospel music, but she loved this particular song, and the track that played after it, "Something About the Name Jesus."

Sydney switched the stereo from Power 105.9, WKPO out of Janesville, Wisconsin, and started the CD player. Delores listened to the words with her eyes closed, and moved her hand to the sound of the music.

Sydney wondered how a person's faith could be so strong. So strong that they could hear the sort of news Delores had heard about her tumor, and then enjoy listening to music on the way back home. She didn't seem bothered in the least, but Sydney had to admit that she was glad. Because if her mother had been sad or had been shedding tears over this, she probably would have fallen apart right along with her. Sydney was actually finding inspiration and strength from her mother, even though it should have been the other way around.

They drove all the way back to Covington Park listening and singing along with the rest of the songs on the CD, and by the time they arrived, Sydney's spirits were lifted back to normal. She didn't know how long it was going to last, but she was going to enjoy this feeling while she could.

"Baby, I know this is hard for you," Wesley said after Sydney told him about her trip to Madison. "But you can't give up."

"I'm not giving up, but I'm so sick of hearing bad news about Mom's condition. It seems like she does real well one minute, and then the next thing you know, there's something going wrong."

Wesley was leaning against the kitchen counter, and he pulled Sydney closer to him. "You have to think of your mother and how she feels, because if she sees that you're having a hard time with this, it will bring her down, and you know you don't want that."

"No, I don't," Sydney said, falling apart.

"Well, you've got to think positively from here on out, no matter how bad things get."

"I feel like I'm being pulled in every direction. I'm dealing with Mom's illness, this thing that my father did, all of these stupid deadlines, and I'm not spending nearly enough time with Victoria," Sydney said.

"Things will get better, and it won't always be like this."

"Sweetheart," she said, looking at him. "Make love to me."

Wesley raised his eyebrows, but had a big smile on his face. "Well, isn't this a first."

"I need you so much," she said.

"And you know I'll always be here for you. That's one thing you don't ever have to worry about," he said.

They kissed in a sensual, loving manner, and then ended up in their bedroom. Sydney was glad that she was finally able to desire sex like any other normal person. It really did make all the difference in the world.

Epilogue

Two years later

Delores had died on a Saturday, and although one whole year had passed, Sydney still found herself shedding tears at any time without the slightest notice. It was still so hard for her to believe that her mother was gone. She'd tried to prepare herself for the inevitable, after her mother's health had begun to deteriorate at a very rapid rate, and her mother had gone out of her way of trying to prepare her as well. She'd told her how everything really did happen for a reason, and that God never, ever made any mistakes, but it hadn't helped Sydney to the extent that she needed it to.

Sydney was stronger than she'd ever been before, and it wasn't that she couldn't accept her mother's passing, since Delores had made it very clear that she had her soul right with God, but it was just that she missed her so much. She missed her love, her smile, and she just missed being in her presence. Her mother had held on for as long as she could trying to allow everyone a chance to accept her illness, but there finally came a time when she couldn't hold on any longer. Her digestive system had shut completely down, and she'd lost all mobility in her arms and legs. She'd wanted Rick and Gina to rid themselves of the denial they were dealing with, and it worried her, because if they couldn't deal with her illness, she hadn't known how they were going to deal with her death. She'd told them in no uncertain terms that she was tired, and that she was "finally winding this thing down."

Sydney had told her mother that she didn't want her to suffer any longer and that she wanted her to know that she was the best mother she and her siblings could have ever prayed for. Delores had smiled and told her that that was what she'd tried to be, and that she had done the very best she could.

She'd talked to all three of her children continuously, and even though Sydney had come to the realization that her mother did have to leave, it still hadn't seemed real until the day it happened. Then she'd felt like her whole world had come to an end, and while her mother had explained to her how bad the pain was going to feel, it hadn't helped her.

Delores had told her how she'd heard many people say that their hearts felt like holes were in them whenever they endured a certain amount of emotional pain, but that she really didn't believe anything could compare to losing a mother or she suspected, losing a child. She remembered how she'd felt when her own mother passed away, and she'd told Sydney that her heart really *was* going to feel like a hole had been drilled through it, and that she was going to feel like it would never, ever fill up again. She told her that, for a while, each day was going to feel worse than the last, but that eventually, with time, she would begin to feel better. That she would eventually begin living her life again. She told her that she would never overcome the loss, but that she would find herself smiling at all the wonderful memories they'd shared together. She told her that she was going to be okay, and that she thanked God for Wesley.

She told Sydney how she'd watched her and Wesley over the years, but how she'd really paid special attention to their relationship when she'd had to stay with them right after her surgery. She'd wanted to make sure that Sydney was going to have him to lean on, and Delores had told her she was satisfied in knowing that Wesley was, in fact, going to take care of her when she was gone. She'd been so content after learning that, and she was content to know that Rick and Samantha seemed very happily married as well, and that there was no doubt that Samantha was going to take care of Rick. She promised Delores that she would, but Delores had already determined that beforehand.

But she still worried about Gina, because even though Gina was moving on with her life, and the twins seemed to be much more adjusted since their father's death, she wanted Gina to have someone to lean on as well. Someone who would be there to hold her in the middle of the night when she felt lonely, and someone to tell her that everything was going to be all right when she went through tough times.

Sydney had promised her mother that she would be there for her sister always, but Sydney could tell that her mother still hadn't been completely satisfied with that. She'd told Gina that she could only imagine how hard life could be raising small children all alone, and that she prayed that Gina would eventually find a man who would love her and her children in the manner they deserved.

Delores worried about Victoria as well, because she'd always had such a close relationship with her granddaughter, and she'd told Sydney that her leaving was going to bring them much closer as mother and daughter over time. They still had their disagreements and tiny breakdowns in communication, but Sydney did have to admit that Victoria was clinging to her a whole lot more since her grandmother's death.

Sydney sat on her patio looking across their backyard as the cool summer wind blew through her hair. She thought about everything that had happened over the last two years. She remembered the terrible things her stepfather had done to her, which she still hadn't completely come to terms with, but the sessions with her psychologist had allowed her to make major strides in dealing with them. Then there had been her mother's terminal illness and Gina's domestic violence situation.

She'd said it a hundred times, but it just hadn't seemed fair for so many tragedies to burden one family. As she continued to sit and think, however, she recalled what her mother had told her the last time she'd wondered this very thing.

She told her that if a person never experienced any trials or tribulations in their lives, that they would never humble themselves, and that the world would be an even worse place to live in than it already was. Sydney hadn't thought too much about it at the time, but now she knew her mother had been right.

Because if everything in life did turn out perfectly, why on earth would a person ever need to pray? And the fact of the matter was, they wouldn't.

Author's Note

If you or someone you know is experiencing domestic violence, sexual abuse, or caregiving of an ill or elderly loved one, please call one of the hotline numbers listed below.

National Domestic Violence Hotline
(800) 799-SAFE
Rape, Abuse, and Incest National Network (RAINN)
(800) 656-HOPE
National Family Caregivers Association (NFCA)
(800) 896-3650

Grab These Other
Dafina Novels
(trade paperback editions)

Every Bitter Thing Sweet
1-57566-851-3

by Roslyn Carrington
$14.00US/$19.00CAN

When Twilight Comes
0-7582-0009-9

by Gwynne Forster
$15.00US/$21.00CAN

Some Sunday
0-7582-0003-X

by Margaret Johnson-Hodge
$15.00US/$21.00CAN

Testimony
0-7582-0063-3

by Felicia Mason
$15.00US/$21.00CAN

Forever
1-57566-759-2

by Timmothy B. McCann
$15.00US/$21.00CAN

God Don't Like Ugly
1-57566-607-3

by Mary Monroe
$15.00US/$20.00CAN

Gonna Lay Down My Burdens
0-7582-0001-3

by Mary Monroe
$15.00US/$21.00CAN

The Upper Room
0-7582-0023-4

by Mary Monroe
$15.00US/$21.00CAN

Soulmates Dissipate
0-7582-0006-4

by Mary B. Morrison
$15.00US/$21.00CAN

Got a Man
0-7582-0240-7

by Daaimah S. Poole
$15.00US/$21.00CAN

Casting the First Stone
1-57566-633-2

by Kimberla Lawson Roby
$14.00US/$18.00CAN

It's a Thin Line
1-57566-744-4

by Kimberla Lawson Roby
$15.00US/$21.00CAN

Available Wherever Books Are Sold!

Visit our website at **www.kensingtonbooks.com**

Grab These Other
Dafina Novels
(mass market editions)

Some Sunday
0-7582-0026-9

by Margaret Johnson-Hodge
$6.99US/$9.99CAN

Forever
0-7582-0353-5

by Timmothy B. McCann
$6.99US/$9.99CAN

Soulmates Dissipate
0-7582-0020-X

by Mary B. Morrison
$6.99US/$9.99CAN

High Hand
1-57566-684-7

by Gary Phillips
$5.99US/$7.99CAN

Shooter's Point
1-57566-745-2

by Gary Phillips
$5.99US/$7.99CAN

Casting the First Stone
0-7582-0179-6

by Kimberla Lawson Roby
$6.99US/$9.99CAN

Here and Now
0-7582-0064-1

by Kimberla Lawson Roby
$6.99US/$9.99CAN

Lookin' for Luv
0-7582-0118-4

by Carl Weber
$6.99US/$8.99CAN

Available Wherever Books Are Sold!

Visit our website at **www.kensingtonbooks.com**

Grab These Other
Thought Provoking Books

Adam by Adam
0-7582-0195-8

by Adam Clayton Powell, Jr.
$15.00US/$21.00CAN

African American Firsts
0-7582-0243-1

by Joan Potter
$15.00US/$21.00CAN

African-American Pride
0-8065-2498-7

by Lakisha Martin
$15.95US/$21.95CAN

The African-American Soldier
0-8065-2049-3

by Michael Lee Lanning
$16.95US/$24.95CAN

African Proverbs and Wisdom
0-7582-0298-9

by Julia Stewart
$12.00US/$17.00CAN

Al on America
0-7582-0351-9

by Rev. Al Sharpton
with Karen Hunter
$16.00US/$23.00CAN

Available Wherever Books Are Sold!

Visit our website at **www.kensingtonbooks.com**

BOOK YOUR PLACE ON OUR WEBSITE AND MAKE THE READING CONNECTION!

We've created a customized website just for our very special readers, where you can get the inside scoop on everything that's going on with Zebra, Pinnacle and Kensington books.

When you come online, you'll have the exciting opportunity to:

- View covers of upcoming books
- Read sample chapters
- Learn about our future publishing schedule (listed by publication month *and author*)
- Find out when your favorite authors will be visiting a city near you
- Search for and order backlist books from our online catalog
- Check out author bios and background information
- Send e-mail to your favorite authors
- Meet the Kensington staff online
- Join us in weekly chats with authors, readers and other guests
- Get writing guidelines
- AND MUCH MORE!

**Visit our website at
http://www.kensingtonbooks.com**